Wizard Redeemed

Book Seven

Intergalactic Wizard Scout Chronicles

Rodney W. Hartman

ISBN-13: 978-0-9982166-4-5 (R&K Publishing)

ISBN-10: 0-9982166-4-X

Cover Design by Angie Abler

Editing services by The Pro Book Editor

DEDICATION

This book is dedicated to my grandson, William. Your enthusiasm and cheerfulness affect all those around you. I look forward to seeing you grow as God leads you down the path he has planned for you. I love you, buddy.

ACKNOWLEDGMENTS

I want to thank my wife for putting up with the many hours I spent pounding away on the keyboard while continuing to encourage and support me in my chosen profession. Thank you, Karen. I appreciate all you do more than you will ever know.

Other Books by Rodney W. Hartman

Intergalactic Wizard Scout Chronicles

Wizard Defiant	Book One
Wizard Cadet	Book Two
Wizard Scout	Book Three
Wizard Omega	Book Four
Wizard Rebellion	Book Five
Wizard Betrayed	Book Six
Wizard Redeemed	Book Seven

Wizard Scout Trinity Delgado Series

Trinity Unleashed

Ring Defender Series

Fire Defender	Book One

CHAPTER 1

[Begin Transmission]

Wizard Scout Richard Shepard stood in the galley of the recon ship *Defiant* waiting for the re-hydrator to finish reconstituting the simulated beef. Two pots of meat and vegetables were already simmering away on the stove. After glancing over his shoulder at the growing crowd around the mess table, he knew he was going to need a lot more. The size of the *Defiant's crew* had grown a lot since the first time he'd come onboard. A single pot of stew was no longer nearly enough.

Pulling a smaller pot from underneath the oven, he added water and vegetables but no meat. *Not everyone on the ship likes meat. Jeena will eat meat if push comes to shove, but she prefers a vegetarian diet. It's the least I can do for her,* Richard thought.

Looking out the door of the galley into the mess area, he spotted his bondmate, Jeena. The elf's long silver hair, done up in a high ponytail, crept over her shoulder as she leaned over to whisper something into Dren's ear. His adopted niece laughed as only teenagers can. Jeena's molten-silver eyes sparkled as she added her own laughter. Dren turned and whispered something into her brother's ear. Brachia placed his hand over his mouth and laughed.

Scanning the other crewmembers at the table, Richard smiled. The crew was making small talk while they waited for lunch. *"I'll say one thing,"* he thought in the part of his mind he shared with his battle computer Nickelo. *"The crew of the* Defiant *is sure a*

1

diverse lot. We've got humans, elves, dwarves, gnomes, and even a teenage orc working together. For being the only orc, Timerman seems to be fitting in well with the others. Good thing, since he's the only one in the crew that doesn't have another of their kind onboard."

"Do not forget about the two-meter-long dragon we have on the Defiant," *replied Nickelo.* "Bright Wing *is in the engine room."*

"I'm not forgetting. You know, it's hard to believe that it's only been five days since the battle of the fleets around Estos. A lot has happened since then. I'm surprised War-king Bistoria hasn't organized a counterattack against the Conglomerate yet."

"Oh, I calculate your friend Liz will convince her father to do something soon," said Nickelo. *"She has been officially promoted to Admiral of the Fleets for the rebellion. I seriously doubt you will be involved with that fight in the foreseeable future. I also calculate Jeena and your mission will be in the magic dimension on Portalis. Based upon previous missions you have been sent on by* 'the One,' *I calculate a ninety-seven percent probability Portalis is the key to this whole interdimensional conflict."*

"Don't mention 'the One,'" Richard said feeling a rising anger inside him. *"My interest's in keeping the Empire in one piece.* 'The One' *can take care of his own war."*

"It is all interrelated," said Nickelo. *"Your bondmate is part of the war. I calculate the elves' Tree of Light will play a major part in the final battle. I seriously doubt the rebellion in this dimension can succeed without winning the war in the magic dimension as well. Jeena's elves are going to need your help as much as your friends in the physical dimension."*

Richard looked at Jeena through the open curtain separating the galley from the mess area. She was watching him, wearing one of the dazzling smiles he'd come to love over the past few days. Once again, he was drawn to the swirling molten-silver of her eyes. He felt a sudden tightness in his chest and sensed her emotions through their bond link.

What I sense is so much more than love, Richard thought. *How can I help but be humbled?*

A tingle throughout his body jerked Richard out of his thoughts. The galley and the mess area began focusing in and out of view. He locked eyes with Jeena. Wide-eyed, she began to rise from the table, fear evident on her face.

"No!" was all Richard had time to shout before Jeena and the *Defiant* faded from view.

"Do what must be done. I am 'the One.'" said a voice in Richard's head.

Then everything went black.

CHAPTER 2

Damp stone walls came into focus along with the sound of shuffling feet. Cold air blew across Richard's bare skin. He was naked. A large creature standing on his left bumped against him. Glancing over, Richard saw a bare, gray-skinned chest. Looking up, he stared into the face of the largest male orc he'd ever seen. One of the two yellow tusks sticking out of his mouth was broken off at the halfway point. Taking a step to his right and raising his hands in preparation for launching an attack, Richard bumped into a blue-skinned humanoid. The blue creature was tall, thin, and also naked. Other orcs and blue humanoids stood all around saying and doing nothing. Reaching out for his Power reserve in preparation for taking out the nearest orc, Richard found nothing.

I can't find the link to my Power reserve.

None of the orcs seemed to be taking any interest in him. Richard lowered his hands.

What's going on? The orcs don't appear to be an immediate threat. Don't do anything rash. I need to figure out what's going on before I start trouble. I'm in a tunnel. Why?

Through the stench of orc, Richard caught intermittent whiffs of fresh air. To his right, a glimmer of sunlight was visible through what he took to be the tunnel's entrance a hundred and fifty meters behind him. The tunnel itself was almost twenty meters wide and half as high. Metal canisters attached to the walls at head-height gave out beams of white light illuminating the tunnel's mud-colored walls. Standing along the tunnel wall to his front was at least a score of soldiers in some type of power-armor with rifles at the ready. He'd seen the weapons before. They were the magic-based equivalent of the Empire's plasma rifles. Richard noticed two raised metal platforms with a half dozen soldiers manning crew-served weapons. Turning his head, he noted a similar number of armored soldiers standing against the rear wall.

Angry shouts drew Richard's attention. He spotted large, hairy, four-armed creatures walking between the orcs and blue humanoids, striking out with vicious looking whips. He'd seen the four-armed creatures in the past. They were Thargs, the bullyboys of a reptilian race in the magic dimension called Dragars.

Richard tried to reach out with his passive scan to get a count of life forms, but his mind remained blank. *I can feel my Power reserve in the distance, but only faintly. The connection is too faint to even do something as simple as a passive scan.*

Richard made a manual count of those around him. *By my estimate, there are at least fifty of these orcs in the tunnel. There are nearly as many of those blue humanoids. I count twenty of the Thargs with whips or meter-long black metal rods. They're obviously weapons of some kind. The Tharg guards aren't wearing armor, but some of them have handguns stuck in their belts.*

When one of the Thargs walked by, Richard was tempted to break the hairy creature's neck and shove the whip it carried down its throat. The sight of the armored soldiers along the walls changed his mind.

There's too many of them. They'd cut me down before I took out a half dozen of them.

Although he doubted 'the One' had allowed his battle computer to come with him, Richard called out in his shared space anyway. *"Nick? Are you there, buddy?"*

As expected, no answer was forthcoming.

Crack!

The leather strands of a cat-o'-nine tails lashed across the back of the blue humanoid standing to Richard's right. The blue creature screamed and grabbed at his back. One of the leather strands from the guard's whip had caught Richard on the right arm. It cut deep, but he forced himself not to flinch.

I'm obviously just one of many prisoners. I've got a feeling the only way I'm going to figure out what's going on is to draw the least amount of attention to myself as possible until I get a better handle on things.

A warm feeling on the upper part of Richard's right arm drew his attention. He glanced to see the bloody stripe left by the whip congealing together. *At least my self-heal's still working. The cut is almost healed. Why I can't use my Power for anything else, I don't know. If I had all my wizard scout abilities, I'd risk grabbing a weapon and fighting my way out. As it is, there are too many unknowns to try it right now. What's* 'the One' *up to? Why has he hamstrung me?*

Richard's anger at *'the One'* threatened to spill out into action against his jailers, but he kept it contained with the greatest of effort.

Don't do anything to draw attention. Not yet. I need to find out where I am before I do anything drastic. If I can't contact Nick, maybe I can get help from another source.

Sending out the strongest emotion of concern he could muster, Richard called out into the void for his wolf-like dolgar friends. The call seemed different as if there was no one there to hear it. Richard searched the area in his mind where the timeline for his DNA baseline was, finding it easily enough.

Crap. That can't be right. According to my timeline, I'm two million years in the past. What's going on?

A sense of panic started welling up inside Richard, but he forced it back down into the darkness of his soul where it belonged. He'd been a marine once. Marines didn't panic.

Panicking won't help. I've got to come up with a plan. The question is what?

The huge orc to Richard's left shifted position, forcing Richard to step to his right and bump into the blue humanoid. The blue creature stumbled and fell to the tunnel's stone floor. As soon as the blue humanoid went down, a four-armed Tharg walking nearby stepped forward and lashed his whip across the blue creature's back.

A pitiful scream gurgled out of the blue humanoid's mouth.

Richard sensed an emotion of excitement from the Tharg guard as he raised his whip and beat on the poor creature all the more. Another of the unarmored guards joined the first. They began whipping the blue humanoid in tandem. Richard took a half step in the direction of the blue humanoid to lift the poor creature to its feet. A calloused, yellowed hand with knuckle-length claws resembling hardened pieces of rusty iron grabbed his left arm, holding him in place. Following the hand and arm up, Richard discovered it belonged to the big orc to his left. The orc shook his head in a human-like gesture. He started to shake free of the orc's grasp when one of the other blue prisoners took a step forward and reached out toward his fallen comrade. The blue humanoid made it only a step before a red ball of energy burst out of its forehead, splattering those around it with bluish blood and brain matter.

Richard felt warm liquid run down the side of his face. He made no move to wipe the blood away. Tracing the ball of energy back to its source, he noticed one of the armored soldiers at the side of the tunnel aiming its rifle in his direction. Several of the other soldiers had their weapons raised as well.

Richard sensed an overwhelming emotion of eagerness. *They want the prisoners to revolt. They're just looking for an excuse to fire.*

The big orc released Richard's arm. Remaining where he was, Richard forgot about helping the fallen prisoner. He looked back at the two unarmored Tharg guards still beating it. The blue creature was curled up on the floor, its screams growing weaker with each blow. Another unarmored guard walked over and joined the fun.

I could kill all three of them, Richard thought. *But then what? I can't take on fifty armed soldiers in power-armor. Even if they don't kill me right off the bat, they're bound to discover I can self-heal. If they do, they could keep me alive and torture me for years. I've got to wait for a better opportunity.*

The blue prisoner's screams lessened before dying away completely.

A sense of shame washed over Richard, but he shoved it deep inside him. *Getting killed won't help,* he thought. *If the orc to my left hadn't stopped me, I'd be the one on the floor with a hole through my head. When my wound healed, even the stupidest Tharg would've noticed. I can't afford to draw attention to myself until I figure things out. I just can't. An opportunity will come sooner or later to get away. I just have to wait.*

After a few more swings at the lifeless body, the three Thargs lost interest and moved away. A half dozen of the unarmored

Tharg guards moved to the front of the prisoners and began forcing them into some semblance of a line. The guards used both their whips and black rods. One of the guards moved in front of Richard, shoving him back with its upper arms. Part of Richard's temper escaped from its cage before he could catch it and he knocked the guard's hands away.

The guard shoved the end of his metal rod into Richard's stomach. The force of the blow along with an electrical shock knocked the wind out of him, and he fell to his knees. The guard immediately raised his whip and brought it down across Richard's back. Biting back a cry of pain, Richard tried to rise. Another electric shock sapped his strength, preventing him from doing more than rising to a half crouch.

A large, calloused hand grabbed Richard by the left arm and pulled him to his feet. He followed the hand and arm up to his savior's face. He was greeted by two large bloodshot eyes along with two yellowed, finger-length tusks protruding from a wide mouth. He recognized the broken off tusk of the big orc that had stopped him from helping the blue prisoner.

The Tharg guard raised his whip and struck the big orc across the chest. The orc didn't bother grunting. He just let go of Richard's arm, staring straight ahead while seeming to take no notice of the bloody streaks across his chest. The guard raised his whip to strike again. The sound of a scream from another of the blue prisoners farther down the line drew the guard's attention. Richard sensed an emotion of excitement from the Tharg as it rushed to help one of its companions whip the screaming prisoner.

Richard studied the orc to his left. The yellow-skinned creature was almost a head taller than the orcs he was used to seeing on Portalis. The self-discipline of the orc to ignore the whipping was beyond anything he'd previously witnessed.

He's just as ugly though, Richard decided.

Glancing to his left and right at the row of prisoners, Richard noticed he was the only human in the line. Lack of clothing made the muscles on the orcs stand out. It was blatantly obvious they could easily overwhelm and kill the unarmored Tharg guards with their bare hands if they so desired.

Why don't they defend themselves? Are they smart enough to know the soldiers backing the guards up would shoot them all down? Can an orc even control their emotions enough to make that kind of logical decision?

An image of a young orc flashed in Richard's mind. The image was that of Timerman, the teenage orc on the *Defiant*. *I've only known Timerman for a few days, but he's as intelligent as any human. He's almost as good of a navigator as Sergeant Ron. Maybe this orc is one of Timerman's race. Maybe none of these orcs are from Portalis.*

Richard came out of his thoughts when two of the guards began laying out a length of rusty chain alongside the line of prisoners. Two more guards followed the first pair, hooking shackles to each of the prisoners' ankles and wrists. A third pair of Thargs attached a smaller line from the main chain to the prisoners' shackles.

Glancing out the corner of his right eye, Richard noticed Thargs shackling the ankles of the lifeless body of the blue prisoner they'd killed earlier to the main chain. The pair of Thargs rose and moved in front of Richard. One of the pair placed a heavy metal shackle on Richard's right ankle, then another on his left. Two more shackles were placed on his wrists. The rough-cut edges of the cuffs bit into his flesh. He felt the beast which was his temper trying to claw its way out of its cage. The sight of a dozen soldiers aiming rifles at his chest forced him to keep his anger under control.

The guard snapped the last shackle shut, locking it with a large key hooked to its belt by a thin wire. The Tharg stood and looked at Richard while making a loud gurgling sound.

Is that laughter? Richard wondered trying his best to keep any hint of emotion off his face.

When Richard failed to react, the Tharg bent down and snapped the other shackles shut before moving on to the big orc with the broken tusk. The same gurgling sound came out of the Tharg's mouth as he locked the orc's shackles in place.

Laugh away, Chuckles, Richard thought. *When you don't have all these soldiers standing behind you, I'm going to shove that key down your throat so far that you'll need a locksmith to get it out.*

Once all the prisoners were attached to the common chain, one of the guards growled. When the big orc next to Richard turned and faced left, Richard followed suit. The other orcs did the same, but only a few of the blue prisoners turned. The guards lashed out with their whips at the prisoners still facing to the front. In short order, all of the prisoners were facing left. More than one of the blue prisoners had bloody streaks on their backs and shoulders. The guard with the key made a loud gurgling sound. The other guards made the same gurgling sounds that Richard was fast associating with Tharg laughter.

That's right, Chuckles, Richard thought. *All of you keep it up. Your day's coming.*

The guard with the key made a woofing sound. The big orc ahead of Richard stepped out, dragging the main chain along with him. Richard stepped out as well. Once again, most of the blue creatures failed to move. The guards lashed out with both whips and rods. By the time the entire chain gang was moving, two more lifeless blue bodies were on the ground.

At his second step, Richard's right leg encountered resistance. *The body of the dead prisoner is still attached to the main chain,* he thought. *I can't walk and pull the body behind me at the same time.*

Two lashes from a nearby guard's whip across Richard's back convinced him otherwise. If it had been up to only his strength, Richard doubted he would've made it far dragging a hundred kilos of dead weight behind him with every step. Thankfully the big orc to his front seemed to time his steps with Richard, taking some of the load from the corpse.

Is the orc doing it on purpose or by accident? Richard wondered.

Within fifty meters, the twenty prisoners ahead of Richard in the chain turned into a side hole on the left side of the main tunnel. As he made his own turn, he looked back the way he'd come. The light of day was barely visible two hundred meters away.

I'll come back here after those armored guards are gone. When the time is right, I'll kill Chuckles along with his unarmored pals and retrace my steps. I just have to wait a while until the entrance is less guarded. Getting back here will be no big deal. All I have to do is remember the route.

When Richard drew past the corner of the side tunnel, the last of the daylight disappeared. It was replaced by a dim greenish glow seeming to emanate from the walls of the side tunnel. *No,* he thought. *Not from the walls. It's as if the green light is in the air itself.*

Once all the prisoners were in the side tunnel, Chuckles woofed again. The big orc ahead of Richard stopped so suddenly that he bumped into the orc's back. Glancing over his shoulder, Richard noticed the guards at the rear of the chain pushing the last dozen or so prisoners forward. Before long, all of the prisoners were bunched up thirty meters past the entrance to the main tunnel.

Chuckles woofed a command before moving next to a lever located on the side wall of the tunnel. Richard noticed one of the Thargs a few meters to his rear pulling a mask out of a bag at his waist and placing it over his mouth and nose. Chuckles donned a similar mask, then made a loud gurgling sound as he grabbed the lever and began pulling it downward.

"Hit the deck!" Richard yelled as he fell to the floor covering his face and head with his arms. He sensed the big orc ahead of him diving to the stone floor as well.

Boom!

Chalky dust filled the air as the sound of the explosion reverberated throughout the tunnel. As far as Richard could tell, all of the orc prisoners had fallen to the floor along with some of the blue humanoids. The reaction time of several of the other blue prisoners wasn't quite fast enough. Even before the debris settled, Richard knew from their high-pitched screams that several of the blue prisoners had been caught in the blast.

Peeking between his arms, Richard noticed one of the blue prisoners located four positions to his rear lying on the ground, staring at a finger-long length of bone protruding from his left ankle. The prisoner grabbed its wounded leg, screaming. Chuckles walked up the line until he was even with the injured prisoner. Pulling out his rod, he began beating the blue creature. The sadistic Tharg was soon joined by two other guards. Within seconds, the injured prisoner stopped screaming and lay still.

After a final hit, Chuckles kicked the lifeless body before continuing up the line. Richard rose to his feet. So did the big orc with the broken tusk to his left. As soon as the big orc rose, all of the orcs stood in unison and faced to the front of the chain line. Richard quickly faced the front as well. A few of the blue prisoners followed suit. Those who didn't were given a few lashes by the nearest guards. Soon, all of the prisoners who remained alive were standing and facing front.

The Thargs removed their masks. Chuckles walked past Richard making a gurgling sound. Richard risked a glance to his rear. The majority of the dust had settled enough to see that the entrance to the main tunnel was no more. In its place was a solid wall of rubble.

They've blocked off my escape route. Now even if I get free of these chains and kill the guards, how am I supposed to get out of the tunnels?

Chuckles growled.

The big orc to Richard's front stepped out. So did Richard. He noticed that at the first step of the big orc to his front, all of the orcs took a step.

Are they keying off him? Richard wondered. He thought back to his warning about the explosion. *I seriously doubt any of the orcs speak intergalactic standard. I think the orc in front of me dropped to the floor a split-second after I did.* Richard tried to remember if the other orcs had done the same or if they had only dropped after the orc to his front had moved. *I can't remember. It happened too fast. Probably doesn't matter anyway.*

The next hour turned into a litany of steps as Richard moved his left foot forward followed by a hard pull of his right dragging the blue body behind him. By the time the hour was over, two more of the blue humanoids' lifeless bodies were added to the weight of the main chain.

Chuckles growled.

The big orc in front of Richard stopped. Richard and the remaining blue prisoners also stopped.

Either the blue guys are getting more alert, Richard thought, or the un-alert ones are already dead.

One of the nearby Thargs growled a command.

The orcs bent down and began digging at the tunnel walls with their bare hands. The soft rock gave way to their hardened claws.

Crack!

Richard fell to his knees. White hot pain across his back tracked the path of each of the cat-o'-nine-tail's straps. Glancing back, he saw Chuckles raising his whip for another blow. He heard the gurgling sound he'd come to hate. Reaching out, Richard tore at the tunnel wall with his bare hands. The wall was composed more of hardened dirt than of stone. Two fist-sized portions of the wall crumbled to the floor. Pulling back his hands, Richard saw drops of blood fall to the floor from his torn fingers. He heard another round of gurgling behind him.

A blue prisoner a dozen positions down the chain raised two bloody hands at a guard, saying something in a language Richard didn't understand. Whether the Tharg guard could understand or not, didn't matter. At the blue prisoner's apparent complaint, the guard raised his whip and lay into the prisoner all the while making the hated gurgling sound. Chuckles rushed over with his whip and joined in. When the two Thargs stopped their whipping, one more lifeless body adorned the main chain. After that, none of the prisoners complained about digging with their hands.

Dig, Richard thought. *Dig. Their time's coming, but you've got to figure a way out of this place first. So stay alive and dig.*

He dug.

What are we digging for? Richard wondered. *My self-heal is keeping my fingers healed, but it still hurts. Is this just some form of sadistic torture, or are we looking for something? If they want us to find anything, why don't we have tools?*

Hours passed. Large mounds of hardened dirt and soft rock formed piles along the tunnel. Guards walked down the line, stopping at the prisoners with smaller piles and beating them. Richard compared his pile with the big orc's next to him.

There's no way I can compete, Richard thought. *The orc's claws allow him to dig in the soft stone at a pace I can't hope to match.* The sound of high-pitched screams came from down the line. Richard braced himself to push up to a standing position. *They're killing those who can't keep up. I'm going to have to fight now whether I know a way out or not.*

A movement to his right drew Richard's attention. He noticed the big orc next to him scoop up an armful of debris off his pile. The orc tossed the dirt and rock onto Richard's pile.

What the hell? Richard thought.

One of the Tharg guards stopped behind Richard. Making a snap decision, Richard shoved his fingers into the stone and pulled out two blood-streaked fistfuls of rubble, adding it to his pile. The Tharg gurgled and moved on without using his whip.

Richard glanced out the corner of his eye. The big orc continued to dig, appearing to pay him no mind. "Thanks," Richard whispered.

The big orc made a barely audible growl and continued digging.

An hour later, Richard heard a commotion from some prisoners to his left. When he turned, he noticed one of the blue humanoids lifting a spherical-shaped rock up to a guard. He sensed excitement from the guard. Chuckles ran over to the prisoner with the rock. Grabbing the spherical stone out of the prisoner's hands, the Tharg woofed a command. All of the prisoners sat down and leaned against the tunnel wall. Richard did the same. As Chuckles passed his position, Richard got a better look at the stone. He stiffened.

That's not a rock. It's a dragon egg. Realization swept over Richard. *I know where I am.*

The memory of a mission on the *Defiant* where he'd landed on a planet-sized asteroid riddled with tunnels flooded his mind. While there, he'd been given a vision by a green sphere of millions of dragons laying their eggs in the hot mud of the asteroid. After a time, the mud had hardened. His vision had shown Dragar starships landing on the asteroid. He'd seen their Tharg minions forcing prisoners to dig in the soft rock with their bare hands for dragon eggs. From a later mission for *'the One,'* he knew those same eggs were destined to be Dragar sacrifices.

I must be in a time-bubble on that asteroid, Richard thought.

Another memory flashed into Richard's mind. It was a map of the part of the tunnel he'd been in on the earlier mission to the asteroid, placed in his mind by his battle computer at the time. The map had a green route on it leading from where he'd encountered the green sphere, back to the surface.

The only problem is, Richard thought, *I don't know where in the tunnel system I am. Nothing in this section is familiar. The map doesn't do me any good if I don't have a point of reference.*

The relaxation break for finding the dragon egg lasted almost an hour. Eventually, quiet time ended and the Thargs got their prisoners digging again. They dug for another two hours without finding any other dragon eggs.

A rumbling came from farther down the tunnel. Turning his head in the direction of the noise, Richard noticed three carts being pushed by chained prisoners. The four-wheeled metal ore carts came lumbering down the center of the tunnel. One of the carts stopped a few positions down the line from Richard. The prisoners nearest the cart began scooping their piles of stone and dirt into the cart. When they were done, the cart moved a few meters down the line where the process was repeated. When one of the carts stopped near Richard, the big orc next to him began loading the residue of his work onto the cart. Richard followed suit, taking the opportunity to inspect the prisoners pushing the carts. They were neither the blue humanoids nor were they orcs. It was difficult to tell in the greenish light of the tunnel, but Richard thought the cart prisoners' skin was yellowish. In his opinion, they appeared to be some distant offshoot of humans.

They remind me of pictures of cavemen from Earth history more than they do modern humans.

Once the carts were full, the cavemen prisoners departed with their loads. The orcs and what few blue prisoners remained alive went back to digging. Richard did likewise. Eventually, another group of chained prisoners came walking down the tunnel carrying buckets. The new prisoners were a different species than any of the others he'd seen thus far. They resembled chimpanzees, in his opinion.

One of the chimps dipped a ladle into its bucket. When it pulled the ladle out, a stream of dark liquid dripped onto the tunnel floor. The chimp raised the ladle toward Richard's mouth. The stink of the liquid preceded the ladle.

Richard knocked the offensive container away, splattering the liquid onto the floor.

The chimp appeared unperturbed as it stepped in front of the orc with the broken tusk, refilled the ladle, and held it out. The orc wrinkled his nose but grabbed the ladle and drained it dry. When the chimp refilled it, the orc emptied it again. He did so three times before the chimp moved to the next prisoner.

The big orc with the broken tusk sat down with his back against the wall before turning to Richard and motioning with his hand to a spot on the floor. Richard sat down as well. The orc made a soft growl accompanied by several unintelligible sounds. Richard shrugged his shoulders.

"If you're trying to make small talk," Richard whispered, "I haven't got the faintest idea what you're saying."

The orc bared his teeth. Even in the greenish light, they

appeared yellow. The broken-off tusk appeared more yellow than the rest.

Pointing at the orc, Richard decided to give him a name. "Yellow-tooth." Pointing at his own chest, he said, "Rick."

The orc pointed at his chest and made an unintelligible sound. He then pointed at Rick, making a noise that sounded more like 'Chekrak' than it did 'Rick.'

Another of the chimpanzee-like prisoners carrying a bucket approached from the opposite direction of the first. It stopped in front of Yellow-tooth. Reaching into its bucket, the chimp extracted a piece of meat. At least Richard assumed it was meat. It was hard to tell from the covering of slime. The smell of rot assailed Richard's nostrils. Ignoring the odor, Yellow-tooth grabbed the ball of meat and shoved it into his mouth. The big orc made a gagging sound, but after a few chews, Richard noticed him swallow.

The chimp moved in front of Richard and held out another piece of the rotted flesh. Richard was about to knock the chimp's hand aside when he changed his mind at the last moment. Taking the ball of slime, he set it on the floor between him and the big orc. The chimpanzee-like creature frowned, but in a human-like gesture, shrugged its shoulders before moving down the line.

Yellow-tooth made a soft growl. When Richard looked, the orc pointed a claw-tipped finger at the piece of meat and then at Richard's mouth.

Shaking his head, Richard pointed at the meat and then at the orc. Yellow-tooth gazed at him for several seconds before taking the meat. Instead of popping the fist-sized ball of slime into his mouth as Richard expected, Yellow-tooth passed the meat to the next orc in line. Richard noticed that orc pass it to the next orc as well. The orcs continued passing the meat down the line all the while appearing to use great care not to draw the attention of any guards. Finally, the ball of meat made it to an orc who was only half the size of the others.

A child? Richard wondered. He took a closer look at the orcs in his chain. Some were nearly as large as Yellow-tooth. He guessed a few of the other orcs would only come to the larger orcs' shoulders. A glance at the shorter orcs' chests confirmed what he suspected. *Females.*

Richard noticed the female orc sitting next to the smallest orc shove the half-rotten meat into the child's mouth. The young orc tried to spit it out, but the female forced it to chew and swallow. *Its mother?* he wondered.

Once the feeding was complete, the orcs curled up into balls on the floor. Soon, loud snoring could be heard all along the chain.

Richard tried curling up into a ball as well, but he couldn't sleep. *I'm a wizard scout. I don't need to eat or drink. My self-heal will keep me alive, but I've got to think of a way to escape. The explosion blocked the way we came. I've got to find a point of reference to the map Nick gave me. I've got to stay alive until then. They can't keep us digging in the same spot for long, the tunnel would collapse. They'll have to move us. Sooner or later, they'll take us somewhere familiar. When they do, I'll kill the guards and make my escape. All I've got to do is stay alive until then.*

Richard dozed a few minutes to keep his mind fresh, but mostly he thought. He had a lot of time to think.

I wonder what Jeena's doing. Does she even know I'm gone?

CHAPTER 3

"I want to know how we are going to get him back," Jeena said in a tone she hoped conveyed she wasn't in the mood for half measures. Glancing down the length of the *Defiant's* mess table, she waited for someone to answer.

Sergeant Ron sat at the head of the table while Wizard Scout Terrie Shastot and his wife, Angela, sat at the other end. Her bondmate's niece and nephew, Dren and Brachia, sat on one side of the table along with the elf mage Comstar and the leader of the dwarves' security team, Felspar. The ship's armorer, Sergeant Hendricks, sat near the dwarf. On the opposite side of the table from Jeena was the leader of the gnome mages, Calatron, and the *Defiant's* two newest crewmembers, the elf teenager Asquan and his orc friend, Timerman, along with the ship's Trecorian fighter pilot, Tia. Wizard Scout Terrie Shastot's battle helmet was in front of him on the table just as Rick's battle helmet was in front of her. In addition to the people at the table, Jeena also knew the ship's battle computers, Margery and Danny, were also listening in to the meeting. The final attendee was the two-meter-long silver dragon, Bright Wing. The dragon was curled up on top of a cupboard behind Sergeant Ron. The remainder of the *Defiant's* crew appeared to be giving the impromptu meeting a wide berth.

"Well?" Jeena said slapping the palm of her hand on the table. "I am waiting."

Dren looked at her brother before looking over at Sergeant Ron. The *Defiant's* captain shrugged his shoulders.

Jeena gripped her staff tighter with her left hand as she drummed the fingers of her right on the table. She'd called the emergency meeting ten minutes earlier. Thus far the results had been less than desirable. Her patience was beginning to wear thin.

She turned to look at the *Defiant's* elf mage. "Comstar, you were Rick's roommate on the *Defiant*. You *claim* to be a master mage. I want to know what we can do to return my bondmate to the ship."

The old elf seemed to wince at the word *claim*, but his face otherwise remained emotionless. He emulated Sergeant Ron by shrugging his shoulders. "It is really not as bad as it seems, Jeehana. Rick is a time-commando. He is always disappearing every couple of weeks on one mission or another for *'the One.'* Ask any of the others. You have only been on the *Defiant* for five days. Your bondmate will be back. He always comes back. It is just something you will have to get used—"

Jeena rose out of her seat slamming the butt of her staff onto the metal deck. The entire ship shuddered. "I will not accept this as business as usual. I am surprised all of you have. My bondmate is missing. We have to get him back."

"Calm down, Jeehana," said a wide-eyed Sergeant Ron rising to his feet. "The *Defiant's* a delicate piece of equipment. You can't go beating on her like that. As for Rick, it's like Comstar said. *'The One'* is always sending him on missions. There's nothing any of us can do about it. There's no use getting yourself all worked up about something over which we have no control."

Gritting her teeth, Jeena stared at the old ship's captain for several seconds before answering. "You think I am worked up, Captain? Believe me, this is nothing to how I am going to get if I do not get some answers. I will show you a worked-up version of me none of you want to see."

"Jeehana," said Dren apparently hoping to stop a useless argument before it got started. "What do you expect us to do? We don't control *'the One.'* Brachia and I explained how he's a network of computers. He does what he wants. Don't you think we'd do something if we could? You've just got to learn to accept—"

"No," Jeena said surprising herself with the anger in her voice. "Do not say it. Maybe the rest of you have accepted the situation, but I refuse to do so. I will not abandon my bondmate. You claim to be his friends. I am beginning to wonder since you have not stopped this before now?"

"Stopped it how?" asked Terrie voicing the question for everyone at the table. "It's easy to criticize, but doing something about it is another thing. I'd do anything for Rick, but there's nothing we can do. None of us even know where he is."

Jeena relaxed the grip on her staff. "That is where you are wrong. I know exactly where he is. I just don't know when he is."

"What?" asked several people simultaneously.

"Where?" said Sergeant Ron in a voice loud enough to override that of the others. "And how?"

Sitting back down on her part of the bench, Jeena glanced around the table, confirming she had everyone's attention before replying. She noticed that even Bright Wing raised her head over the edge of her perch to stare down with her silver dragon-eyes.

"Your bond link," said Bright Wing in near perfect intergalactic standard. "You have a trace on my brother with your bond link, do you not?"

"You are correct, Bright Wing. It is very faint, but I know where he is."

"You do?" asked Sergeant Ron. "So are you going to keep it a secret, or are you going to clue us in?"

"Clue you what?... No, never mind," Jeena said. "It does not matter. What does matter is that Rick is in the place where I first met him as a helper. He is in the place where we helped the green sphere and her brothers escape from their servitude to the Dragars."

"You mean at the Dragar temple on Portalis?" asked Tia. "It was destroyed. You helped destroy it, Jeehana."

Shaking her head Jeena looked at the teenager. "No, not their temple. The first time I encountered Rick and the spheres was in another place. It was the place where Rick told me the *Defiant* first fought the black-dragon ships. My bondmate told me it was at a mining camp on an asteroid."

"Uh," said Tia, "don't take this personally, Jeehana, but I think that's unlikely. After our skirmish there, my father established a military base on the asteroid to prevent anyone from opening another gate without his knowledge. If Rick was there now, I'm sure he'd have made contact with them already."

"Yes," Jeena admitted. "If he was there *now*, he would."

"I'm not following you," replied Tia.

Dren raised her head and smiled. "You're talking time-bubbles, aren't you?"

Nodding her head, Jeena looked around the table before turning her gaze on her bondmate's niece. "I am. I can sense Rick through our bond link, but the connection is very faint. He is alive, and he's on that asteroid. If he was in our time, the link would be stronger. Based upon the weakness of the link, I believe he is far in the past; much farther in the past than when we fought the Dragars at their temple. I believe he is in the time-bubble we encountered on the asteroid."

"All right, Jeehana," said Sergeant Ron. "If you're that sure, then I'll plot a course to the asteroid. If Rick's there, we'll find him."

Jeena surprised everyone by shaking her head. "No. That will not do any good at the moment. I have been questioning Nickelo about time-bubbles a lot over the last few days. Haven't I, Master Nick?"

"Uh, that is correct," replied Nickelo speaking through the external speaker of the battle helmet in front of Jeena. "If you remember, I told you based upon analysis of Rick's previous encounters with time-bubbles, that although they exist in all time at the same time, they are only visible at certain activation points in time. The origination point of the time-bubble on the asteroid was destroyed upon the death of the three spheres during the battle at the Dragars' temple. The time-bubble is no longer accessible from our time."

"No, it is not," Jeena agreed. "That is why we will need to travel to the past to access the time-bubble and rescue Rick."

Brachia frowned. "Jeehana, we can't time travel. Our adoptive father, Keka, repaired our teleporter on Storage at the directions of *'the One,'* but it's time-travel component no longer works, at least not for us. Even that three-headed dragon Rick calls the triplets can only create gates to the magic dimension. They can't time travel without Rick's help. I thought Dren and I explained that to you earlier."

Jeena allowed herself a slight smile for the first time since the start of the meeting. "You did, and you are correct. The triplets need Rick to time travel because the Power the Lady provides them with for dimensional gates is different than what is needed to travel back in time. Only the Lady's link to Rick can be used to manipulate the Lady's Power in the way necessary to time travel."

"Then we're back to square one," said Sergeant Ron. "We can't do anything. That's what we've been trying to tell you."

"That is not quite correct, is it, Master Nick?" Jeena asked.

Her bondmate's computer remained silent for several seconds as everyone at the table looked at the battle helmet on the table in front of her. Finally, the helmet's external speakers crackled.

"I calculate you are referring to your ability as your Lady's high priestess to manipulate links," said Nickelo. "If your bond link to Rick is still active like you say, then you could theoretically draw Power from your Lady through the link, manipulate the Power to the frequency necessary for time travel, and feed the modified Power to the triplets. That still leaves you with one major problem. You do not know where in time Rick is located. I calculate eternity is a big search area."

"You are correct, of course," Jeena said. "I do not know where in time Rick is located. None of the people on this ship know that."

"I fail to understand how any of this is helpful," said Comstar. "When I was enslaved by the Dragars, I traveled through time on many occasions in time-bubbles. Even if you succeed in creating a time-bubble, you still have to know where in time you are going. You just admitted none of us know that information."

Jeena shook her head. "That is not exactly true. I said that none of the *people* on this ship know when in time Rick is located. There are other life forms on the *Defiant* besides people. Aren't there, Master Nick?"

"Now wait a nanosecond, Jeehana," said Nickelo sounding defensive. "If I knew where or when Rick was, I would be the first to tell you. He's my friend. There is nothing in my databanks about Rick's location. Or do you think I am lying?"

"No," said Jeena. "I do not think you are lying. However, I do think you are in a position to find out. So are Margery, Danny, and Terrie's battle computer."

"My name is Taylor," came a male voice over the battle helmet in front of Terrie. "And like Nickelo, I have no knowledge of

Wizard Scout Shepard's location in this time or any other. I am a computer. I do not lie."

Jeena shook her head. "No, you are not a computer. You act like one, but you are a life form the same as the rest of us. Rick shared his knowledge of '*the One*' with me. All of you battle computers are part of '*the One.*' Margery and Danny, that includes you as well." Turning to Dren, she said, "You told me a theory of how the battle computers could be a part of '*the One*' without realizing it. When '*the One*' needs to include them in its discussion, it contacts them. After the discussion, it removes the knowledge of the conversation from their databanks and then cuts off the communication link. Do you still stick by your theory?"

"Yes," said Dren. "But I don't see how—"

"And you, Master Nick," Jeena said placing her right hand on the battle helmet on the table to her front. "You claim not to know when in time Rick is located. Whether you know it or not, I believe you are the reason he is there."

"Me?" said Nickelo sounding offended. "Rick is my friend. I would never do anything to harm him. I tell you there is nothing in—"

"Enough," Jeena said. "Even if you do not remember it, I believe you are a large part of the reason Rick has been going on missions. I am a creature of magic. I am also the High Priestess of the Lady of the Tree. I sense things even Rick does not. For example, I sense a wall of magic inside you, Master Nick. I believe behind that wall is the key to all that has been happening."

"I can't get past that wa—"

"That does not matter right now," Jeena said letting some of her growing impatience come out in her voice. "All that I care about now is getting Rick back. Everything else can wait." Glancing around the room, she locked eyes with each of the people at the table in turn. "This is what is going to happen. One of you battle computers, and I do not care which, is going to contact '*the One.*' You are going to inform '*the One*' that he, she, or it is going to give me the exact point in time where Rick is located. You will also inform '*the One*' that if I am not given that point in time, I will use my link with Rick to manipulate the security network of the central computer and every other computer in this galaxy and the magic dimension as well. I will bring the entire tele-network down around their ears if they push me. Do not doubt my words." Jeena stood and pounded her staff on the floor again. The *Defiant* shuddered even harder than it had earlier.

"Jeehana," yelled Sergeant Ron. "I told you—"

"Quiet," Jeena told the *Defiant's* captain. "You had your chance as have all of you. I am in charge now. The days of *'the One'* using Rick without his permission are over. I happen to know *'the One'* placed a part of itself in Rick's DNA. A part of me is also in Rick. I swear I will use that connection to destroy *'the One'* if I do not get my bondmate back."

Jeena slapped the top of the battle helmet in front of her hard enough to make it bounce a handbreadth off the table. "I am done playing games. Now tell *'the One'* to either give me the point in time where Rick is located or suffer the consequences. If *'the One'* does not like it, you can tell him I do not care. I am going to get Rick back one way or another. I swear it."

CHAPTER 4

At least some of the orcs in Richard's prisoner chain were military in his opinion. Six weeks of captivity had afforded him more than enough opportunity to observe them. The orcs' sense of discipline reminded him of his old military unit in the Marines. From the respect the other orcs gave Yellow-tooth, Richard suspected the big orc chained next to him was one of their military leaders.

Richard's respect for the orcs had increased as the weeks passed. They'd withstood the guards' continuous whippings proudly with nary a whimper. Despite their courage, the constant abuse had slowly taken its toll on even the hardiest of the orcs. Richard only had to glance at Yellow-tooth's bare back crisscrossed with scabs of green blood and festering puss to know the beatings they were taking. Unlike Richard, none of the other prisoners could self-heal. The blue prisoners had suffered worse than the orcs. None of the non-orc prisoners remained alive. The last of their decayed bodies had fallen off the chain from the constant dragging the previous day. With the death of the other non-orcs, Richard knew he stood out like a sore thumb. Thankfully, either the guards were too stupid to notice he could self-heal, or they just didn't care. Either way, he considered himself lucky.

Richard looked around the new tunnel where his chain was now digging. *It's as I expected. The Thargs can only keep us excavating in a section of tunnel until it threatens to collapse. Then they move our chain to a new location to start fresh. I guess I should be grateful we move to new locations so often. It's the only thing that breaks our routine.*

Even as he thought it, Richard knew his line of thinking wasn't completely true. When enough prisoners died so that the empty shackles in the chain outnumbered those holding live prisoners, their routine changed drastically. *The last time that had happened was ten days ago,* Richard thought, *when the last of the blue prisoners in my chain died.*

He remembered how another group of prisoners resembling human-sized salamanders had been brought in to fill the empty spaces in the chain. Regretfully, none of the new salamander prisoners had lasted more than a week before succumbing to the grueling work and beatings. Only the tough orcs seemed able to withstand their imprisonment for more than a few days.

Only the orcs and me, Richard corrected himself. *My self-heal makes sure I stay alive.* After looking at his bloody fingers, he shoved them into the tunnel wall and pulled out another chunk of dirt and soil to add to his pile of debris. *That is if you can call being in this living hell a life.*

Glancing at the big orc next to him, Richard noticed greenish liquid dripping from the tips of the orc's fingers.

The constant digging is slowly wearing away even the orc's hard fingernails, Richard thought. Taking a look at the pile of diggings beside the orc, he noticed that for once it was smaller than his own pile. Reaching over, Richard dropped a double fistful of dirt and stone onto the pile.

Yellow-tooth glanced at him and nodded before going back to digging.

Things have sure changed, Richard thought. *I remember sleeping with one eye open the first few days in order to make sure the orcs in my chain didn't try to eat me. I know them better now. They may not be civilized in the way I think of civilized, but they definitely aren't the barbaric, murderous orcs I've fought in the past.*

Richard glanced back at the big orc next to him before digging out another handful of the soft rock in the wall and adding it to the orc's pile.

I suppose most of the orcs have a small streak of kindness in them. At least they are kind to each other. The three orc children in our chain-gang would've been beaten to death long ago if the orcs next to them didn't keep shoving some of their debris onto the children's piles. The memory of Yellow-tooth sharing his pile of diggings with him on more than one occasion crossed his mind. *I wonder why he helps me? I'm not an orc.*

One of the monkey creatures came walking down the chain line carrying a bucket. Stopping in front of Richard, the chimp pulled out a piece of slimy meat. As usual, Richard accepted the putrid substance, keeping it in his hand until the monkey moved on. When none of the guards were looking, he passed the meat to Yellow-tooth. The big orc passed it to the next orc until it made its way to one of the half-starved orc children. The young orc ate it greedily.

That one isn't going to make it much longer, Richard thought. He glanced down the length of the chain. *Actually, none of the orcs are. They're tough, but the beatings and short rations are taking their toll. I give them a couple more weeks. If something doesn't change, I may wind up being the only one of my original chain left alive. No one can survive this torture for long.*

Richard thought back to a time during his first week in the chain gang when he'd made the mistake of tripping over one of his shackles and falling to the tunnel floor. Like usual, the guards kept the chain line moving. Either a prisoner rose on their own, or they were dragged to death. When he'd tried to regain his feet, the Tharg he called Chuckles had reached out and knocked him back down with his rod. Try as he might, he'd been unable to stand. Each time he almost made it to his feet, Chuckles had knocked him back. Then the unexpected had happened. Yellow-tooth had stopped dead in his tracks and shouted, "Chekrak!" At his shout, the other orcs stopped as well. The guards immediately began whipping the other prisoners in an attempt to get them moving. After taking more than a few strikes of Chuckles's whip, Yellow-tooth had finally started walking again. So did the other orcs in the chain. Thankfully, the momentary halt had given Richard the time he'd needed to stand.

Why did the orcs help me? Richard wondered for the thousandth time. *Is it because I've got a splice of orc in my DNA? Do they sense it? All the orc DNA has ever done until now is given me a bad temper. Surely that's not the reason they help me. There's bound to be more to it.*

A guard walking down the line brought Richard out of his thoughts as the Tharg started kicking the prisoners, forcing them to their feet.

This is different, Richard thought as he stood. *They usually let us rest for a few minutes after we eat.*

Several of the guards joined their companion in beating the prisoners who were slow rising. Chuckles came walking down the line until he was even with Richard. As the sadistic guard raised his whip, Richard braced himself for a taste of the cat-o'-nine. At that moment, Yellow-tooth let out a groan. The cat-o'-nine struck the big orc instead of Richard. Within seconds, multiple strokes of the guard's whip opened new cuts on the orc's back and neck. Somehow Yellow-tooth was able to keep from screaming. The big orc's silence must've been too little to interest Chuckles because the Tharg stopped whipping and moved down the line.

"Raraggg!" woofed Chuckles.

Richard recognized the Tharg word for 'march.' He stepped out at the same time as the orcs in his chain. They continued marching for several minutes. Like always, Richard kept his eye out for anything familiar. Like always, he saw nothing in the tunnel he recognized.

I wonder why they're moving us early, Richard thought. *We've only been in that section of the tunnel for a day. Normally they keep us in one spot for three days.*

After an hour of walking, Richard became aware of a change in the lighting.

The green glow in the tunnel is getting brighter. At least I think it is.

Squinting at Yellow-tooth's back, Richard was sure he could see details in the crisscrossed scars that he hadn't seen earlier.

The lead orc in the chain came to a 'T' intersection. Chuckles ran to the front of the line and shoved the orc to the right. The other orcs in line dutifully turned to the right as they came to the intersection. When Richard approached the 'T,' he glanced down the left tunnel, past Chuckles. For the barest instant, he saw something that caused him to stumble. Catching himself before a Tharg could react, Richard turned to the right, staying in step with Yellow-tooth.

The image of what he'd seen flared in Richard's mind. *It's a green sphere. I saw it plain as day. That's the reason the light's brighter. This has to be the point in the tunnel system where I originally found the green sphere.* Realization came over him. *I know where I am. I'll bet the orange and purple spheres are somewhere nearby. The green sphere and her two brothers are one entity.*

A cat-o'-nine struck Richard's back. He heard Chuckles gurgle. Richard ignored the pain as well as Chuckles's laughter.

Keep smiling, a-hole. Your day's finally here. All I need is the right opportunity. When I get it, you and your four-armed buddies are dead.

After another half hour of walking, the Thargs halted the chain gang. Richard heard the sound of dragging chains along with angry shouts in the distance. Five minutes later, a line of orc prisoners and their guards came into view. From what he could tell, Richard figured over half of the shackles in the new chain gang were empty.

They're short the same as ours. They're going to merge the chains together. That's why we left the other tunnel early.

As the new line of prisoners came to a halt, Richard grew alert. After six weeks of the same routine, he was familiar with the merging of chains.

The guards will be forced to remove a shackle on one of our arms to get rid of the empty spaces between the prisoners. That won't make me completely free, but it should give me enough slack in my other arm and my legs to move more than normal. Still, it won't be easy. The guards are careful when merging chains.

Richard heard some grunts coming from behind him. Like usual, the Thargs were bringing in a few extra guards. He made a count.

Between the two chains, there are now twelve guards; six with the new group and six with mine. Still, none of them are in armor, and most of them only have their whips and rods. If they make a single mistake, I'm going to take advantage of it.

Chuckles began moving up the chain line one prisoner at a time with two of his fellow guards following close behind. Richard noticed the sadistic Tharg come to the first empty spot. Using his key, Chuckles unlocked the chain connecting the empty space to the adjacent prisoner. The two guards following Chuckles removed the unused portion of the chain and hooked the prisoner to one of the prisoners in the other chain.

Richard glanced to his right. An empty set of shackles dangled from the main chain. A plan began forming in his mind as Chuckles and his two companions continued up the line removing empty shackles and adding new prisoners as they came. After a long five minutes, they were at the empty set of shackles to Richard's right.

Relax, Richard thought. *Don't look up. Look down. Look at the floor. Wait until he frees your arm from the main chain.*

Chuckles grasped the shackle's chain about an arm length from Richard's hand. Inserting his key into the lock, the Tharg twisted. When the shackle fell free, the Tharg turned to a prisoner in the new chain in order to chain him to Richard's free arm. Richard didn't give the four-armed guard a chance to complete his maneuver. As soon as Chuckles turned his back, Richard reached up, grabbed a fistful of hair on the back of the Tharg's head, and jerked with all his weight. At the same time, he brought his knee up directly into the back of Chuckles's neck. The Tharg's thick muscles absorbed some of the blow's force, but not enough. Richard knew he'd aimed his knee well when he heard the satisfying snap of the Tharg's neck.

Grabbing the key from Chuckles's suddenly limp hand before it fell to the stone floor, Richard plunged it into the second guard's eye. The guard screamed and fell beside Chuckles's twitching corpse. The third guard raised his whip to strike. Before he could do more than draw the cat-o'-nine back, Richard leaped in the air and delivered a flying jump-kick to the guard's belly. The guard was big, but it was knocked back enough to fall into the waiting arms of Yellow-tooth. The big orc slammed the Tharg's head into the tunnel wall, splattering blood and pieces of brain matter across the stone before tossing the bloody body to the floor.

Taking a quick glance to his rear, Richard saw three more guards rushing forward in close formation. One of the guards drew a stun pistol from his belt. Richard fell to the ground next to Chuckles's body, grabbing the dead Tharg's stunner. Pointing the overly large pistol in the direction of the rushing guards, he pulled the trigger a split second before the other guard fired. As Richard's stunner made a loud screeching sound, all three of the guards dropped to the stone floor. Richard thanked his lucky stars the stunners were wide-area weapons designed to neutralize multiple prisoners with a single shot.

Taking advantage of the short lull, Richard jumped to his feet and used Chuckles's key to remove his remaining chains.

"Chekrak! Dova se quama, ky!"

Richard turned to his left, noticing Yellow-tooth holding out his hands and making a *'give me'* motion with his fingers. Without hesitation, Richard threw the key to the big orc who immediately began unlocking the shackles on himself and the orcs nearest him.

They're definitely organized, Richard thought.

Glancing around for the remaining six guards, Richard saw orcs in the two chains ganging up on the Thargs and pulling them to the floor. He heard screams. They were not made by orcs.

Definitely military, Richard thought. *I've done all I can for them. Military or not, I can't help them or anyone else down here. This is my chance to get out of this place. I'm going to take advantage of it while I can.*

Wasting no time, Richard began running down the tunnel in the direction the map in his mind told him led to the surface. He knew he had a long way to go.

A shout from behind stopped him in his tracks.

Turning back, Richard noticed Yellow-tooth looking at him. On impulse, he yelled, "Chekrak!" and tossed his former chain-mate the stunner he'd taken off Chuckles.

The big orc caught the weapon in midair and lowered the stunner to his side, seeming very comfortable with the handgun.

Definitely military, Richard thought.

As if to confirm Richard's opinion, Yellow-tooth barked a command at the other prisoners. The orcs from both chains formed two lines, the lead orcs all carrying confiscated Tharg stunners. Orc children and females were ushered into the center of the formation.

Definitely not typical orc behavior, Richard thought. *At least I don't think it is.*

Yellow-tooth stood at attention and raised his free arm across his chest. Richard stood at attention and returned the salute, then took off down the tunnel at a dead run. Within seconds he'd left his fellow prisoners far behind.

Right. Take a right. Now left. Another left.

Following the green route on the map in his mind, Richard continued running through the tunnels for twenty-five minutes without encountering anyone. He doubted his luck would hold. He soon found out he was correct. The blare of an alarm began sounding from ahead.

So, someone's finally noticed there's a problem in the tunnels. The easy times are over. Richard had a momentary prick of conscience that he hadn't remained with the orcs. He shook the thought out of his head. *I got them free. I've paid Yellow-tooth and the others back for whatever help they gave me. I can't make it out of these tunnels dragging a hundred half-starved orcs with me. I probably won't even make it out alive traveling by my lonesome. I paid them back. My conscience is clear.*

Despite his words, the obstinate pinprick at the outskirts of his soul continued. If anything, the feeling grew worse.

Well, it's too late now to change things. What's done is done. I've got to concentrate on getting out of here. The orcs will just have to take care of themselves.

Rounding a corner, Richard surprised a Tharg in the process of whipping an orc prisoner in a side tunnel. Leaping into the air, he caught the guard in the throat with the edge of his foot. The guard went down, spewing blood out of his mouth. Stopping long enough to strip off the guard's utility belt, Richard tossed the orc the key off the belt. Then he strapped the belt around his waist, pulled the guard's stunner out of its holster, and examined the weapon. A yellow light-bar on the grip was fully lit.

I sure hope that mean's it's fully loaded.

Once he finished inspecting the handgun, Richard returned it to the holster before running back to the main tunnel. When he left the orc, the prisoner was squatting next to the dying guard, unchaining his shackles.

Run! Run! Run! Richard thought. *I've got to get out of here. Left; left; left, now right; now down.* As Richard ran, he monitored his progress on the map his battle computer had placed in his mind. He knew he was getting near the entrance. *There. I think I remember that red rock. Slow down; you're getting close.*

Stopping twenty meters short of a four-way intersection,

Richard crouched low against the wall. The cross tunnel ahead was not the one he sought, but from looking at the map, he knew he was getting near it. He forced himself to be extra cautious.

Without a link to my Power reserve, I can't use even a simple passive scan. Without my wizard scout abilities, I've got no idea what I'll be facing when I get to the entrance. All I'll have to rely on will be my eyes, ears, and common sense.

Richard could almost hear his battle computer telling him that he was often short of the latter.

Well, I'll admit Nick's probably right most of the time. I wish he was here now to give me some advice, but he's not, so it's up to me.

The sound of metal on stone drew Richard's attention. He lay flat on the tunnel floor while straining to hear. Soon the echoing sound of stomping feet and reflection of lights on the walls of the intersection announced the approach of a team of guards. One guard flashed a light down the side tunnel, but luck was with Richard. The guards kept running past the intersection. Within seconds they disappeared from view.

Good. They're the normal unarmored guards. They don't have regular soldiers patrolling the tunnels yet.

Once the last echo of the guards' feet faded away, Richard began moving again. He ran through the intersection, taking a dogleg to the left. Suddenly he came upon three humanoids wearing what appeared to be gas masks. They were hooking hoses to a large canister in the back of a motorized cart. While they weren't guards, Richard could tell they weren't soldiers either. None of the humanoids were the four-armed Thargs. All three appeared to be human or close enough to it not to make a difference. Two of the humans were working on the hoses while the third stood behind them with a handgun at the ready.

Technicians, Richard thought as he activated the stunner he'd confiscated from the guard he'd killed earlier. With the first whine of the stunner, all three humans fell to the ground in a heap. Grabbing the handgun from the human who'd been standing guard, Richard gave it a quick inspection. From what he could tell, it was a magic-based weapon similar in size and shape to a Deloris blaster.

The trigger mechanism looks simple enough. Pointing the pistol down the tunnel, he pulled the trigger. Nothing happened. Inspecting the weapon closer, Richard noticed a small lever resembling a safety. Flicking it downward, he pulled the trigger again. This time the pistol bucked in his hand. A blue streak of energy ricocheted off the wall ten meters down the tunnel before disappearing around the corner.

It's a lightweight energy round. I doubt it'll penetrate armor, but the range should be a whole lot better than the stunner.

Kneeling next to the human who'd been standing guard, Richard rolled him over and spotted two stun grenades on the human's utility belt. He'd seen the stun grenades used before when some prisoners in another chain had tried to riot. The grenades didn't produce shrapnel, but the concussion was powerful enough to stun if it exploded nearby.

Removing the utility belt he'd confiscated earlier, Richard started to buckle on the new one before changing his mind. He pulled the technician's pants and shirt off and put them on before adding the new utility belt with its grenades and the holster for the pistol. He took the stunner from the other holster and shoved it into his newly acquired belt. He bent down and removed one of the man's boots. One look at the man's eight toes convinced him trying on the stunned technician's footgear would be a waste of effort.

Not completely human after all. Too bad. I could've used some boots.

Although rushed for time, Richard took a moment to inspect the large canister the technicians had been handling. Two plastic hoses were attached to the canister via some pipes with twist knobs. He noticed a small device made out of metal and glass that had all the appearance of a pressure gauge.

The technicians are wearing masks. I think they were going to gas the tunnels. Everyone in the tunnels below this point not wearing a gas mask would probably be killed.

Looking for a way to disable the canister without releasing the gas, Richard found nothing obvious. After a few seconds, he gave up.

I don't have time to figure it out. He looked at the unconscious technicians. *As soon as these three wake up, they'll probably release the gas. I know I would if I was them.*

Concentrating on the image of thousands of helpless prisoners below, Richard twisted the necks of each of the humans until he heard a snap. Once again, something pricked at him, but the memory of all the prisoners he'd seen beaten to death over the last six weeks overrode his conscience. He continued walking toward the tunnel entrance, trying to make as little noise as possible.

There's bound to be a reception party when I get near the entrance.

Walking at a crouch with the confiscated stunner in his left hand and the technician's handgun in his right, Richard drew closer to what he figured was the final turn in the tunnel before freedom. He spotted several stacks of boxes and a large intersection just beyond them. Hiding behind the boxes, he sniffed the air. It smelled fresh. Bright lights overhead cast shadows in the main tunnel of the intersection. Some of the light extended into the side tunnel, illuminating everything on the other side of the boxes.

I'm not going to sneak by anyone with those lights. I can't stay here either. The alarm's been sounded. Someone's bound to come this way soon. I'll just have to start walking down the tunnel and hope my luck holds out.

Thus resolved, Richard stood and moved around the boxes, hoping for the best. His luck lasted all of ten steps. Without warning, a half dozen energy beams sliced through the air around him. The stink of ozone and burned flesh filled the air. Jumping behind the corner of a little alcove cut into one wall, he felt a burning sensation in his left arm.

I've been hit.

A quick glance confirmed a finger-sized hole surrounded by charred flesh in the upper muscle of his left arm. The wound began to throb as the initial shock wore off, then Richard sensed his self-heal repairing the damage. He crouched lower in the alcove, trying to buy time for the first ninety percent of his wound to heal. He had the distinct feeling he wasn't going to have the time. While the firing had stopped, a quick peek around the corner of his hiding spot revealed two human-like creatures walking down the center of the tunnel with rifles pointed at his hiding spot. Bright lights behind the two made it apparent they were soldiers wearing light armor.

Well, they might be soldiers, but they're definitely not frontline troops. Experienced soldiers would never light up their own comrades that way. If those two knew their business, they'd already be trying to bounce some rounds into my hidey-hole. They're inexperienced. That may mean all the difference in keeping me alive.

Long shadows stretched out before the two soldiers as their companions continued to silhouette them with their lights. The pair would soon be at an angle where they would be able to shoot directly into his alcove.

Eyeing the two weapons in his hands, Richard made a quick analysis of their effectiveness against the approaching troops. *I doubt either this stunner or the handgun will penetrate even the light armor those soldiers are wearing. I'm going to have to do this the hard way.*

Bracing his feet against the wall, Richard tensed his muscles but stayed where he was for the moment. The guards appeared to be in no hurry. They continued approaching his hiding place at a methodical pace, weapons at the ready.

You've given your enemy too much time, boys, Richard thought in silent admonishment. *You should've killed me already. You're about to find out you lost your chance because now it's my turn.*

Pulling the pins on both of his stun grenades, Richard threw one out followed a second later by the other. The first grenade skidded along the floor, stopping against the right foot of the lead soldier.

Boom!

The first grenade exploded with a blinding flash. As the lead guard was knocked off his feet, the second guard began firing blindly at Richard's position. The second grenade exploded throwing off the second soldier's aim. The first soldier screamed from his position on the floor. When the second soldier looked down, Richard launched himself out of the alcove, directly at the second soldier. The soldier jerked upright just as Richard body-slammed him. Snatching the rifle out of the man's grasp in midair, Richard forced the barrel into the center of the soldier's chest and pulled what he hoped was the trigger.

A series of bangs sounded as a half dozen military-grade rounds tore through the soldier's armor, knocking the man against the far wall. Richard's momentum carried him into the wall as well. A sharp pain shot up his left arm followed by a snapping sound.

Crap. My arm's broke.

He had a fleeting thought that the bullet wound in the arm had just started to heal. Richard let out a little groan from the pain but refused to stop moving. Bouncing off the tunnel wall, he dove in the direction of the first guard who was just starting to bring his rifle to bear. Kicking the soldier's weapon to the side, Richard raised the rifle he'd taken from the soldier he'd killed and aimed at the first soldier. The man tried to bring his own weapon back in line with Richard, but he was too slow.

Bang!

One of Richard's rounds caught the man directly in the center of his visor. The hardened glass exploded inward as a spray of black liquid gushed out the back of the soldier's helmet, splattering against the opposite wall. A horrible stench filled the tunnel.

Definitely not human, was all Richard had time to think before more beams of blue energy began zinging through the tunnel as the two soldiers' companions began firing their weapons.

The distinctive sound of metal hitting stone caught Richard's attention. A split-second later, a round metallic shape bounced down the tunnel in his direction.

Grenade, Richard thought.

Diving behind the body of the first soldier he'd killed, Richard prayed the man's armor would provide at least some protection. From the brief look he'd gotten of the grenade, he knew it was not a stun grenade.

Boom!

The sound was deafening. Both Richard and the soldier's body flew a dozen paces down the tunnel floor, rolling as they went. He felt liquid running out of both ears. The explosion had ruptured his eardrums. Somehow during the roll, he managed to keep hold of the dead soldier's rifle. Blindly aiming in the general direction the grenade had come from, he held the trigger down, spraying a score of rounds at the other soldiers. He didn't expect to hit anyone, so was surprised when their return fire slowed. He caught a glimpse of several soldiers diving for cover. He pulled the trigger on his rifle again. Nothing happened.

Out of ammo, and I don't have time to figure out how to load it.

Spying two round metal shapes on the belt of the dead soldier he'd used for cover, Richard grabbed both grenades, pulled their pins, and threw them toward the intersection.

"See how you like a taste of your own medicine!" Richard yelled as he ducked behind the body again for cover.

The grenades exploded in succession. Boom! Boom!

As soon as Richard saw the flash of the second grenade, he jumped to his feet and ran toward the intersection. As he passed the assault rifle of the other soldier he'd killed, he kicked the weapon upward, catching it in midair. He fired a short burst at a couple of shadows in the smoke and dust ahead. The shadows fell backward. When Richard reached the intersection, he jumped over two bodies and fired a long burst as he rounded the corner. Three soldiers hiding behind a stack of crates returned his fire, but they were *spraying and praying.* Their rounds went wide of their intended target. Adjusting his aim, Richard cut down two of the soldiers with a concentrated burst from his assault rifle. Before he could bring his rifle to bear on the third soldier, his weapon stopped firing.

Crap! Out of ammo again.

The third soldier wasn't wearing a helmet. The soldier aimed his weapon dead center at Richard's chest and gave a nasty smile. In desperation, Richard threw his empty rifle at the soldier's head. The man ducked below the flying weapon, pulling the trigger of his own rifle as he did. The soldier's aim was off. Several of the magic rounds hit the floor in front of Richard. One of the rounds ricocheted, hitting Richard in the leg and knocking him down. A flash of pain caused everything to go white for a split-second. Even blinded as he was, he knew he'd probably just lost his left kneecap. With a scream of agony, he waited for the soldier to finish him off. The expected round didn't come. When his vision cleared, he noticed the soldier struggling to replace a small battery pack underneath his rifle.

"You're out of ammo, a-hole," Richard said through clenched teeth. Drawing the technician's pistol from the holster on his utility belt, he took aim and put a single round through the guard's right eye.

The echoes of his shot died away. All was quiet except for the distant alarm bell.

Richard was sure the calm wouldn't last long. His leg hurt like hell. He forced himself to look down. The wound was just as bad as he feared. The flowing blood and bits of protruding bone confirmed his kneecap was gone.

Thank the Creator a side effect of self-healing is a partial dulling of the pain. Otherwise, I'd be passed out by now.

Ripping off part of his trouser leg, Richard wound a makeshift tourniquet just above his knee. Even with his self-heal, Richard figured it would be at least five minutes before he'd be able to put much pressure on his leg. Glancing at his left arm, he saw it was mostly healed. He picked up a two-meter-long length of metal rod to use as a makeshift crutch, then hobbling over to the soldier he'd just killed, and picked up the man's rifle. A check of the weapon's battery compartment confirmed what he'd suspected.

The soldier got into too much of a hurry. The battery is cockeyed in the opening.

After jiggling the jammed battery a couple of times, Richard succeeded in getting it out. Easing the battery back into its slot, he heard a click. He removed the soldier's belt, replacing his old belt with it. Clipped to the new belt were four extra batteries and two grenades. Despite the pain in his left leg, he began feeling more hopeful as he hobbled in the direction of the mine's entrance. When he got within ten meters of the opening, Richard felt a shiver run down the back of his neck. No one was in sight, but he had a bad feeling nonetheless.

'The One' *sometimes communicates through tele-bots to give me a sense of intuition when things aren't right,* Richard thought.

Using the metal rod to hold himself erect, Richard pulled the pin on one of his antipersonnel grenades and then bounced it off the left wall of the tunnel in such a manner that it rolled out the entrance, disappearing around the right corner of the opening.

"Aracck!" came a shout accompanied by the sound of scrambling feet.

Two soldiers ran from the right side of the entrance, diving for a stack of boxes near the left side. Richard mowed the pair down with a long burst from his rifle. Although the soldiers appeared to be wearing light armor, it was apparently no match for the military-grade rounds. Spurts of dark liquid shot out the backs of both soldiers as they fell to the ground. A second later, Richard's grenade exploded around the right corner, sending a cloud of dust across the opening. When the dust cleared enough to see, Richard noticed a bloody helmet rolling past the entrance. Pulling the partially expended battery out of his rifle, he replaced it with a fully charged one.

I'm not running out of ammo this time.

Hobbling as fast as he could toward the entrance, Richard sensed his self-heal working overtime to bring his knee back into baseline. His speed picked up considerably as he closed the distance to fresh air and freedom.

It's still going to be a couple of minutes before I can walk without the aid of my makeshift crutch, but I don't care. I'm going to be free.

Stepping past the entrance, Richard noticed two more bodies wearing light armor crumpled on the ground to his right. One of the soldiers was still alive but bleeding from his chest. The soldier tried raising his weapon to a firing position. Aiming his rifle at the soldier with the intent of putting a round into the man's head, Richard changed his mind at the last moment. Instead of firing, he slammed the butt of his makeshift crutch into the side of the soldier's head.

"Sorry, buddy," Richard said as he hobbled past the unconscious but still living soldier. "I respect your courage, but I can't leave a conscious enemy to my rear."

The tunnel's entrance opened up to a rock-strewn clearing with high cliffs to the sides and rear.

It's far from how I remember it, Richard thought, *but then I'm a couple of million years in the past, so that's no surprise.*

Richard spotted a gravel road snaking out a kilometer to his front before disappearing around a hill. The bright sunlight made it difficult to see after six weeks underground. He felt Power from his self-heal envelope his eyes. The terrain became clearer. He spotted three orange-colored vehicles resembling tracked dump trucks parked fifty meters to his right front and began hobbling toward the vehicles as fast as he could on his damaged knee.

I've got to get away from here quick. There's bound to be more guards on the surface.

When he got within ten meters of the nearest truck, Richard's hopes began rising even higher. Although he knew he was no closer to getting back home two million years in the future, he didn't care.

I'm out of the mine. That's what matters. One step at a time. I'll figure out how to get home somehow. If I can get that truck cranked, I'll put some distance between me and this place. Then I'll have time to think.

Crack!

An invisible sledgehammer slammed into the back of Richard's right shoulder, throwing him spinning to the ground. His rifle skidded across the gravel and came to rest half a dozen meters away. Grabbing his pistol out of its holster, he rolled onto his right side, scanning back and forth in an attempt to spot a target. He spied a four-armed Tharg wearing light armor running in his direction, carrying rifles in two of his four hands.

Ignoring the pain in his shoulder, Richard brought his pistol up in an attempt to line the sights on the weaving soldier. The sights were blurry. He fired but missed. The charging soldier fired both rifles before Richard could get another round off. Two blue streaks of energy sizzled through Richard's left arm and shoulder. His pistol went flying into the air. Grabbing his last grenade with his right hand, he got it pulled off his belt just before the furry Tharg was on him. A hard kick from the soldier sent the grenade flying out of Richard's hand with its pin still in place. The soldier put an overly large foot on Richard's throat and pressed the barrels of both rifles against Richard's head.

"Sheknak ceadar noshay!" the Tharg shouted as he spit a gob of foul liquid into Richard's face.

Struggling for breath, Richard sensed more than saw the Tharg start to increase pressure on the triggers of the rifles. In a moment of clarity, he noticed three stripes painted on the soldier's armor. Despite the situation, Richard gave an inward smile. *At least it's a sergeant. I couldn't live with myself if an officer killed me.* As his surroundings began to black out, Richard had a final thought. *I've always been told you never hear the shot that kills you. I guess I'm about to find out.*

Crack!

Bloody gore, splintered bone, and brain particles burst out of the sergeant's forehead. The Tharg flew over Richard's body, landing in a heap on the side opposite the mine entrance. Regaining his sight, Richard looked for the source of the shot. He spotted a large, gray figure with two tusks, one broken off at the halfway point, near the mine's entrance. As he watched, Yellow-tooth stepped clear of the tunnel, lowering a rifle from his shoulder.

Definitely military, Richard thought as he struggled to a kneeling position.

Crawling to his makeshift crutch, Richard leveraged himself into a standing position. Blood oozed out of holes in his right shoulder and left arm. He vaguely acknowledged that the bleeding from his knee had finally stopped.

"Chekrak!" shouted the big orc raising his rifle over his head. Half a hundred other orcs came running out of the tunnel. Several of them carried rifles. As he watched, the orcs began stripping weapons and equipment off the bodies of the soldiers Richard had killed.

Most definitely military, Richard thought appreciatively.

An image of thousands of orc prisoners in chains flashed into Richard's mind along with a feeling he should go back in the tunnels.

"Save them," came an unbidden thought. *"I am* 'the One.'"

"Save them?" Richard shouted at the sky. "Are you crazy? I just got out of that hellhole. I'm not going back in there. I can't save them anyway. It's not possible."

"Save them!" said the voice in his mind speaking more firmly.

For a moment, Richard mulled the problem over in his mind. A score of Yellow-tooth's orcs had already taken up positions around the tunnel entrance. Half of them were now armed with confiscated weapons. A few were in pieces of confiscated light armor.

Shaking his head, Richard shouted at the heavens again. "It's not possible, I tell you. There are hundreds of guards and soldiers in those tunnels. I can't save them. Besides, they're orcs. Why should I help?"

No reply was forthcoming.

A memory of Yellow-tooth stopping the chain that day when he was being dragged flashed into Richard's mind. Other memories of the big orc sharing his pile of debris with him on more than one occasion even though it meant taking a whipping came as well. He remembered how the orcs shared their food with their younglings.

Several orcs ran past Richard, heading for the orange trucks. Within seconds, he heard the roar of engines. Two trucks roared past him toward the mine's entrance. The third stopped next to him. An orc standing on the running board next to the driver jumped off, grabbed Richard, and threw him into the bed of the truck before jumping in beside him. The engine roared to life, its tracks spinning in the gravel before gaining traction. A dozen heartbeats later, the truck slid to a stop behind the other two. Semi-healthy orcs began loading their less fortunate comrades onto the beds of the trucks.

The hell with it, Richard thought as he rolled over the lip of the truck's tailgate onto the ground. Surprisingly, his left leg held his weight. The throbbing in his shoulder and arm lessened as well as his self-heal worked overtime to bring his body back into baseline.

Glancing skyward, Richard yelled, "Fine. I'll do it. But I'll need my abilities back. For once, don't be a jerk!"

A wave of Power washed over Richard. Once again he sensed the links running to each of his Power reserves. Pulling Power from the reserve he used for offense and defense, Richard formed a passive scan letting it sweep out around him. He sensed thousands of life forms in a chaotic symphony of movements below ground.

The prisoners are in revolt.

Glancing at Yellow-tooth, Richard saw the big orc bending over an orc half his size lying on the ground. Richard recognized it as one of the orc younglings from his chain. A female orc knelt beside the child, pressing her hands on the young orc's chest in a futile attempt to staunch flows of green blood oozing out of three holes. Liquid dripped from the female's cheeks onto the child.

Is she crying? Richard wondered. *Do orcs even know how to cry?*

A memory of the *Defiant's* teenage orc pilot popped into Richard's mind. He'd only known the young orc for a few days, but he'd found Timerman to be an intelligent creature with a wide range of emotions.

Before he knew what he was doing, Richard found himself kneeling beside the female orc and her child. Reaching out with his left hand, he grabbed the child's wrist.

This is going to hurt, Richard thought. *I'm not even fully healed myself. Emp-healing sucks.*

Richard had killed enough orcs during his life that he was intimately familiar with their anatomy. Wrapping Power from the reserve he used to heal others around the child, he compared how the young orc was with the way he knew the orc should be. He pulled the difference into himself.

"Arrgh!" he groaned.

Holes appeared in Richard's chest at the same time as red blood and flesh shot out his back. As soon as all of the child's wounds were replicated on his body, Richard sensed the holes in the young orc's chest close over. The child's heartbeat steadied as he drew in a deep breath.

Richard let go of the child's wrist when he felt Power healing his replicated wounds. Falling to the ground, he curled up into a fetal position. After a few moments of intense pain, he sensed rough hands raising him to a sitting position. A large gray face with a broken yellow tusk shook him, shouting in a language Richard couldn't understand. Glancing to his left, he noticed the young orc standing near his mother. Both were looking at him. He noticed all of the nearby orcs looking at him. Shaking free of the big orc, Richard stood on his feet. His left leg was fully healed. Even his right shoulder and left arm were fully healed.

My self-heal doesn't work that fast, Richard thought. *'The One' must have accelerated the healing somehow.*

Sensing the thousands of life forms picked up by his passive scan, Richard had a feeling he was going to need the faster healing. As he watched, he noted dozens of the life forms disappear.

The Thargs are killing their prisoners. There's no way I can save them on my own. If I can somehow convince Yellow-tooth and his orcs to go back with me into the tunnels, then we might have a chance. They'd make good allies.

With no other plan in sight, Richard pointed at Yellow-tooth and then the mine's entrance. "We need to go back and help the others. The other prisoners are being slaughtered."

The big orc continued staring at him. So did the other orcs. They all remained silent as if waiting for something.

The hell with it, Richard thought. *Lead by example. That's what my old Marine first sergeant used to say.*

Grabbing a rifle off the ground, Richard began running for the entrance.

"Chekrak!" came a shout behind him.

Yellow-tooth ran up carrying his rifle and two belts of extra batteries. He grabbed Richard by the shoulder, pulling him to a stop, then handed him one of the belts. Looking over his shoulder, Yellow-tooth shouted commands to the orcs near the trucks. Half of them began loading the wounded along with the females and young onto the vehicles. The other half, most of who were carrying weapons of one sort or another, came running up behind Yellow-tooth.

Looking at Richard, the big orc raised his rifle in the air and shouted, "Chekrak!"

"Chekrak!" shouted the other orcs also raising their weapons in the air.

What the hell, Richard thought. He raised his rifle into the air and shouted, "Chekrak!"

Then into the entrance he ran with two score orcs hot on his heels.

CHAPTER 5

Matthew turned the dial on the anti-tele-bot rod before pressing the activate button. No one was in the hallway, but he knew it wouldn't do to draw some security program's interest by destroying one of the tele-bots. He pulled the hood of his camouflage suit tighter around his face before moving forward. Within ten minutes he was at the private entrance to his mother's office. As he'd hoped, the door was unguarded since she was attending a meeting in the palace's main conference chamber.

My mother's duties as empress are always forcing her to attend meetings. I haven't even gotten a chance to see her for the last five days. She got back to the palace last night and has been in meetings ever since.

Reaching out with his mind the way Gaston and his friend Rick had shown him, Matthew located the flow of energy going to the private door's security mechanism. With a twist, he looped the flow back on itself. Holding his breath, he counted to ten before turning the door's handle. No alarms sounded. He opened the door just enough to accommodate his body and slipped inside.

So far so good.

His mother's office was large and full of art from around the galaxy. It looked the part of an office for the Intergalactic Empire's empress. Finding an out of the way spot near a statue of some species' god, he settled down to wait. He had a lot to think about.

I've got to know what's happening. I've got to know the truth. The Intergalactic Empire News and the other government-

controlled news agencies are no help. Even the independent agencies aren't helpful. Each agency has a different opinion on who did what.

Matthew stared at his mother's desk. It was still hard for him to believe his mother was the empress.

When I talked to her over the secured halo-pad, she swore the Conglomerate had nothing to do with the defeat of the Empire's military by the Crosioians last week. She's my mother. I want to believe her, but I've got to know for sure. She says Crosioian hackers broke through the central computer's security and gave false orders directing the Conglomerate fleets to withdraw. According to her, Rick and his friend Liz are traitors in league with the Trecorian Alliance.

Matthew didn't believe the last part. He'd spent a year on Portalis with Rick. He didn't want to disbelieve his mother, but...

He waited over two hours, barely moving since he'd deactivated the rod's control over the security tele-bots to keep from drawing suspicion. Occasionally, he stretched one of his legs to keep them from going to sleep. Other than that, he remained still.

Finally, the main door to the empress's office opened. Two guards came inside. One lifted a black box, sweeping it from one side of the room to the other. Matthew held his breath waiting to see if the stealth shield Myers and Rick had taught him was as good as he hoped. After a second sweep of the office, the man lowered the black box. Both guards left the room, shutting the door behind them.

Thank you, Rick and Gaston, Matthew thought as he breathed a sigh of relief. The year of training they'd given him on Portalis was paying off.

A shuffling noise from the hallway outside his mother's private entrance drew Matthew's attention.

The guards are back. I might be stuck here for a long time. What was I thinking? If mother catches me, she'll attach a couple of her security teams to me at the hip. I'll never have a moment's privacy. Belatedly, Matthew wondered if he'd made the right choice. *Doesn't matter. The die is cast. I'm committed.*

The main door to the office opened. In walked his mother surrounded by a slew of courtiers and security personnel. Matthew noticed Myers take up a position along the wall to the side of his mother's desk. The man's eyes stared straight ahead, but Matthew sensed a line of Power scan across the room.

He's checking the room. His scan's got a stealth shield around it, but I'm still picking it up. Either he's getting sloppy in his old age, or all that training we did together has made me more sensitive to his Power.

The line of Myers's Power passed over Matthew and continued. Suddenly, Matthew sensed the line stop and back up. It crossed over his position several times. Matthew looked at Myers. The Conglomerate's chief of security seemed to be looking dead at him.

He senses me. He knows I'm here.

After a couple of seconds, Matthew sensed the scan move past him, continuing around the room. When he looked at Myers again, the ex-wizard scout was once more looking straight ahead. Matthew gave a sigh of relief, wiping a drop of sweat from his brow.

That was too close. I thought sure he spotted me. I guess I was wrong.

The next hour was filled with one boring discussion after another.

Why my mother wants to be the empress is beyond me. All she does is attend meetings and take a lot of grief. I'm sure she's doing her best to help the Empire, but no one appreciates her. Matthew had a momentary twinge of conscience as he remembered he was spying on her. *That's different. She thinks I'm still a child and doesn't tell me a lot. I'm almost twenty now. I'm sure I could help her if I knew what was really going on. She's my mother. I have to help her whether she thinks I'm old enough or not.*

Eventually, everyone left the room except his mother and her chief of security. Barely breathing, Matthew leaned forward. He sensed a tenseness of emotions in the room. If he was going to find out anything, he had a feeling it was going to be now.

His mother nodded at a metallic box located on the corner of her desk. Myers opened the lid, removed his battle helmet from his belt, and placed the helmet inside the box.

Why's he doing that? Matthew wondered.

Neither his mother nor Myers said anything until the lid on the box was slammed shut.

Matthew's mother rose from her desk and walked over to the ex-wizard scout. "I can see you're a little perturbed," said his mother. "Well, too bad. I did what had to be done."

"A hundred million of our people were slaughtered," said Myers. "How could you do that? You should've told me what you were planning. I had to find out watching IEN."

Matthew's mother grew red-faced. She was angrier than he'd ever seen her.

"First off, they weren't *our* people," said his mother. "They weren't loyal to me. I'm the empress, but those regular Empire units would have been the first to rebel against my authority. They all got what they deserved. As for telling you, I am the empress. I don't have to tell you anything. Besides, you're gone so much nowadays. When was I supposed to tell you? You are always popping in and out. I can't depend on you anymore."

"You know I'm doing it for you," said Myers. "Do you think I went on those time-commando missions because I enjoyed them?"

"I have no idea what you do or don't do," Matthew heard his mother say. "I expect results, and so far I haven't seen any. I did what I had to do."

Myers shook his head. "You let Governor Jenkins lead our military into a trap. He was working with the Crosioians. Did you know that?"

Matthew leaned even farther forward, listening for every nuance of his mother's reply.

"Gaston, you are a fool sometimes. Jenkins only does what I tell him. Thanks to the Trecorians and their allies, the Crosioians took even heavier losses than our traitorous regular military. Secretary Reaster says the Crosioians' master computer is out of action as well. As of this moment, the Empire forces that remain loyal to me are the dominant power in the galaxy. I reign supreme."

"Don't kid yourself, Diane. The Trecorians are dangerous. Plus, Admiral Bistos and the others got a lot of the regular military forces safely into Trecorian space. Not to mention those fleets from the magic dimension. You've got a nest of pactars on your hands."

Instead of dressing down her chief of security as Matthew expected, his mother drew close to the man and placed her hand on his shoulder.

"That's why I need you, Gaston. I need you to get that last bottle of DNA gas so we can be a real family. Then I need you to help me track down and kill these traitors."

"One of those so-called traitors is my brother," said Myers. "We need him in order to get the DNA gas. I told you Shepard destroyed the Dalinfaust's avatar. From what the demon in my battle helmet tells me, the Dalinfaust is being tortured as we speak in the demonic plane. Unless some master demon takes action, the Dalinfaust should be imprisoned for another nine hundred and fifty years. He won't be sending me on any more missions to the magic dimension. We need Shepard alive to take me there."

"So you've told me," said Matthew's mother. "Sometimes I don't think you love me. If you did, you'd have gotten the bottle of DNA gas for me long ago. We can't be a real family until you do."

For a moment, Myers took his eyes off the empress and scanned the room. Matthew noticed the chief of security's eyes stop at his hiding spot. He expected Myers's next words to give him away. After a couple of seconds, the ex-wizard scout looked back at his mother.

"We don't have to wait," said Myers. "We could be a family right now. All you have to do is tell Matthew the truth."

Matthew strained his ears to hear his mother's response.

"I'll tell him one day, but now is not the time. Once you get the DNA gas for me, then I'll tell him."

Tell me what? Matthew wondered.

Leaning forward as far as he could without making noise, Matthew cocked his head and strained to hear every nuance of the security chief's next words.

"I'm beginning to think you won't," said Myers. "A man should know who his father is."

"Matthew's still a boy," said the empress. "When the time's right, I'll know it. Then I'll tell him."

For an instant, Matthew thought Myers's eyes locked with his before returning to look at his mother.

"You'll tell Matthew that I'm his father?"

My father? Matthew thought.

Through his shock, Matthew heard his mother say, "Yes. I'll tell him the truth, but only when the time is right. I'll tell him that you're his father. Until that time, I think it is best that he continue thinking his father's dead. I don't want to speak about this again, Gaston. I mean it."

"Fine," said Myers. "I won't bring it up again. I have to know one thing, Diane. Did you know Jenkins was leading the Empire's regular military into a trap last week? Did you know he was conspiring with the Crosioians? Did you know a hundred million of our soldiers and sailors were going to be sacrificed?"

Matthew heard his mother laugh. Her eyes narrowed. He'd never seen such a vicious look on her face. He hardly recognized her.

"You're a fool, Gaston," said his mother. "You always have been. You have no idea what it takes to run an empire. Did I think a hundred million of the military's regular forces were going to die? No. I hoped more than that would die. Jenkins was supposed to lead all half a billion of them into the Crosioians' trap. Only our Conglomerate forces were supposed to come out alive. If I knew where Jenkins was, I would have him tortured before sending him to a disintegration chamber. He made a mistake. I don't tolerate mistakes."

"Governor Jenkins is dead," said Myers. "His body is missing, but the techs confirmed the blood in the bedchamber was his. They estimate ninety percent of his blood was splattered around the room. Whoever killed him may come after you next. You've got to protect yourself."

Matthew thought he saw a flash of fear come into his mother's eyes before it disappeared.

"That's what I have you for, Gaston," said his mother. "You know as well as I that your brother is responsible for Jenkins's death. I need you to get that last bottle of DNA gas. Then I need you to track down your brother and kill him. Wizard Scout Richard Shepard is a traitorous dog, and he deserves to die. Do you understand me?"

Myers stared at Matthew's mother for several seconds before glancing back to Matthew's hiding spot. Looking back at the empress, he said, "I understand completely, Diane. I think you made a mistake with Jenkins's trap, but what's done is done. You have a full rebellion on your hands now. I just hope you're prepared to take the consequences of your part in the betrayal."

"You have no idea what I am prepared to take, Gaston," said

Matthew's mother. "You just do your part and find that DNA gas. I will handle the rebellion."

The two talked a few minutes longer, but Matthew barely heard.

My mother betrayed the military. She's responsible for all those deaths. And Gaston? He's my father? Why didn't Mother tell me?

Matthew sat in silence long after his mother and Myers departed. When he finally moved, the guards were no longer at their post by the private entrance. It was well past midnight. The halls were once again empty. Coming to a decision, he made his way back to his room. He grabbed his C-PAST and a few possessions and threw them into a bag. Making his way over to the halo-phone, he opened up a secure channel and sent a two-line encrypted message to Captain Ronald Deloris on the *Defiant*.

"Hold me a spot. I'm on my way."

CHAPTER 6

Pain beyond the imagination of mere mortals racked the depths of the Dalinfaust's soul. Although intense, the pain was bearable. The Dalinfaust reinforced his defenses around a small section of his mind, keeping the area clear of the pain. In that one small section of his being, his thoughts were clear.

My brothers Efrestra and Cancontus are too weak to keep both Zenthra and myself helpless with their pain spell at the same time. If the fool Zenthra hadn't allowed his computer avatar to be destroyed, the three of them could have overwhelmed me and kept control. They should know that two brothers are not enough. My Power may be weak at the moment, but I am still able to communicate with my minions. I can still advance my plans.

The demon thought about how the human and his dolgars had destroyed his black dragon avatar, forcing his soul back to the demonic plane to be tortured for a thousand years. His anger burned, giving him the will to ignore even the worst of the pain attempting to invade the clear section of his mind.

The human is my master's variable, but I will make him pay. His time is coming. Any tortures Efrestra and Cancontus are doing to me will pale beside what I will do to that human. First, though, I must escape from my brothers' prison. If I can contact Zenthra, we can work together to overpower our two brothers. Zenthra is weak and a fool, but his Power combined with mine will be more than a match for Efrestra and Cancontus.

A wave of pain greater than any thus far attempted to break into the clear space of the Dalinfaust's mind. His need for revenge kept the pain at bay. He threw it back into the swirling mass of pain that was the part of the demonic plane where he was imprisoned. The clear section of his mind remained pain-free.

The fool Lord Crendemor has the Staff of the Lady of the Tree. He will undoubtedly attempt to use it to open the gate on his own. That he has not already opened the gate means the staff is giving him more trouble than he anticipated. I cannot allow him to succeed. Lord Crendemor is no longer a reliable pawn. I must use the human's brother as my tool. He is nearly as powerful as the master's variable. I must use the brother to help me break free. The fool cares for the woman. I will use his so-called love to bend him to my will. Once he sets me free, then both he and his precious empress will get the reward they deserve.

In spite of another wave of pain, the Dalinfaust laughed. *It is time to begin. Soon I will escape this prison. Once I am free, let the master's variable and all he cares for beware. He will pay. Oh, how he will pay.*

CHAPTER 7

Matthew hid around the corner of the parked tanker while surveying the hangar where he knew the experimental X-shuttle was located. From the top-secret meetings he'd attended during the past few months, he knew the prototype fighter-shuttle was the leading edge of technology for the Conglomerate. Based upon a multitude of boring accounting meetings, he also knew the Deloris Armaments Corporation had spent extravagant sums in their attempt to complete the project on time.

They didn't make it, Matthew thought. *The X-shuttle is still only in the prototype stage. I'm betting Mother wanted it in production before last week's battle. Despite what she told Gaston, I believe enough of the Empire's regular military forces escaped to Trecorian space to cause major problems. Mother is going to need more of these X-shuttles to hold the Conglomerate's territory.*

Thinking back to one of the classified briefings, Matthew remembered that the prototype fighter-shuttle had the same hyper-drive his Mother had installed in the *Defiant*. As a result, the X-shuttle could make thirty hyper-jumps instead of the normal twenty without requiring an overhaul of its hyper-drive. In addition, the X-shuttle had been given a miniaturized version of the stealth shield used to hide destroyers. While a destroyer's stealth shield couldn't hide it up close, the X-shuttle was different. Due to its small size, the fighter-shuttle had proven invisible to all types of scans farther out than a light second.

Even one of the Empire's R-three-fifteen sensor ships wouldn't be able to detect the X-shuttle, Matthew thought. *I need the X-shuttle to get off Risors.*

Reaching out with a line of Power, Matthew probed the hangar for security checkpoints. He found more than he'd bargained for.

He whispered to his C-PAST, "I knew security would be topnotch, but I didn't expect this much, Johnny."

"Perhaps it is best," said Johnny in a mechanical voice lower than normal speech but louder than a whisper. "You have only piloted the X-shuttle in the simulator. I have serious reservations about your ability to pilot the real thing. Surely you know you can't circumvent all that security. Your telekinetic abilities are good, but they are not that good."

"Doesn't matter," Matthew whispered. "I'll never get off this planet using regular transport. My mother would have me back in no time, locked in my quarters for the next twenty years. The X-shuttle is my only hope of escape."

"Nonsense," said Johnny raising his voice. "I think—"

"Keep your voice down," Matthew whispered sorry he'd started the conversation with his C-PAST. He should've known he'd only start an argument. "I've got to try. Now keep quiet before you give me away."

"It's too late for that," said a deep voice behind Matthew.

Spinning around, Matthew came face to face with the Conglomerate's chief of security, ex-Wizard Scout Gaston Myers. The man was only an arm-length away. Although he was still dressed in his light-blue business suit, Matthew wasn't fooled. He knew the man was more dangerous than a battalion of special operation's soldiers. Glancing between the flaps of the business suit jacket, Matthew noticed the utility belt he knew held the wizard scout's battle helmet and phase rod.

"Gaston," Matthew said frantically looking around for some means of escape but seeing none. "I...uh..."

The short, toad-faced man smiled. "You should've put you C-PAST on mute. Not that it would've mattered. I've been following you ever since you left the palace."

The man peeked around Matthew, eyeing the security hangar. "I'll say this for you, Matt, you're ambitious. That hangar's got even better security than your mother's office. I supervised the security installation myself. Your stealth shield's good. I'm impressed, but even I couldn't penetrate that building's security. You wouldn't get past the second set of doors before the guards would have you chained up and on your way back to your mother."

"I suppose that's the same thing you're going to do," Matthew said finding his tongue. "You're both murderers. You let the Crosioians slaughter our troops. How could you?"

Matthew noticed the muscles tighten on the security chief's face. The man's eyes looked shinier than normal. *He looks hurt,* Mathew thought. *Is that even possible?*

Shaking his head, Myers said, "Not me. I knew nothing about it. I swear I was as surprised as anyone to hear about Governor Jenkins's betrayal. I know you were in your mother's office. You heard Diane. I doubt more than a handful of Conglomerate personnel knew Jenkins's plan. Our soldiers are good people for the most part. They wouldn't have put up with it if they'd known. They'd give your mother trouble now if the truth came out."

Matthew snorted. "Ha! Words come cheap. You're still working for my mother. You're just as culpable."

Myers shook his head again. "No. I love your mother, but I wouldn't have gone along with the governor's plan if I'd known ahead of time. You've got to believe me."

"Why should I?"

Matthew noticed Myers glance around before looking back at him. "Because…because I'm your father. I know you heard your mother admit it. You're my son, Matt. I've wanted to tell you for years, but Diane wouldn't let me."

Matthew wanted to deny it, but his mother's words kept coming back to him. In his heart, he knew it was true. He shook his head. "It doesn't matter. You're with her. I can't be. I'm not a traitor to the Empire."

"Nor am I," insisted Myers.

"You're Mother's chief of security. You've chosen your side. You're one of them."

"No longer. I'm done. I can't be a part of the Conglomerate any longer, no matter how much I love your mother."

"Prove it," Matthew said calling the man's bluff.

Myers locked eyes with him for several seconds before replying. "I will. Come with me."

The chief of security took three steps toward the hangar.

Matthew didn't follow. He reached into his jacket pocket, fingering the small-wattage plasma pistol he'd hidden inside and weighing his chances.

Myers stopped and turned around. "Don't be a fool. I'm a fully trained wizard scout."

Easing his empty hand out of his pocket, Matthew dropped it to his side. He'd gambled and lost. *He's going to take me back to the palace,* he thought. *I lost my only chance to get away.* An image of his friend Tia appeared unbidden in his mind. His stomach felt empty. For all he knew, she'd been killed in Jenkins's trap. A feeling of hopelessness swept over him.

"That's better," said Myers. "Now follow me...son. Be sure and cue off me."

The man's last comment confused Matthew. Nevertheless, when the chief of security began walking toward the hangar, he followed. *What else can I do? He's a wizard scout.*

Myers led him to the main door of the hangar. Six guards in heavy power-armor sporting Conglomerate patches and carrying phase rifles blocked their way.

A soldier with sergeant stripes painted on his armor stepped forward. "Sorry, sir. There's no admittance today. Everything's been locked down since last week. Not even the techs are allowed inside for now."

Myers raised his right hand. "Of course they're not. I gave the order myself. I assume you know who I am."

"I do," said the sergeant sounding unimpressed. "But orders are orders."

"Yes, they are," agreed Myers in a calm voice. "Present your security tablet, Sergeant."

The sergeant pulled a notebook-sized tablet out of a pouch attached to his left side. Matthew recognized the tablet as one of the latest security devices. Myers placed his right hand on the tablet. A blue glow surrounded his hand. After a couple of seconds, the glow disappeared.

"Identity confirmed," came a computerized voice from the tablet. "What are your orders?"

"File an orbital flight plan," said Myers. "Matthew Deloris and I are going on a special test flight for the empress. We're taking the X-shuttle." Looking at the sergeant, the chief of security said,

"Any questions?"

The sergeant shook his head as he placed the tablet back in his pouch. "None, sir. You may proceed."

Just before they passed through the door, Matthew looked back. He noticed the sergeant speaking into a handset on the wrist of his power-armor. Stepping into the hangar, Matthew followed his father through one security checkpoint after another. In less than ten minutes, Myers occupied the pilot's seat and Matthew the copilot's in the cockpit of the X-shuttle.

A ground crew arrived and began rolling the fighter-shuttle through a series of locked doors. As they did so, Myers went through the preflight check. By the time he was finished, the X-shuttle was outside the hangar. Once the ground personnel cleared the area, Myers pressed an icon on his control console. The rear door to the X-shuttle rose, sealing them inside. As Matthew continued to watch, his father pressed another icon, and the X-shuttle vibrated as the hyper-drive came online.

"What are you doing?" Matthew said. "We can't use a hyper-drive until we clear the atmosphere."

Myers looked over, giving a rare smile. "Actually, the rule is that we *shouldn't* use it until we clear the atmosphere. It's normally too dangerous. That's why starships use ion thrusters until they're far enough away from a planet for the hyper-drive to be used safely."

"Then why—" Matthew started to say before the ex-wizard scout pointed at something through the X-shuttle's windscreen.

"That's why," said Myers.

Following the direction indicated by his father, Matthew spotted a score of vehicles with flashing lights heading their way. A glance at the view screens for the rear videos showed a dozen guards in power-armor running from the hangar's main door in their direction.

"Hold on," said Myers as he hit an icon on his control panel with the ball of his fist.

Whoosh!

Matthew was crushed back into his seat as the X-shuttle leaped skyward. Blackness overcame reality, and Matthew knew no more.

* * *

A soft hum accompanied by a mild vibration was Matthew's first sense of the universe around him. Every muscle in his body ached. He struggled to open his eyes. With great effort, he succeeded in prying open his left eye. He recognized the inside of the X-shuttle. He was still in the copilot's chair, but someone had lowered the backrest into the prone position. Turning his head slightly, Matthew spied his father in the pilot's seat touching various controls. With a final touch, the chief of security looked to his right.

"Ah, you're finally awake. I suppose an emergency hyper-drive takeoff is a little rough when you can't self-heal."

Opening his right eye, Matthew blinked several times. When his eyes focused on the windscreen, he noticed the blurred lights of hyper-space. He pressed the button on the side of his chair's armrest to raise himself into a sitting position.

"What happened?" he asked trying to get an anchor point for his confused mind. "I don't remember anything after we took off."

Myers snorted. "Well, it was touch and go there for a while, I can tell you that. Your mother caught on quicker than I thought. She's got layers of spies even I don't know about. Still, we succeeded in getting away." The chief of security patted the control console. "This baby's worth every credit the Deloris Armaments Corporation invested in it. We had a dozen warships on our tail as soon as we got outside the atmosphere. The X-shuttle outflew them all. Once we were outside visual range, I activated the ship's stealth shield. No one's bothered us since."

Matthew eyed the man. "Why are you doing this? Mother will never forgive you."

"Why?" asked Myers getting a shiny look in his eyes again. "I told you that I couldn't be a part of her plan anymore. I'm with you…Son. I got you off Risors. What else can I do to convince you?"

Matthew eyed the control console, trying to remember his sessions in the simulator. The controls in the actual X-shuttle looked more complicated than during the simulation. One thing he did recognize was the navigation display. He didn't like what he saw.

"If you were trying to help me, we'd be heading for Trecorian space. You're going in the opposite direction."

Myers drummed the fingers of his right hand on the armrest of his chair. "Why would you want to go to Trecor?"

"You know why. That's where the survivors of the Empire's regular military are located. That's where the *Defiant* is. My grandfather will know what to do. He's bound to be near Trecor."

"That's where you're wrong, Matt. I have it on good authority your grandfather is on his way to Earth in the *Defiant* as we speak. That's where we're going."

"Earth? Why?" Matthew said still trying to give his foggy mind time to clear. "How do you know?"

Myers reached inside the flap of his business suit and pulled out a flattened black object. The object changed shape into a battle helmet in three-quarters mode as the chief of security placed it on his head.

"I know because I'm a wizard scout," said Myers. "I may be wearing a business suit, but I keep my battle computer close at hand. The *Defiant* is on her way to Earth. Trust me on that account. Sergeant Ron plans to gate to the magical dimension and rescue your uncle. We're going to join them."

"Uh…my uncle?" Matthew said growing more confused.

Myers frowned. "Much as I hate to admit it, Shepard's my brother. That makes him your uncle. He's on a mission for *'the One.'* Apparently he's in trouble, from what I've been told. Sergeant Ron and the rest of the *Defiant's* crew are going to save him."

Matthew thought things were falling a little too neatly into place. "I'm not sure—"

"Tia's with them," said Myers.

"Tia?" Matthew asked forgetting his other concerns. "She's alive?"

"That's right. She returned to the *Defiant* before the battle on Estos last week. She's on the *Defiant* now. You're going to get to see her. You asked me to prove I wasn't with the Conglomerate any longer. I'm taking you to see Tia. Won't you trust me?"

Matthew looked at his father long and hard, trying to gauge the man's motives. An image of Tia flashed in his mind forcing all doubts away.

"All right," Matthew said. "I'll trust you…Father. For now."

CHAPTER 8

The *Defiant* approached the space station using ion thrusters to assist the tugs moving her into their assigned berth. Jeena sat in the communication officer's chair directly behind Sergeant Ron. The *Defiant's* copilot seat was occupied by Comstar while Timerman sat in the navigator's chair across from her.

Looking over Sergeant Ron's shoulder, Jeena eyed the large blue and white ball behind the space station. "So that is where Rick was born? It is beautiful."

"Yep, that's Earth," said Sergeant Ron as he gave the control panel a final pat before looking over at Comstar. "She's all yours, partner. Do you think you can take her the rest of the way in by your lonesome?"

The old elf grabbed the steering controls for the ion thrusters. In an emotionless voice, he said, "Aye, aye, Captain."

Jeena allowed herself a small smile. Although he might try, Comstar couldn't hide his excitement from her. She also sensed a little bit of nervousness from the old elf. She noticed a drop of sweat trickle down the side of his face.

Turning away from Comstar and back to Sergeant Ron, Jeena waved a hand to encompass the part of the space station visible through the windscreen. "The thing is massive. It is just as large as the Crosioian station Stella, Bright Wing, and I destroyed when we recovered the bottles of DNA gas. Rick told me your people were advanced, but the idea they could build something so huge in less than a week boggles the mind." Jeena glanced over at Comstar.

"Did I use the word boggle right? Rick has been trying to teach me some of the different vernacular of the intergalactic standard language so I will blend in when we are in the physical dimension."

Without taking his eyes off of his instrument panel, Comstar gave a tense laugh. "Believe me, Jeehana, you will never *blend in*, as you say. Your molten-silver eyes will always draw attention regardless of whether you are in the physical or magical dimension."

"He's right," said Sergeant Ron. "You'd stand out no matter where you were. As for the word boggle, you used it correctly. And you're right. It would boggle my mind as well if this space station was built in the five days since we fought the Crosioians on Estos. However, it wasn't, was it, Timerman?"

Jeena looked at the other side of the cockpit at the young orc in the navigator's chair. He just stared at her without saying a word. "Timerman?" she asked trying to move things along.

The teenager shook his head as if coming out of a trance. "Oh, sorry. I just like looking at your eyes. They...uh...never mind. Uh, the space station. Until five days ago it was orbiting my home planet of Redestan in the magic dimension. Our United Galaxy Alliance and your galaxy's Trecorian war-king agreed to have it transported here until a permanent home for the triplets could be built near Earth."

Jeena remembered how Rick had helped the three-headed dragon he called "the triplets" form a gate between the magical and physical dimension. That was how the naval fleets of the magical dimension's United Galaxy Alliance had been able to send their warships into the physical galaxy just in time to save the Empire's regular military forces from annihilation. She also remembered how she had been told the triplets had set up a permanent gate between the two dimensions near Earth since her bondmate's birthplace was the sister planet of her own world of Portalis.

"The station is quite busy," Jeena said. "I can sense the energy sources coming from the ships in the station's berths. I believe there is almost an even mixture of magic- and technology-based starships."

The *Defiant* shuddered accompanied by a slight metallic bang.

Jeena glanced out the windscreen. "We are in our berth. You

did an excellent job of landing," she told Comstar. "I did not feel a thing until we touched the side of our docking berth."

Comstar released the controls for the ion thrusters and touched an icon on his control panel. Turning in his seat, he said, "It was mostly the tug's doing. I just kept us level."

Despite his words, Jeena could tell from the old elf's emotions that he was pleased. Unlike humans, elves were sensitive to each other's emotions. She smiled. Comstar smiled back.

"That's a strange looking shuttle," said Timerman pointing to the left side of the windscreen. "It reminds me a little of the Yardorian elves' design, but at the same time, it has a look of technology to it."

Jeena looked out at the ship in question. While she hadn't been exposed to enough of the ships that moved through the space between the stars to tell the difference between one dimension's designs and another's, she knew something was definitely strange about the shuttle.

"I sense both magic and technology energy coming from the ship," Jeena said. "I know you told me the *Defiant* and some of the United Galaxy Alliance's warships are a mixture of the two technologies, but the energy readings I am sensing go beyond that. They blend in so well it is almost a new form of energy in its own right."

Sergeant Ron touched an icon on his console. The windscreen turned solid white. Jeena remembered Rick telling her the windscreen was really a computerized display for outside video cameras.

"Well," said the *Defiant's* captain, "whatever it is, fortunately, it's not our concern. We're just here long enough to get the triplets to create an access point to the time-bubble around that asteroid of Rick's." Sergeant Ron stood up. "So, are we going to go in the station or are we going to sit around flapping our jaws all day?"

Jeena stood up. She knew in theory since her bondmate was in a time-bubble in the past that any delays in the current time would have no effect on how soon they could get back to him. She still had no desire for anyone to *flap their jaws.*

"Oh, we are going, Sergeant Ron," Jeena said. "That is something you can bet on."

* * *

Following Sergeant Ron, Comstar, Timerman, Terrie, and Tia through what Jeena had been told was an airlock, she entered the space station proper. Like the *Defiant*, the inside of the station appeared to be composed primarily of a gray metal. She touched it, feeling a vibration of magic in the material, and frowned.

Comstar must have noticed the expression on her face. "The physical dimension's technology uses a metal called brerellium steel for many of its starships. The magic dimension's counterpart to brerellium is a magic-based metal. Coincidently, the Dragars' word for the magic-based metal translates to steel in intergalactic standard.

Jeena nodded her head. Between her first visit to the *Defiant* and her current stay, she'd picked up a lot of the intergalactic standard language. *One of these days,* she thought, *I will not even have to use a translation spell to speak to my new friends.*

A group of seven humanoids was waiting at the end of the airlock. Two were human stock, one was elvish, and the other four were orcs.

Jeena had to remind herself that they weren't the orcs she was used to dealing with on Portalis. *These orcs are Timerman's people,* she thought. *They are just as advanced in space travel as Rick's Empire. They just use magic instead of technology.*

The smallest of the orcs stepped away from the others. Jeena recognized the orc as a female. "Captain Deloris," came a rough yet feminine voice from a small speaker attached to the orc's belt. "I am Admiral Ostar, commander of this station. War-king Bistoria advised us of your pending arrival. He told us you would be meeting with the triplets to coordinate a gate. The triplets are aware of your mission and are prepared to help in your task. Before you coordinate your gate with the honored dragon, War-king Bistoria has requested you give your opinion on two defectors that arrived at the station a few hours ahead of you."

Sergeant Ron scratched his beard and eyed the orc admiral before replying, "Defectors, eh? Not sure why we'd be interested in any defectors. By the way, I'd appreciate it if'n you wouldn't call me captain. Sergeant Ron will do just fine."

The orc admiral nodded her head. "As you wish, Sergeant Ron.

Now, if all of you will follow me."

Jeena couldn't tell if she was perturbed, or if she didn't care what she called the ornery old ship's captain.

As the orc admiral led the way through the maze of metal corridors, she told them of the efforts of both the United Galaxy Alliance and War-King Bistoria to integrate the armed forces of the two dimensions.

"The day of the Great Battle is fast approaching," said Admiral Ostar. "If our forces are to have any hope of defeating the Dragars, we must learn to work together." She pointed at the two human males in her staff. "Colonel Armos and Commodore Tilfinos are from the Empire and Trecor's high commands respectively. Staff members from the United Galaxy Alliance are on War-King Bistoria's staff."

Tia spoke before Sergeant Ron could reply. "Father, err I mean, War-King Bistoria told me the UGA was leaving one of its fleets in the physical dimension to help with our fight against the Conglomerate and the Crosioian Federation."

The orc admiral stopped and looked at the impetuous teenager. "Ah, yes, you are one of the war-king's daughters, are you not? I have talked to your sister, Admiral of the Fleets Bistos, on several occasions via scrying devices. Like me, she is not so sure either the Conglomerate or the Crosioian Federation is our primary enemy."

"What?" said Tia before anyone could stop her. "The Crosioians killed a hundred million of the Empire's best during the battle for Estos. The Conglomerate is just as responsible as them."

For an orc, Jeena thought the admiral was very patient. The orc admiral didn't immediately dress down the teenager for interrupting. "Ah, to be young again and not care about proprieties or etiquette, but alas those days are long gone."

The three orcs on her staff nodded their heads.

"Actually," said Sergeant Ron, "I have to agree with Ensign Bistoria here. The Crosioians almost wiped the Empire's regular forces out in a single stroke. The Conglomerate led the Empire fleets into a trap and left them at the mercy of the Crosioians. If your alliance hadn't come to our dimension to help, we'd probably all be dead."

Jeena had to agree with Tia as well. While the Empire wasn't her people, they were her bondmate's. She automatically spoke for him in his absence. "If the United Galaxy Alliance didn't think the Crosioians and the Conglomerate were their enemies, why did the UGA send your fleets to help the Empire and Trecor fleets?"

The admiral smiled. "High Priestess Jeehanathoraxen, is it not? Part of the reason we sent our fleets to help in the Empire's fight against the Crosioian Federation was to get help in return in our fight against the Dragars. That was not the only reason. The cooperation between our forces in the magical dimension and the physical dimension was foretold by Chekrak. The only hope for both our dimensions is if we work together to prevent the opening of the gate to the demonic plane. The deaths of a hundred million of the Empire's troops pale in comparison to the slaughter that will occur in both dimensions if the gate is opened."

"Try telling that to the parents of the hundred million who died," said Sergeant Ron.

The orc admiral faced the *Defiant's* captain. "Yes, the Empire lost many of its armed forces. The UGA lost more than a few as well. So did Trecor. I must also point out that the loss of life on the side of the Crosioian Federation was even higher. Our intelligence staff estimates over two billion of their ground and naval personnel are dead or wounded."

"Somehow my heart doesn't bleed for them," said Tia.

Before the teenager could say anything more, Jeena keyed in on an unfamiliar word the admiral had used.

"Chekrak," Jeena said. "What is a Chekrak?" The answer came from behind her.

"Chekrak is not a what," said Timerman. "Chekrak is a who. He is a prophet of legend. He foretold of the Great Battle and the attempt to open the demonic gate. Every orc and elf in the United Galaxy Alliance knows of Chekrak. He rescued Sevantor from the Dragars. Chekrak foretold of the time the magic and physical dimensions would work together. He told Sevantor the Dragars were the servants of our real enemies. He told us to be ready when the *defiant ones* came to seek our aid. Chekrak prophesized when the *defiant ones* came that the day of the Great Battle would be nigh."

The orc admiral, as well as the orcs and elf on his staff, nodded their heads. The two human staff officers looked as confused as the rest of the *Defiant's* crew except for Timerman.

"Your young friend is right," said Admiral Ostar. "All that we have done is as foretold by the great prophet and warrior Chekrak. Did you really think the United Galaxy Alliance would commit its forces to helping you based upon your powers of persuasion alone, Sergeant Ron? The way was paved for you by Sevantor. He was told the prophecy by Chekrak. Sevantor organized the first resistance against the Dragars. He was the first leader of the United Galaxy Alliance. For a hundred thousand years, the UGA has defended our galaxy against the Dragars. The battle has been hard, but it will soon end. The time of the Great Battle approaches. Then we will see an end to our fight one way or another."

Jeena looked at Timerman. "You will have to tell me more about your prophet Chekrak when we get a chance." She glanced back at the orc admiral. "In the meantime, perhaps we should see these defectors of yours. I do not wish to tarry from our mission longer than necessary."

"Perhaps that is best," agreed the admiral.

Turning, Admiral Ostar led the way through several more corridors and down an elevator. Soon they entered a room with a large window allowing the occupants to look into another room. Several orcs and elves along with two humans wearing orange jumpsuits sat at display terminals with various colored lights flashing on panels in front of each display.

The displays reminded Jeena of the Empire's computers, but she knew they were not technology. She sensed their magic. Glancing through the large window into the other room, Jeena saw a short human male in a gray jumpsuit sitting at a table. Next to him sat a teenage human male. The short man had been scratching at the table top when she entered the control room. She saw him glance up, seeming to look directly into her eyes. Jeena thought she saw a slight smile on the man's lips before it disappeared.

"Gaston," said Terrie and Sergeant Ron at the same time.

"And Matt," said Tia. "Can they see us?"

One of the orc technicians shook his head. "No. The window is a one-way scrying device. We can see them, but they cannot see us.

"Ha!" scoffed Terrie. "Gaston's a wizard scout, one of the best. He knows we're here. You can bet your last credit on it."

"You say they defected?" asked Sergeant Ron. "You know who

they are, right?"

The admiral nodded. "Yes. They showed up outside our protective shield. No warning; nothing. They were just there. The young male is the son of the Empire's empress. The older man is her chief of security. They have been cooperative ever since they arrived."

"Were they armed?" Jeena asked.

"Yes, but they both gave their weapons and equipment up readily enough," said the admiral. "The man's gear is locked in a secure vault. They have no weapons now."

"Gaston is a weapon," said Sergeant Ron. "Are you sure that room's secure? Gaston's a shifter. He can go right through walls unless they're made of creallium."

"So he told us," said the admiral. "As I said, he has been very cooperative. As for security, the room is encased in multiple layers of magic spells. Even one of your so-called shifters could not escape without outside assistance."

"Let 'em see us," said Sergeant Ron. "I want to talk to them. The boy is my grandson."

The admiral nodded at one of the orange-suited orcs. The orc touched an image on his display. The large window shimmered. Jeena sensed a flow of magic disappear from the window.

"Grandfather!" said Matthew.

Jeena noticed the teenager's eyes scan the room. They stayed on her for a couple of seconds before continuing on. She noticed the boy's eyes stop again and widen.

"Tia," the boy whispered.

Tia said nothing.

"Why are you here, Matt?" asked Sergeant Ron.

"I came to join you," said Matthew. "Didn't you get my message? I couldn't stay on Risors. Not after what Mother did."

Jeena watched Sergeant Ron's internal struggle on his face. His cheek muscles twitched while his eyes were locked with his grandson's for several seconds.

"Yeah, I got your message, but I didn't think you could get away." Sergeant Ron glanced at the others in the control room before looking back at his grandson. "I believe you, Matt, but the stakes are too high. There's nothing I can do to help you now. I'm sorry."

The teenager looked like he wanted to protest but merely nodded.

Jeena looked at the short man. "You are him, are you not? You are Rick's brother. I sense your frequency. Rick and yours are similar."

The short man nodded. "That's right. So you're the one who's been helping him. I can sense the link you have to him. I sensed it when we were trying to stop the Dragars on Portalis. I understand you're the one who recovered the bottles of DNA gas with Wizard Scout Stella."

"I am," Jeena admitted.

"Why are you here, Gaston?" asked Terrie. "As the Conglomerate's chief of security, I've got to believe you were knee deep in the empress's treachery."

"Then you'd be wrong," said Myers. "I didn't find out until after the fact. I'm a soldier. I wouldn't have betrayed my comrades in arms."

Jeena waited while Terrie and her bondmate's brother had a staring contest. Finally, Terrie nodded. "All right, I believe you, but that doesn't matter. I'm going to recommend that you be assigned the most secure cell in the military prison on Diajor. If I get my way, you'll be there the rest of your life. A lot of wizard scouts died because of the empress. You're just as responsible in my book."

Myers shrugged his shoulders. "That's fair enough. I'd probably feel the same if I was in your boots."

"Then I guess there's nothing more to say," said Sergeant Ron.

"I guess not," replied Myers.

Jeena noticed Matthew open his mouth. Before the teenager could say anything, the short man reached out and touched the boy's arm, shaking his head.

"Don't say anything, Matt," said Myers. "They've got their minds made up. Of course, without the X-shuttle, they won't get past the Dragars to rescue Shepard, but that's not our problem, is it?"

Jeena had already started to follow the others out of the control room but whirled back to face her bondmate's brother. "What are you saying? What do you know about my bondmate?"

The others stopped as well, gathering behind Jeena.

"Oh, I know quite a bit," said Myers. "My battle computer has told me a lot. You see, I'm a time-commando just like your precious Shepard."

Jeena looked at the man suspiciously. Her bondmate had not talked about his brother much, but what he had told her did not endear the man to her heart. "*'The One'* has been sending you on missions like Rick?" she asked stalling for time until she could figure out the man's motives.

"No, not *'the One,'*" replied Myers. "Someone else. Who doesn't matter. What does matter is that I know the asteroid where Shepard is being kept prisoner is surrounded by the Dragars' invasion fleets. They are there waiting for the command to attack our time. Even if you can get your so-called triplets to create a gate to the asteroid at the right point in time, the *Defiant* will never make it to the asteroid's surface in one piece."

Jeena noticed the man smile and didn't like it.

"What are you suggesting?" asked Sergeant Ron. "If you think we're taking you with us, you've got another think coming. You lost my trust when you sided with my daughter against the Empire."

"Diane is the Empire," said Myers. "You're just..." He stopped and bit his lip. "That's neither here nor there. The end result is you need the X-shuttle to save Shepard. That's why I brought it here."

"Ha!" said Sergeant Ron. "You brought it here to help Rick? Somehow I find that hard to believe."

"Oh, I want a couple of things in return," said Myers. "For one, Matthew's totally innocent. I want you to free him and take him with you."

"And your second demand?" Jeena asked. She didn't know much about the teenager, but she did know Rick liked him. It wasn't her decision, but if taking the teen boy would help rescue her bondmate, she was all for it."

"The second thing is that I want the last bottle of DNA gas," said Myers. "Those are my terms."

"We don't have—" Jeena started.

"You've got nothing to bargain with," said Sergeant Ron cutting her off. "If the X-shuttle is the one parked next to the *Defiant*, which I suspect it is, then we can just take it. We don't need you."

Myers smiled. "You can try. The X-shuttle's security is tighter than anything you've got time to figure out. Only I know the access code."

"If you think we're taking you with us," said Terrie, "you've got another think coming."

Myers smiled. "That wasn't one of my terms, old friend. If you take Matthew and give me the bottle of DNA gas, I'll give you the access code. Matt's had plenty of hours in the X-shuttle's simulator. He can fly the thing. You'll need him."

Sergeant Ron shook his head. "Well, the joke's on you, Gaston. We don't have any bottles of DNA gas lying around, and we don't know where any are. Do we guys?" The *Defiant's* captain looked around the room expectantly. Jeena noticed him stop when he got to her. He scratched his beard. "Uh, do we Jeehana?"

Jeena thought back to a sensation she'd gotten fifty-one years earlier when she'd visited Drakomar, the capital city of the dark elves.

"Jeehana," said Terrie, "do you know something we don't? Are you trying to tell us you kept a bottle of the DNA gas you took off the Crosioians' space station?"

Shaking her head, Jeena looked first at Terrie and Sergeant Ron, then through the window to the room containing her bondmate's brother. "No, I do not have a bottle of DNA gas." She noticed the partial smile on the short man's face disappear. *He thought I had one. Why?*

"Then there's no deal," said Myers. "I'd advise not trying to defuse the booby trap on the X-shuttle. It's got an energy source that'll take out half this space station in the blast."

Sergeant Ron folded his arms across his chest. "We've got four battle computers on the *Defiant*. Between that and Charlie's diviner ability, I think we can manage."

Myers shrugged his shoulders. "Suit yourself. I've got nothing but respect for Charlie. He can circumvent most technology."

Sergeant Ron dropped his arms and opened his mouth to speak.

"Unfortunately," said Myers, "the X-shuttle's energy source isn't technology. It's magic. I believe you've encountered it before, Sergeant Ron. It's what gives the X-shuttle its stealth ability. Diane acquired the stealth shield technology from the Crosioians, who got it from the Carsoloians. It was a prototype model developed by a Professor Jaskok. I think you knew him, didn't you, Sergeant Ron?"

Jeena looked at the *Defiant's* captain. He was frowning. "Sergeant Ron?" she said. "What is he talking about?"

The *Defiant's* captain glared at Myers before looking back and scratching his beard. "Well, a few years back, Charlie and I had some trouble on a planet called Cavos. The Carsoloians had developed a stealth shield better 'n anything in the galaxy. It used a blue gem, which gave off magic energy as its power source. The stealth shield was destroyed, or at least that's what I thought."

Myers smiled. "You thought wrong. The empress got the technology from the Crosioians, and I fetched her one of those blue gems while I was on one of my time-commando missions. The stealth shield works. Ask the admiral here. She didn't even know we were around until I lowered our shield."

Sergeant Ron looked at Admiral Ostar. The orc glared at Myers before nodding her head at Sergeant Ron. "It's true. Neither our magic-based sensors or the technology-based ones installed by War-King Bistoria detected anything."

Myers smiled again. "That's right. The X-shuttle's stealth shield is a merging of technology and magic. Neither can detect it alone. The booby trap is the same combination. Charlie's good at technology, but the magic part would get him."

Jeena saw her bondmate's brother point at her. "She's a magic-based diviner. Maybe between Charlie and her they could deactivate the booby trap given time, but that's something you don't have, is it?"

Moving forward until she was only a handbreadth from the observation window, Jeena locked eyes with the short human. "We do not have any DNA gas," Jeena said. "I am told Rick is your brother. Are you going to let him die?"

Myers snorted.

Jeena was tempted to slam her staff on the window, blow a hole in it, and drag the short man out while beating some sense into him. His disregard for her bondmate's wellbeing was obvious.

"No gas, no deal," said Myers.

Jeena gave a tightlipped smile. It must have looked out of place because her bondmate's brother stopped smirking long enough to stare at her.

"You know something, don't you?" said Myers with the eagerness in his voice giving it a high-pitched sound.

"As I told you, we do not have a bottle of DNA gas, but I might know where one is," Jeena said.

The smirk reappeared on Myers's face. "So you did keep a bottle for yourself when you snatched them from the Crosioians? I thought as much. Where is it?"

Jeena shook her head. "No, I told you I do not have any. I used fifteen in the battle at the Dragars' temple. Rick told me the other fourteen were used by your parents to destroy the Holy Gem during the same battle."

Myers frowned, then opened his mouth to speak.

Jeena didn't give him the chance. "Buuuttt…, I sensed the same energy as those bottles of DNA gas half a century ago. If I tell you where I sensed it, will that be enough for you to give us the access code? That is all we know. Take it or leave it. Either way, we are done here. We will take our chances in the *Defiant* as originally planned if necessary."

Myers got a faraway look in his eyes.

Jeena got the distinct impression he was communicating with someone. *He's got the same look Rick has when he's discussing things with Master Nick.*

Turning to Admiral Ostar, Jeena said, "You mentioned that you confiscated his equipment and put it in a secure location. Did his equipment include his battle helmet? Is it in a place that would prevent him from communicating with it?"

The admiral nodded her head. "His battle helmet and the rest of his gear are in our security vault. War-King Bistoria assigned two wizard scouts to this space station as part of the triplets' security. We tested the vault with one of their battle helmets. The wizard scout was unable to communicate with her battle computer. The room on the other side of this window was also tested. I'm confident the spells around the room keep prisoners incommunicado. It is escape proof. Nothing in either the magical or physical dimension can get in or out as long as the spells are active."

Jeena looked back at her bondmate's brother. The faraway look was gone from his eyes, and he was staring at her once again. The smug smile on his face bothered her. Despite the admiral's assurances, she wasn't as confident.

"I've decided to go along with your deal," said Myers. "Tell me the location where you sensed the DNA gas, and I'll give you the access code to the X-shuttle."

Jeena looked at Sergeant Ron.

The *Defiant's* captain merely shrugged his shoulders.

Terrie stepped beside her and looked at his fellow wizard scout. "No tricks, Gaston. You'll give us all the access codes and not leave some hidden backdoor or backup trap for us?"

Myers nodded affirmatively.

"Is that wizard scout honor?" asked Terrie.

Jeena thought she saw the short wizard scout's face turn slightly pink before he looked away. After a second, he turned back to Terrie.

"I give my word as a wizard scout," said Myers. "If you give me the location of a bottle of DNA gas, I'll give you the access code for the X-shuttle." He smiled. "I'll also give you the code to deactivate the backup booby trap as well."

Jeena glanced at Terrie.

After a thoughtful moment, Terrie looked away from Myers and faced Jeena. "I believe him. No wizard scout has ever intentionally broken their word."

Turning back to the window, Jeena eyed the short wizard scout for a few seconds. *He is nothing like his brother,* she thought. *He is keeping a stealth shield up. I cannot sense his emotions directly, or his Power, yet at the same time, I feel the same sensation I got from the Dalinfaust. That cannot be. Rick told me the Dalinfaust's dragon avatar had been destroyed. The Dalinfaust should be trapped in the demonic plane for another nine hundred and fifty years before he can return to bother Rick and me again. Should the Creator bless us to be alive then, we shall be ready.*

Jeena shrugged the sensation off. "Very well," she told her bondmate's brother. "I sensed what I believe was a bottle of DNA gas fifty-one years ago when I was at the dark elves' capital city of Drakomar."

Myers frowned. "Dark elves, you say?"

When she nodded, Myers stood and paced the floor of the small room that was his prison. He looked down at Matthew before looking back at Jeena. "A city is a big place. I'm not sure you've told me enough to warrant the access codes."

"That is all I know," Jeena said. "I will tell you that I believe a dark elf named Lord Crendemor may be in possession—"

"Crendemor!" said Myers. "Are you sure?"

The short man's reaction caught Jeena by surprise. "You know him?"

Myers nodded. "I've met him a few times. So he was in Drakomar, you say?"

Nodding, Jeena said, "He was when I sensed the DNA gas. I felt it for only a few seconds, but it was definitely there. Then it was gone. My guess is that he put some kind of shield or something around it."

"Is he still there?" asked Myers.

Jeena shook her head. She was too honest to lie. "No. Crendemor betrayed me to the Dalinfaust. After my rescue and return to Silverton, word was sent to the council of dark elves. They searched for Crendemor, but he could not be found. They sealed his quarters with protective spells against his return. I believe the bottle you seek is there. That is only my belief. I do not know it for a fact."

Myers looked at her for several seconds before turning to Matthew. "The access code is one-eight-three-one-nine-point-nine-six. To clear the backup booby trap..." Myers bent over and whispered in the teenager's ear.

"Hey!" said Sergeant Ron. "That wasn't the deal. You're supposed to tell us."

"And you're supposed to take Matt with you," said Myers placing a hand on the teenager's shoulder. "Besides me, he's now the only one who knows the code. You'll have to take him with you if you want it."

Matthew stood, shaking the wizard scout's hand off his shoulder. "A deal's a deal, *Father*," he said. The teenager looked at Sergeant Ron. "The backup access code is nine-four-five-one-three-point-two-one."

Sergeant Ron looked at his grandson for several seconds. Jeena held her breath along with the rest of the dead silent control room.

The *Defiant's* captain nodded. "I'm proud of you, Matt." He turned to Admiral Ostar. "Keep Gaston under your best lock and key. We're taking my grandson with us. We're taking the X-shuttle as well. If you've got any concerns, take it up with War-King Bistoria. We'll be back to get the *Defiant*."

"And if you don't come back?" asked the orc admiral.

"Then we'll be dead."

Sergeant Ron turned to Jeena. "I don't know about you, High Priestess, but I think it's time we saw the triplets. I'm not sure what kind of problems Rick is having, but you can bet he's knee-deep in trouble."

Jeena smiled. "Isn't he always?"

CHAPTER 9

Once the crew of the *Defiant* and Matthew were gone, Myers sat in his chair staring down at the tabletop. As far as the techs in the control room could tell, he appeared resigned to his fate. On the inside, he was anything but resigned.

"You had best be right," Myers said in the area of his mind shared with his battle computer. *"The Dalinfaust was wrong about the elf having the DNA gas. If the elf is wrong about where it is, then I got myself locked up for nothing."*

"Relax," hissed the demon which was his battle computer. *"The Dalinfaust said the elf high priestess was the key to getting the last bottle of DNA gas. He did not say she had it in her possession."*

"You told me the elf did," Myers said allowing his growing anger to accompany his thoughts. *"You said she kept one of the bottles for herself. You told me if I allowed Matt and myself to be taken captive that I would get the bottle of DNA gas."*

"So you shall," said the demon. *"I may have stretched the facts a little, but the end result of my algorithm is that you will get the bottle of DNA gas. That's all that is important."*

Myers reached out with an active scan and probed the interior of his cell. Each time his line of Power touched one of the surrounding protective spells, his scan was thrown back.

"How am I supposed to get out of here?" Myers asked *"The room's impregnable. Or did you forget to include that little detail in your algorithm."*

"I calculate you are making a joke," said the demon. *"Unlike your old battle computer Wanda, I can appreciate humor, but do not press me too far. The Dalinfaust ordered me to help you acquire the DNA gas, so I will do so. The Dalinfaust's Power was weakened when your brother destroyed the Dalinfaust's avatar, but he is far from helpless. The pieces of his essence in the four phase rods keep part of him here in the physical dimension. When you take your phase rod to the magical dimension, the Dalinfaust will be present there as well. With the energy from the DNA gas combined with the Power of the four essences in the phase rods, the Dalinfaust will be able to free himself from the demonic plane without having to wait the full thousand years."*

"The DNA gas is mine," Myers said suspiciously. *"I'm only going along with this plan to get the bottle. That was the agreement."*

"Foolish mortal," said the demon letting his disdain for living organisms accompany his words. *"What cares the Dalinfaust about the bottle of DNA gas once he is free of his prison? It shall be yours. The Dalinfaust has promised that your precious Diane will have eternal life. He always keeps his word. Do not tempt him. You shall both get the reward you deserve."*

"As long as we understand each other," Myers said. At the same time, he promised in his private space that he wouldn't trust either his battle computer or the Dalinfaust. He well knew the demon's words usually held double meaning.

"There is nothing to understand, mortal. You will get what you deserve if you follow the Dalinfaust's instructions. Your son is with the others. The Dalinfaust can no longer teleport you between dimensions on his own. As long as he is in his prison, he will need assistance to transport you to the magical dimension. Once the triplets open an access point into the time-bubble around the asteroid, the Dalinfaust can use your connection to your son to utilize the time-bubble and gate you to Portalis. Once there, you will go to the dark elves' capital and find the bottle of DNA gas. When you have it, I will tell you where to take it to free the Dalinfaust. Once he is free, you may take the DNA gas to your precious empress. After that, the Dalinfaust will have no further use for you. As far as he is concerned, you may both live your lives as you see fit from that point on. So may your son. All three of you

are so far beneath the Dalinfaust's notice that he cares not what you do."

Myers stared at the top of the table for several more seconds. His mind was spinning a hundred kilometers a second as he weighed risks and rewards. *"My son is not to be harmed."*

"Have I not said as much? The Dalinfaust only needs your connection to your son as the triplets create the gate to the time-bubble around the asteroid. Your precious son is in no danger. All that matters is for you to go to Portalis and fetch the bottle of DNA gas."

Myers raised his head and looked at the observation window. Its spells had been reactivated. All he could see was his own reflection in its mirrored surface. *"Fine, then let's do it. So how am I getting out of this place? I'll need my equipment as well."*

"Of course you will," said his battle computer. *"Your phase rod must be taken to the magical dimension."* The demon laughed. *"You wouldn't want to leave your trusted battle computer behind either, would you? Where you go, I go. You will never be free of me."*

A shudder ran down Myers's spine. He forced himself to stay steady. *Diane is all that matters,* he thought in his private space. *Once I get the DNA gas, I will get free of the demon somehow. First, I must get the bottle for Diane. Then the Dalinfaust and his demon watchdog can go square to hell!*

CHAPTER 10

Richard pointed at the side tunnel to the left with his head. Two orcs with rifles took up positions on either side of the opening. He continued moving down the main tunnel at a fast pace with two score orcs hot on his heels, only a few of which were armed with military-grade rifles. The ragtag group had placed rear security at five intersections in just under six minutes.

Considering we don't speak each other's language, he thought, *they're taking my commands easily enough. Why, I don't know, but at this point in time, I'm not going to question it.*

A familiar tingle passed down Richard's spine. He'd felt it often in the past when the tele-bots around him tried to warn him of pending danger. He stopped where he was, holding up his hand as he took a knee. He looked at the 'T' intersection ahead. All seemed quiet. Even the alarms in the tunnels had stopped ringing earlier. A quick check of his passive scan revealed nothing past the intersection.

Drawing Power from his reserve, Richard formed an active scan, wrapping it in a stealth shield. He reached out to the intersection and probed on either side. He sensed magical energy. Ever so carefully, he moved his active scan through the energy field, sensing a score of life forms split evenly on both sides of the 'T' intersection.

Turning to Yellow-tooth, Richard pointed at one of the grenades on the big orc's utility belt. Holding up two fingers he pointed at the right-most tunnel. Then he pointed at the left side of the 'T' intersection with both fingers.

Four orcs stood holding grenades in their hands. At a nod from Yellow-tooth, they pulled the pins and tossed the grenades down the tunnel, bouncing them off the back wall of the intersection. Two grenades rolled into each of the side tunnels.

Richard was impressed. *Without my battle suit,* he thought, *the range would've been too far for me to have thrown. The strength of the orcs is phenomenal even after weeks of captivity and abuse.*

Boom! Boom! Boom! Boom!

At the fourth explosion, a score of orcs sprinted forward, half turning down the left tunnel and the remainder running into the right. A furious barrage of rifle and pistol shots was accompanied by loud screams. None of the screams sounded orc to Richard.

When the last of the ambushers' life forms disappeared from his passive scan, Richard ran forward. Yellow-tooth and the rest of the orcs followed. Richard stepped into the intersection just in time to see an orc slamming the armored head of a Tharg into the tunnel wall. An armored, headless torso of a four-armed Tharg lay twitching on the rough stone floor near the orc's feet.

Definitely strong, Richard thought. *New safety tip. Never let an orc get me in a headlock.*

Yellow-tooth barked a command. The orcs began distributing weapons and ammo belts from the dead. Yellow-tooth held out two grenades to Richard.

Shaking his head, Richard tossed his rifle and ammo belt to one of the unarmed orcs. *They're going to need it more than me,* he thought. *With my Power fully restored, I could probably clear out the entire tunnel system on my own given time. The problem is that's the one thing I don't have.* A glance at his passive scan confirmed that more of the prisoners' life forms were disappearing every second.

Yellow-tooth said something Richard couldn't understand. When he didn't respond, the big orc shouted an obvious command. The orcs around him started moving down each of the two side tunnels.

Richard grabbed Yellow-tooth's right arm. When the big orc looked at him, Richard shook his head and held up his hand in a stopping motion. "Wait!"

The big orc shouted another command. The orcs stopped and

went down on one knee with weapons at the ready.

Reaching out with his mind, Richard located an energy source. As he suspected, it appeared to be some type of magical monitoring device. He followed the line of magic to other sources of energy. Something inside him responded to the magic. It was the same something that had helped him hack his way into magic-based computers and security systems during past missions. He had a fleeting memory of his DNA being infused with part of the gaseous form of *'the One'* when he was still an embryo. Letting that part of him reach into the magic-based network controlling the devices, Richard twisted the flows of magic energy back on themselves.

A flurry of small explosions echoed throughout the tunnel.

There, Richard thought. *Unless I miss my guess, they've lost their scrying devices. I'm betting most of their automated weapons systems are out as well. Now we're on even footing.*

Releasing Yellow-tooth's arm, Richard did his best to emulate the guttural sound he associated with the orc word for 'move.'

The orcs did not move.

Well, so much for my language skills, Richard thought. Changing tactics, he pointed down each of the side tunnels and yelled, "Go! Go!"

The orcs began running down each tunnel. Yellow-tooth gestured at Richard with one hand and then at the left and right tunnel in turn. The puzzled look on his face made it an obvious question.

Richard shook his head. Wrapping himself in Power, he pointed to the stone floor. Shifting into the void, he levitated downward. The big orc didn't seem as shocked as he'd expected. Just before Richard's head sank into the floor, he saw Yellow-tooth nod and take off down the right tunnel.

After fifteen meters levitating through the stone, Richard broke into a lower tunnel right in the midst of four armored Thargs firing into a chain of fifty human-looking prisoners. Wasting no time, he reached out with Power, splitting it into four lines and sending one to each of the Thargs. Wrapping the lines around the Thargs' spinal columns, he gave a twist. All of the four-armed guards dropped unmoving to the stone floor.

Only a few of the prisoners remained alive, but the ones that could move immediately jumped on the Thargs and began stripping them of armor and weapons. One of the humans grabbed a set of keys and began unlocking chains.

Turning in the direction leading to the intersection where he'd seen the technicians with the poison gas equipment, Richard took off running for all he was worth. As he did, he checked the level of his Power reserve.

Crap. I'm at about ninety percent already. I've got to keep from shifting into the void if I can help it. It takes too much Power. Nick would probably point out that I can't keep doing that little 'snap the spinal cord' maneuver very often either. I've got to get myself a weapon.

A large concentration of life forms was located off his path down another side tunnel. Several of the life forms disappeared from his passive scan. While desperate to reach the poison gas equipment before the Thargs got it operating, something inside Richard tugged at his heart. He shook his head. *I ain't ever going to get there at this rate.*

Despite his frustration, Richard obeyed the pinprick to his conscience and turned down the side tunnel. He passed an entire chain of fifty tall blue prisoners running in the direction from which he'd come. He let them pass as he picked up even more speed. Turning another corner, he ran straight into the rear of a chain of elves trying to get away from a half-dozen armored soldiers firing automatic weapons into their group.

The animal that was Richard's temper burst out of its cage. "Try picking on someone who's not helpless," he shouted.

His previous intention not to waste Power fell to the wayside as he shifted into the void, passing through the fleeing elves. Within two heartbeats he was in the midst of the soldiers. Dropping his shift to conserve Power, he grabbed a large-bore rifle out of one of the soldier's hands and fired point-blank into the visor of another.

The soldiers were not Thargs, and their armor was far from top of the line. The round from Richard's rifle penetrated the soldier's visor, making a bloody mess on the inside. Sweeping out with his leg, he tripped two more soldiers. In the confusion, he shot another in the neck joint of his armor. The soldier flew back and hit the tunnel wall, then slid to the stone floor. The two soldiers still standing swung their rifles in Richard's direction. He beat them to the punch by tearing apart their spinal cords with lines of Power. Spinning on his heels, he fired two rounds into the visors of the soldiers he'd tripped. They stopped moving.

His temper partially abated, Richard sensed the Power reserve he used for offense and defense. It was noticeably lower. *I can't keep this up. I'm below eighty percent now.*

Turning, Richard looked at the elves. Most that were still alive were trying to flee, but their progress was hampered by the weight of the score of dead bodies hooked to the chain. One of the elves closest to Richard shouted something. Then he shouted again. The other elves stopped trying to run. After glancing back, several of the elves bent down and began trying to assist their wounded comrades as best they could. Three of the elves were wearing dragon-skin collars. He sensed links from the three elves going to large Power reserves. Energy from the collars was wrapped around the elves' links to their reserves, apparently preventing access.

Magic users of some kind, Richard thought. *They could be useful.* He sensed the energy locking the devices around the elves' necks, then the magical traps in the collars set to explode at any attempt to remove them. *That won't do,* he thought.

Reaching out with lines of Power, Richard twisted the flows of magic in the collars back on themselves. The collars' magic flared before dissipating back into the universe from which it came. Gripping the collars with telekinesis, he tore the thin pieces of dragon skin off the elves' necks.

One of the elves he freed was the one who'd ordered the others to stop running. Like all of the elves, he was male. The elf raised his hand, feeling around his neck. Looking at Richard, he said something. The elf's words were no more intelligible to Richard than that of any of the other prisoners he'd encountered.

Richard snorted. *The big jerk in the sky lets me understand languages when he sends me on other missions, so why not now?* Like usual, Richard didn't have an answer. "Doesn't matter," he muttered. "I've got things to do."

Bending over the body of the soldier he'd taken the large-bore weapon from, Richard stripped off the man's belt. He strapped it around his waist, then removed what appeared to be one of the Dragars' DNA batteries. With more than a little regret, he swapped out the partial battery in his acquired weapon for a fresh one.

The unborn dragons that were sacrificed to create these batteries are already dead, he reasoned. *There's nothing I can do about that. All I can do is use the magic from their sacrifice to kill as many Dragar thugs as I can.*

The lead elf said something again, but Richard ignored him. He turned and ran back down the tunnel leaving the chain of elves behind.

I did what I could for them. I can't stop to heal their wounded. I could save a few, but thousands of others will die if I don't get to that poison gas before the Thargs. Those elves are on their own. Jeena will just have to understand.

The image of his molten silver-eyed bondmate flashed in his mind. He missed her. *No time for sentiment now,* he thought. *I've got things to do.*

Richard sensed a dozen life forms about to come around the next corner. He raised his rifle into a firing position, aiming it down the tunnel where he estimated the first life form would appear. Before the life form did, he recognized its frequency. He held his fire as six of the monkey-like creatures that had previously distributed food to his chain turned the corner. Without hesitation, the monkeys ran past him in the direction of the exit.

After the monkey creatures passed, Richard ran around the corner, straight into two unarmored Thargs sprawled on the tunnel floor in a pool of blood. Broken pieces of buckets were scattered around the bodies. Pieces of the rotten meat normally fed to the prisoners were stuffed into the mouths of the dead guards. An image of the six monkeys ganging up on the two guards flashed in his mind. *Vicious little beggars. If even the monkeys are revolting, we might actually have a chance.*

Several loud booms sounded behind Richard in the direction where he'd left the elves. He noticed three bursts of magic energy appear on his passive scan.

I guess they were magic users after all. Good. That ought to shake things up a bit.

Continuing on, Richard closed the distance to the intersection where he'd left the poison gas equipment. Using his passive scan, he spotted a score of life forms scattered around the intersection with another two-score spaced out in the tunnel opposite him.

Picking up speed and raising his rifle into a firing position,

Richard said, "What the hell. No guts, no glory."

Turning the corner, he started to pull the rifle's trigger as the intersection came into view. Milling around the wheeled cart containing the poison gas was a mixture of gnomes and dwarves. Two gnomes were standing on the cart-sized engine, attempting to pry open its metal top. He immediately eased off the trigger without firing.

Several dwarves armed with rifles and pistols aimed their weapons in Richard's direction. He shouted the dwarf word for friend followed by its gnome counterpart. He doubted the dwarves and gnomes understood languages from Portalis but figured it was worth a shot. Just in case, he wrapped himself in Power, preparing to shift into the void.

A white-haired gnome with an equally white beard shouted something in a language Richard didn't understand. The dwarves lowered their weapons.

"Rick," said the white-haired gnome in a language Richard understood. "By all that's holy, you're the last person I expected to see in this Creator forsaken place."

Searching deep inside his memory, Richard tried to place the gnome's face. Slowly, a memory of his mission to destroy the Dragars' temple on Portalis floated to the surface of his mind. It suddenly hit him who the gnome was.

"Rembis," Richard said. "What are... No, never mind. It doesn't matter. We've got to get this container of gas to the tunnel leading to the guards' barracks area. Do you think your friends and you could give me a hand?"

Richard remembered when he'd first met the gnome mage. Rembis had been young then. The gnome had been one of the Dragars' slaves on a fighter-shuttle attacking the city Richard and his friends were defending. As he remembered it, once he'd hijacked the shuttle, the young gnome had been very helpful sharing knowledge of Dragar equipment and tactics.

Pointing at a leather collar around his neck, Rembis said, "Do you think you can help me get this off like you did the last time?"

Without taking the time to reply, Richard wrapped Power around the dragon-skin collar, deactivated the magic, and ripped the collar off the gnome's neck.

"Thanks," said the gnome. "I feel like a young fool for letting myself get captured again, but no time for that now. Sounds like you have the same idea we have. If we can get this cart to the tunnels leading to the Thargs barracks, we should be able to take a lot of them out of action before they can get a major counterattack going. So far we've only had to deal with the normal guards and a few roving patrols."

A glance at the large assortment of weapons and the hodgepodge of armor on the dwarves and gnomes told Richard they'd had to deal with more than a few patrols. The half dozen Tharg corpses scattered around the cart reinforced his impression.

"So you'll help?" Richard asked.

Rembis said something in a language Richard didn't understand. A dozen dwarves gathered around the mechanical cart and began pushing it down the tunnel.

"I'm not exactly sure where to go," Richard admitted.

"Then it's lucky we're here," said Rembis. He pointed at one of the gnomes on top of the cart tugging at the metal covering over the equipment's engine compartment. "Balso here has worked in engineering and tunnel repairs for the last six months. He's got most of the tunnel system memorized."

Richard noticed several burn holes in the side of the engine compartment. Pointing, he said, "Too bad. If we could get the engine running, we'd make better time."

"Tell me about it," said Rembis. "Balso thinks he can get it running if he can get inside. I've got my doubts, but you know how stubborn young gnomes can be."

Eyeing the old gnome, Richard remembered the year he'd spent with the younger version of Rembis before the final attack on the Dragars' temple. The younger Rembis had been more than a little hard headed at times. "I certainly can."

Rembis waved a hand at the cart and mumbled words Richard heard but quickly forgot. A ball of blue energy left the old dwarf's hand, settling around the engine compartment. Green sparks leaped out from the engine and intermixed with the gnome's spell. The green sparks increased in intensity until the blue energy faded away.

"Just as I feared," said Rembis. "All the Thargs let me memorize was low-level spells. The magic in this equipment's security shield is too powerful for my current spells."

As the dwarves continued manhandling the heavy cart down the tunnel, Richard reached out with his mind and located the main flow of energy in the equipment. He traced the flow to a part that *felt* like a security program. He unraveled two lines of magic and circumvented the flow's key. Converting his line of Power to telekinesis, he used a technique the *Defiant's* mechanic, Charlie, had taught him to locate weak points in equipment. With a pull on two metallic catches, the lid to the engine compartment popped open.

"I told you I'd get it," said Balso smiling.

The old gnome winked at Richard. "I see you're just as proficient at circumventing magic as I remember. Seems like yesterday, doesn't it?"

Richard shrugged. From the difference in the gnome's appearance, he had a feeling it had been several centuries for the old gnome. *Come to think of it,* Richard thought. *It's been several centuries for me as well, counting my missions for* 'the One.'

Glancing around, Richard noticed four of the other gnomes and two of the dwarves were also wearing the dragon-skin collars. With little to lose, he shorted out the collars' security and used a twist of telekinesis to tear the security devices off their throats.

"Thanks," said Rembis. "I should have thought to ask. Guess I really am getting old." He pointed at one of the two dwarves whose collar's Richard had removed. "Stonemite, grab Jade and see if you can help some of our wounded now."

The newly released dwarves waved thanks to Richard, then moved to kneel beside the more unfortunate prisoners and waved their hands in intricate patterns while muttering words Richard heard but quickly forgot. He sensed surges of magic energy envelope the wounded prisoners. At the same time, his passive scan showed an increase in their life forces.

"Priests?" Richard asked.

Rembis nodded. "The best. They haven't been able to heal before now with those blasted collars around their necks." The old gnome looked at Richard before pointing at the cart. "Don't mean to tell you your business, but it's going to take a few minutes to drag this monstrosity to the tunnel leading to the guards' barracks. Most of the soldiers might get out before we arrive."

Nodding his head, Richard said, "Yeah, I was thinking the same thing. If you can tell me where it is, I'll go on ahead and try to slow them down."

"I will do you one better," said Rembis. He glanced up at the young gnome on top of the poison gas cart. "Balso, go with Rick and guide him to the intersection on level thirteen that leads down to the guard barracks." The old gnome turned back to Richard. "I respect your abilities, wizard scout, but you're not going to stop them all by your lonesome." He pointed at a red-bearded dwarf with a patch over one eye and a long scar down the side of his face. "Take Stoneclaw here and half the dwarves. A couple of my gnome mages can go to back you up. The rest of us will be there as soon as we can."

So it was that Richard found himself running down the tunnel following a meter-tall gnome with a score of half-naked dwarves trailing behind with an assortment of rifles and pistols in their hands. He glanced at the dwarves as he ran, noting the fire in their eyes.

I wouldn't want to be a Tharg or Dragar today, Richard thought. *These guys are out for blood.* He smiled. *Come to think of it, so am I.*

CHAPTER 11

Tia squeezed into the bench seat on the inside wall of the X-shuttle, then strapped the flight harness over her shoulders and waist. She elbowed the two dwarves sitting on either side. "Hey, give me some room. For being so short, you two take up a lot of room."

The dwarf on her right, Stovis, laughed as he patted his belly. "Can I help it if I like to eat? Besides, Sergeant Hendricks had us take half the armory with us. We've got no idea what we'll be facing."

Glancing at the assortment of rifles, pistols, war hammers, battle-axes, missile launchers, and auto-cannons crammed into the confined space of the shuttle, Tia nodded her head. They really didn't know what they'd be facing. All any of them knew was that their friend was in trouble, and they were going to do their best to get him back home in one piece.

The dwarf to Tia's left happened to be Felspar, the leader of the *Defiant's* security team. He waved his hand at the inside of the X-shuttle. "It doesn't help that this thing has seating for fourteen while the high priestess convinced Sergeant Ron to cram twenty-two of us in here. The only ones left on the *Defiant* are Sergeant Hendricks and your brother."

Tia thought back to the fit Daniel had thrown when Sergeant Ron had told her brother he was staying back. *I don't blame him. Daniel is a Trecorian the same as me. There isn't a Trecorian alive who can resist a good fight when the cause is noble.*

Tia looked at Felspar. "Be that as it may, I'm so squished

between the two of you that I can barely breathe." She jammed her elbows into the sides of the two dwarves as hard as she could. They barely moved. "Not everybody's made out of hard-as-rock muscles like you guys."

Stovis laughed. "I can't make myself any smaller. Matt hasn't even gotten the shuttle out of its docking berth yet. You're just going to have to deal with being crowded for a couple of hours."

Tia looked toward the front of the X-shuttle. Matthew was hunched over the instrument panel, nodding his head as Sergeant Ron tried to help him figure out the controls. As irritated as she was with the teenager for not contacting her since their mission on Portalis, she couldn't help being a little sympathetic. *If what Myers told us is true, we're all entrusting our lives to someone who's only flown the X-shuttle during simulator training.*

A flash of silver in the corner of Tia's eye caused her to look up and find the elf high priestess standing over her. The elf's waist-length silver hair caught the dome light of the shuttle, reflecting rainbows of colors onto the inside walls. Like always, Tia tried to avoid the high priestess's eyes, but she wasn't quite fast enough. The molten-silver of the elf's gaze drew Tia's attention despite her resolve. She momentarily forgot her cramped space as she was drawn deeper into the mysteries contained within the swirling-silver. Tia had a feeling the high priestess's eyes held all the answers if she could only think of the right questions.

"Stovis," said the high priestess breaking eye contact, "why don't you trade seats with me. My spot between two gnomes will give you room to spread out. I think I would be a much better fit sitting next to Ensign Bistoria."

The potbellied dwarf grinned and patted his stomach. "That's an excellent idea, Jeehana. Tia may look small, but the way she's strapped weapons and ammo on every part of her body takes up a lot of room."

The high priestess's words broke Tia's spell. She looked away from the elf, noticing the empty spot on the opposite bench where the elf had been sitting. The two gnome mages on either side of the empty seat appeared none too happy to hear the stocky dwarf would be taking the place of the slender elf.

"It's all right, High Priestess," Tia said. "I'm fine. I was just complaining. Soldiers like to complain sometimes."

The elf smiled. "So Rick tells me."

As Stovis unstrapped and rose from his seat, Tia took the opportunity to take a closer look at the high priestess. Having served on the *Defiant* previously, Tia was used to Comstar, but he was a male elf, and he was old. In her opinion, the high priestess was a species unto herself.

The elf had traded in her robe for an all-black jumpsuit complete with utility belt and holster. Besides the two hand grenades on her belt, two thin wands made out of a dark brown wood were jammed in the belt. Tia sensed energy in the wands. In lieu of a rifle, the high priestess carried her staff in her left hand.

Tia had a thought that the elf's warlike appearance somehow only added to her beauty. The elf was easily the most beautiful female she'd ever seen. Tia had even caught Matthew staring openmouthed at the high priestess as they'd made their way from the control room to the X-shuttle. Remembering the incident, she found herself forcing down a wave of jealousy.

Once Stovis took his place in the seat on the opposite side of the shuttle, the elf high priestess gracefully sat down beside Tia.

Tia became very aware of her sometimes less than graceful moves. *The elf makes sitting in a jump-seat look like she's sitting on a throne. I wonder if she ever does anything wrong. Kinda makes me want to reach out and slap her for being too perfect.* Although Tia knew she was thinking foolish thoughts, she couldn't help it. The double set of phase pistols across her own chest and the vest of grenades she wore made her feel anything but feminine. *No wonder Matt was looking at her instead of me.*

No sooner had the high priestess sat down than the X-shuttle jerked. Looking out the cockpit's forward video display, Tia found they were backing away from the space station. She watched Matthew moving the ion controls ever so gently to spin the X-shuttle a hundred and eighty degrees before engaging the main engine. She felt a slight acceleration.

The high priestess shifted in the seat to Tia's right. As Matthew increased the shuttle's forward velocity, the elf leaned against Tia's shoulder. When Tia looked at the elf, she was surprised to see that the high priestess's eyes were shut and her lips were moving.

Is she praying? Tia wondered. The idea that the elf might be a little frightened cut down Tia's rising jealousy a little.

As the shuttle's acceleration leveled off, the elf straightened in her seat and opened her eyes.

Tia quickly looked away.

"My apologies, Tia," said the high priestess. "I suppose I am not used to these metal ships yet. If truth be told, I have not even ridden on a wooden ship on one of Portalis' lakes, much less an ocean." She smiled. "Rick says I am a landlubber at heart. He said that means—"

"I know what it means, High Priestess," Tia said.

The elf smiled. "Jeehana. Won't you call me Jeehana? Rick considers you a good friend. I would like to be your friend too if you will let me."

"I'm just a common soldier," Tia said unsure how to react. "I'm not sure—"

The elf laughed.

Tia did not get the impression the elf was laughing at her. "Did I say something funny?"

The high priestess smiled. "I was just thinking that if you are a common soldier, then let Trecor's enemies beware. Rick has told me some of the exploits you have had together. He says you have saved his life more than once. He is very fond of you, as I am sure you know."

Tia felt her face grow warm. "Uh...I like Rick too. Did he tell you he saved my life when I was shot in the neck with an orc crossbow?"

"No," said the elf. "He did not mention it. I have found that I have to pry things like that out of him, but he was full of praise for your sister and you."

"Yeah, well, he and Liz were very close for a..." Tia let her words trail off when it dawned on her who she was talking to. "Uh, I'm sorry, High Priestess. What I mean is—"

"Jeehana. Please call me Jeehana. I hope you do not mind me calling you Tia? Ensign Bistoria seems too formal for friends."

"Uh, sure. Tia is fine, uh...Jeehana."

"Good," said the elf. "I am thankful Rick had your sister and you for friends." She looked at Tia for a couple of seconds. "Is your sister as pretty as you?"

"I'm not pretty," Tia said feeling herself grow warm again. "I told you, I'm just a soldier."

The elf gave what Tia could only describe as a dazzling smile. The swirling in the high priestess's molten-silver eyes appeared to speed up.

"You are too modest," said the high priestess nodding toward the cockpit. "I have seen our young pilot looking at you more than once. As an elf, I can sense emotions. He is way beyond fond of you. I sense the same emotions from him when he looks at you that Terrie and Angela have when they are near each other. Rick tells me that emotion is what humans call love."

The heat in Tia's face grew even warmer. "Uh...I don't think he—"

"Do not fool yourself," said the elf. "I sense the same emotion from you when you look at him. Rick told me a little about your uh...situation. May I give you a piece of advice, Tia?"

Looking down at the floor to buy some time, Tia wasn't sure whether she wanted to hear what the high priestess had to say. A part of her was tempted, but another part was flashing caution lights fast and furious. After a couple of seconds, curiosity overcame her caution. She looked back at the high priestess, doing her best not to stare directly into the elf's eyes.

"What do you want to tell me, Jeehana?"

The elf looked at Tia for several seconds without saying a word.

In spite of her attempt not to look directly into the elf's eyes, Tia was irresistibly drawn to them. She sensed something in the high priestess as if the elf was opening the smallest part of a window into herself. Tia sensed an emotion. It was warm and very intense. Slowly Tia realized the emotion wasn't coming from the elf. The emotion originated from the front of the shuttle. She drew in her breath as she realized it was coming from Matthew. The emotion was love—strong and pure love.

The high priestess looked away, breaking the connection.

Although the emotion itself was gone, its memory was firm in Tia's mind. *He loves me,* she thought. *He really does love me.*

The high priestess looked at the front of the shuttle before turning back to Tia. "Do not let a mere war or politics keep you from the other part of your soul. Rick and I almost missed our chance. This may be Matthew and your only chance to make amends. Do not go through life regretting a lost opportunity. You and Matthew were created for each other. I can sense it."

The elf shifted her staff to her right hand before placing her left hand over Tia's right. The hand felt warm to Tia. She could also feel the elf's hand reverberating with Power. The high priestess locked eyes with her. This time Tia wasn't drawn in but more interested in the elf's words.

"Tia, I believe that in your heart you know Matthew is the one for you. Do I believe wrong?"

Lowering her head to stare at the metal deck, Tia searched her heart before shaking her head. Although she did not say the words out loud, she couldn't lie to herself. *I do love him. By the Creator, I really do.*

CHAPTER 12

"Get ready," said the demon who was Wanda. *"The dragon is preparing the time-bubble gate combination. Use your son as a conduit to the gate. When you have the connection, give me control. The Dalinfaust will use his link to me to transport you to Portalis."*

It's risky, Myers thought in his private space. *I've been able to keep the demon from having direct contact with Diane and Matthew until now. The demon wants to use my connection to my son to manipulate the triplet's gate. I know it's risky, but the reward will be worth it. If I sense even the slightest attempt by the demon to contact Matthew, I'll close the connection. I'm sure I can stop the demon if the need arises.* "I'll need all of my gear," he told his battle computer.

The demon that was Wanda laughed. *"You need not trouble yourself to worry about such mundane matters. You are my wizard scout. I will take care of you. You may always rest assured I am watching your back. I will also make sure you get what you deserve. When the Dalinfaust teleports you to Portalis, I and all of your equipment will be teleported as well. You are in good hands as long as you have me."*

Knowing better than to trust the demon but left with little choice, Myers followed his link to his Power reserve, found the path from his reserve to the Power reserve he'd previously shared with his father, and shared the same Power reserve with his son. He ignored a weak point in the larger reserve where a series of deadly traps blocked a link to another being. He knew where the link led but had no desire to go there even if he could. It was the link his father had once attached to his brother during the battle for the Academy's spaceport. Following the perimeter of the large Power reserve, Myers found that which he sought.

There. That's the link to Matthew's part of the shared reserve. All I have to do is remove the booby-traps I've set on this side and the connection will be complete.

"Yes," said Wanda. *"Hurry. We have very little time. If you want to save your precious Diane, you must hurry."*

Anger burned within Myers at the demon's intrusion on his private thoughts, but nonetheless, he removed the traps at a rapid pace. They were his traps after all. When the last trap was removed, he sensed the essence of his son.

"Place a stealth shield around yourself, fool," growled Wanda. *"Even if your son does not detect us, the high priestess might. She is more powerful than even she realizes. Be wary, but be fast."*

Wrapping himself with Power, Myers converted it to his best stealth shield, then cautiously entered the link to their shared Power reserve until he was in the portion reserved for the teenager.

"I'm in," Myers said. *"Now what?"*

The demon laughed. *"Leave that to me."*

CHAPTER 13

"It's almost time, Jeehana," said Sergeant Ron from the shuttle's cockpit. "We're approaching the point in space given to us by the triplets."

Jeena unbuckled her flight harness, giving a last nod of encouragement to Tia, then took three steps to stand behind Matthew and Sergeant Ron. Drawing Power from her reserve, she waved a hand as she whispered the words of a telekinesis spell. Using the magic energy, she locked herself in place on the shuttle's metal deck. *It is liable to get bumpy,* she thought. Drawing more Power, Jeena touched the link she shared with her bondmate. She felt him far off and very faint, but she did sense him. She sent another line of magic back to the triplets in the space station. The glow of magic from their location confirmed they were ready to do their part. So was she.

"The triplets and I are ready, Sergeant Ron," Jeena said. "Tell me when."

"Matt," said Sergeant Ron, "activate the X-shuttle's stealth shield. If Gaston's right, we're going to be in the middle of a hornet's nest if we're not careful."

The teenager touched an icon on his control panel.

Jeena sensed strong magic surround the shuttle. *No,* she thought. *It is not magic, but it is not technology either. The combination of the two really is a new type of energy.*

"Now," yelled Sergeant Ron.

Jeena shouted the final word of the spell connecting her to the triplet's Power. The gem at the top of her staff glowed brightly, causing her to raise her other hand to shield her eyes. The X-shuttle vibrated and bucked back and forth. Jeena glanced at the forward video displays, noticing a translucent sphere faintly glowing to their front.

"Head for the sphere, Matt," said Sergeant Ron.

Jeena barely heard the old man's commands. The vibrations in the shuttle increased incrementally the nearer they got to the sphere. Through sheer force of will and with the help of her telekinesis spell, she remained on her feet. She heard shouts of surprise mixed with cries of pain from her rear as the rest of the crew was thrown around in their flight harnesses.

"Something's not right," said Matthew. "Should I change course?"

"Negative," replied Sergeant Ron. "Keep going. Everything's fine." Looking over his shoulder, he shouted at Jeena, "Everything is fine, isn't it?!"

The energy from the triplets is resisting me, Jeena thought. Tracing the link to her bondmate, she pulled the barest snippet of Power from the other half of her soul and merged it into the energy from the triplets. The vibrations in the shuttle lessened noticeably. Inserting a drop of her bondmate's Power into the glowing sphere on the shuttle's forward display, Jeena willed it to obey her commands. *It still resists me,* she thought.

Reaching deep inside her, Jeena searched for the piece of her that she knew was a part of her bondmate. Using that part as an anchor, she commanded the triplet's energy to do her will. This time it obeyed. She felt the vibrations in the metal deck lessen, then disappear altogether.

For the barest instant, she sensed something…else. *It is not the triplet's Power or the gate this time. It almost feels like what I sensed when I was in the presence of the Dalinfaust. But that cannot be. Rick and his dolgar friends destroyed the demon's avatar. The Dalinfaust is banished to the demonic plane for another nine hundred and fifty years.*

The feeling disappeared as fast as it came. Jeena sent out a scan of magic, attempting to relocate the source of her feeling, but found nothing. She shrugged her worries off. She had other concerns at the moment.

As Jeena watched, Matthew guided the shuttle directly into the center of the sphere. The moment he did, she cast the second spell taught her by the triplets. A wave of energy swept through the shuttle. Her cells were torn apart. Suddenly all was dark.

A split second later, the inside of the shuttle came back into focus. Everything was quiet. A glance at the video displays confirmed the glowing sphere was no more.

"Are we through?" came Terrie's voice from the rear of the shuttle.

Jeena glanced back at the disabled wizard scout in the bench seat nearest the drop ramp. Looking closer, she saw his left hand entwined in the right hand of his red-headed wife, Angela.

Her brain foggy, Jeena tried to familiarize herself with her surroundings. She noticed that Terrie was wearing his battle suit and carrying a modified M12 with a magic wand strapped underneath the barrel. His wife was in power-armor, holding a similar M12 in her free hand. Jeena glanced at the remainder of the *Defiant's* crew. They were all looking in her direction and, in her opinion, they all looked very deadly.

They only need the command to go, Jeena thought, *and then someone, a lot of someone's, are probably going to die.*

Glancing around the cockpit area, Jeena noticed Sergeant Ron adjusting icons on his console. The holograph display between the pilot and copilot seats activated. An image of the surrounding space appeared. A bright dot in the hologram's center denoted the mining asteroid. Tens of thousands, if not hundreds of thousands of other dots filled the hologram.

"Gaston was right," said Sergeant Ron. "It's the Dragars' invasion fleets. This must be their staging area." He spun his seat around to look at Jeena. "Are we at the right point in time? Did it work?"

Jeena touched her bond link. She felt the other half of her soul, strong and vibrant. Sensing the low amount of Power in her bondmate's reserve, she gathered Power from her own reserve and sent it down the link. Along with Power, she sent the same emotion her bondmate had sent her when she was a prisoner of the Dalinfaust underneath Dillonath Mountain. She had recognized the meaning of the emotion then and had no doubt her bondmate would recognize it now. The meaning of the emotion was clear.

"I am coming."

CHAPTER 14

A red-bearded dwarf fired a long burst of rounds down the tunnel. As soon as his clip ran out, he yelled, "Reload!"

Richard and another dwarf on the opposite side of the tunnel fired their weapons on full automatic, spraying red balls of magic energy down the tunnel.

The heavy return fire from the Tharg guards lessened slightly, but only slightly.

Another dwarf pulled the pin on a grenade and stood to toss it down the tunnel.

Richard sensed a ball of magic heading toward the dwarf. Before he could get a defensive shield up, a line of magic from one of the gnome magic users shot out and formed a translucent wall of blue in front of the dwarf. The Thargs' magic spell hit the shield, bursting into a ball of flames. None of the flames succeeded in touching any of the dwarves or Richard.

The dwarf threw his grenade, sending the metal sphere bouncing down the tunnel until it disappeared around the corner.

Boom!

"That was our last grenade," said the red-bearded dwarf, Stoneclaw. "How much longer until Rembis and the others get here with that blasted piece of machinery?"

Checking his passive scan, Richard noted the position of Rembis and the others. He didn't like what he saw. "At least five minutes. I guess we should've left more of our team with him."

A virtual wall of return fire from the Thargs ricocheted off the gnome's defensive spell. Two rounds made it through, hitting the dwarf who'd thrown the grenade. The rounds knocked the dwarf back and sent blood spewing from his chest. Another dwarf dragged the wounded prisoner into a nearby alcove. Richard sensed Power wrap around the injured dwarf.

Priest, Richard thought. *At least I don't have to worry about healing right now. Not that I could. I'm down to less than fifteen percent Power in my primary reserve as it is, and the reserve I use to heal others is already empty.*

The ten-minute battle had taken its toll in Power and ammo, and Richard knew he wasn't the only one running low on ammo.

Stoneclaw fired his rifle at a fleeting shadow down the tunnel, in single-shot mode. Several of the other dwarves were firing in single-shot mode as well. In comparison, full automatic fire continued to come up the tunnel from the direction of the Thargs. Stoneclaw laughed. Richard barely heard the sound over the noise of weapons firing.

"I'm thinking we are not going to be alive in five minutes," said Stoneclaw. "That is unless you have a secret plan you have not bothered mentioning, human."

Richard had no secret plan. Even worse, he sensed life forms strong in Power moving up the tunnel from the barrack's area. He recognized them for what they were—magic users.

Turning to look over his shoulder, Richard pointed at Balso, the nearest of the gnome mages. "We need some help. Don't you mages have fireballs or lightning bolts or something?"

The young gnome shook his head. "Not at the moment. The Dragars aren't in the habit of letting their captive mages memorize offensive spells. Defensive spells and supportive spells like the translation spell I cast on you, sure. Fireballs and lightning bolts? Not so much."

A glance at his passive scan showed the Dragar magic users were getting closer. Richard took a moment to sense the other parts of the battle occurring in the underground labyrinth that was the mine. *It looks like the prisoners are getting the upper hand on the Thargs that were guarding the prisoner chains,* he thought. *Their victories are going to be short-lived if these Thargs break out of their barracks. They're armored and have plenty of ammo. The prisoners won't stand a chance.* Richard noted his Power reserve. *I'm at thirteen percent. That's just about enough for one desperate charge.*

His marine training kicking in, Richard slapped his last full battery into his rifle. The thought of running away didn't enter his mind. The dwarves and gnomes in his team were his comrades now. Marines didn't desert their teammates. Bracing his right leg against the tunnel wall, he prepared to form a defensive shield.

Maybe my shield will last long enough to get me around the corner and into the Thargs, he thought. *If I can do enough damage, it might give my team a chance to close before the Dragar magic users arrive.*

"I calculate an eighty-nine percent probability your plan will not work," came a thought in Richard's head. *"But then what do I know. I'm just a battle computer."*

Before Richard could reply, the link he shared with his elven bondmate flared with Power. A wave of energy flowed over him, enveloping him in its warmth. He felt Jeena at the other end of their link and sensed an emotion that could only mean one thing, *"I am coming."*

"Nick," Richard mentally shouted into his shared space. *"Where? How?"*

"Do you really want to discuss the details right now?" said Nickelo. *"Or would you be satisfied knowing that your high priestess, Sergeant Ron, and the majority of the* Defiant's *crew are in a shuttle, making an approach toward the asteroid. I calculate we are fifteen minutes out. I also calculate we are easily within range for you to summon your equipment to you. That elf of yours made sure Sergeant Ron brought it onto the shuttle with us."*

Richard knew he wasn't the smartest man in the galaxy, and he sometimes didn't think fast, but one thing he knew he was good at was reacting to fluid situations. Without wasting time on further questions, he did what he did best; he acted. Reaching out with his mind, he summoned his battle helmet to him. A black helmet appeared in the air, and he grabbed it before it hit the floor. It changed shape into three-quarters mode as he brought it toward his head, and he shoved it on.

"Welcome home, old buddy," Richard said in his shared space. *"I could use a little help."*

"What else is new?" asked Nickelo. *"It's a good thing you previously tagged a lot of your primary equipment so you could*

summon it the way the commandant taught you. Now, enough dillydallying. Feed me the results of your passive scan while you summon the rest of your equipment. I'll have some recommended courses of action by the time you are finished."

Acting on his battle computer's suggestion, Richard summoned the rest of his battle suit and weapons along with his dimensional pack. Stripping off his makeshift clothing, he put his battle suit on in record time.

"Seal me up, Nick."

"Compliance."

The battle helmet's visor lowered to merge with his throat armor.

Richard heard the rush of air as the battle suit sealed, enveloping him in the toughest armor the Empire's technicians could devise. He grabbed the phase rod off his left hip and activated it in full destructive mode. A sense of hunger permeated the tunnel. Several of the nearby dwarves stepped back. To their credit, Stoneclaw, Balso, and Rembis remained where they were, but they did stop firing long enough to stare at Richard openmouthed.

Sending an image of his trusty M63 lightweight plasma assault rifle to his dimensional pack, Richard reached over his shoulder and pulled out a fully-loaded weapon.

Richard had a thought. *"Nick, can I summon weapons and ammo for these guys?"*

"Not magic weapons," said Nickelo. *"From what Brachia and Dren told me, the warehouses on the planet Storage only contain equipment from the physical dimension. You could summon technology weapons for the dwarves, but then you would have to spend a few minutes training them in how they work. I calculate you do not have the time."*

Richard knew his battle computer's statement about the Storage warehouses not containing magic wasn't entirely true. He'd once placed a twin of the blue gem his niece and nephew had placed on High Priestess Remozorz's staff in his dimensional pack. He assumed it was in one of the warehouses on Storage. He'd also sent 2,500 smaller blue gems to the planet for safekeeping. Nevertheless, he opted not to argue the point with his battle computer at the current time.

Switching to an alternate plan, he pointed at Stoneclaw. "Give me thirty seconds, then come charging around that corner. You'll have plenty of weapons and ammo when you get there."

"But—"

Richard didn't give the dwarf time to ask questions. He pulled the starburst grenade off his utility belt, pulled the pin, and tossed it down the tunnel, bouncing it around the corner with a little help from his telekinesis. Although the starburst was only intended as a signaling device, he'd used it to blind opponents in the past. Crossing his fingers, he hoped to do so once again.

"Everyone close your eyes," Richard commanded. "Now!" At the same time, he thought the command to switch his visor to max filter.

Boom!

The black visor of Richard's battle helmet momentarily lightened before turning black again.

"Normal night vision mode, Nick," Richard thought as he pushed himself off the tunnel wall, raising his M63 to firing position.

The tunnel took on a reddish tint as his battle computer switched the helmet's visor to night vision mode. Richard pulled the trigger on his M63, sending a virtually solid stream of plasma-energy rounds bouncing off the far wall of the tunnel, into the massed life forms he detected just around the corner. As he ran the twenty steps to the tunnel intersection, he noticed that the return fire from the Thargs had stopped.

"Hmm," said Nickelo. *"I guess your little starburst trick succeeded again. You like to use that a lot, don't you?"*

"Hey. If something works, I use it. So sue me."

Turning the corner, Richard ran smack dab into two score Thargs stumbling into the walls and each other. Lashing out with his phase rod, he caught an armored Tharg on the side of the helmet. The thick metal cracked under the force of the blow and the phase energy running up and down the rod's length. At the same time, he sensed the demon essence in the rod suck life force from the unfortunate Tharg. The guard gave a scream filled with terror and pain. Richard swung his phase rod into a second Tharg who was attempting to raise his rifle. The Tharg fell to the floor with a smashed visor and a bloody face.

"Nick, take control of the M63. Concentrate on the unarmored soldiers. I'll handle the ones in armor with my phase rod."

"Compliance. I'll start with that magic user over there."

Richard felt the right arm of his battle suit raise and a flurry of phase rounds fire into a group of Thargs. In the center of the group stood one of the reptilian Dragars waving his hands in intricate patterns and shouting words Richard couldn't understand. Two plasma rounds caught the magic user in his forehead, flinging him against the tunnel wall.

"Nice shooting, Nick."

"I aim to please," laughed Nickelo. *"Pun intended. By the way, your Power reserve is at ninety-six percent. Your elf sent you a large amount of her Power at the cost of her own reserve. I recommend you send some back so it can regenerate her reserve. This might be a long battle."*

Richard kicked himself for not remembering to send Power back to Jeena. Unlike other bondmates who could only create Power when they mated for the first time in the Presence of the Lady, Jeena and he could create Power by passing some of their own down their bond link to each other. Taking ten percent of the Power in his reserve, he sent it down the link to his bondmate. At the same time, he thrust the tip of his phase rod into the thick chest plate of a Tharg attempting to point a pistol at his head. The Tharg's armor held, but Richard sensed microscopic explosions of phase energy turning the internal organs of the Tharg into a soupy mess.

"This is taking too long," Richard said noticing another mass of life forms heading his way from the direction of the Thargs' barracks.

"I'm plotting the information from your passive scan onto your battle helmet's heads-up display," said Nickelo. *"You will notice I have identified the magic users as red dots."*

Richard saw a dozen red dots intermixed with a hundred yellow and orange dots heading his way.

At that moment, Stoneclaw and his dwarves came charging around the corner, firing at any Thargs still moving. Richard put up a defensive shield to his rear to keep from getting hit by some of the more trigger-happy dwarves as he yelled, "Hey, I'm on your side, remember?"

The dwarves stopped firing and began stripping weapons and armor from the bodies of the Thargs.

"Hold this position at all costs," Richard told Stoneclaw. "I'm going to see what's keeping Rembis and that gas cart."

The dwarves began firing enthusiastically down the tunnel with their newfound weapons and ammo. Richard sensed a ball of energy from the nearest Dragar magic user heading their way. The young magic user Rembis called Balso countered it with a defensive spell, causing it to fizzle in a series of sparks.

Figuring the dwarves and gnomes could hold the intersection for a few seconds on their own, Richard sprinted back the way they'd come. He sensed a group of life forms heading his way at a pace much faster than he figured the gnomes could push the heavy gas cart. Raising his M63, he prepared to take out as many of the enemy as he could before they could attack the dwarves from the rear.

The first of the life forms came charging around the corner. The life form was a tall, half-naked humanoid with gray-leather skin and two yellow tusks protruding from his mouth. One of the tusks was broken off at the halfway point. Richard relaxed the pressure on the trigger of his M63 as Yellow-tooth and the rest of his orcs continued around the corner, pushing the heavy gas cart ahead of them. Yellow-tooth pointed a large-bore rifle in Richard's direction.

"He doesn't know it's you," warned Nickelo.

Switching his helmet to clear visor, Richard shouted. "Chekrak! Chekrak!"

The big orc lowered his weapon. Pointing a free hand at Richard, he said, "Good armor." Yellow-tooth jerked his thumb at the gas cart. "Where does Chekrak want this?"

"Nick," Richard said in his shared space. *"The orc's speaking intergalactic standard."*

"Not hardly," replied Nickelo. *"You've had a translation spell cast on you. The effects haven't worn off yet. I don't even need to use the battle helmet's translator. By the way, your elf told Taylor to tell me to tell you to get up to the surface pronto."*

"Taylor?" Richard said more than a little confused. *"Terrie's battle computer? I thought you were only able to communicate with Margery and Danny. You've told me often enough that you*

were in quarantine from the other battle computers so you wouldn't emotionally infect them."

"Well, things change, so keep up," said Nickelo. *"Besides, the point is that there are several fleets of Dragar warships scattered in space around the asteroid in all directions. According to Taylor, two of the Dragar troopships are on final approach for the pit outside the mine's entrance. I calculate they are planning on putting this prisoner riot down hard. The* Defiant's *crew in the X-shuttle will just have time to land and get you off the asteroid before the Dragars' soldiers surround the mine entrance."*

Richard shook his head. *"No. There are thousands of prisoners in this revolt. I started this whole mess. I can't just leave them."*

In the voice he used when trying to get his wizard scout to listen to reason, Nickelo said, *"Rick, the X-shuttle has seats for fourteen. It already has twenty-one people plus Bright Wing inside. There is barely room for you. How do you think you are going to get everyone away? Even if you could capture the two troopships that are landing, which you can't, you still would not be able to get the other prisoners off this asteroid. The orbiting warships will bombard the asteroid or destroy the troopships when they try to take off. Your friends from the* Defiant *have risked their lives coming here to save you. Don't let them die trying to do something that can't be done. It's hopeless."*

Along with his words, Nickelo forwarded a series of images from Taylor. Richard saw Jeena dressed in a black jumpsuit with her silver hair trailing down her back, standing behind Sergeant Ron and Matthew. He saw an image of space around the asteroid. Hundreds of thousands of black starships of every size dotted the area. They all had the emblem of a red-striped black dragon on their hulls. Another image showed the layout of the mines complete with various colored dots indicating the life forms inside. Richard instinctively knew the white dots were his fellow prisoners. They were scattered all throughout the mine's tunnels.

"See," said Nickelo. *"Over four thousand prisoners are located throughout the mine. It would take hours to get them organized and above ground even if you had ships to put them on, which you don't. Now stop arguing and get to the surface. Save yourself. The fate of three galaxies depends on you. The others prisoners are expendable. Deal with it."*

The memory of orcs taking a beating for him when he'd fallen down popped into Richard's mind. He remembered the orcs passing food to their young and Yellow-tooth sharing his pile of stones.

"No," Richard said using command voice. *"I'm not leaving without them. What was the plan to get us back to our time in the future once you all found me?"*

A series of specs scrolled down the battle helmet's heads-up display. The binary code moved too fast for a human mind to comprehend, but Nickelo interpreted the information for Richard in their shared space. Richard *saw* the triplets create the time-bubble gate combination with Jeena's assistance. Realization came to him that the triplets had made the access point in the time-bubble just large enough for the shuttle to return. He knew even if he could somehow capture the two troopships, they couldn't pass through the triplet's access point.

"Crap!" Richard said out loud. "It's too much to deal with. The hell with it. First things first." He pointed at Yellow-tooth. "Get that cart to Balso. Have him saturate the guards' tunnels with gas. Leave half of your orcs with Balso and Stoneclaw to hold this intersection. We don't need a counterattack from our rear."

Yellow-tooth gestured at the orcs and gnomes around the cart. They hurriedly pushed the cart down the tunnel in Balso's direction. "What about the rest of us?" he asked.

Pointing up the tunnel, Richard said, "The rest of you are coming to the surface with me. The Dragars are landing troopships. We're going to have a whole lot of company very soon."

The big orc nodded his head. "We will die fighting," said Yellow-tooth. "That is a fitting death for soldiers."

"We're not going to die," Richard said not caring that he was probably telling a lie. "Chekrak isn't going to allow it."

CHAPTER 15

Jeena looked at the holograph display. While she was far from an expert at technology, even she could tell things were not looking good. "Are we going to beat those troopships to the ground?" she asked.

Sergeant Ron shook his head. "No way. They'll already be disembarking troops by the time we get down. I've got detailed maps of the pit around the mine. There's a place we can touchdown out of sight, then we can have Rick meet us there and get off the asteroid before the Dragars know we're there."

A crackle came from the external speaker of Terrie's battle helmet. Jeena and Sergeant Ron looked back toward the rear of the X-shuttle.

"Actually," said Taylor, "according to Nickelo, his wizard scout is refusing to leave unless all the prisoners can be saved as well. Wizard Scout Shepard is coming to the surface now, but his intent is only to hold the entrance against the landing Tharg soldiers."

"What?" said Terrie. "You're supposed to be my battle computer. Why am I just finding out about this now?"

"Because you didn't ask," said Taylor. Something sounding like a laugh came from the helmet's speaker. "Hmm. For some reason, I find my reply amusing. I may have made an error contacting Nickelo directly. I calculate a one hundred percent probability I have been emotionally contaminated."

"Great. That's just great," said Terrie. "As if we don't have enough problems all ready."

Jeena tapped the base of her staff on the metal deck. The X-shuttle vibrated. As soon as all eyes were on her, she said, "How many prisoners are there?"

"The count is currently four thousand eight hundred and thirty-seven," replied Taylor. "I calculate there will be less as the battle continues."

"Four thousand!" exclaimed Sergeant Ron. "Is Rick crazy? We'd be hard-pressed to put five more in here. How does he think he's getting the others off that asteroid?"

"Hmm," said Taylor. "Nickelo indicates his wizard scout has not taken the time to figure that part out yet. Nickelo says Wizard Scout Shepard has ordered us to return to the future while we have the chance. Nickelo says he will try to figure some way to save his wizard scout on his own."

"The hell with that," said Sergeant Ron. "Anyone here want to go back?"

Jeena took a quick look around the shuttle. Even Bright Wing was shaking her head no.

"Fine then," Jeena said summing the situation up the way her bondmate sometimes did. "Matthew, I want you to put the X-shuttle down in that hidden spot Sergeant Ron mentioned." Jeena looked back at the rest of the crew. "As soon as we touch down, everyone except Matthew will exit and head for the mine entrance. We will help Rick hold it until he thinks of some way to pull this off." She looked at each of the crew in turn. "I am told wizard scouts are phenomenally lucky. If only a miracle can save us, then I have faith my bondmate will create one. I think you all have the same faith as well."

Sergeant Ron laughed. "I hope Rick's as good at pulling off miracles as you are at making speeches, Jeehana. Regardless, we're going in. May the Creator help us all."

* * *

Richard bulled his way past the stream of prisoners heading away from the mine entrance. Some carried makeshift litters laden with wounded of every race imaginable.

"Two troopships have touched down," said Nickelo. *"Your elf and the others are on short final."*

"I told you to tell them I ordered them to leave," Richard said

beginning to lose his temper. Nothing was going right.

"I did tell them," said Nickelo. *"If the situation was reversed, would you leave them to die?"*

Richard knew the answer but kept it in his private space.

A measured amount of Power came down his bond link, mixed with his, and created more Power. He sent a portion of the created Power back up the link.

"We've got to get everyone deeper into the tunnels," said Yellow-tooth. "The first thing the Thargs will do is bombard the entrance before they commit their troops."

Boom!

A wave of dust and screams came down the tunnel from the direction of the mine entrance.

Richard turned to Yellow-tooth. "Take charge here. Get everyone to the lower levels. I'll try to slow the Thargs down a little."

The big orc hefted his large-bore rifle. "I will go with you."

Richard flashed the orc a grin. "Not this time, big guy. Where I'm going, I don't think you can follow."

Before the orc could protest further, Richard wrapped himself with Power and shifted into the void. As he levitated into the nearest wall, he reached out with an active scan toward the surface and spotted a large energy source heading for the mine entrance.

"I calculate that is some type of magic-based armored vehicle," said Nickelo. *"It appears to be about the size of one of the Empire's Leviathan heavy cats."*

Making for the vehicle from below the surface, Richard positioned himself directly underneath the energy before popping out of the ground. Four metallic legs held up the body of a ten-meter tall monstrosity firing beams of magic energy at the mine entrance. Two troopships about the size of Empire regimental assault ships sat on the asteroid's surface six hundred meters away. Foot soldiers in power-armor and scores of magic-based armored vehicles were streaming down ramps extending out the sides of the ships.

"See, Rick. You can't stop that. I highly recommend you make your way to the rendezvous point with the X-shuttle and get off this Creator-forsaken rock."

Ignoring his battle computer, Richard levitated up through the belly of the armored beast. Inside, he shifted out of the void firing a burst of plasma rounds at two very surprised Thargs loading balls of swirling-red gas into an opening in the wall of the vehicle. The Thargs went down before either could bring their side-arms to bear. Sensing two life forms in the rear of the vehicle, Richard tossed an anti-personnel grenade through an opening before sprinting for the cockpit.

Boom!

Two more life forms disappeared from Richard's passive scan.

"I am mystified by your actions," said Nickelo. *"Nevertheless, you are my wizard scout, so I am obliged to help. What are your orders?"*

A plan started to form in Richard's mind. *"As soon as we take control of the cockpit, I want you to hack into the vehicle's computer system. It's bound to be networked to at least one of the troopships. Use that as an entry point to take over those two ships. Once you get in their systems, we'll use the troopships' automated weapons to take out the attacking armor along with the foot soldiers. If we're lucky, we can use defensive weapons inside the ships to take out most of their crew."*

"Uh, I don't know, Rick. I think—"

"Just do it," Richard said as he ran shoulder first into the metal door separating the cockpit from the rest of the vehicle.

The door gave way to the strength of the battle suit's assistors. Richard fired a burst of plasma rounds at three Thargs inside the cockpit. All three fell to the floor, leaving pieces of brain matter dripping down the windscreen.

Richard sat in the center of the three seats and stared at the strange control systems. A realization swept over him that he had absolutely no idea how to drive the armored vehicle.

"What did you expect?" asked Nickelo. *"You barely know how to operate the Empire's larger cats. Fortunately, I have hacked into this vehicle's computer. I am hacking my way into the troopships' networks now. What is your command, oh greatest but most foolish of wizard scouts?"*

Richard had been a Marine. He instinctively chose to attack. *"Get this thing turned around and engage the nearest enemy vehicle. We've got to take the pressure off the mine's entrance until Yellow-tooth can get the prisoners to the lower levels."*

"Compliance."

The four-legged armored vehicle spun on its two rear legs. Multicolored beams of magic shot out, catching a similar four-legged vehicle in the cockpit. A flash of fire and smoke erupted from the vehicle as metal and crew parts flew into the air.

"Their shield wasn't set up to protect against friendly fire," said Nickelo. *"I sense the computers in the other vehicles making adjustments to their shields now. They will not go down so easily. I am adjusting our shields as well."*

The vehicle jerked to the side, knocking Richard out of his seat.

"Hmm," said Nickelo. *"I calculate I got our right-side shield adjusted just in time. By the way, I have almost completed my hack into the troopships' network. I need your help to get through the last of the security programs."*

"Roger that," Richard said as he formed an active scan and merged it with his battle computer's probe. Using a technique shown him by his friend Charlie, Richard let his mind become part of the vehicle's computer. Following Nickelo, he entered an area that could only be the network to the two troop ships. He sensed strong magic.

"The security programs are similar to the magic-based computers you've hacked into before," said Nickelo. *"Get me past this next wall of magic, and I can do the rest."*

Concentrating on the swirling barrier of energy ahead, Richard followed the lines of magic, copying them movement for movement. The confusing lines of magic slowly took on a familiar form. Picking out a weak point, he twisted the flows back on themselves, creating an opening in the wall of magic.

"Will that do?" Richard asked.

"I calculate it will," said Nickelo sounding pleased. *"Give me a few nanoseconds."*

Richard's mind was in hyper-mode. The wait seemed interminable.

After a near eternity, his battle computer said, *"I am in. By the Creator, Rick, I swear you are the luckiest wizard scout this side of Sirius Minor. The security program you hacked is the primary security for both troopships. I am in the process of taking over their automated weapons now. I calculate we will make short work of the attacking troops as well as the crew. Just give me a few more—"*

A flash of light so bright even the max filters on Richard's battle helmet couldn't protect his eyes from its effects erupted from the farthest troopship. The last image Richard saw was a rolling wave of rocks, pieces of starship armor, vehicles, and soldiers flying in his direction. Blinded, he sensed the cockpit of his vehicle rising into the air.

"Shift!" yelled Nickelo.

Wrapping himself in Power, Richard shifted into the void just as he felt heat blistering his skin. He felt his self-heal repairing what little damage occurred, including his burned-out optic nerves.

"What happened?" Richard said still blinded.

"One of the troopships exploded, creating a domino effect that set off the second ship. Based upon the size of the explosions, I calculate everything on the surface within a two-kilometer radius was destroyed. If you hadn't shifted into the void, I would be willing to bet the billowing mushroom clouds I sense would contain microscopic pieces of wizard scout no amount of self-heal could repair."

"Crap, Nick. I didn't want you to destroy the ships. We needed them to rescue the other prisoners."

"I swear it wasn't me," said Nickelo sounding more apologetic than Richard had ever heard him. *"I was just getting ready to fire the automated weapons when the first ship's reactor exploded. I had already calculated we could take control of both ships. I had come to the conclusion your plan was going to work. Surely you don't think I would be foolish enough to destroy our only hope of completing our mission?"*

"Well," Richard said not entirely convinced, *"if you didn't cause the explosion, what fool idiot did?"*

* * *

Bright Wing reappeared in the X-shuttle just as Matthew turned on short final.

"See?" said Sergeant Ron. "I told you it would work. Bright Wing overloaded one of the ship's magic reactors. The explosion took out the second ship and everything on the surface as well."

"Are you sure all the prisoners were in the tunnels?" Jeena

asked.

"Hell, yeah," said Sergeant Ron sounding confident. "What idiot would be stupid enough to be in the middle of all those charging enemy vehicles? Besides, you still sense Rick, right?"

Jeena nodded her head. Her bondmate's presence was strong at the other end of their link. She had no doubt he was still alive.

"See?" said Sergeant Ron again with a big smile. "I just love it when a plan comes together. Sometimes I amaze even myself."

While Jeena had a lot of respect for the cagey old ship's captain, she hadn't been as enthused about the plan as he'd been. *Still,* she thought, *it seems to have worked. Those assault ships were destroyed along with their ground troops. The path to the mines is clear. Once I find Rick, I'll convince him to come back to the shuttle if I have to cast a paralysis spell on him to do it.*

A wave of sadness came over Jeena. She thought about the thousands of prisoners who would be left behind to meet their doom. She hardened her heart. *Sometimes sacrifices have to be made for the good of the many. Rick is the one in the prophecy; I know it. He must be saved. The fate of three galaxies rides in the balance.*

"Incoming," said Terrie. "I can sense them with my passive scan."

Jeena noticed Sergeant Ron punch an icon on his control panel. A holographic image of their part of the asteroid showed six blips coming out of orbit and heading their way.

"Fighters?" asked Tia.

"Negative," said Sergeant Ron continuing to fiddle with a control at the base of the holograph. The blips transformed into black warships. "It's four destroyers and two light cruisers. I'm guessing they're coming in for a bombing run."

"Can Bright Wing—" Jeena started.

"Negative," came Taylor's voice out of the external speaker on Terrie's battle helmet. "I am in contact with Nickelo. He has hacked into the Dragars' communication network. The Dragars' tactical computer analyzed the method to destroy their troopships. They have adjusted their shields to prevent teleportation. Nickelo says he calculates a ninety-two percent probability the attacking ships will use ammonia gas bombs to quell the prisoner revolt in order not to damage their mines."

Sergeant Ron looked up at Jeena. "So what are your orders, boss?"

Without hesitation, Jeena said, "We need to get to Rick." She gave a tense smile. "We are going to see how lucky my bondmate really is." Touching Matthew's shoulder, Jeena pointed at the forward display screen, in the direction of the mine's entrance. "I want you to land right there. We do not have time to waste."

* * *

Richard ran up to the mine entrance just as the shuttle he'd sensed with his passive scan came skidding to a halt. The rear ramp dropped, spewing out a half dozen dwarves armed with an assortment of modern and medieval weapons. At the same moment, Yellow-tooth and a score of orcs ran out of the mine. Both dwarves and orcs raised their weapons at each other.

"No!" Richard yelled amplifying his voice over his battle helmet's external speakers. "We're on the same side."

Then he saw her. Dressed in a black jumpsuit, silver hair flying, Jeena came running down the ramp. With her left hand wrapped around her staff and her right hand clutching a phase pistol, he thought she was the most welcome sight he'd ever seen. He also thought she was the most beautiful creature in the entire universe. When she locked eyes with him, Richard smiled. He'd missed her. He opened his arms to give her a hug.

"Are you crazy?" said Jeena strolling up and shoving Richard in the chest with the butt of her phase pistol. "We have to get out of here now. The Dragar ships are on final approach for a bombing run. You are going to get on this shuttle if I have to drag you onboard."

Richard felt the smile disappear from his face. He lowered his arms. "No." He pointed back at the orcs. "I'm not leaving without them. I'm not leaving any of the prisoners."

The molten silver in Jeena's eyes churned furiously before settling down to a more normal swirling movement. "Then we are all going to die, Rick. Is that what you want?"

"Two minutes until those warships start their bombing run," said Nickelo over the helmet's external speakers. "Just thought I'd mention it in case someone's interested."

Richard stared deep into Jeena's eyes. "I can't leave them. I've been responsible for too many deaths over the years. I've got to save them. Don't ask me why; I just know I have to do it. I need your help."

The elf's silver eyes softened even more.

Richard sensed her emotions through their bond link. He felt her Power, sensing she was slightly below full. As a type of peace offering, he sent a small amount of Power down their link. She accepted the Power just like she had done when they'd tried to save the green sphere and the sphere's brothers. He remembered how they'd closed the time-bubble gate only to learn it came at the expense of the spheres' lives.

"I would do anything for you, Rick," said Jeena, "but how can we save them? What you are asking is impossible. Isn't it?"

Richard thought his bondmate's last words sounded unsure as if beyond all logic, she hoped he had some miracle up his sleeve. The only problem was that he had no such miracle. He was out of ideas. A tingle at the back of his mind drew his attention. He thought of the green sphere and her brothers again. He thought of their time-bubble. He thought of how the Dragars controlled the energy the spheres used to create access points in their time-bubble. A memory of how the dwarf, Emerald, had formed a Circle to save a city popped into his mind. He remembered how he had helped form a Circle to defeat the demon, Cancontus.

Richard looked deep into his bondmate's eyes. "Do you trust me?"

"You know I do."

Nodding his head, he said, "Follow me."

Richard reached out with his mind and let it travel deep into the lower levels of the mine. He sensed Jeena's mind following close behind. He traveled directly to the point where he'd spotted the green sphere earlier that day. It was the same spot where he'd found the sphere during his first mission on the asteroid. He reached out with his emotions and touched the green sphere.

"Hello," Richard said using a combination of emotion-speak and dragon-speak.

"Hello," replied the green sphere.

To Richard, the green sphere's emotions felt hesitant as if she was unsure if she'd imagined the emotion.

"We need your help," Richard told her.

"We?" asked the green sphere.

Richard sensed an emotion from Jeena touch the green sphere.

"Yes," said Jeena in emotion-speak. "We are the *helpers*. We have met before, but it will be in your future."

Richard didn't try to understand why he heard his bondmate's emotion-speak as clearly as if she were speaking in intergalactic standard. He was just grateful that at this moment in time, she could.

"Ah," said the green sphere. "Time can get so confusing. How do I know you tell the truth if we are not to meet until my future?"

"Because I am a dragon friend," Richard said.

"Who named you thus?" asked the sphere.

"You did," Richard said. "I am also an elf friend. I need you to help us now so that we may help you in your future."

"How will you help my brothers and me in the future?" asked the green sphere sending out emotions mixed with curiosity and something that felt like hope.

"My bondmate and I will free your brothers and you," Richard said. "We are the helpers. You can trust us."

"What is it you ask of us?" asked the green sphere still sounding unsure.

"We need you to create an access point in this time-bubble to our time in the future. The fate of three galaxies depends on you helping us."

"We cannot," said the green sphere accompanying her words with a feeling of regret. "The Dragars control our Power. Without Power, we cannot create the access point you request."

Richard touched his bondmate with his mind, letting all the love he felt for her flare into a bright light of emotion. "We will provide you the energy you need."

"How?" asked the green sphere.

"How?" echoed Jeena sounding as confused as the sphere. "What can possibly provide the energy the spheres need to manipulate the time-bubble?"

Richard let an emotion of a smile touch his bondmate and the sphere. "A Circle," he told them. At the same time, he shared a memory with the sphere and Jeena. It was a memory of how he'd formed a Circle with the spheres and the slaves and his fellow wizard scouts during their battle against the vampires and the demon, Cancontus.

"Rick," warned Nickelo in their shared space. *"You are telling the sphere what will happen in her future. You cannot tamper with time. Chaos could ensue. It is dangerous."*

"Dying's pretty dangerous too," Richard replied in his shared space. *"I know what I'm doing. Just be prepared to help."*

"Aren't I always?" Nickelo asked.

Switching his concentration back to the sphere and Jeena, Richard sent them an image of what he hoped to do.

"You will free my brothers and me?" asked the green sphere, hope evident in her emotions.

"Yes," Richard said. "My bondmate and I will destroy the Dragars' temple and stop the sacrifices of your dragon kin." He sent the green sphere an image of the three-headed triplets. "This is your offspring. Your future self made me promise to save them. I kept my promise. Countless generations of your offspring live in freedom because of what you do here today. The Dragars will not enslave your heirs as they have you. They will be free."

The green sphere released an emotion of hope. "Do you swear, dragon friend?"

"I give you my word as a wizard scout. If you help us now, we will help free your future self, stop the sacrifices, and do all we can to keep your heirs free of the Dragars."

"Rick…" came a troubled emotion from Jeena.

Richard knew what concerned his bondmate. "We will not lie to you," he said. "Freeing you means—"

"My brothers and I know what it means," said the green sphere. "Death will be a small price to pay in order to be free of the Dragars. Do not concern yourself. We are satisfied. Now, we sense that time grows short. Shall we begin?"

"Nick, feed the green sphere the exact moment the shuttle left the future. I want an access point in this time-bubble one second after that time."

"Compliance," said Nickelo in their shared space. *"I should point out that while the atmosphere on this asteroid is breathable now, it is poisonous in the future. I suspect between the gas generator spewing poison into the Thargs' part of the mine and the gas bombs the warships will be dropping in less than a minute,*

that the air will be permanently polluted. It will not support the prisoners even if you are somehow able to organize them to come to wherever the spheres create their access point."

"*Crap,*" Richard thought in his shared space. "*Every time I get a plan going, something gets it out of whack.*"

"*I think that is called life,*" said Nickelo.

"*Whatever,*" Richard said. "*Do you have any suggestions?*"

A series of emotions came to Richard from his bondmate.

"You are asking the wrong person," said Jeena in emotion-speak.

Richard was confused. "You can hear me talking to Nick? Why haven't you mentioned it before?"

"Because I have not been able to hear him in the past," came Jeena's reply. "I suspect my hearing is temporary due to our shared connection with the green sphere."

"But—"

"Do you really want to discuss this now, or would you rather hear my solution?"

"Uh, a solution would be preferable," Richard said.

"Good," came Jeena's reply accompanied by an emotion Richard thought felt an awful lot like smugness. "From your memory of the Circle, I am guessing you plan to form a Circle with all of the prisoners as well as the spheres. Assuming you include me in the Circle, I can cast a 'breath' spell. Based on what I can tell from your memory, my spell should affect all who are part of the Circle."

A glance at his passive scan told Richard the warships were closing in fast. With no time to discuss the situation further, he reached out with his mind and formed a Circle as he went. He started with Jeena, which was easy since their modified bond link was basically a two-person Circle of its own. He expanded the Circle to include the green sphere. He located the orange and purple spheres and brought them into the Circle. As the three spheres came online, he reached outward and touched each of the life forms in the mine in turn. With his mind in hyper-mode and his battle computer's help, Richard bypassed the non-prisoners

Almost immediately, Richard noticed the Circle wasn't forming correctly. As he attempted to connect the links to the prisoners located in the tunnels, the two-way links that should have solidified into a continuous set of links connecting the spheres, the *Defiant's* crew, and all of the prisoners into a single Circle kept shorting out.

"It's not working," said Nickelo. *"I highly recommend you and the rest of the* Defiant's *crew get in the X-shuttle and get away while you can."*

"No," Richard said desperately attempting to form the Circle. *"Either help me form the Circle or shut up. I'm not leaving."*

"I don't know how to help you," said Nickelo.

Fortunately, someone did. A feeling of peace swept over Richard which he sensed originated from his bondmate. As he continued to attempt forming the Circle, Jeena touched the malfunctioning links in the Circle and gently requested the flows of Power do her will. The short-circuiting links settled down, sharing their Power with each other. As Richard watched, the Circle strengthened, forming one continuous link and touching all prisoners, the spheres, the *Defiant's* crew, Jeena, and him.

"The elf is a diviner specializing in magic," said Nickelo. *"Take advantage of it. The warships have fired their gas bombs. It's now or never."*

Remembering how he had previously used Circles to pull Power from the universe, Richard did so once again and concentrated that Power on the three spheres. He sensed lines of energy form a triangle between the spheres. At the same time, he sensed Jeena cast a spell and pass it from one link in the Circle to the next. Then everything went black.

CHAPTER 16

The Trecorian colonel looked at the hologram of Admiral of the Fleets Elizabeth Bistos.

"Admiral," said the colonel sounding a little heated, "we don't have facilities to house an additional four thousand people for five more days. Most of them aren't even human. What am I supposed to feed them?"

"I've got a war to run, Colonel," said Liz. "I don't have time or the desire to handle your logistical problems. War-King Bistoria guaranteed me your full cooperation, so make it happen."

At the mention of the war-king's name, the Trecorian colonel calmed noticeably. "I'll make it happen, Admiral, but that doesn't mean I'm going to like it."

The holographic image of Liz looked in Richard's direction.

"So are you satisfied?" asked Liz. "The troop carriers will arrive early next week to transport the colonel's guests to the coordinates you have provided." She gave a tense smile. "I don't mind telling you that you have a tendency to create problems for your higher-ups."

"I had a few problems of my own," Richard said, "so whatever hassles I've caused your colonel over the last few hours doesn't concern me all that much. I'm just thankful the green sphere and her brothers were able to create the access point and transport the prisoners and us back to our current time on this asteroid without any additional losses." He turned to Jeena. "If you hadn't cast those mass breath spells on the prisoners, the ammonia gas this asteroid calls air would've done them in for sure."

"You definitely got lucky," said Liz. She looked at the silver-haired elf standing next to Richard. "Thanks for pulling his bacon out of the fire. I have to warn you, though, that he can be a lot of trouble. I also have a strong feeling we are going to need him in the days ahead."

Richard noticed the two females exchange smiles.

"He is a lot of trouble," agreed Jeena still smiling. "How did you ever put up with him?"

"With a lot of patience," replied Liz giving a final nod at Jeena before looking back at Richard with a tightlipped smile. "While I would love to chat, I have a lot on my plate. I wish you luck, wizard scout."

Returning his friend's smile, Richard said, "Same to you, Liz. Take care. Tell Tim I said hello."

Admiral of the Fleets Bistos looked at Richard for a full five seconds before replying, "You've changed, Rick. You're more caring. I like this version of you a lot better." She smiled again. "I will be sure to tell my husband you said hello. He considers you a friend, as do I."

The hologram blinked out. After a few words of discussion with the colonel on how the ex-prisoners were going to be provided for, Richard and Jeena left the command center and headed for the X-shuttle. Thankfully, the green sphere had included the shuttle in the gate through the time-bubble's access point.

"So what is our next step?" asked Jeena. "Do we stay in the physical galaxy and help in the fight against the Conglomerate? Or do we return to Portalis and take up the battle there?"

Richard glanced at his bondmate as they walked through the metal corridors of the command center. Most of the Trecorian soldiers they passed did double-takes at the elf. He didn't blame them. He thought she made even a black utility suit look good.

"To be honest," Richard said, "I haven't got the faintest idea what we should do next. I guess I've been a time-commando so long that I'm used to being sent on missions by 'the One' instead of having to figure out what to do on my own."

Jeena gave what sounded like a very unladylike snort. When Richard looked at her, she explained.

"Those days are over," she said. "I had a long talk with the battle computers. Decisions will be a team effort from now on."

She flashed a quick smile. "The bad news is that with freedom comes responsibility. So I ask again, what are we going to do next, Wizard Scout?"

By this time, they were in the hangar where the X-shuttle had been brought. Richard noticed several orcs standing near the crew of the *Defiant*. One of the orcs looked larger than the others, and Richard recognized Yellow-tooth immediately. His fellow chain-mate appeared to be in deep conversation with Timerman. When the teenager glanced up, he motioned for Richard to come over. The young orc motioned for Captain Ron to join them as well.

Making their way toward the teenager, Richard and Jeena arrived at the same time as the *Defiant's* captain. Timerman wasted no time in pointing at Yellow-tooth. "Do you know who this is?"

"Uh, I call him Yellow-tooth," Richard said. "I didn't get a translation spell until a few hours ago." Looking at the big orc, he smiled. "I think you tried to tell me your name a few times, but I could never pronounce it."

The translator Yellow-tooth now wore at his side crackled. "You did better with my name than you think, Chekrak. My name is Sevantor. When translated in old Orcish, my name means '*the one with the yellow tooth.*'"

The reference to the name Chekrak puzzled Richard. "Why did you say Chekrak? What does it mean?"

The big orc gave what looked like a snarl but was the orc's version of a smile. "Chekrak means '*little brother*' in ancient Orcish. You are Chekrak. You look human, but I sensed a part of my species in you the first day we met. The legend of Chekrak was foretold by the ancient prophets. It was said that our *little brother* would come in a time of need and lead us to the path of victory."

Something inside Richard rebelled against being part of a prophecy. *I've got free-will,* he thought. *Prophecy doesn't control what I do.*

"I calculate prophecies are just high probabilities that something will occur," said Nickelo in their share space. *"They are not guaranteed outcomes. I suppose that is where your free-will comes in."*

Kicking himself for thinking in his shared space, Richard decided to forego any prolonged philosophical discussion about free-will with his battle computer. He looked at Yellow-tooth instead. "So now what? The troopships will be taking everyone to a planet in our dimension that is connected to the magic dimension. Some previous Dragar prisoners we freed from one of those black ships are already settled there. I think your people could make a good home on that planet."

"He can't go!" said Timerman. His gray skin took on a pinkish tinge when everyone turned to stare at him. "Uh, I mean, I think we should take Sevantor back to where the Dragars took him captive."

"What do you know that we don't?" asked Sergeant Ron sounding more than a little suspicious. When the young orc hesitated to answer, the *Defiant's* captain snapped, "Speak up! That's an order."

The teenage elf, Asquan, elbowed his way through the larger orcs until he stood next to Timerman. "He is not sure he should answer in front of Sevantor," he said. "I, on the other hand, think it is important for Sevantor to know the whole story. He will need all the motivation he can get when we take him back."

Timerman glanced from Asquan to Sevantor and back to Asquan. "I don't think—"

"I'm the captain," said Sergeant Ron, "so I'll be the one doing the thinking around here." He pointed at the teenage elf. "Out with it. Why do we need to take him back?"

Asquan pointed at Richard. "Because he is the Chekrak of which the legends speak." He waved a hand at Yellow-tooth. "I know this to be true because he is Sevantor." Looking back at Sergeant Ron, the young elf said, "Did you not think it was strange that you were able to convince the United Galaxy Alliance so easily that they should send their fleets to the physical galaxy to help in your fight against the bat-creatures?"

"Easy?" said Sergeant Ron. "That's the same thing that orc admiral on the space station asked me. As it so happens, Comstar and I had to talk until we were blue in the face to convince the UGA to help us. They didn't do it for free either. Trecor and the Empire are expected to help them against the Dragars in return."

"I know," chimed in Timerman coming to the defense of his friend. "Still, the only reason you were able to convince them was because of Chekrak and Sevantor. I've told some of the *Defiant's* crew about how Chekrak freed Sevantor from his Dragar captives.

Sevantor was…" The teenager looked at the big orc. "I mean, Sevantor *is* a great war-leader of the original Redestan orc empire. He was able to convince the Redestan orcs to stop their eternal battle against the Yardorian elves and combine forces to resist the Dragars. That was a hundred thousand years ago. Without Sevantor's intervention and leadership, the Dragars would have overwhelmed our galaxy in the magic dimension long ago. We've got to take him back."

"It takes a lot of Power to gate back in time," Richard said thinking of how much of a drain on the Tree of Light's Power it had taken to transport the X-shuttle back to rescue him. The tree may need every drop of Power in the battle that is coming our way. The triplets are already using some of the tree's Power to gate ships between the two dimensions. The Power requirements for gating back in time are a hundred-fold of what's required to pass between dimensions."

"But if Sevantor doesn't go ba—" started Timerman.

"Enough!" said Jeena.

Everyone stopped talking and looked at the elf. Even several groups of Trecorian mechanics standing near partially disassembled vehicles stopped what they were doing and stared.

Indicating Richard with a wave of her hand, Jeena said, "My bondmate is correct in that we should be frugal with the Lady's Power. She risked much giving Rick unfettered access. We need to ensure her trust is warranted. On the other hand, I believe everyone is forgetting to ask the most important person what they would prefer to do." Turning to Yellow-tooth, Jeena said, "Honorable Sevantor, we can transport you and your orcs to the planet of magic of which Sergeant Ron spoke. I believe your people would enjoy a life of relative peace there, if you so choose. Or, Sir Matthew and Sergeant Ron can use the X-shuttle with the help of the triplets and return you to the time and place from which you were taken captive. I ask you now, what would you like to do?"

Richard noticed the big orc study Jeena for several seconds. Yellow-tooth turned to face several of his fellow orcs. After they gave almost imperceptible nods, the big orc looked back at the elf. "My people and I have fought elves in the Yardorian alliance for nearly a thousand years," he said. "We have killed many elves, and they have killed many orcs. A few years ago, the Dragars began attacking both of our empires. The black ships invaded my home planet, killing many and taking others prisoner to work in their mines."

The big orc surveyed the mixed group of humans, dwarves, elves, gnomes, and orcs. "I have seen the Dragars and their Tharg servants at close hand. I have seen their fleets of warships massed to attack at a time of their choosing. They cannot be reasoned with. They cannot be stopped by a single empire."

Richard noticed his ex-fellow prisoner lock eyes with him.

"You are *little brother*," said Yellow-tooth. "When you appeared next to me in the tunnels, I sensed orc in you even though your body was that of a human. I also sensed elf and other races. I began thinking if all these parts could coexist in one body, surely my race could work with others to defeat the Dragars who are our real enemies."

"He's pretty articulate for an orc," Richard confided to his battle computer.

"Hush," said Nickelo. *"I calculate we are at a point of juxtaposition. I do not want to miss anything. You would do well to pay attention yourself."*

I am paying attention, Richard thought, keeping his rebuttal in his private space.

Richard switched gears back to the scene before him. The big orc had stepped in front of Jeena. His muscled bulk contrasted sharply with the lithe, silver-haired elf.

Jerking a thumb at Asquan, Yellow-tooth said, "The young one spoke to me earlier. He told me of what is to come. My people face a hundred thousand years of battle against the Dragars until the time of the Great Battle." The big orc looked down at Jeena. "You spoke of peace for my people if we go to the planet of magic, but I think you know as well as I that it would only be a short-lived peace. The day of the Great Battle is upon us. I would be honored to stand beside you, my new friends, and fight the Dragars, but my part in the battle is in the past. My orcs and I must return from whence we came." He swept his arm to encompass the entire hangar bay. "I have seen all these species working together for a common cause. I will do my part to pave the way for you by returning to your past."

Yellow-tooth placed his massive right hand on Jeena's left

shoulder. She didn't flinch.

"You and the young Asquan have shown me that some elves can be reasonable. When I return to my time, I will seek out those elves of like mind and make peace. I will devote my life and that of my offspring to joining our two races together to deny the Dragars the victory they seek."

Removing his hand from Jeena, the big orc turned toward Richard. "You are my friend. You are Chekrak. I will tell my people that the day will come when Chekrak and the crew of the *Defiant* will come to our aid. When the *defiant ones* come, they will be ready."

Holding out his gray, warty right hand in Richard's direction, Yellow-tooth waited.

Richard sensed a feeling of approval from his bondmate through the link they shared. He glanced in her direction long enough to see her nod.

Grasping the orc's hand in his, Richard shook it. "It has been an honor to fight beside you, Sevantor. I give you my word of honor as a wizard scout that your work in the past will not go wasted. My friends and I will not rest until the Dragars and their allies are swept from the three galaxies." Staring into the bloodshot yellow eyes of the orc, he added, "I am going to miss you."

The orc nodded and snarled. "And I you. Farewell my friend, Chekrak."

CHAPTER 17

The next two days were hectic as Rick, Jeena, and the crew of the *Defiant* took Sevantor and his orcs back to their time in the magic dimension a hundred thousand years in the past. Upon returning to the physical dimension, Richard called an emergency meeting in the ship's dining area with Sergeant Ron, Jeena, Terrie, Matthew, Tia, Rembis, and himself.

"The transport should arrive at the asteroid in a few days to take the other survivors to the magic planet," said Terrie as he sat with the others around the mess table. He looked at Sergeant Ron. "By the way, I'm getting tired of referring to it as *'the magic planet.'* We should probably give the place a name."

Sergeant Ron laughed. When the others looked at him, he said, "I was just thinking Ronville had a nice ring to it."

One of the speakers mounted in the bulkhead crackled. "The planet has a name," said Margery. "It is three-six-one-five-four-seven. It is a logical name because it was the three hundred, sixty-one thousandth, five hundred and forty-seventh solid object identified by the Empire's survey parties."

"That's a number, not a name," said Terrie. "And it doesn't exactly roll off the tongue." He smiled at Sergeant Ron. "Ronville isn't exactly giving me a warm and fuzzy either."

A thought came to Richard. "How about New Hope?"

"I like it," said Comstar who had just walked up the stairs from the *Defiant's* cargo bay. "I would suggest running it past the current inhabitants, but as an ex-slave on one of the Dragar ships myself, I can tell you I approve."

All eyes were on the old elf. Even Richard was anxious to hear more. While Comstar had been his roommate on the *Defiant* before Jeena came onboard, the old elf had rarely spoken about his past.

"When I was a slave on the Dragar destroyer, I had no hope. The *Defiant* freed me and gave me hope back. The magic planet is the home of the other ex-slaves. I believe they will approve of Rick's name."

"Hey," Richard said, "I was just making a suggestion. I assumed there would be others. I've never been that good at words."

"Comstar's right," said Sergeant Ron. "No use continuing to try and find something once it's been found. New Hope it is." He smiled. "Of course, like Comstar said, we should probably ask the residents. They might prefer Ronville instead." He winked. "You never know."

"Ha!" said Terrie. "Believe me, I know. I'll have Taylor contact the communication station on New Hope and see what they think. If they approve, the central computer can update the star charts."

When everyone nodded their approval, Terrie changed the subject. "Okay, that was easy. Now we move on to something harder. What do we do next? We've got the Conglomerate consolidating their forces around Risors. The Crosioians are currently licking their wounds, but it won't be long before they'll start a new offensive. Counting their allies, they still outnumber the Empire and Trecorian fleets ten to one. On top of that, War-King Bistoria has provided the United Galaxy Alliance with a fleet of Trecorian ships and what's left of the Empire's ninth fleet."

"The Crosioians may take longer to regroup than you think," said Sergeant Ron. "Those bat folks rely on their master computer more than we do our central computer. Since Rick knocked out the demon Zenthra's control over the master computer, it will take some time to bring it back online to peak efficiency. That may give War-King Bistoria time to act against the Conglomerate."

"Good," Richard said in a vicious tone. He remembered his friend Sharon being cut in half by a Crosioian plasma beam during the battle on Estos. "I've got a score to settle with the Conglomerate. After that, I've got one to settle with the bats as well."

"The Conglomerate isn't our enemy," said a voice from the far end of the table.

Richard looked to find Matthew staring at him. "How can you say that, Matt? Of course they're our enemy. The Conglomerate's in league with the Crosioians. A hundred million of the Empire's soldiers are dead, and another two hundred million captured. I know your mother is the empress, but—"

Matthew slapped the table with the palm of his hand before jumping to his feet. Richard noticed Tia start to reach a hand toward the teenage boy next to her. Before she completed the maneuver, she withdrew her hand back under the table.

"No one, not even you, Rick, has to remind me what occurred," said Matthew through clenched teeth. "Be that as it may, I've worked with the Conglomerate for the past year. They're just like everyone else in the Empire because they are *part* of the Empire."

"The Conglomerate is respons—" Richard started.

"No!" said Matthew. "My mother is. So are a few ambitious leaders in the Conglomerate hierarchy. The average soldier, sailor, clerk, and whatever in the Conglomerate are just as mystified by what happened last week as you and I. The Conglomerate is not our enemy. Creator help me, my mother is the one responsible." The boy hung his head.

Richard heard no sound, but he noticed the boy's shoulders shaking. Tia stood and placed an arm around Matthew, then led him away from the table, toward the stairs. The boy didn't resist.

"He is not a boy," said Nickelo in Richard's shared space. *"He may have been a boy last week, but no longer. It takes a full-grown man to see things as they really are. He is right too. The Conglomerate is not our enemy. I calculate some that you think of as enemies may be needed to stop the demons from overrunning the three galaxies."*

Richard shook his head but said nothing until Matthew and Tia had disappeared down the stairs. "He doesn't understand," he said to no one in particular. "When he matures, he'll know what's right."

A sensation of irritation came down the link Richard shared with his bondmate. He thought he sensed a feeling of sadness as well. When he looked at Jeena, he noticed her eyes were closed, and her lips were moving slightly as if whispering.

"Praying," observed Nickelo in their shared space. *"It wouldn't*

hurt you to try it once in a while."

"*I pray occasionally,*" Richard said not at all appreciating getting lectured by a computer on spiritual matters.

"*Asking for the chow line to move faster isn't exactly what I had in mind,*" laughed Nickelo. "*You have matured a lot over the years, but I calculate you've still got a ways to go.*"

"*Whatever,*" Richard muttered, ending the conversation.

Sergeant Ron cleared his throat. When Richard looked, the *Defiant's* captain was staring straight at him.

"My grandson's right," said Sergeant Ron. "The individuals in the Conglomerate aren't evil, they're just being led down the wrong path. I reckon if there was a leadership change, the Conglomerate would merge back into the Empire's fold with no problem."

Richard shook his head. "I don't believe that, and I'm surprised to hear it coming from you. The Conglomerate are traitors. None of their ships made the hyper-jump to Estos last week. They're all just as responsible for the deaths of our people as the Crosioians. Are we just supposed to forgive and forget?" He shook his head again. "Next thing I know, you'll be telling me we should forgive the Crosioians."

Sergeant Ron's brow wrinkled as he gritted his teeth. Before he could respond to Richard's verbal attack, someone else beat him to the punch.

"We should be willing to forgive the Crosioians as well," said Jeena.

"What?" Richard said fairly shouting the question. "Never! They killed the commandant. They killed my father. I will never forgive them."

Richard looked at Sergeant Ron for support. "You were on Velos during the Crosioians' attack. You know. Tell her."

Sergeant Ron started to open his mouth but closed it abruptly and looked at the deck instead.

Richard glanced back at Jeena. "You weren't there. You don't understand. The Crosioians killed my father."

"Humans killed both of my parents and my sister," said Jeena staring hard at Richard. "I do not hold that against *you*, do I?"

A harsh reply was on Richard's lips, but he bit it back before it hit air. The intense sadness he sensed accompanying his bondmate's words helped him control his mouth. He had no desire to cause her additional pain. He consoled himself by repeating the one thing he knew to be true. "They killed my father."

Jeena looked at Richard for several seconds, her silver eyes churning. "Yes, they did," she admitted.

Richard relaxed. *Finally,* he thought, *she understands. The only problem is that her silver eyes are continuing to draw me in, telling me she definitely doesn't understand.*

"How many?" asked Jeena.

The question puzzled Richard. "How many what?"

"How many Crosioian fathers have you killed? How many mothers, brothers, and sisters?"

"That's not the same. We are at war. I'm a soldier. I'm only doing my duty. Besides, they're bats. They don't think like us." He looked around the table at the others for support. "They *murdered* my father."

Richard tried to hold his gaze with Jeena's, but the churning silver seemed to accuse him the more he looked into her eyes. Combined with the disappointment he felt through his bond link, he felt suddenly ashamed. "It's not the same," he insisted, averting his eyes to the top of the mess table.

Richard heard the scrapping of metal on metal as someone moved their bench away from the table. Soft footsteps drew closer. A gentle hand rested on his shoulder. A feeling of emotion more potent than love flowed down his bond link.

"I do not say these things to hurt you, Rick," whispered Jeena into the silence of the mess area. "Who am I to criticize? I have murdered thousands of Crosioians all in the name of accomplishing my mission."

Richard looked up into his bondmate's shiny silver irises. "Don't say that," he said. "You would never murder anyone."

A feeling of regret passed down their link from Jeena to him.

"Murder, kill," said Jeena. "What's the difference? After Stella and I took the bottles of DNA gas from the Crosioians' space station, I attached strands of the black hole to the station. Every Crosioian onboard—male, female, young, old—died instantly. I killed children as well as soldiers."

"That was diff—"

"No, killing is killing," she said. "Once a life is gone, can you bring it back?" When Richard didn't answer, Jeena said, "Nor can I. As a priestess of the Lady of the Tree, I know that all life is precious. I have spent many nights thinking of those Crosioian lives I took that day on the space station. Perhaps one of them was the Crosioian that would have sought peace with the Empire. Perhaps I destroyed the only chance for peace that existed. I will never know."

"Jeena, I don't think—"

"It does not matter, my bondmate. What's done is done. I only bring this up because I think Matthew was trying to tell you, that he was trying to tell all of us, we need to know who our real enemy is, and that it may not be as simple as we think."

"I happen to agree with Rick," said Tia. "The Crosioians are our enemy. Trecorian losses were nowhere near as heavy as that of the Empire, but we still lost thousands. The Crosioians must pay for what they've done."

Jeena nodded her head. "Yes, they killed many, and we killed many of them. Perhaps peace with the Crosioians will never occur. Perhaps our war with them will continue until they either kill all of us or we them. Who am I to say? This I do know. Our real enemies are the demons. They hate all living things. Even the Dragars will be wiped out if the demons succeed in opening one of the gates to the demonic plane."

Richard felt Jeena squeeze his shoulder. "We need allies, Rick. I do not say the Conglomerate or the Crosioians will ever fight on our side. I only say we must be willing to forgive if the opportunity presents itself. Just as Sevantor was willing to forgive the elves in the deaths of his kin for the betterment of three galaxies, we must be willing to do the same."

The idea of forgiveness did not sit well with Richard. "I will never forgive anyone who had a part in the commandant's death. The Crosioians killed my father. That's all there is to it."

Jeena removed her hand. Her voice took on an edge Richard had not heard before. "Did they, Rick? Are you so sure?"

Richard stood and turned to face his bondmate.

She was tall, their eyes at almost the same level. The elf's molten-silver eyes churned faster than he'd ever seen, but he didn't flinch.

"Yes, I'm sure. I was there. You weren't."

Instead of backing down, his bondmate locked eyes, drawing him in.

Instinctively, Richard sensed a truth coming that he didn't want to hear.

"You are right, Rick," said Jeena. "I was not there. However, Margery was. She was the commandant's battle computer. She shared the memory of that day with Danny, who shared it with me. Your father was killed when the Crosioians' dreadnaught crashed into the DNA center on Velos. Do you think the Crosioians were so fanatical that they purposely killed themselves to attack your father and you?"

Richard didn't answer. He didn't care why they'd crashed their ship. He only knew his father had died because of it. He tried to look away from his bondmate, but her silver eyes kept pulling him in no matter how much he struggled.

"The demon Zenthra crashed the dreadnaught," said Jeena, "not the Crosioians. The demon is not the only one who shares in the blame for your father's death. Margery says the commandant shared his Power with you to help you escape. She told me his reserve was already damaged, and that the strain was too much. He died saving you."

The memory of that day came flooding back in Richard's mind. The Crosioian dreadnaught had exploded after crashing into the DNA center, creating a massive firestorm. Shifting into the void, he'd saved his father and Chief Instructor Winslow, but due to his small Power reserve, they were unable to complete their escape through the fire. He remembered how his father had shared his Power to give them the time needed to get away. The strain had been too much on his father's reserve. It had ruptured, killing the commandant in the process.

"Why was the commandant's Power reserve weak?" asked Jeena.

The question caught Richard off guard. He sensed a trap and refused to answer. He tried to look away from his bondmate, but her silver eyes prevented escape.

"Your brother damaged your father's reserve, didn't he?" asked Jeena. "Do not deny it. Margery and Danny already told me."

"Yes," Richard said spitting the words out. "And you're right. He shares part of the blame. He sabotaged my parents' reserves.

He is as responsible for my father's death as is Zenthra and the Crosioians. Anyone who played a part in killing my father deserves to be punished. They are all my enemies. I will never forgive any of them."

Jeena stared at Richard for several seconds. The churning in her eyes slowed. He felt a great sense of sadness come down their bond link.

"Forgive me, my bondmate, but I must ask one more question," said Jeena.

Richard stared at the elf. Her eyes no longer held him, but he didn't turn away. *Someone else is responsible as well,* he thought. *I have to know who. I must know who all of my enemies are.*

Jeena reached out with her right hand and touched Richard's cheek before letting her hand drop. A tear tracked down her right eye.

"I ask you this one final question, my bondmate. Who taught your brother the skills he needed to sabotage your parents' Power reserves? Your parents might be alive today if that person hadn't done so. Can you forgive the one who did?"

Richard's stomach dropped. A blackness swept over him. His shoulders shook, and his vision blurred. He shook his head whispering, "No. No."

Richard felt soft arms wrap around him and hold him tight.

"Nothing is as simple as it seems, Rick. The demons are your real enemies. Not the Conglomerate; not the Crosioians; not your brother, and certainly not you. You must learn to forgive, Rick. You must learn to even forgive yourself."

CHAPTER 18

A slight distortion in the air near the tunnel wall was the only evidence of the intruder. He was being careful, very careful.

"You should have killed those guards," hissed Wanda. *"It would have been so easy."*

"I'm not here to kill," Myers said growing increasingly irritated at the demon that was his battle computer. *"I'm here to get the DNA gas. So where is Crendemor's quarters? How much farther?"*

"We are nearly there," said Wanda. *"I do not sense the DNA gas yet, but the dark elf may have hidden it with spells. I calculate his room will be trapped. We must be cautious. You cannot help the Dalinfaust if you are dead."*

"I'll try to watch my step," Myers said. *"I'd hate to disappoint your master."*

"He is your master as well," said Wanda. *"You would do well not to forget it."*

Myers kept his feelings about the Dalinfaust in his private space. It would do no good to stir up unnecessary trouble.

"It's taking too long," Myers said. *"My Power reserve's large, but even it's feeling the strain. The protective spells around the city have taken two days to penetrate. If I stay here much longer, I'll be discovered."*

"I calculate a forty-two percent probability of discovery," said Wanda. *"The odds are still in your favor. Your Power reserve is at thirty-seven percent. It will be enough to complete the mission if you are efficient. Perhaps if you gave me full control of your battle*

suit, I could help you more."

Myers laughed. It was not a friendly laugh. *"It will be a cold day in hell when I give you full control."* The mere thought of being at the demon's mercy sent a shiver down his back.

"As you will. You are the wizard scout, and I am just your obedient battle computer. I exist to serve."

"Sure you do," Myers snorted. *"The only question is who are you serving?"*

"Why you, of course, Wizard Scout. See. The door ahead is your destination. Now we must work as a team to circumvent the dark elf lord's traps. It will serve neither of us if we are detected. We must recover the bottle of DNA gas so the Dalinfaust can be free."

Myers didn't argue the point. He knew why he wanted the bottle of gas, and it had nothing to do with the Dalinfaust.

Bypassing the traps around the dark elf lord's room proved more difficult than Myers anticipated. The defensive spells were subtle as well as powerful. The process was further complicated by passing dark elves. At the approach of any elves, he was forced to stop what he was doing and levitate to the ceiling, hoping all the while his battle suit's camouflage would prevent detection. After two hours, the door to Crendemor's quarters creaked open. The slight distortion in the air that was Myers slipped inside.

"Recommend you deactivate your battle suit's camouflage," said Wanda. *"We may need all of our Power to penetrate the next barrier."*

Myers started to ask 'what barrier?' when a stream of calculations appeared in the space of his mind that he shared with the demon. The data pinpointed an area of the far wall near a large bed that was releasing strange energy. For some reason, the energy seemed vaguely familiar.

"It is residual DNA energy combined with some type of spell energy," said Wanda.

Additional calculations ran down Myers's heads-up display. Suddenly the demon that had taken Wanda's place began to laugh.

Myers frowned. *"What's so funny?"*

Wanda stopped laughing. *"The dark elf is better at spells than either the Dalinfaust or I realized. The spell energy appears to be a semi-permanent teleport spell. The energy is familiar to you because it replicates your dimensional pack."*

"What are you trying to say, demon? Out with it. I don't have time for games. I need to get that bottle of DNA gas. I've waited too long for it already."

Wanda laughed again. *"Yes, and that is what is so humorous. You see, my dear wizard scout, Crendemor created a spell version of your dimensional pack. The cavity inside that wall is connected to a warehouse on the planet Storage. That is why the energy is so familiar."* The demon laughed once more. *"All these years you have been doing missions for the Dalinfaust in the hopes of acquiring the bottle of DNA gas. During all that time, all you needed to do was send the request to your dimensional pack and the bottle of DNA gas would have been sent to your pack."* Laughing even harder, the demon said, *"You could have given your sweet empress the bottle long ago. Do you not see the humor in the situation?"*

Myers reached out with an active scan, probing the cavity inside the wall. He sensed slight traces of DNA energy, but only a trace. Throwing caution to the wind, he wrapped Power around the stone protecting the cavity and tugged with telekinesis. The stone fell to the floor, revealing a black space beyond. He felt a cold breeze blowing from the hole.

"It is empty, Wizard Scout. Crendemor has obviously moved the bottle of gas. It is no longer on Storage."

Ignoring another burst of laughter from the demon, Myers ran to the wall and stuck his hand in the hole. The cavity was empty. Ripping the dimensional pack off his back, he imagined a bottle of DNA gas. No Power left his reserve. Opening the pack, he peered inside. It was empty.

"I told you the dark elf has moved the bottle of DNA gas," said Wanda. *"Your lack of trust is liable to hurt my feelings."* The demon laughed even harder.

Myers sent Power into every corner of the room, searching with an active scan for…anything. He found nothing of interest. In a fit of anger, he grabbed the edge of the dark elf's bed and threw it against the wall with all the strength of his battle suit behind it. The bed shattered into a dozen pieces that clattered loudly to the floor.

"I calculate that was foolish," said Wanda. *"Someone in the hallway may have heard your little temper tantrum. Have I not*

taught you better?" Again, the demon laughed.

"Why are you laughing?" Myers said angrily. *"You need the DNA gas as much as I. How do you plan on freeing your Dalinfaust now? Whatever plans you have, you'll have to do on your own because I'm done. Without the DNA gas, you have no hold on me."*

The demon stopped laughing. *"You are only free when the Dalinfaust says you are free. As it so happens, my master has another plan, and you will help. Otherwise, your precious empress and your son will pay the price."*

"If you so much as touch—"

"Temper, temper," said the demon. *"The bottle of DNA gas is not lost; it has only been moved. I calculate an eighty-seven percent probability I know where it is now located."*

"Where?" Myers snapped.

"We will need to travel far," said the demon that was Wanda. *"Time is too short to walk, and the Dalinfaust is not yet strong enough to teleport you on his own. But fear not, valiant wizard scout. The Dalinfaust is sending you a ride."*

Before Myers could ask 'what ride?' a scaly, gray cat head poked out of the stone floor of the bedroom followed by a gray, lizard-like body with four legs ending in razor-sharp claws. Except for the lack of fur, the creature reminded Myers of a lizard-skinned cat the size of a horse. The cat turned its two fire-red eyes in Myers's direction and roared, revealing a mouthful of finger-length fangs.

"Ah," said Wanda. *"Your spirit-cat has arrived. Mount and let us be on our way."*

"Our way where?" Myers said refusing to get on the creature until he knew more.

"Why, Wizard Scout, to the place where Lord Crendemor has hidden the DNA gas. We ride to the city of the elves. We ride to Silverton."

CHAPTER 19

Tia nodded her head approvingly as she watched the teenage elf evade a trio of incoming Dragar dragon-fighters.

"That's good, Asquan," Tia said over the controller's headset, "but you could've come out of your roll behind the tail of the dragon-fighters if you'd used your right-side maneuvering thrusters."

"Roger that," said Asquan taking the criticism in stride. "Do you want to reset the simulation and let me try again? I'm still not used to all the capabilities of this Zip fighter."

"No time," said Sergeant Ron cutting in on the simulator's communication link. "Rick and Jeehana are gonna be leaving us in another hour. I've got something that needs to be done before they head back to Portalis."

"What's that?" Tia asked.

"Never you mind," said Sergeant Ron. "Just be in the mess area at a quarter till. I'll explain everything then."

Shrugging her shoulders, Tia punched the End Simulation icon on the controller's console. The area around the dragon-fighter to her front shimmered, leaving Asquan sitting in a lone chair in a makeshift cubbyhole made out of used ammo containers.

"Hop to it," Tia said. "You heard Sergeant Ron. He wants us upstairs pronto."

"Roger that," said the elf sounding even more cheerful than usual. "Maybe the captain is going to tell us we will be seeing some action soon. Don't get me wrong, I enjoy the simulator training, but it is a far cry from the real thing."

Tia tried not to smile at the young elf's enthusiasm. *It wasn't too long ago I was the same way,* she thought.

"Ha," said Danny intruding on her thoughts via the headset. "You are as hungry for action as the elf. I calculate both of you as well as your friend Timerman are much too blood-thirsty for your own good. If this war drags on another forty or fifty years, you will be wishing you had even a few minutes of peace."

"I'll worry about that when the time comes," Tia said. "In the meantime, I've got a meeting to make." She ripped off the headset and tossed it on the controller's console, cutting off any reply from Danny.

The makeshift hologram simulator was only a dozen steps from the stairs leading out of the cargo bay. After Asquan joined her, they made their way to the mess area together. They found the entire crew of the *Defiant* crowded into the room. The ship was designed for a crew of twenty-two, so with a total population of twenty-seven counting the *guests*, cramming them all into a single room was a chore, to say the least.

Half of the crew were forced to stand along the sides of the room while the rest sat around the metal table on benches. Peering over the heads of a couple of dwarves, Tia spotted Matthew and her brother, Daniel. She elbowed her way past two gnome magic users as she made her way forward.

Kester, the youngest of the gnome mages assigned to the *Defiant*, barked, "Watch your step. You nearly smashed my foot."

Looking down, Tia said, "Sorry. I told you before that maybe you should consider using an enlarge spell on yourself when you're in crowds. Face it, you're hard to see sometimes."

"Ha," said the gnome mage. "If I was going to cast any magic, it would be a dozen shrink spells on some of the less courteous of you giants onboard. I'm betting that would make a little more room on this ship. So how about watching your step?"

"I said I was sorry." Tia tried to sound apologetic but was having trouble suppressing a laugh. When the gnome turned away, she continued making her way toward Matthew and her brother. *Geesh,* she thought. *Gnomes are so sensitive. Of course, I suppose if I was in a starship crewed by humanoids twice my size, I'd probably be a little offended if they tried walking all over me.* She made a mental promise to be more considerate in the future when around any of the gnomes or dwarves in the crew.

Reaching Matthew and Daniel, Tia squeezed her way between the two males. Her brother gave her a dirty look but scooted over.

"What's going on?" Tia whispered out the side of her mouth to Matthew. She felt the warmth of his body against her left arm. While the tension between them had eased considerably after a long talk two days earlier, she knew it wasn't completely gone. They had both silently agreed to avoid talking politics and anything to do with Matthew's mother. Tia knew that agreement couldn't last forever, but for now, she had no desire to destroy the tentative peace between them.

Matthew shrugged his shoulders. "I've got absolutely no idea. I know my uncle and Jeehana are heading back to Portalis soon, but there wouldn't be a ship-wide meeting just to say goodbye."

Tia agreed there was more to the meeting than a bon voyage party. "I heard Rembis is going with them. I wonder if the gnome mage knows what he's getting into. I worked with him a lot when I was flying that shuttle on Portalis last year. He was young then. It's strange seeing him as an old gnome with a long white beard."

"Yeah," agreed Matthew. "This time-travel stuff can get confusing. I don't see how Uncle Rick keeps things straight in his head."

Tia had a feeling her wizard scout friend didn't, but she kept her opinion to herself. "How do you feel about finding out he's your uncle?"

Matthew was quiet for a half dozen heartbeats. Just when Tia thought he wasn't going to reply, he turned to look directly at her. He'd had a growth spurt during the past year, so he was taller than her now. She was forced to look up into his eyes.

"I've always liked Rick, so finding out we're related was a nice surprise, to be honest. Discovering Gaston is my father was a different matter. I'm still trying to process that bit of information."

Tia nodded her head. Growing up with a fully-functional core family around her, she knew she couldn't fully appreciate how Matthew was feeling. She also knew now wasn't the time or place to probe further. She decided to change the subject. "What do you think about—"

A voice came from the stairs leading to the cockpit. "I'm sure you're all wondering why you've been crammed together," said

Sergeant Ron coming down the short flight of stairs.

The *Defiant's* captain was followed closely by Rick and Jeehana. Behind them came Terrie and his wife, Angela. Tia sensed high energy readings coming from Terrie's direction. Reaching out with her senses the way she'd been taught by Rick and Gaston, she pinpointed two energy sources in Terrie's right breast pocket.

"I've sensed similar energy before," Tia whispered smiling. "This is beginning to be a habit."

Matthew whispered back, "What are you talking about?"

Tia shook her head. "Never mind. You're going to find out soon enough." She had a thought. With a laugh she said, "I hope this turns out better than last time, though. I'm not in the mood for another extended trip."

Matthew's brow wrinkled. "What are you—"

"Quiet down," said Sergeant Ron as he made his way to the front of the mess table followed by Rick, Jeena, Angela, and Terrie.

Rick and Jeena stood in front of the *Defiant's* captain with their backs to the crew. Terrie and Angela flanked Sergeant Ron, facing everyone. Tia smiled, growing more confident that she knew what was going on. *Good,* she thought. *I'm glad for Rick. I've no doubt Liz will be happy as well.*

When the crew quieted, Sergeant Ron smiled. "I'm sure you've all noticed Rick and Jeehana have been occupying the same living quarters on the ship. Now, I ain't no legal expert, but I'm thinking regardless of whatever ceremonies they partook in during their time in the magic dimension, I doubt it applies in our galaxy if lawyers were to get involved. So…" His smile widened. "…after a long talk with our two companions, I've convinced them to stop living in sin on my ship. After all, they've got to set a good example for some of our more impressionable young people onboard."

Tia noticed the *Defiant's* captain look at her and wink, then felt her face grow warm. Glancing out the corner of her eye, she noticed a slight reddening of Matthew's face too.

"Without further ado," said Sergeant Ron, "let's get this ceremony started. Rick, Jeehana, in all seriousness, I want you to know I consider it a privilege to officiate your wedding." Speaking over the comments of some of the crew, the *Defiant's* captain began. "Dearly beloved…"

The wedding went without a hitch. Halfway through, Tia felt Matthew clasp her hand. She entwined her fingers in his and held tight for the rest of the ceremony. From the pressure of Matthew's grasp, she had a feeling he had no intention of ever letting go. She made a silent promise never to let anything get between them again. *War or no war,* she thought, *we're supposed to be together. That's just the way it's going to be.*

When it came to the part in the ceremony where Sergeant Ron asked about the rings, Tia saw Terrie reach into his pocket and pull two paper-thin bands of creallium out with barely visible red sparkles at the top of each ring. She didn't need her active scan to know the rings were the sources of energy she'd detected earlier.

"Hey," whispered Matthew, "those are the same rings Rick gave Jerad and Trinity last year."

Tia shook her head. "Similar, but they aren't the same. These have red gems. Jerad and Trinity's have blue gems. The magic energy coming off them is also different. I think Comstar and Calatron must have cast different spells on them this time."

Tia remembered seeing Calatron, the leader of the gnome mages on the recon ship, poring over spell books with Comstar more than once during the last week in preparation for casting the spells.

Matthew's brow tightened as he leaned forward. After a couple of seconds, he relaxed. "I see what you mean. Some of the spells are the same, but some are different. Both rings have strength and hardness spells on them like Jared and Trinity's. I suppose they have to in order to keep from getting damaged."

Tia nodded. "Yeah, those are the same as on the other rings. I suspect Rick and Comstar will be placing a stealth shield on the rings, the same as they did for Trinity and Jerad's. Rick wouldn't be much of a recon guy if he wore his ring the way it is now."

"Can you make out the other spells on their rings?" asked Matthew. "I think Jeehana's has some fire-based spells. I can't make out the ones on Rick's."

Tia concentrated on Richard's ring, sensing energy similar to that given out by Terrie when he healed people. "I think there are some healing spells on his ring. I also sense some type of scan and detection spells. I wonder what that's all about."

Before Matthew could give his opinion on the subject, Sergeant Ron looked at the couple and fairly shouted, "I now pronounce you man and wife! You may kiss the bride."

Tia thought she noticed Rick turn a little pink. "Well, I'll be," she whispered to Matthew. "He's shy. Didn't my sister teach him anything?"

To Tia's surprise, the normally reserved high priestess wrapped her arms around her newly declared husband and gave him a kiss passionate enough to make Tia blush. Once the elf pulled back, both Rick and Jeena faced the crew smiling at the various comments aimed at them.

"All right," shouted Sergeant Ron. "Show's over. Everyone get back to work. This ain't no cruise liner, and you aren't paying guests, so move it."

Despite Sergeant Ron's words, the crew lingered long enough to give their congratulations and say their goodbyes. After half an hour, only Sergeant Ron, Jeena, Rick, Terrie, Angela, Brachia, Dren, Bright Wing, Rembis, Matthew, and Tia were left in the mess area. They each took a bench seat at the mess table.

Tia glanced at the rings on the couple's left hands. She could no longer sense energy from them. As she'd suspected, Comstar and Richard had cast stealth spells and manipulated energy links in such a manner as to hide the rings from detection. Even at a range of two meters, Tia could no longer sense the rings with either her passive or active scan.

"What's with the rings?" asked Matthew voicing the same question Tia wanted to ask. "Are you planning on starting a new career in the wedding ring business? You gave rings to Jared and Trinity when they got married, and now you've made some for Jeehana and you."

Before Richard had a chance to answer, his battle computer chimed in over the battle helmet's external speaker. "Actually, since High Priestess Jeehanathoraxen's little talk with *'the One,'* he has been more forthcoming with information. According to Margery and Danny, the rings will play a part in the final battle. Unfortunately, *'the One'* hasn't seen fit to inform us what their part will be."

"Are you saying the rings Rick gave Trinity and Jerad will play a part also?" asked Matthew. "What can four rings do?"

"Actually," said Brachia, "a total of eight rings were created. Dren and I had our father, Keka, check the warehouse inventories on Storage for rings. There are four still waiting in one of the miscellaneous warehouses. From what our father could find out, four pairs of rings were created. Their purpose is unknown."

"We did learn one interesting thing," added Dren apparently determined not to be outdone by her brother.

Matthew spread his arms with a questioning look. "Well? I give up. What did you learn?"

Dren smiled. "The rings are inset with a chip that's an exact duplicate of the ones used in battle helmets."

"Only smaller," said Brachia. "A battle helmet's normal brerellium encased chip is larger than the entire ring."

Tia beat Matthew in asking the next question. "Then what good are they? From what Danny's told me during the times I've been assigned to the *Defiant*, he's a living gas that's compressed into the brerellium chip that's in battle helmets. Are there forms of living gas smaller than battle computers that can fit in the rings?"

Laughter came out of the intercom on the wall of the mess area. Tia glanced at the intercom on the opposite wall from where she sat. "All right, Danny. What did I say that's so amusing?"

"Sorry," replied Danny still chuckling. "Maybe I did a poor job of explaining gaseous life forms to you. Battle computers are compressed gas. We can expand massive distances or compress into microscopic spaces. Size doesn't matter. The ability comes in handy on occasion. That is why I can easily fit into either a battle helmet's chip or the chip inside Jeehana's ring."

"Which as it so happens," said Richard, "is what Danny is going to do. He'll be leaving the *Defiant* and going with Jeena and me to Portalis."

"Danny's leaving?" Tia asked suddenly realizing how attached she'd become to the ex-battle computer. "Who's going to handle the targeting computations on the ship's fighters?"

"Hey," said Margery breaking in over the intercom. "Do you have so little faith in me? I can handle the calculations on the *Defiant* and our fighters at the same time with no problem. I am an advanced computer. I can handle trillions of calculations in a single nanosecond. I can—"

"Sorry," Tia said in an attempt to put salve on Margery's hurt feelings. "Don't get your panties in a wad. I was only asking."

"Well, in that case," said Margery, "apology accepted. Trust me. You will be in good hands while Danny is gone."

"Oh, I trust you," Tia assured the *Defiant's* computer. "I was just a little surprised Sergeant Ron agreed to it."

"Hey," said Sergeant Ron. "I may be the captain of this ship, but Margery and Danny are living beings. They make their own decisions. They think Portalis is an important piece of the puzzle. We'll just have to get along without Danny."

"So how long will you be gone, Rick?" asked Matthew. "I was just starting to get used to the fact that I had an uncle."

Tia noticed Richard smile.

"I'm not dying, Matt," said Richard. "Jeena and I will just be leaving for a bit. We'll be back. I'm just not sure when."

"Speaking of leaving," said Sergeant Ron, "I assume you heard that your brother escaped. No one knows how, but he's gone."

Richard bit his lip as he nodded.

"He might have gone back to my mother," suggested Matthew.

A soft voice came from the other end of the table. "I don't think so."

Tia looked at the high priestess. "Why not, Jeehana? I think that would be his obvious destination."

Jeena shook her head. "He was too interested in that bottle of DNA gas. Also, I felt a disturbance when we entered the triplet's time-bubble gate. I have a feeling that Rick's brother somehow managed to make his way to Portalis. I am not sure when in time he went, but I believe he is there. He could be far in the past for all I know. There is no way to tell for sure. What I do know is that he will do anything to get the gas."

Tia noticed Matthew look down at the table. She had no doubt all the talk about his mother and father was having an effect and decided to help him out by changing the subject. "When will you and Jeehana be leaving, Rick?" she asked.

Richard looked at Jeehana.

The high priestess looked away from her bondmate and toward Tia. "The sooner we leave the better. The Tree of Light was damaged. We left in such a hurry that I was unable to determine how bad he was hurt." She turned to Richard. "I will go wherever and whenever you wish, my bondmate, but at the same time, I think it is important for us to return to Silverton as soon as possible."

Richard nodded. "I concur. Things have stalemated somewhat here. War-King Bistoria and Liz are more than capable of handling things in the physical dimension without us."

"So what are my orders, Rick?" asked Sergeant Ron.

Tia noticed the *Defiant's* captain give her a wink, making it obvious he didn't take orders from anyone; only suggestions.

Richard drummed his fingers on the table before shrugging his shoulders. "I'm not even sure what my plans are for Jeena and me. I haven't thought about anyone else to be honest."

Nickelo laughed over the external speaker. "You know Rick's not much on planning, Sergeant Ron. I do have a suggestion if you are willing to listen."

"I'm all ears," said Sergeant Ron.

"I calculate it would be advantageous to have the *Defiant* in the magic dimension," said Nickelo. "Rick and Jeehana can coordinate that with the triplets before they leave. The United Galaxy Alliance needs to be updated on the size of the Dragars' fleets that you spotted in the past, around the asteroid. You could do that and still be available to help Rick and Jeehana if the need arose."

Terrie shook his head. "I don't see how. That shield around Portalis prevents any ships from landing."

"True," conceded Nickelo. "However, things change. I calculate a lot of changes are coming down the line. We have to be in a position to take advantage of them. You can bet the Dragars have not assembled their fleets for no reason. The orcs' Great Battle is coming. How soon, I do not know, but it is definitely getting closer."

"What about us, Uncle Rick?" asked Dren. "Do you want us to stay on the *Defiant*?"

Richard shook his head. "No. I think you and Brachia will be more helpful on Storage. Since we'll be operating in the current time, if we need something special from Storage, I'd feel better if I knew the two of you were there to make things happen. If Jeena and I need something new from my dimensional pack, maybe you could speed things up. Besides, I'd rest easier knowing you guys were on Storage where it's safe. Wizard Scout Telsa is already there, so you won't be lonely."

"We're not children, Uncle Rick," said Brachia. "Omar and I will protect Dren. You don't need to worry."

Tia thought she saw a smile start on Richard's face before he got it under control.

"Oh, I'm not worried about Dren and you," said Richard with a wink toward Dren. "I was more worried about the Crosioians and the Balorian Pirates."

Brachia smiled, but Dren was all business.

"What do you think you'll be needing?" asked Dren.

"I've got no idea," said Richard. "Just be ready."

"All right," replied Dren sounding doubtful. She looked at Brachia and then back at Richard. "How are we supposed to get back to Storage? Will we be teleporting?"

"Teleport?" laughed Sergeant Ron. "You've obviously gotten too used to having a teleporter at your beck and call. Rick and I have already hashed it all out. You'll be traveling in the lap of luxury right here on the *Defiant*. We'll drop the two of you off on Storage and then hightail it to Portalis. Now, don't think you'll be lazing around like guests on the trip. I'll expect both of you to pull your share of the load."

Brachia snapped to attention and gave Sergeant Ron a salute. "Aye, aye, Captain!"

"And don't call me Captain. I keep telling you I'm a sergeant. I work for a living. Isn't that right, Rick?"

Richard winked at his bondmate before giving Sergeant Ron a grin and saluting. "Sir, yes, sir!"

CHAPTER 20

As far as Jeena was concerned, the worst thing about riding on a spirit-horse through dimensions was being encased in total darkness most of the time. She doubted she'd ever get used to it. Half-seen landscapes occasionally flashed by as the stallion shifted in and out of dimensions, but for the most part, they rode in the dark. The feel of her bondmate's arms wrapped protectively around her gave her comfort. Even so, the ride still felt strange beyond words.

"Actually," said Danny speaking to her from the ring on her left hand, *"the stallion is not really a horse. He is a spirit creature that prefers equine forms. You should be honored that he has actually wrapped tendrils around you to secure you to his back. The poor gnome in front of you only has your arms securing him in place. Based upon his heart rate, I do not think he will be making a habit of asking to accompany Rick on future rides."*

Jeena unconsciously tightened her grip around Rembis. She wasn't sure what would happen to the old gnome if she let go and wasn't planning to find out.

"I am not sure honored is the word I would use," Jeena said in the space of her mind she used to communicate with her ring's battle computer. *"Truthfully, I am thankful the spirit-horse decided to secure me in place. Rick said the stallion senses our bond link. I suppose that is why I am being treated better than poor Rembis."*

"Could be," agreed Danny. *"I would not depend on your link endearing you to the stallion too much though. According to Nickelo, the spirit-horse has not displayed an abundance of*

affection for your bondmate over the years. By the way, I think we are getting close to our destination."

Jeena reached out with her senses. What her scan brought back definitely felt familiar. After a dozen heartbeats, a blazing sun came into view temporarily causing Jeena to shield her eyes with her right arm.

"Sorry," came Richard's voice from behind her. "I should've warned you we were getting close."

Lowering her arm, Jeena blinked a few times to clear her eyes. She spied Silverton's white walls in the distance. The top of the Tree of Light was visible over the roofs of even the tallest of the city's buildings.

"Put me down," said Rembis squirming out of Jeena's grasp. He leaped clear of the stallion, landing in what was to him chest-deep green grass. Glancing back, the gnome said, "Don't either of you ever ask me to ride a dimensional shifting creature again. I'll stick to good old-fashioned teleports from now on, thank you very much."

The tendrils holding Jeena to the spirit-horse's back slipped away. Kicking her right leg over the stallion's neck, she joined Rembis on the ground. Her bondmate dismounted as well.

"We are on Dragon's Ridge," Jeena told her companions as she pointed toward the city. "This is one of my favorite picnic areas. You can get a view of the entire valley from here." Looking down at the old gnome, she asked, "Have you ever visited Silverton before, Master Rembis?"

"Can't say I've had the pleasure," admitted the old gnome.

"Dragon's Ridge, you say?" asked Richard.

Jeena looked at her bondmate. He was still wearing his battle suit although the red visor was raised out of sight, giving her a clear view of his eyes. He seemed to be scanning the entire valley with a faraway look in his eyes as if he were seeing things invisible to either the gnome or her.

Waving her hand to encompass the landscape before them, Jeena went into story mode. "A great battle was fought in the valley you see before you. A demon in the form of a giant at the head of a massive army of orcs tried to destroy Silverton. Legend has it that a hero dressed in black armor fought a fierce dragon on this very ridge during the battle. There is a tapestry in the palace depicting the scene. I will have to show it to both of you when we get the chance."

The faraway look remained in Richard's eyes for a dozen heartbeats. Finally, he nodded, saying, "I saw the tapestry that night at the palace. I think the weaver took a little artistic license in the depiction of the battle with the *dragon*."

"Artists usually do," Jeena said studying her bondmate. "Especially when the piece of art is created thousands of years after the fact. It has been my experience that the reality of something is often less exciting than the actual event." She locked eyes with Richard. "You were here, were you not? Were you the one who fought the dragon?"

Her bondmate stared at her for several seconds before nodding his head. "I fought something, but it wasn't a dragon." He pointed at Silverton's main gates. "The real battle was down there. King William and his half-sister, Mendera, along with the unicorn, Swiftmane, are the ones who defeated the demon. I was all the way up here when they needed me down there."

Jeena shifted her staff from her right hand to her left. "I think it is going to take some time to get used to the fact that you participated in things I was raised on as legends. The battle for Silverton happened sixty thousand years ago. I would like to hear more about what you have done over the years, but perhaps we should keep it between the three of us for now. I fear some on the Council of Light might use any such information to our detriment."

"Fine by me," replied Richard. "I don't remember most of what I've done over the years anyway. Sometimes it scares me to think of what horrible things I might have done that I'm not even aware of."

"Well, don't let it bother you, my friend," said Rembis. "From what I know of you, I doubt you've done anything to be ashamed of. If I thought any different, I wouldn't have volunteered to come with you to Silverton."

Richard nodded appreciatively, but Jeena had the feeling her bondmate was taking the gnome's words with a grain of salt. "Enough dillydallying," she said using a word her bondmate's battle computer had taught her. She was anxious to get back to her duties as high priestess, and *dillydallying* was the last thing she wanted to do. "It is still a good hour's walk yet to the city."

"We could ride," suggested Richard.

"Ha," said Rembis. "You ride. I will walk. My riding days are over."

"I agree with Master Rembis," Jeena said. "I doubt riding your demon of a horse into the city would endear either of you to the average citizen of Silverton."

The stallion bared its teeth and growled before turning translucent and sinking into the ground.

"Hmm," Jeena said. "I think I hurt his feelings."

"Could be," said Richard. "He understands a lot more of our language than I understand of his. I'm actually surprised he hung around so long after we dismounted. Maybe he's getting soft in his old age."

Jeena tried to decide if her bondmate was joking or not, sensing no humor through their link. "I'd suggest we change clothes now, Rick. You will be a lot less intimidating to my fellow elves if you wear your healer robes. Do you mind?"

Her bondmate shrugged his shoulders. "Fine by me. I'm not planning on doing any fighting while I'm in Silverton anyway." He looked at her. "Are you going to change into your robe? Or are you staying in your jumpsuit?" He smiled. "If my opinion matters, you look good the way you are."

Smiling, Jeena said, "Oh, your opinion matters, but I think I will change just the same. The other lords on the council might not appreciate me the way you do."

"I certainly hope not," replied Richard smiling even more.

Jenna sensed what she could only describe as a frisky emotion coming from her bondmate's end of their link. She felt her face growing warm but pointedly ignored her human as she removed the pack he'd given her from her back. She pulled out a pretty good facsimile of her normal light blue priestess robe that Richard had summoned for her earlier. She shook out the neatly folded robe and examined it.

"Whoever handles clothing on Storage does excellent work," Jeena said admiring the embroidery of her family seal on the left breast of the robe. "It is not elven silk, but it is close enough. This robe will serve me much better than my bonding dress."

Richard smiled. "Oh, I kinda liked your bonding dress better. I think it served you well. It certainly drew my attention while you were in it."

A definite warmth flowed over Jeena's face and neck. She sensed an emotion coming down the link from her bondmate that was anything but businesslike. She glanced at the gnome.

The gnome stared back, then huffed, "Well, if you think I'm going to slink away to give you two some alone time, you've got another think coming. I've got more important things to do than stand around waiting on you two to finish your honeymoon."

With her face growing even warmer, Jeena grabbed her robe and fairly ran to the backside of the ridge. When she was out of sight of the males, she removed her black jumpsuit and replaced it with the robe. After stuffing the jumpsuit into her backpack, she strapped her utility belt around her waist and adjusted the holster on her left hip. When she was done, she slung her pack over her shoulder and headed back toward the males.

"Are you going to keep the phase pistol?" asked Danny. *"That might seem a little out of place to some of your fellow elves."*

"Let it," Jeena said. *"Magic is my primary defense, but it let me down once. I do not plan on ever being caught helpless again. If that means using technology to supplement my magic, then so be it."*

"Fine by me," replied Danny. *"I was just asking a question."*

Once she reached the crest of the ridge, Jeena spotted her bondmate and the gnome waiting. Richard had changed into a plain brown robe more befitting of a human healer. She had to admit he looked much less fearsome. As far as she could tell, he wasn't even wearing his utility belt with his phase rod and pistol.

When her bondmate caught her eye, he smiled. The bit of red on his left ring finger glinted in the bright sunlight. She smiled back and shifted her left hand so her ring's gem caught the morning sunlight as well. Elves had no tradition of wedding rings since a bond link declared to all an elf's attachment. Just the same, she was beginning to warm to the idea of their two rings being a symbol of their commitment. Casting thoughts of rings to the side, Jeena joined the two males.

Jeena pointed at her bondmate's waist. "You didn't keep your phase rod?"

Richard smiled as he reached into a slit in the side of his robe. He pulled out the handle of his deactivated phase rod. "I decided to keep this on me, but I'll make sure it stays out of sight. I put everything else in my dimensional pack except for my battle helmet. I strapped it to the side of my pack to keep Nick around."

"That is probably best," Jeena agreed. "Master Nick is always welcome." She pointed her staff in the direction of Silverton. "Shall we?"

Setting a quick pace, Jeena had the three of them standing in front of the city's main gates within an hour. As was normal in times when there was no threat of attack, the gates stood wide open. A squad of soldiers armed with swords and bows stood to one side.

A sergeant made her way forward and saluted. "Hail High Priestess Jeehanathoraxen. It is good to see you return." The sergeant turned to glance at Richard and Rembis. "Elf Friend, you are welcome as well." She looked back at Jeena. "I assume you are taking responsibility for this gnome."

"I am," Jeena assured the sergeant. "I will present him to the Council of Light shortly. I would like to visit the Tree of Light first and pay my compliments to the Lady."

"Of course," said the sergeant. "Much has happened since your, err…departure. Your guests and you may pass, High Priestess."

With a nod, Jeena led the way forward with her bondmate to her right and the gnome to her left. The sergeant's comment about *much happening* bothered her, but she refrained from questioning the soldier further. No doubt the high lord would bring her up to date on current events soon enough.

For their part, the gnome and her bondmate seemed content to let her guide them through the city as they gawked at Silverton's architecture and citizenry. Before they had gone a quarter of the way to the city park, Jeena noticed an increase in traffic along their path.

"I have a feeling word is spreading of your return," said Richard indicating a small crowd ahead with a nod of his head. "I think you've got a welcoming committee."

Jeena smiled at her bondmate's modesty. "Ha. The citizens of Silverton have seen me often enough not to make a special effort to do so now. I have no doubt they are here to get another look at the legendary elf friend."

An emotion of what might have been embarrassment made its

way down their bond link.

"Perhaps they are here to see the gnome," said Danny in her mind. *"Did you think about that?"*

Jeena ignored the battle computer. She was fast becoming used to the fact that not everything a battle computer said was worth taking the time to respond.

A familiar tickle at the back of Jeena's mind drew her attention. "The Lady knows we are here," she told the others.

"Did she tell you something?" asked Richard sounding suddenly interested.

Shaking her head, Jeena dispelled the notion. "No. Either she has nothing to say, or we will find out soon enough anyway." She pointed ahead. "We will take the park path to the Tree of Light." Glancing at the gnome, she added, "It is unfortunate we did not arrive at night. I suspect the silver elms would be lit up in all their glory at our arrival."

They entered the city park and made their way along one of the many white-stone paths heading in the direction of the park's center where the Tree of Light was located. A half dozen older elf children were trailing a quarter of a bowshot behind and pointing at their group. When Jeena stopped, the children stopped as well. She had no trouble recognizing two of the children. One was her niece, Terika. The other was Matisa, her adoptive sister. Waving the children forward, Jeena waited patiently for them to get the nerve to approach.

"I think you have some admirers," Jeena whispered out the side of her mouth to Richard. "Please be on your best behavior."

"Aren't I always?" replied Richard.

Jeena, Rembis, and Nickelo all said "No" at the same time.

Reaching over his shoulder, Richard slapped the top of his battle helmet where he'd strapped it to the side of his dimensional pack. "You stay out of this, wise guy, or I'll stick you in my pack with the rest of my equipment. Then you can stay on a shelf on Storage and amuse yourself until I need you."

"I do not think that would be advisable," said Nickelo.

Jeena thought her bondmate's battle computer sounded a little nervous. She had a feeling whatever shelf was being mentioned was not a very nice place. She decided to put the battle computer out of his misery. "My bondmate was just joking, Master Nick. I have no doubt Rick knows how valuable you are."

"Well," said Nickelo perking up, "at least somebody here recognizes my worth."

Since the children had arrived, Jeena made no more remarks to her bondmate's battle computer. Although he might not know it, she knew full well they were at a crossroad of her bondmate's acceptance in the elven community. The six children now standing before them were Silverton's unofficial leaders of the other elf children. How ever these six went in their acceptance of a human elf friend in their midst, the other children would soon follow.

If the children give their trust to Rick, most of the adults in the city will do so as well.

Being the oldest of the children, her adoptive sister Matisa opened her mouth to speak. She turned red and immediately closed her mouth without uttering a word.

That does not bode well, Jeena thought.

To Jeena's relief, her niece Terika smiled, taking the lead. "I am glad to see you are back, Aunt Jeena. Everyone was worried after you left. Some of the other children tried to say you had been eaten by a vicious demon-horse. I didn't believe them."

Returning her niece's smile, Jeena said, "No, I am fine as you can see." Turning to her bondmate, Jeena said, "Rick, this is my niece, Terika." Pointing at Matisa, she added, "This chatterbox is my adoptive sister, Matisa." Switching roles, Jeena introduced her bondmate. "Terika, Matisa, this is Elf Friend Richard Shepard. We have been on a metal ship that flies between the stars."

All six children seemed suitably impressed. Jeena introduced Rembis to the children.

"You look very tall for a gnome," said Terika who was occasionally known for being suspicious. "Are you sure you are a gnome?"

Rembis gave a big grin. "I was last time I checked. Maybe I'm actually half giant, and I didn't know it until now."

All of the children laughed. Jeena and Richard did as well.

"Are you going to the Tree of Light?" asked Matisa. "May we go with you? Everyone has been waiting for you to come back!" Again without waiting for Jeena to reply, the young elf added, "Since the elf friend is your bondmate, is he now my adoptive brother?"

Jeena raised a hand to her chin. "Hmm. Possibly," she said trying to remain non-committal. "I hadn't really thought about how our bonding would affect family ties."

"Then he is my uncle as well, right, Aunt Jeena?" asked Terika apparently not wanting to be outdone by Matisa.

Suspecting she'd purposely been caught in a childish trap, Jeena shrugged. "I suppose so." She glanced helplessly at her bondmate, unsure how he'd take the news. She needn't have worried.

Richard bent on one knee so his head was level with that of the children. "I would be honored to be your adoptive brother," he said nodding at Matisa. Turning to Terika he added, "I would also be honored to be your uncle. I would consider it a triple honor if all of you would call me Rick. We don't have elf friends where I come from, so I'm not used to the title."

The children smiled although a couple of the smiles were a tad on the timid side.

Jeena mentally blessed her bondmate for the initial overture of friendship, but she had a feeling it would take many years before he was fully accepted by her fellow elves. *It does not matter,* she thought. *He will grow on them. They just need to get to know him like I do.*

"Ha," said Danny in her mind. *"You have been with him for a total of nine days. I calculate you have a lot to learn about him before you really know him."*

"Hush," Jeena mentally replied, *"or I will take this ring off and toss it in Rick's pack. Then you can sit on a shelf on Storage until I need you."*

"Since I calculate you are joking," said Danny not sounding the least worried, *"I am not impressed. However, I will 'hush' as you say."*

Several of the children seemed taken by the gnome more than by the elf friend. Soon four of the children were running ahead hand in hand with the old gnome in the direction of the Tree of Light. To his credit, Rembis played along good-naturedly, laughing with the children as they went.

"Maybe I should be jealous," said Richard. "Rembis seems to be the hit of the party."

"We stayed," said Terika who had interposed herself between Jeena and her bondmate.

Although Jeena noticed her niece wasn't so bold as to touch her new uncle, she was walking very close to his side nonetheless. Matisa, on the other hand, was walking to Jeena's left, keeping her aunt between her and the human.

"Give her time," came Danny's thought. *"Rick appears hard when people first meet him, but he's a teddy bear at heart."*

"A what?" Jeena asked trying to envision how bears fit into the picture.

"Never mind," replied Danny. *"It is a quote from a book Nickelo sent me called* Cute Sayings and Slang of 20th through 21st Century America *by Robert R. Fitzgerald. You should get Rick to summon you a copy when you get the chance. I find it fascinating reading."*

The white-stone path opened up onto the clearing containing the Tree of Light. Rembis stopped and stood openmouthed, gazing at the massive tree. The others in the group stopped beside the gnome. Jeena didn't blame them. She never tired of looking at the Creator's gift to her people.

"It's beautiful," remarked Rembis finding his tongue.

"Yes, he is," Jeena said.

"He?" asked the gnome looking back. "I thought the Lady was a she."

Jeena laughed. "You must spend some time in our library reading the history of my people, Master Rembis. The Tree of Light is a story worth hearing. When High Priestess Shandristiathoraxen found her bondmate, High Lord Carndador, near death in the forest, she took him to the Tree of Light. Unable to heal the high lord, the tree shared life force with the high priestess's bondmate, absorbing him into the tree. So you see, the tree is a he."

"What about the Lady?" asked Rembis.

"She is my friend Shandria," said Richard moving next to Jeena. "Shandria's bond link binds her to the tree and to her bondmate."

Jeena looked over at her own bondmate and smiled. "That is correct. I did not know it until the Lady told her story on the night of our bonding ceremony. You helped the Lady recover the seed, did you not?"

Richard nodded his head.

Jeena stared at him for several seconds, unsure how she felt. The human standing before her, while her bondmate, was also the stuff of legends. It was hard to believe even for her.

"High Priestess," came the familiar voice of Chief Forester Mistros as he hurried toward her from the direction of the tree. "Praise the Lady you have returned. I have much to tell you, and there is still so much to do."

Jeena turned back to her bondmate.

Before she could speak, Richard said, "Go. You've got things to do. I'm quite capable of looking after myself."

When Jeena started to protest, Terika chimed in. "Leave the elf friend to me, Aunt Jeena."

"Do not forget about me," said Matisa. "Between Terika and me, we will make sure the elf friend stays out of trouble."

"See?" smiled Richard. "I'm in good hands. Besides, we're linked. It's not like I'm going anywhere. You can always find me. Heck, if you could find me two million years in the past, I've got a feeling you'd have no trouble finding me in the here and now in Silverton."

As her mind began thinking of all the things she had to do, Jeena conceded to allow her niece and adoptive sister to take charge of her bondmate. "Then I will leave you in the hands of your two guides" She turned to face the gnome magic user. "Master Rembis, I believe Master Jathar could find great use for you in our mage guild if you are of a mind."

Rembis laughed. "Mind? I'd be honored. I have got enough questions about elf spells to last all afternoon. Just point me in the right direction."

"I will take him," said an older elf boy standing behind Matisa. "I have to meet my sister at the mage guild anyway."

"See?" said Rembis. "I have a guide too."

Jeena nodded. "So I see." She turned to Richard. "After I get things straightened out here, I will need to report to the high lord and the Council of Light. I will see you at our home tonight."

Richard smiled. "Our home. I like the sound of that."

Turning to go with the chief forester, Jeena smiled. "As do I, my bondmate. I very much like the sound of that."

CHAPTER 21

Fighting against the waves of pain Efrestra and Cancontus were inflicting, the Dalinfaust succeeded in touching the soul of his other brother, Zenthra.

"Have you come to mock me as well?" asked Zenthra, his thoughts full of vitriol and uttermost hate.

"No, brother," said the Dalinfaust struggling to keep the contempt he felt for the weakest of his brothers out of his voice. *"I came to offer you a chance for release and revenge. Working together, we can free ourselves from the prisons Efrestra and Cancontus have created for us."*

"Impossible, fool," snarled Zenthra between cries of pain. *"Our Power is limited until the time limit is up. All we can do is suffer and endure our thousand years as we plot our revenge. Thus it has always been, and thus it will always be."*

The Dalinfaust nearly lost control of his anger but succeeded in keeping it hidden from his worthless brother. *No, not quite worthless,* he thought. *I need his Power to escape. I must speak to his ego. He will help if I can only play him right.* The Dalinfaust decided to explain what his idiot brother should have been able to discern for himself. *"This time is different. Never before have two of us been imprisoned at the same time."*

"Our Power is still reduced while we are in our cells," snorted Zenthra between groans. *"Even if we worked together, Efrestra and Cancontus would be too strong for us to break free. We are helpless until our thousand years are up. I have been unable to even do something as simple as contacting my minions. If you try*

to contact yours, I am confident you will fail as well."

Anger burned in the Dalinfaust. *The fool. Does he not wonder how I have managed to communicate with him?* Forcing his anger aside, the Dalinfaust kept the thoughts he directed at his brother semi-cordial. *"Ah. Normally you would be correct, brother. On the other hand, you and I are the smartest and strongest of the four."* The Dalinfaust almost choked while implying Zenthra was either smart or strong, but somehow he succeeded in completing his compliment without laughing *"Also, I am not completely imprisoned. Four parts of me exist in the physical and magic dimensions. I have been using those parts to contact my servants. I can also use those parts to channel your commands to your minions, if you so desire."*

"What good is that?" said Zenthra. *"We will still be trapped and tortured."*

"Only for a short while longer if we work together," explained the Dalinfaust trying his best to remain patient. *"I have a plan to break free of this prison, but it will take both of us. Even now one of my servants is seeking the last bottle of DNA gas. Together, you and I can manipulate its energy to shatter our bonds. We will be free to exact our revenge on those who destroyed our avatars."*

The Dalinfaust sensed a wave of hate from Zenthra. *Good,* he thought. *My brother's desire for revenge will make him easier to manipulate.* He also sensed suspicion from his brother. *"You doubt me?"* asked the Dalinfaust.

"Even if parts of you exist outside this prison," said Zenthra, *"and even if your servants gain the DNA gas, they will need to disable the four corners of one of the gates to free us. You would need to have prepositioned at least four separate parts of yourself outside this prison to do any good. I doubt you were that farsighted."*

"Then you would be wrong, brother," said the Dalinfaust once again using all his will to control his temper. *"Even now one of my parts is in the hands of my servant on Portalis, heading toward the elves' gate located under their Tree of Light. Two other parts are safely hidden on the planet called Storage in the physical dimension."*

"What of the fourth part?" asked Zenthra finally beginning to gain interest.

"The fourth part is in the hands of our master's variable," said the Dalinfaust. *"He is already positioned near the gate."*

"The master's variable will not serve you willingly," said Zenthra.

"No, he will not," agreed the Dalinfaust. *"Still, he will serve me nonetheless."*

"What about the two parts on Storage? How do you plan to get them here?"

The Dalinfaust let his brother think about it on the off chance that he could figure it out for himself. After a time, it became apparent Zenthra could not.

"That is where you come in, my dear brother," the Dalinfaust explained. *"I will give you a connection you can use to contact your Dragar servants. I know you have assembled their fleets two million years in the past. All l need you to do is order one of their dreadnaughts to perform a small mission for us. Upon their success and that of my other servants, we can be free."* The Dalinfaust sensed curiosity from his brother.

"Where would you have me order my dreadnaught to go?" asked Zenthra still failing to grasp his brother's intentions.

"That is easy, dear brother. Your warship will go to the planet Storage. Once they destroy the planet's occupants, they will recover my two parts stored there and bring them to Portalis in the current time. Combined with the two parts already on Portalis, we can use the elves' gate to break out of our cells and regain our full Power. We will be free."

"Should my Dragar servants take any captives when they destroy Storage?"

The Dalinfaust laughed for the first time since he'd been imprisoned. *"No. We have no need for captives. All of the miserable life forms in the three galaxies will be annihilated when we open the gate to the demonic plane. The life forms on Storage will be but the first. They must* all *die. They* will *all die."*

CHAPTER 22

Lord Crendemor watched the guard complete his report to High Lord Trenadine.

"Are you sure?" asked the high lord.

"I saw the high priestess and the elf friend myself," replied the guard. "They were at the Tree of Light when I left to come here."

The high lord glanced at the other council members. Lord Crendemor kept the hatred he felt out of his eyes as best he could. Apparently he succeeded, because the high lord paid him no heed.

My two enemies are here again, Crendemor thought. *If I bide my time, I can destroy them both in one fell swoop. I must be cautious though. I cannot act until I am fully ready. I am too close to gaining mastery over the Staff of the Lady of the Tree to jeopardize my plans for a mere act of revenge. I have invested too much time and effort to spring my trap prematurely.*

"We must neutralize the human's weapons," said Lord Sheshna. "I was not at the bonding ceremony since I was standing watch-guard, but Lord Thalos assures me the sword of red fire was demonic in nature. We cannot allow such a weapon to roam free among our people."

"You have made your point often enough over the last nine days," said High Lord Trenadine. "I told you before that we would have the high priestess ask the Lady for guidance before we did any action that may alienate the elf friend."

"I think—" began Lord Sheshna.

High Lord Trenadine rose from his chair. "I said we shall speak to the high priestess first." He turned to the guard. "Ask the high priestess to report to the Council of Light at her earliest convenience." After glancing at Lord Sheshna, he added, "Tell her our need is great."

Lord Crendemor noticed Lord Sheshna frown, but the old elf remained silent. Crendemor decided to follow the old lord's lead. *No use drawing unnecessary attention to myself,* he thought. Looking down at his pale hands, he frowned in disgust. *Although I was born a high elf, I have grown too used to the hands of my dark elf form over the years. I find the pasty hands of my current form repulsive. Once I have used the Lady's staff to open the gate, I will make my transformation to a dark elf permanent. The high elf race is weak and pathetic. When the gate opens, their time on Portalis will be at an end.*

High Lord Trenadine rose to look at each of the council members in turn. "I know some of you have other duties that are pressing. I am sure Lord Sheshna, Lord Thalos, and I can attend to the questioning of the high priestess."

Lord Crendemor nodded his head along with the others. Rising, he made his way to the door, thinking, *I have much to do. The pieces are starting to fall into place. I must be ready.*

CHAPTER 23

Richard threw the saucer-shaped piece of plastic at the older of the elf children. The agile youth caught it readily enough before tossing it on to one of the other children.

"Good catch," Richard yelled. "Are you sure none of you have played this game before?"

At least half of the dozen young elves forming the large circle shook their heads.

"We throw twine balls," explained Terika as she flipped the plastic saucer to a boy on the opposite side of the circle. "This is way more fun! Aren't you glad we stayed to play for a while before we took you home?"

"Definitely," Richard said. He meant it. They'd been playing for over an hour under the branches of the Tree of Light, and he was having as much fun as the elf children.

Switching to his shared space, Richard said, *"Thanks for the idea, Nick. I wish we'd had one of these at the orphanage when I was growing up. The sisters weren't much on playing games."*

"I told you there was a ninety-five percent probability the children would like it," said Nickelo sounding smug. *"It has certainly made you a hit with the younger elves."*

Richard laughed as Jeena's adoptive sister, Matisa, jumped into the air, caught the saucer, and threw it at him before she hit the ground. The plastic saucer bounced off the edge of his hand before he could get a good grip.

"Hump!" said Nickelo privately. *"You can catch live hand grenades in midair, but you can't catch a plastic toy? What is the*

world coming to?"

"You missed," laughed Matisa.

"Hey," Richard said pointing up, "the sun was in my eyes."

Terika glanced upward. "The sun is behind a cloud."

Richard raised a hand, pretending to shield his eyes as he looked skyward. "So it is. I stand corrected. I guess I must be tired."

"You are a wizard scout," came a thought from Nickelo. *"You do not get tired."*

"Whatever," Richard thought back. Picking up the dropped saucer, he tossed it to one of the boys before saying, "That's it for me, kids. I guess I'm getting old. I think I'll take a rest break on that stone wall for a few minutes."

Terika and a couple of the others pleaded with Richard to stay, but he finally succeeded in bowing out of the game and made his way to the wall. Sitting on top of the waist-high stone surface, he let the peace of the Tree of Light wash over him as he watched the children. They laughed as one of the boys did a flip in the air, catching and throwing the plastic saucer before he hit the ground.

"Didn't take them long to get by without me," Richard said laughing.

"I guess that proves you are not indispensable," Nickelo replied in their shared space. *"Makes you feel humble, doesn't it?"*

Richard gazed at the area under the tree's branches where the children continued their game. *"I thought Jeena told me the ground under the tree was off limits. From the looks of things, the foresters are just working around the children without saying anything."*

"Things change," said Nickelo. *"I took the liberty of using your battle helmet's audio sensors to listen to a few conversations while you were playing with the children. I dis—"*

"You were spying on the elves?" Richard asked.

"It was not spying," said Nickelo sounding offended. *"I was merely gathering useful information in a discreet manner. Now, do you want to hear what I found out, or do you want to argue semantics?"*

"You were spying," Richard insisted enjoying the fact that for once, he had his battle computer on the defensive.

"Fine. I was spying. The end result is that the Tree of Light

apparently enjoys the children playing under his branches. Ever since we've been gone, the younger elves have been playing games of tag in the morning while climbing the tree's branches. I calculate the tree has been lonely. I believe hearing the children laugh gives him pleasure. Besides, the reason for staying off the ground below the branches was to protect any nuts that might fall. So many were created the night of your bonding ceremony that I calculate the elves' foresters are no longer worried about protecting the nuts."

Richard nodded, then busied himself watching the children play. In between observing them, he watched his bondmate supervising the foresters and talking to the other priests. While she seemed poised on the outside, he sensed her worry and concern through their bond link.

I don't blame her, he thought. *The scars on the tree from our bonding ceremony look serious. Of course, I'm not all that familiar with trees, so what do I know.*

"Sometimes not too much," said Nickelo laughing as he intruded on Richard's thoughts. *"However, I would not worry about the tree too much. I calculate a ninety-seven percent probability your high priestess has everything well under control."*

Richard noticed a guard walk up from the direction of the palace and stop just outside the outer branches of the Tree of Light, then motion to a nearby forester. After speaking for a few seconds, the forester hurried away in the direction of Jeena on the far side of the tree. Curious, Richard walked toward the guard. The blue-caped guard nodded at his approach.

"Trouble?" Richard asked.

The guard shrugged his shoulders. "Who am I to say, Elf Friend?" The guard smiled what seemed like a genuinely friendly smile to Richard. "My orders were to summon the high priestess to the council chambers." The guard looked at Richard for several seconds before speaking again. "I served with Commander Leethor and Trooper Meshoan in the scouts before transferring to the council guards. I heard how you saved Meshoan's life. I thank you, Elf Friend."

Richard thought back to the attack by the orcs the previous week and his healing of the elf Meshoan. Details in his memory were sketchy at best. He was sure the healing had hurt, but he had no memory of it.

"'The One' *removes the memory of a tough healing,"* explained Nickelo in their shared space for what was probably the thousandth time. *"It is a good thing he does, or I calculate you would never heal anyone again."*

"You can bank on it," Richard thought back. Looking at the guard, Richard said, "It was nothing. To be honest, I barely remember the healing."

The guard squinted and started to speak, but Jeena walked up before he did and he raised his right arm and fist across his chest in a salute. "High Priestess, the high lord has requested your presence in the council chamber."

Jeena gave Richard a tired smile as if to say 'My work is never done.' She looked back at the guard. "Give my regards to the high lord. Tell him I am planning on reporting to the council as soon as I finish getting things organized here."

Richard noticed the guard bite his lower lip before glancing at the ground and then back up. "The high lord said to tell you it was most urgent, High Priestess."

Jeena sighed. She glanced at the Tree of Light before returning her attention to the guard. "Tell the high lord I will be there shortly. I must see to the needs of my bondmate first."

"The high lord said—"

Richard noticed the silver in his bondmate's eyes flash.

"I said tell the high lord I will be there *shortly.*" In a softer voice, Jeena added, "Please."

The guard saluted before hurrying away in the direction of the palace.

"I don't want to be a bother," Richard said. "I can take care of myself. You go on."

Jeena smiled. Richard sensed stress, tiredness, and a little amusement through their bond link. The molten silver in her eyes seemed to speed up.

"I have no doubt you can see to your own needs," said Jeena with a laugh. "As to being a bother, I knew you were trouble the first time I laid eyes on you. I have a feeling both of us are going to be a lot of *bother* to the other in the years ahead."

Richard couldn't argue the point.

"You said we could take Uncle Rick home," said Terika who

had just walked up with a small group of the other children. "You haven't changed your mind, have you Aunt Jeena?"

"No, I guess not," said Jeena. "I just thought that maybe I should—"

"It'll be fine," Richard said figuring the best way he could help his bondmate was to get out of her hair and let her work. "With these two to watch out for me, what could happen? I'm sure I'll be in good hands."

"Well, all right," said Jeena allowing herself to be convinced. "I will be home as soon as I can."

Richard noticed Jeena stare at the ground before looking back at him. He sensed something like embarrassment through their bond link. "Is something the matter?" he asked, wondering if he'd done something wrong.

Terika burst out in laughter. "Aunt Jeena is not known for her housecleaning abilities. Fortunately for her, my mother and Lord Reale are. They spent two full days cleaning your home while you were away."

"They did what?" said Jeena frowning. "My books and—"

"Relax," laughed Matisa moving beside Terika. "They did not touch your scrolls and books other than straightening them up a little. I helped some too. We all know how particular you are with books. We just did enough to make your bondmate feel welcome when the two of you returned." The young elf girl turned to Richard. "My mother even left a few of Father's clothes for you. Of course, she had to let them out some, but I believe they will fit."

"See?" Richard told Jeena. "I'm in good hands."

"Very well," Jeena said admitting defeat. "Then I shall see you at home later." She placed her left hand on Richard's shoulder. "Do not make any plans for tonight."

Richard smiled thinking about what plans the beautiful elf might have for him. Some of his emotions must have passed down their bond link because he noticed her turn a slight pink.

"What I mean," explained Jeena, "is that I am going to recommend there be a bonding ceremony tonight. Two bonding ceremonies have been conducted since we departed. Neither of them resulted in a seeding. Even the recharging stands did not work. I will need to ask the Lady to be sure, but I suspect the way we healed the Tree of Light's offering link requires us to be here for it to work correctly. I want to test my theory. We have used a lot of the Tree of Light's Power helping the triplets create gates and time-bubbles. That Power must be replenished."

"So we'll be doing one of those watch-over things tonight?" Richard asked. To be honest, he was kind of anxious to see what one looked like when he wasn't the one getting bonded.

Jeena nodded. "That is correct. Now, I must be off. It takes time to plan a bonding ceremony."

Terika and Matisa each grabbed one of Richard's hands and began dragging him away.

"I'll see you tonight," Richard shouted over his shoulder.

The emotion that came down his bond link left little doubt he would.

CHAPTER 24

The blue glow from the gem at the top of the staff increased intensity as Lord Crendemor concentrated on making the Lady's staff do his bidding. Pinkish colored beads of sweat popped out on his forehead. He squinted, trying to ignore a drop of the stinging liquid as it made its way into his right eye. In spite of all he could do, he blinked. The blue glow decreased.

"No!" Lord Crendemor yelled. "I was so close!"

He looked around for someone to vent his anger on. The only other humanoid in the dimly lit cavern was the blood-soaked body of an elf tied on top of a nearby table. Her white skin and lifeless eyes made it obvious she was immune to any acts of frustration.

After reciting a calming mantra, Crendemor rose from his chair and picked up the Staff of the Lady of the Tree. The energy in the staff struggled against him but to no avail. He had long ago learned how to gain the upper hand. The blood of the elf he'd used to coat the staff streamed down the length of the wood, running over his fingers. Raising the staff, he forced magic energy through, intertwining its energy with the four corners enclosing the gate spell he'd cast earlier. The gate enlarged slightly before collapsing back on itself and disappearing completely.

Crendemor threw the staff on the stone floor in disgust. "It should have worked!" he yelled at the walls of his long-hidden sanctum.

Laughter echoed through the chamber. "Temper, temper, elf. Are you having problems?"

Crendemor mentally kicked himself for losing control in front of the Dalinfaust. Reciting a calming mantra, he remained silent until the heat in his face dissipated. Turning, he scanned the shelves lining the wall until he spied the round globe wedged behind two glass bottles that contained the hearts of past elf victims. He knew that he should ignore the demon but couldn't resist making a jab at his longtime adversary.

"So, you have decided to come and taunt me again," Crendemor said. "Any problems I have will soon be alleviated. You, on the other hand, are looking at another nine hundred and fifty years of torture by your brothers. I would suggest you concern yourself with your own problems before worrying about mine."

Frowning, Lord Crendemor edged closer to the shelf containing the scrying device he'd used in the past to communicate with the Dalinfaust. The round globe emanated Power. He pulled the head-sized glass ball from behind the two jars and set it on the worktable next to the deceased elf.

The globe looks brighter than it has in many years, Crendemor thought growing nervous. *The demon should be getting weaker, not stronger.*

A yellow eye appeared in the white smoke swirling inside the globe. The eye seemed to focus on the corpse of the elf. "Ah. I see you paid attention all those years while watching me torture my victims. Bravo. The greater the fear and pain of the victim, the more potent the energy in their blood." The eye moved from the dead elf to focus on Crendemor. "Still, the staff does not work, does it?"

Lord Crendemor was tempted to place the globe back on the shelf and ignore the demon's bantering but did not. *He knows something. He is trying to play me. He has information I do not.*

After a dozen seconds of silence, the Dalinfaust spoke again. "You have done well since I have been away, elf. The spells the gnome high priestess placed around your sanctum were formidable. Even after nearly ninety thousand years of deterioration, few mortals could have broken through."

"I do not need your empty brags on my abilities. What do you want, demon? Out with it, or I will destroy this scrying device like I should have done when I first entered my old laboratory."

The Dalinfaust laughed. "Yes, elf. You may destroy the device, but if you do, you will be passing up an opportunity to regain favor in my eyes."

The laughter bothered Crendemor more than the demon's words. "Ha!" Crendemor replied. "I am not the one trapped and helpless. I will have gained control of the staff and opened the gate long before you are released from your prison."

"Perhaps," agreed the Dalinfaust. "Although, perhaps not. I may not be as helpless as you seem to think, elf. Destroy the device if you like, but one day soon you may find me standing next to you in the magic dimension."

A drop of sweat trickled down Lord Crendemor's cheek. He wasn't scared, but the sound of confidence in the demon's voice was disturbing.

"You have my interest, demon. Say what you have to say. I must return to the council chamber soon. Why have you contacted me now?"

The yellow eye in the globe blinked. "That is more like it, elf. Even if you could gain control of the staff, it would not open the gate under the Tree of Light."

"That cannot—" Crendemor started before catching himself. "I was with the gnome when she closed the gate at Drepdenoris Mountain. Even from a distance of a thousand leagues, the staff easily gained control over the gate's magic."

The demon laughed again. "The minds of mere mortals continue to amuse me. You gain the smallest bits of knowledge and think you know all. The gate under the dragon's mountain was only partially opened. Only one of the four corners had been weakened by the spell I gave the necromancer. The gnome high priestess used the staff to renew the energy in the faulty corner and reclose the gate."

That piece of knowledge was not new to Crendemor. He had been with the foolish gnome when she'd used the staff to close the gate. Even at a distance, he'd sensed its flow of magic wrap around one of the four gate corners, strengthening its magic.

"You amuse me in return, demon," Crendemor said forcing a laugh out of this throat. "I was with the gnome, remember? I know all she did. I have learned much over the last fifty years. The staff bends to my will. I will soon be able to manipulate the staff's magic enough to control all four corners of the gate. The fool of a gnome shared all her knowledge with me. It is only a matter of time before I succeed."

Once again, the demon laughed. He laughed long and hard.

Doubts appeared in Crendemor's mind. *The demon is too confident. Have I made a mistake? My plan has been perfect. What have I done wrong?*

Lord Crendemor turned away from the scrying device and looked at his sanctum. Even after 90,000 years of abandonment, the magic of the place was strong and vibrant. Devices of torture were intermingled with worktables containing corpses in various stages of decay. A pentagram formed by bottles containing the blood of his victims drew his attention. The pentagram spell was strong, but even so, it appeared flawed.

Turning back to the scrying device, Crendemor stared deep into the yellow eye floating in the swirling smoke. "As I said, my time is short. If you have something to say, demon, say it. Otherwise, we are done."

The laughter stopped. "You will never succeed on your own, elf. The gnome did not share all she knew with you. The High Priestess Remozorz was not quite the fool you thought."

Crendemor's mind raced, but he forced his features to remain calm. "How so?"

"Ah," said the demon. "I knew you were not a complete fool. You have been a valuable asset to me at times in the past. I may allow you to be my servant again."

Anger burned in Crendemor's eyes. "I am no one's servant. I control the staff. You are the one in prison, not I."

The yellow eye blazed. "You control nothing, elf. You will never gain control of the staff without my help. You have tried for the past fifty years to wrest control of the staff's magic and open the gate. The reason you fail is because you are a creature of magic. The staff, on the other hand, is a mixture of magic and technology."

Lord Crendemor froze. Questions popped into his mind, but he forced his mouth to remain closed. He knew it would not pay to let the Dalinfaust see his confusion.

The Dalinfaust continued. "You see, elf, the two human children who accompanied the gnome high priestess placed a piece of technology inside the staff. It is hidden well by stealth shields, but it is there nonetheless. You have done better than you know in that the staff's magic can no longer resist your will. However, you lack control over the staff's technology. The human children attuned the technology to work with the magic of priests, not mages. It will never open the gate for you without my help."

I know technology, Lord Crendemor thought. *I use it, but it is foreign to me. I am a mage. If the demon is telling the truth, I may have to start anew. All I have done over the years will be for naught.* He stared deeper into the yellow eye. "What help can you give me that I cannot do on my own?"

"Ah, good. You are realizing the truth. You are and will forever be my servant. My time-commando is on his way here. He is a creature of technology. The simple controls the human children placed on the staff for the gnome are insufficient for our needs. My time-commando's battle computer can wrest control of the technology using his link to my time-commando. You will control the staff's magic. Together, the two of you can open the gate."

Crendemor frowned as he thought of possibilities. He'd worked with the time-commando in the past. "Your human is unreliable. Why would he help open the gate?"

"Fool," scoffed the demon. "Do you think I tell my servants all my plans? He comes for the bottle of DNA gas you have hidden here in your sanctum."

"I need the DNA gas to supply the Power to open the gate," Lord Crendemor said, then immediately chastised himself for giving that information to the demon.

The Dalinfaust laughed. "I read your mind better than you think, elf. Yes, the DNA gas will make starting the spell easier, but it is not the only way. I care not whether the human gets his precious gas. You will use the bottle to force his cooperation."

Lord Crendemor wondered if he could use the bottle of DNA gas to make the human his puppet. *Perhaps the two of us can open the gate without the Dalinfaust's help. Once it is open, I can kill the human. The demon armies will be mine to command.*

The Dalinfaust chuckled. "You are so predictable, elf. Do you think the gates were constructed so mere mortals alone could open them? The gates require energy from all three dimensions; magical, physical, and spiritual. The human will supply the technology. You will handle the magic. I will be the spiritual part of the spell to open the gate."

This time Lord Crendemor laughed. "Events are happening too fast. Do you think our opponents will sit around for nine hundred and fifty years until you are free? You are imprisoned. Perhaps I can convince one of your brothers to assist me. I do not need you—"

The yellow eye blazed, filling the cavern with its glow. "Fool! My brothers are weak. Only I have the knowledge and skill. Only I saw fit to remove four parts of me and place them in devices of technology to be used when needed. The four corners of the gate require demon essence to allow technology and magic to work in concert and open the gate."

The demon's words triggered memories in Lord Crendemor's mind. He knew the devices the demon mentioned. "You are talking about the phase rods of the humans. Your time-commando has one. My enemy has another. Where are the other two?"

"They are on the planet Storage in the physical dimension," replied the Dalinfaust sounding unconcerned.

"Do you still have the ability to teleport me to the physical dimension?" Crendemor asked.

"No," admitted the Dalinfaust. "Not yet. However, there is no need. One of the Dragar dreadnaughts will retrieve the two phase rods on Storage and bring them here."

"Portalis is shielded," Crendemor said. "No ship can land on this planet."

The yellow eye squinted, closing to a single slit. "Never assume you have knowledge I do not, elf. You are a useful servant, but I have others in the wings waiting to take your place. The Dragars will bring the two phase rods to you. That is all you need to know. My time-commando will bring the third when he comes for his DNA gas."

"What about the fourth?" Lord Crendemor asked knowing full well his opponent was even now in Silverton. "My enemy will not willingly allow his phase rod to be used in your plan."

The yellow eye opened seemingly amused. "No, not willingly. In the meantime, I will teach you the spells you will need and the knowledge to use the DNA gas to begin the opening process."

Lord Crendemor glanced at the bloody corpse on the table to his right. "I will need more blood to make the spells work."

"Yes," said the Dalinfaust. "You will need the blood of elf

children. A lot of elf children."

Thinking of how carefully the elves watched over their children, Lord Crendemor doubted he could ever capture enough children to make a difference. "That will not be easy, demon."

"Leave that to me, elf. I have a plan."

CHAPTER 25

The two children rushed out the rear ramp of the *Defiant* as soon as it dropped. A human-sized cockroach stood at the bottom with his two upper appendages opened wide.

"Keka!" yelled Brachia as he jumped into his adoptive father's embrace. "I missed you."

The translator on the cockroach's belt crackled. "As I have missed you, little one." Holding out a free appendage in the direction of the teenage girl still standing on the ramp, Keka said, "Are you so grown that you can't give your poor Keka a hug?"

Dren smiled. Throwing away her silly sense of teenage reserve, she ran into her father's appendages. "I'll give you all the hugs you can handle. I've missed you too, Keka."

"I hate to break up this little tear-jerker," said Sergeant Ron strolling down the ramp, "but we've got a war to fight, remember?"

Dren broke away from her adoptive father and looked back at the *Defiant's* captain. "We'll do our part here, Sergeant Ron. Will you be leaving right away?"

Sergeant Ron glanced over the numerous empty berths of the ancient spaceport. "Naw. I think we'll stay here a couple of days before heading back to the triplets. I don't suppose it would hurt to see if there's a little extra trading material around in some of the warehouses here. You never know when something might come in handy."

"Sergeant Ron, you can't just take things that don't belong to you," said Tia as she walked down the ramp arm in arm with

Matthew. "I think there's a word for that."

"Yeah, Grandfather," smiled Matthew. "It's called stealing. I hear they put people in prison for that."

"Ha, let 'em try!" Sergeant Ron replied. "Besides, it wouldn't be stealing. I'm sure Rick would summon anything I needed out of that bag of his if'n he was here. I just don't know what they've got in their warehouses, so I don't know what to ask him for."

A dozen hover vehicles pulled up and a score of octopus-looking technicians wearing orange vests and carrying various pieces of equipment exited. They immediately set to cleaning space residue off the *Defiant's* outer skin.

"Now that's what I like to see," said Sergeant Ron fairly beaming. "Service with a smile."

Dren noticed the old captain take a closer look at the natives of Storage.

"Or without a smile," said Sergeant Ron. "Do those octopuses even have mouths?"

"Oh, yes, we have mouths," said the closest technician through the translator on his belt. "We actually have two; an inner and an outer." The octopus creature twisted one eye on a raised stalk to look at the recon ship before swiveling the stalk back to look at Sergeant Ron. "We do not get many ships at the spaceport nowadays. My maintenance staff is at your disposal, Captain. What do you require?"

"Funny you should ask," grinned Sergeant Ron wrapping an arm around what might have been the octopus's shoulder. "It just so happens I've got a long list inside. Step into my office."

Dren watched Sergeant Ron disappear inside the *Defiant,* then turned to Tia and Matthew. "So what are you two going to do for the next two days? Got any plans?"

Tia shrugged her shoulders. "Other than get Matthew to familiarize me with the controls of that X-shuttle, I've got nothing on my agenda."

Looking back at the *Defiant*, Dren took a closer look at the shuttle anchored to the back of the recon ship. "Sergeant Ron doesn't leave anything behind, does he? What's he think he's going to need that shuttle for? It'll just get in the way if he gets in a firefight. From what Matt told me, the shuttle has very little in the way of weapons."

Matthew released his grip on Tia and turned to look back at the recon ship. "Yeah, well, that's part of the reason Sergeant Ron is staying planet-side for two days. He's hoping to get the Storageans to install armaments on the X-shuttle. I think he's trying to figure out how to use it as a heavy fighter-bomber or something like that."

Dren laughed. "Leave it to Sergeant Ron. If anyone can do it, he can." A thought came to her. "Keka, do you think Matt and Tia can stay with us for a couple of days? They might enjoy a tour of some of the warehouses."

Keka nodded. "I am acceptable to your suggestion. I will clear it with the port authorities. You can take them on the tube-train and show them a few of the sights. I will meet you in the lab later this afternoon."

"Omar and I are going too," said Brachia breaking away from Keka and grabbing Matthew's hand. "Come on, Matt. We men can lead the way for the fair damsels."

Dren watched her little brother drag the teen boy in the direction of the nearest tube-train access. She noticed Matt turn back to Tia and shrug his shoulders while mouthing, "What can I do?"

Tia laughed. "I guess it's just you and me, Dren."

"Ha, don't count on it," Dren replied. "My little brother might be a super-genius, but he sometimes forgets the simplest things."

"Like what?" asked Tia.

Dren reached into her pocket and pulled out a handful of tokens. "I'm the one with the money."

Both girls burst out laughing as they began walking toward the tube-train access.

Tia had a feeling it was going to be a very good day.

CHAPTER 26

The children tugged Richard up the marble steps. "Hurry. You're too slow."

"Hey, you're both wearing trousers," Richard said smiling. "I'm in a robe. My feet will get tangled if I try running up these stairs."

"See," said Terika. "I told you we should have taken him to Aunt Jeena's home first to change clothes."

"It is his home now as well," pointed out Matisa. "Besides, it would have taken too much time. Silverton has so much to see, Brother Rick. It will take days to see just the major points of interest."

"Longer," said Terika. "There are things a lot more exciting to see than this old library. I think we should have gone to the mages' guild. We could have watched the novices practice their spells."

"I like the library just fine," Richard said untangling his right foot from the hem of his healer robe. "If what Jeena tells me is true, she likes to read. I should see where she spent most of her youth."

Terika and Matisa laughed.

Richard thought they had nice laughs. From what little time he'd spent with the children, they weren't nearly as reserved as the elf adults.

"Oh, you do not know the half of it," said Matisa still laughing. "Wait until you see your new home. Libraries in some towns do not have as many books and scrolls as are scattered around the rooms in your home."

Richard envisioned stacks of books in crowded rooms. He had a feeling the children were exaggerating more than a little about the number of books his bondmate kept.

When they reached the top step of the library's entrance, Richard turned to look at the city. The top of the Tree of Light dominated the city center, towering over the other buildings.

"That's because very few of the city structures are more than two stories," said Nickelo in their shared space. *"The library and the palace are exceptions."*

Richard noticed four tall buildings resembling hundred-meter-tall obelisks. One was located in each quadrant of the city. The roofs of the tall buildings were each of a different color. One was blue, one was red, another was green, and the last was yellow.

"What are those?" Richard asked pointing to one of the obelisks.

Matisa let go of his hand long enough to point at each of the obelisks in turn. "Oh, that is the south corner. That is the west. There are the north and east."

"Corners?" Richard asked. "They don't look like corners to me. They look more like monuments." He smiled. "I think you have to have walls to have a corner."

Matisa placed her hands on her hips and stared at Richard. She wasn't smiling. "Not corners of walls, Brother. They are corners of a spell."

"The buildings are not the corners," corrected Terika releasing Richard's other hand. "They are just built over the corners of the gate spell."

The word *gate* drew Richard's immediate attention. "I thought the gate was located somewhere under the Tree of Light."

Terika nodded. "It is. I have never seen it, of course, since I have not been in the Presence of the Lady." She gave Richard a disbelieving look. "You were there. Did you not see it? The gate is a large boulder at the bottom of the lake in the Presence of the Lady. The gate is dormant, so it just looks like a house-sized stone, but surely you noticed the carvings on the rock."

Richard thought back to when he'd taken a swim in the lake during his bonding ceremony. "I, uh, had other things on my mind."

Matisa blushed. Terika did not. After glancing at each other, the two children grabbed Richard's hands and began pulling him toward the two massive bronze doors of the library.

Richard braced his legs and held the girls back, saying, "Before we go inside, can I ask the two of you something?"

The elf children faced him, smiling. Seeing the serious look on his face, their smiles dropped and were replaced by looks of concern.

"Have we done something wrong?" asked Terika.

"No, of course not," Richard assured his new niece. "On the contrary, both of you have been very friendly. I was just wondering why."

The two elves looked at each other before looking back at Richard.

"Are children where you come from not friendly?" asked Matisa.

"Yes," Richard replied before reconsidering his answer. "Well, sometimes. I guess it depends on the situation and their ages. What I was wondering, though, is that I'm a human and you're elves. Jeena warned me that some elves held animosity toward humans. She told me most females avoid touching humans."

Both girls dropped their hold on Richard's hands.

"Are you saying you do not want us to touch you?" asked Terika.

"Yes, uh, I mean, of course not," Richard said trying to phrase his question better. "I was just trying to figure out why neither of you seem averse to touching *me*."

Terika looked at the pavement, moving a small stone with the toe of her leather boot. Matisa glanced at her niece as if waiting for her to reply for both of them. Richard thought that a little strange since Matisa appeared to be the older of the two.

"I calculate Terika is the leader of the pair," said Nickelo in their shared space. *"You might want to keep that in mind."*

Terika stopped playing with the rock and looked at Richard. "It is true that elves are not fond of humans. I will not go into details or the history. It is just the way it is. You are human, but you are also the elf friend. You are the first elf friend named by the Council of Light in fourteen thousand years. The Lady herself named you elf friend for all to hear during your bonding ceremony. My friends and I have talked about our...uh...feelings during the time Aunt Jeena and you were gone. Matisa and I decided we would make sure we treated you like family. We convinced most of the other children they should as well."

"Because you *are* family," added Matisa.

"Are your parents okay with that?" Richard asked unconvinced.

"My parents are lords of the council of light," replied Matisa. "My mother encouraged me to accept you as one of our family. She said we owe it to Jeena to do so."

Switching to Jeena's niece, Richard asked, "What about your parents?"

Terika began moving the stone with the toe of her boot again. After a couple of seconds, she kicked the stone away and looked Richard full in the eyes. "I told my mother what I planned. She approved."

Richard caught the unspoken 'but' in her reply. "I gather your father doesn't approve." He shrugged. "I can't say I blame him. Jeena told me how humans killed her parents and sister. If I were Ceril, I'd probably hold a grudge as well." He glanced away for a second before looking back. "I'm glad you decided to be my friend; both of you."

A smile crossed Terika's face. "You are family, Uncle Rick. My mother has always told me that you can choose your friends, but you are stuck with your family."

An image of his brother Gaston flashed in Richard's mind. He laughed. "Amen to that, sister."

"I'm your niece," said Terika. "Matisa is your sister."

"So you are, and so she is," Richard said holding out both of his hands. "Now, shall we take the grand tour of the Library?"

The children smiled. Each took one of his hands in theirs while shoving against the massive doors with their other. The doors swung open easily as all three entered together.

CHAPTER 27

The demon Zenthra transmitted his final commands through the communication channel established by his brother. He burned with anger and hatred at being so reliant on the Dalinfaust.

I have no choice. The time will come, though, when I will be free. Then we shall see which of us is the more intelligent. My brothers may think they are smarter, but their wit is no match for mine. They will all kneel before me one day.

Zenthra started to laugh. His laughter was cut short by a bout of pain washing over him. When the pain eased, he checked the status of his Dragar servants.

They have positioned the dreadnaught for the jump.

Although his access to the Dragars' computer network was not what it had been, Zenthra had to give his brother credit. *Imprisoned and tortured as the Dalinfaust is, he somehow managed to acquire enough Power to provide an entry point and hack into the Dragars' computer network. I must learn his secret so I may do the same if the need ever arises again.*

Using various shipboard computers, Zenthra counted the magic weapons, missiles, and combat troops on the dreadnaught. *It will be more than enough to overwhelm what few defenses the Storageans have at their disposal. The two armored regiments onboard the dreadnaught should be more than adequate to retrieve the two phase rods.*

Zenthra tried to think of some way he could use the two parts of the Dalinfaust's essence in the phase rods to gain control over his brother. After considering options for several nanoseconds, he gave up.

I will have to go along with my brother's plan for now. Once I am free, I will hunt down the human who destroyed my computer avatar and take him captive. His torture will become legend among my fellow demons. Then I will enslave everyone in the physical galaxy and destroy them at my leisure. The demon armies will follow me, *not my brother. Somehow, I will think of a way to make it happen. For now, I will play the part of the fool and advance my brother's plan as he has requested.*

Zenthra sent the command for the jump. The black dreadnaught blinked out of existence two million years in the past, reappearing in the current time, in the physical dimension. Once the jump was complete, Zenthra scanned the surrounding space. The sensors on the black warship spotted a few stray starships in its vicinity, but none seemed aware an enemy had appeared in their midst.

Good, Zenthra thought. *The Dragars' stealth shield is holding. It will take two days to maneuver the dreadnaught within striking distance of the planet Storage. The foolish inhabitants will not know what hit them. My servants will retrieve the two pieces of the Dalinfaust, destroy the planet's warehouses, and kill every living thing on Storage.*

Zenthra laughed as he imagined the master's variable trying to summon items out of his dimensional pack and getting nothing back. *He will get nothing because the burned residue of an entire civilization will be all that is left on the planet.*

Zenthra gave the order for the dreadnaught to advance. He laughed again. Even a new bout of pain from his two brothers failed to subdue his good mood.

Two days, he thought. *In two days, I will be free.*

CHAPTER 28

The lizard-like cat clawed its way out of the ground until all four paws were hovering a handbreadth above the dried leaves on the forest floor. The night was dark, but ex-Wizard Scout Gaston Myers cared little for the lack of light. What he couldn't see through the night vision filter of his battle helmet, he sensed with his passive scan.

Spotting the lone elf in the clearing, Myers unhooked the strap of his saddle and slid to the ground. The lizard cat hissed, raising a claw as if to strike. A thought from the demon in Myers's helmet gave the creature pause. The claw lowered, although the hissing continued.

Ignoring his reluctant mount, Myers made his way toward the elf. From what he could tell, the figure was a young high elf similar in age to a human male in his mid-twenties. The high elf wore an elaborate blue robe. The elf hefted the white-carved staff in his left hand and stepped forward to meet Myers halfway.

"I think I liked you better as a dark elf," Myers said. "The white skin and blond hair don't suit you."

"It is good to see you too, my friend," snarled Lord Crendemor. "I see you are as lacking in manners as ever."

"You are no friend of mine," Myers hissed through gritted teeth. "I would as soon kill you as look at you."

"As I you, my friend," smiled Crendemor. He waved his free hand at his body. "Alas, this is not my true form. The bumbling oaf whose appearance I have taken has long ago succumbed to the worms and turned to dust." Pointing at the lizard-cat, he said, "I see you have found new transportation."

"It gets me around," Myers said hesitating to get caught up in small talk. He'd been around the dark elf far too long not to know the elf was dangerous. Behind any smile was a dagger waiting to slip between someone's ribs.

"I sense you are impatient to get started," said Crendemor. "Alas, it shall not be today. The high priestess has returned along with your brother. A bonding ceremony will undoubtedly be scheduled for tonight. The Presence of the Lady will be filled with fools donating Power to something beyond their ken. In the early morning hours two days hence, we shall spring our trap."

Myers eyed the elf. "Where is the bottle of DNA gas?"

Crendemor gave the tightlipped smile Myers had grown to hate. "It is safe. Never fear. You will be given it as soon as you have done your part. Once the bottle's energy has started the spell, the Dalinfaust has no more need for the gas. You may have it for your empress with his blessing."

Myers didn't trust either the demon or the dark elf but knew he had no other choice. He needed to do whatever it took to get the DNA gas for Diane.

"So what am I supposed to do for the next two days? Sit around with my thumb up my rear waiting for you to tell me it's time?"

Crendemor's eyes blazed, but the tightlipped smile never left his face. "No, my friend. I have a mission for you. You will not be bored. I assure you."

CHAPTER 29

Lord Sheshna looked down the table, past the high lord. "Why do you not answer, High Priestess? We are waiting."

Gripping the edge of the stone table with both hands, Jeena silently recited a calming mantra. When the knuckles of her hands returned to a more normal color, she glanced around the high lord and locked eyes with Lord Sheshna. She told the old elf, "Perhaps I do not answer because the question makes no sense. The elf friend does not report to the Council of Light. If the council does not wish my bondmate to reside in Silverton, I am sure he will leave if that is what the council desires."

"Not at all," said High Lord Trenadine ever the peacemaker. "Of course we are not asking the elf friend to leave. I have no doubt all the lords are grateful to the elf friend for healing the Tree of Light."

"Partially healing," corrected Lord Sheshna. "The past two bonding ceremonies have yielded no seeds. One can only wonder if perhaps the Lady no longer approves of the human."

Jeena glared at Lord Sheshna. "Do not presume to speak for the Lady. I am the high priestess, not you."

"Perhaps that is in question too," said Lord Sheshna a little heatedly. "A high priestess should not be leaving her duties to her subordinates on a whim. Perhaps—"

"Perhaps you should stop speaking of things you know nothing about," Jeena said before biting her tongue to keep from saying more.

"Please," said High Lord Trenadine. "This is getting us

nowhere." He looked from Lord Sheshna to Jeena and back to Sheshna. "You requested the high priestess here to voice your concern about the lack of additional seeding."

"I have already agreed to conduct another bonding ceremony tonight," Jeena said. "I told you the Lady believes the offering link will work correctly as long as Elf Friend Richard and I are here."

"Yes, so you have told us," said Lord Sheshna. "In his confidence that you would do so, the high lord sent messengers to the mountain villages earlier today to have them bring their expended magic items to tonight's ceremony to be recharged." Sheshna glanced at his longtime ally Lord Thalos before saying, "My concern is that the human—"

"The *elf friend*," Jeena said. "I find it condescending that you appear to go out of your way to call him human instead of using his title. Or due to your advanced years, have you forgotten that you are the one who recommended to the council that my bondmate be named Elf Friend?"

Sheshna turned red and started to rise but stopped when Lord Thalos placed a hand on his shoulder.

The gruff military officer stood instead. "I am a soldier," said Lord Thalos. "I have been for more centuries than you have seen, High Priestess. Lord Sheshna has voiced concern that the weapons of the elf friend may be the reason the Tree of the Light has been unable to produce seed since your bonding night."

Jeena started to protest, but the old general raised a weather-beaten hand. "Be that as it may, I ask you here and now. Should we or should we not be concerned by the elf friend's weapons?"

"Rick would never—"

"I did not ask if we should be concerned about the elf friend," said Lord Thalos. "I asked if we should worry about his weapons. We all sensed the evil in his sword when he drew it during your bonding ceremony. Do you deny it was demonic evil?"

Jeena bit her lip hard enough to draw blood. She sensed concern through the link to her bondmate. Forcing herself to control her temper, she sent an emotion that she hoped meant 'all is well' back down the link. The feeling of concern dissipated somewhat, but it didn't disappear completely.

The ring on Jeena's left hand tingled. *"Wise decision to calm things down,"* came Danny's thought. *"I calculate it would do you no favor to have Rick come storming in here because he thinks you are in trouble. Much as I like your bondmate, he is not known for his tact."*

In spite of the situation, Jeena smiled at the thought of her bondmate being tactful.

"Do I amuse you?" asked Lord Thalos. "Or do you believe my concern about the demon essence is a mere joke?"

Eyeing the old general for a half dozen heartbeats, Jeena shook her head. "No, Lord Thalos. Rarely do either you or Lord Sheshna amuse me. As to the sense of demonic evil in my bondmate's phase rod, it is no joke. However, Lord Sheshna's earlier request to have the elf friend hauled before the council and questioned like a…a—"

"The elf friend would not be *hauled in here*, as you put it," said High Lord Trenadine. "Lord Sheshna and some of the other council members merely wish to discuss the potential threat of the elf friend's sword with hi—"

"Not just his sword," said Lord Sheshna. "What do we know of any of his equipment? Until we ascertain its potential danger to our citizens, perhaps we should—"

Envisioning her bondmate's reaction to Lord Sheshna's questioning, Jeena stood and slapped the table. "Enough. My bondmate is the elf friend. He was blessed by the Lady. I will not see his motives questioned by you or anyone else."

The side door of the council chamber opened, revealing Lord Othellian, the second oldest member of the Council of Light. The old female took one look at the standing Lord Thalos and the high priestess before giving a knowing smile. "Ah, I see I have arrived just in time." She gestured at Lord Sheshna and Lord Thalos. "I had a feeling you two might use this opportunity to gang up on the high priestess."

"No one is *ganging up* on anyone, Othel," said the high lord.

"That is good to know," said Lord Othellian taking her seat at the table. "Then maybe Lord Thalos and Lord Jeehanathoraxen will consider sitting down so we can all discuss this like civilized elves." When neither Jeena nor Lord Thalos moved, Lord Othellian said, "That was not a request."

Lord Thalos glanced at Lord Sheshna. When the old lord nodded, Lord Thalos sat down. Jeena glared at Thalos and Sheshna gripping her staff so tight her knuckles turned white. At an "Ahem," from Lord Othellian, she relaxed her grip and sat down still glaring at the two lords.

"Now," said Lord Othellian, "we are all going to sit and discuss this until we come to a mutual agreement no matter how long it takes."

The ring on Jeena's hand tingled. *"I calculate it is going to be a long meeting."*

Jeena nodded her head. *"I have a feeling you are right, Danny. It is going to be a very long meeting."*

CHAPTER 30

"I've never seen so many books in one place," Richard said. "Do they all get read?"

Chief Librarian Elisinsar beamed with pride. "The Silverton library is just shy of a hundred thousand years old. High Lord Carndador and High Priestess Shandristiathoraxen started its construction shortly after planting the seed for the Tree of Light. Some of the scrolls in the library were ancient even then." The old elf pointed at a set of darkened stairs in the far wall leading down. "The older books and scrolls are kept in our subterranean chambers. Preservation spells keep the elements at bay." He looked back at Richard and smiled. "You asked if all of our books are read. The answer sadly is no. Although I am sure your bondmate would do so if she had the time and ability. As it so happens, about a third of the libraries contents are written in ancient Letian. No one has been able to read them since before Silverton was a sleepy little village called Silver."

Richard glanced at the row upon row of shelving crammed with scrolls and books on the first floor. He looked upward at the six floors above the main antechamber. Each of those floors contained a similar number of shelves. His passive scan picked up the tens of thousands of energy sources above and below ground, denoting the locations of books and scrolls magical in nature.

"If you can't read them," Richard asked, "then why keep them?"

The chief librarian's eyes widened. He opened his mouth, but no words came out. Terika and Matisa both laughed.

"A word to the wise, Uncle," said Terika attempting to control her laughter. "Do not let Aunt Jeena hear you say that. She thinks books are the Creator's gift to elven kind. She would probably consider it heresy if anyone suggested getting rid of a book."

"As would I," said the chief librarian finding his tongue. "Although I will be the first to admit I am not quite as fanatical about it as the high priestess." The old elf tugged at a strand of his long white hair before walking to a nearby shelf and pulling out a scroll as thick as an elf's arm. "This is a copy of one of the ancient Letian scrolls we keep in our subterranean vaults. This copy is over ten thousand years old. Three generations of scribes painstakingly worked to create this copy from the original text. Although no one can decipher the knowledge contained in this scroll. Who knows what secrets it may contain? Who are we to allow knowledge to disappear just because we cannot read it ourselves?"

When neither Richard nor his two young relatives replied, the old elf smiled. "Ah. You begin to understand. One day someone may translate this text or that of one of the other ancient scrolls. On that day, all the years of preserving the writing will be worth it."

Richard glanced at the rows of shelves again. "Maybe," he said noncommittally. "In the meantime, I'd best be getting home before Jeena comes looking for me." He almost turned to leave before remembering his manners. "Uh, thanks for showing me around."

The chief librarian smiled. "It has been my pleasure, Elf Friend. You are most welcome to come back anytime."

Taking the cue, Terika and Matisa grabbed Richard's hands, leading him out the entrance and back down the steps. The sun was just starting to set behind the mountains far off to the west. The clouds nearest the mountains resembled an ocean full of pink waves.

Freeing his right hand, Richard pointed toward the setting sun. "It's pretty."

"I suppose," said Matisa recapturing Richard's hand. "I have some friends who live in those mountains. Maybe I will get the chance to introduce you sometime. For now, we need to get you home. Father says there will be another bonding ceremony tonight. Terika and I need to get back to our homes to help prepare our meal for the midnight blessing."

"Maybe I'll see you there," Richard said.

"Of course you will," said Terika. "We are family. Families always sit near each other. Now hurry. We do not want to be late."

By the time the two elf children stopped in front of a modest, single-story, white adobe house, the sun had set behind the mountains. The silver glow from the trees lining both sides of the stone-paved road gave enough illumination for Richard to see.

"It's a good thing the trees are shinning," Richard commented. "I noticed there aren't any streetlights."

"Streetlights?" said Terika sounding puzzled. "Why would streets need lights?"

"Uh, so people can see where they're going," Richard said unsure why the young elf failed to figure out something so obvious.

Terika laughed. "Oh. I forgot. Humans cannot see in the dark. Elves do not need lights on their streets to see their way at night."

Richard sighed. "Hmm. Then I guess it's a real good thing the trees are shining because I'm blind as a bat without lights." Pointing at the small house, he asked, "Is this the place?"

"That is your home," said Terika. "It has been in the Thoraxen family since Silverton was called Silver. My father used to live here, but it is all Aunt Jeena's now. Uh...and yours."

Richard picked up a life form inside the house. It was not Jeena. He noticed no lights showing through the paned windows.

"Someone's inside," Richard said. "Don't your homes have lights?" He had a sudden vision of himself bumping into everything if he had to get up late at night.

Terika nodded. "Yes." She started forward.

Richard held her back. "Stay behind me, kids," he said gently pushing the two elves behind him before approaching the door.

In spite of his warning, the two children stayed close on his heels. Richard was about to turn and tell them to say farther back when the door swung inward.

"Terika!" said a voice filled with anger. "Get away from him. You too, Matisa."

Standing in the doorway was a silver-haired, silver-eyed male elf. Light from the nearby trees was bright enough to show the anger in the elf's eyes. Richard noticed that the elf's right hand rested on the hilt of his sword, but the weapon remained in its scabbard. He recognized the elf from his bonding ceremony. With his silver hair and eyes, he was hard to miss.

"Ceril," Richard said.

"Father," said Terika. "I was just—"

"I told you to stay away from the human," said Ceril speaking to his daughter but keeping his eyes on Richard. "You have no idea what humans are capable of doing. Neither do you, Matisa."

What an a-hole, Richard thought.

"Watch yourself, Rick," said Nickelo in their shared space. *"He is your new brother-in-law. It will do neither Jeena nor you any good to create unnecessary tensions in the family."*

"As for you, *human*," said Ceril spitting out the word. "Stay away from my daughter. You may have everyone else fooled, but not me. I know your kind. You are all the same. If it were up to me, I would—"

"Ceril!" came a feminine voice accompanied by the sound of running feet on cobblestone.

Richard took his eyes off Ceril long enough to glance over his shoulder. He saw a blonde female elf running down the street.

"I should have known you would be here," said the blonde elf. The female wove her way past the children and Richard to stand in front of the silver-haired Ceril with her back toward Richard.

Ceril glared at Richard over the blonde elf's shoulder before turning his attention to her. "Therasia, this is between him and me. I will not have—"

"He is the elf friend," said the blonde elf. "I told our daughter she could go with Matisa to show our new brother where to go."

"He is no brother of mine," said Ceril. "I will not have my daughter cavorting with humans. They—"

The blonde female waved a finger at Ceril. "He is your sister's bondmate. Nothing you can say or do will ever change that. He is not the one who killed your parents. You must learn to accept—"

"I will never accept—" began Ceril.

"Look," Richard said trying to make his way past the blonde female. "I don't want to cause any problem. I—"

Fire flared in the silver-haired elf's eyes. "Stay away from my bonded, human."

The elf swung a fist at Richard's face. Years of practice took over. Shifting to the right, Richard caught the elf's arm in a hand lock, forcing him to the ground. The elf was no slouch. He rolled, kicked out with his leg, and caught Richard in the chest, forcing him back.

"Stop it!" yelled the blonde female.

Terika cried, "Father, please!"

Richard stepped back out of range in an attempt to disengage.

Ceril jumped to his feet and drew his sword.

Richard's passive scan flared with energy as the magic in the sword activated. Without thinking, he reached through the side slit of his robe and pulled out his phase rod, activating it in full destructive mode.

Matisa screamed as a feeling of hunger emanated outward from the demon essence in the phase rod. The blonde female rushed to Matisa and Terika placing herself between the children and Richard.

"Rick," said Nickelo in their shared space. *"Are you planning to kill your own brother-in-law?"*

The glare of hatred in the silver-haired elf's eyes left Richard little doubt as to the murderous intent of his opponent. Overriding his militaristic instincts, he thumbed the rod's switch to stun mode. The feeling of hunger disappeared.

The elf thrust his sword at the center of Richard's chest. Knocking the blade to the side with his phase rod, Richard kicked out in a sweeping motion at the elf's legs. Ceril leaped over the sweep, spinning around as he aimed his sword at Richard's neck. Ducking below the glowing blade, Richard thrust out with the tip of his phase rod and hit the elf's sternum dead on. To his astonishment, the rod glanced off what felt like a surge of magic from the elf's tunic.

"He must be wearing magic chainmail underneath," warned Nickelo.

"Ya think?" Richard said as the elf changed tactics and began making intricate designs with his left hand while muttering words Richard heard but quickly forgot.

"Lightning bolt spell," said Nickelo.

"Ceril, no," said the blonde female rushing forward.

A ball of glowing magic appeared in Ceril's left hand. The elf laughed as if in triumph.

Off balance, Richard threw his phase rod and guided it toward the elf's head using telekinesis. The rod hit dead on, knocking the elf back into the side of the stone building. The ball of magic formed by Ceril remained suspended in midair. Its glow increased significantly.

"It's going to overload," yelled Nickelo over the battle helmet's speaker on the side of Richard's pack.

A line of magic reached out from the blonde female and wrapped the two children in a shield. Richard intuitively knew the elf's defensive spell wouldn't be completed in time. Wrapping pure Power around the overloading lightning bolt spell, he drew the magic ball into his hands and pulled his body around it as he fell to the ground. Just as he hit, he converted his Power into a defensive shield, praying it would be strong enough to contain the spell.

Boom!

The electrical shock blew Richard three meters into the air. He came back down, hitting the ground hard. Every muscle in his body burned with pain. He vaguely heard shouts behind him and what sounded like the pounding of horse's hoofs. He heard his battle computer trying to tell him something in his shared space, but his befuddled mind couldn't make out the words. He felt hands turning him over, then stared up through strands of silver hair into two molten-silver eyes.

CHAPTER 31

The meeting dragged on with one useless argument after another as most meetings with Sheshna did. Jeena didn't hate the old elf, but her patience with him had worn out long ago. Her patience with Lord Thalos wasn't in much better shape.

"I do not care what you think, Sheshna," Jeena repeated for what seemed like the tenth time. "If you think my bondmate is going to—"

A feeling of confrontation coming down her bond link drove any thoughts of her rebuttal away. She sensed a similar feeling through the emotional link she shared with her brother Ceril.

"No!" Jeena said jumping from the table. She bolted off in the direction of the palace gardens.

She heard High Lord Trenadine shout, "What is it?"

Ignoring the question, Jeena ran between the columns separating the council chamber from the gardens beyond. Wasting no time, she sent a hasty spell out the end of her staff that blew out a side door in the wall of the garden. After her many years growing up in the palace, she knew palace messengers would be waiting outside. As the splintered pieces of wood continued falling to the ground, she passed through the opening to the street beyond. She heard shouts and running feet behind her but paid them no heed. As she'd hoped, two startled guards stood outside holding the reins of a half dozen rearing horses. The guards were attempting to control the frightened animals. Jeena jerked a set of reins from a guard as she leaped into the saddle of the closest steed. With a hard kick of her boot heels, the stallion bolted forward down the alleyway heading to the main street. Shouting encouragement to her running mount, Jeena weaved the warhorse past startled pedestrians. Above the yells of those she passed, she heard the clattering of multiple hoofs behind her.

Emotions of anger coming through the link with her bondmate and the emotional link to her brother told her all she needed to know. The two people she cared most for in the world were locked in battle.

"Lady, no," Jeena pleaded to the tickle at the back of her mind. *"I should have foreseen this. Please stop this before someone is hurt."*

A drop in the reserve she shared with Ceril told Jeena that her brother was preparing a spell. From the amount of Power being removed, she feared it was going to be a big one.

"No," Jeena shouted digging the heels of her boots hard into the sides of her running mount. Although already at a full gallop, the stallion somehow picked up speed. She turned a corner of the darkened street onto the path leading to her home.

Boom!

A flash of light illuminated figures near Jeena's house. She saw her bondmate being thrown into the air. Her brother was sprawled at the base of the stone wall by her door. A wide-eyed Matisa stood nearby with hands to her mouth. Her sister-in-law Therasia and niece Terika were running toward Ceril.

The light of the explosion ended. As her night vision returned, Jeena noticed her bondmate hit the ground and bounce up several handbreadths before falling back again.

Jumping off the stallion without taking the time to stop, Jeena half-ran, half-fell to her bondmate's side. Kneeling beside him, she turned him over and searched his eyes for any signs of life. "Rick, speak to me."

Her bondmate didn't speak, but a wave of burning pain through their bond link assured her he was still alive.

He blinked, trying to focus on her. "Jee—" he tried to say unable to finish her name.

Jeena sensed Power wrapping around her bondmate. Even as she watched, she felt the pain coming through their link decrease. The ring on her left hand tingled.

"He is a wizard scout," explained Danny. *"His self-heal is*

repairing the damage to his body. He will be fine in another minute. Wizard scouts are hard to kill. Trust me."

Jeena released her bondmate and twisted around, jumping to her feet. Magic flared in her staff as she slammed the base into the stone pavement. The stone cracked as the ground shook. The glass panes of her living room window shattered, sending shards onto her brother as he tried to reach for his fallen sword.

Mouthing a single-word levitation spell, Jeena sent her brother's magic blade clattering down the path past the running horses of Lords Sheshna, Thalos, Othellian, and High Lord Trenadine.

"No!" Jeena told her brother in warning. "If you so much as start a spell, I swear it will be the last words you ever utter, Brother."

Her sister-in-law Therasia interposed herself between her bonded and Jeena. The blonde elf pulled Power from her reserve but made no attempt to form it into a spell. The determined look on Therasia's face told Jeena the normally good-natured elf was just as prepared to defend her bonded as she was to protect hers.

The young Terika wrapped her arms around her father's neck, weeping and crying, "No, Father. No. Please."

High Lord Trenadine quickly dismounted as did the others. The high lord positioned himself between Therasia and Jeena. "I will have none of that. Stand down, both of you." Not waiting to see if the two females complied, the high lord faced Ceril. "What is going on? Explain yourself, Ceril."

Extracting himself from his daughter's grasp but keeping an arm around her, Ceril pointed at Richard who was just rising to a sitting position.

"I was protecting my family from this *human*," growled Ceril, "as any elf would. I told him to stay away from them. When he attacked—"

"Attacked?" said Lord Sheshna keying in on the word. "I warned you, High Lord. Did I not say—"

"Silence," said High Lord Trenadine in a rare fit of anger. He looked at Therasia. "Did the elf friend attack you or the children?"

The blonde elf glanced back at Ceril before returning her gaze to the high lord. "It all happened so fast. When the demon scent came out of the elf friend's sword, I—"

"See?" said Lord Sheshna. "I warned you about the danger of

letting a human walk around with weapons."

"Elf Friend," said High Lord Trenadine ignoring Lord Sheshna. "Did you draw your sword against Ceril?"

Jeena saw her bondmate nod his head as he staggered to his feet. She placed a hand under his arm, holding him steady. The red glow of the phase rod lying on the ground made it obvious to all that the weapon in question had been drawn. Thankfully, she sensed no evil coming from the weapon as she had during their bonding ceremony nine days earlier.

Her bondmate pointed at Ceril. "I drew my phase rod when he drew his sword. It was self-defense."

Lord Sheshna walked over to the glowing phase rod and reached down with his left hand. The red glow disappeared as the rod retracted into the grip. The handle rose into the air and flew into Richard's left hand.

"That's not yours," said Richard.

Even with just the glow of the silver elms for illumination, Jeena noticed Sheshna's face turn a deep red. The old elf raised his staff, but Lord Thalos caught Sheshna's arm and held it in place. When Sheshna looked, the elf general shook his head.

So, Jeena thought, *Thalos has a calmer head than Sheshna. I would have thought the opposite.*

Pointing at the handle in Richard's hand, Lord Thalos said, "That weapon is too dangerous to be roaming around our city."

Richard faced the old general while pointing the handle of his phase rod at Ceril. "No more dangerous than that elf's lightning bolt spell. He's so consumed with hate, he didn't even consider the fact that the spell would've hit his own family as well as me." Looking at Ceril, Richard added, "Did you?"

"I…" muttered Ceril before glaring at Richard. "You are a human. You are a murderer just like the rest of your kind. You should all—"

"My kind?" laughed Richard in an exceedingly unfriendly manner. "I'm not even from this dimension, much less this planet. I may look like the people you call humans on this planet, but you're closer on the evolution scale to them than I am. If you want to hate someone so bad, hate yourself, but leave me out of it."

Jeena sensed the anger ready to explode in her brother. She hurried to defuse it before Ceril made matters worse. "He is right,

Brother. I have been to the dimension my bondmate calls home. He is not from Portalis. He is the elf friend. You have no cause to hate him."

Ceril wiped a trickle of blood from his mouth, spitting more on the ground. "I do not care where he is from. He is a human. They are all the same."

Terika broke free from her father and rushed toward Richard with raised fists. Therasia caught her daughter before she could get past.

"I did not want to believe what Father claimed about you, Elf Friend," said the tear-streaked Terika. "Now I know he was right. You hurt my father. I hate you. I never want to see you again."

Jeena watched her niece bury her head in her mother's breast. Therasia wrapped her arms protectively around her daughter. Matisa stood teary-eyed near her father, High Lord Trenadine. The high lord appeared bewildered as to what to do next.

Lord Sheshna leaped on the opportunity in an apparent attempt to take charge. "Elf friend you may be, human, but we will have that sword and the rest of your equipment as well."

Jeena noticed her bondmate give a tightlipped smile that sent a shiver down her back. *Sheshna is overconfident,* she thought. *He has no idea of my bondmate's capabilities.*

The ring on her finger tingled. *"Do even you, High Priestess?"* asked Danny in their shared space. *"I, for one, do not know the full extent of the wizard scout's abilities. Even with four to one odds, if it comes to battle, my credits are on the wizard scout."*

"Not four to one," Jeena thought back as she stepped to stand beside her bondmate. *"Four to two."*

* * *

Richard sensed an emotion come down his bond link that seemed to say "I am with you" when Jeena stepped next to him. He looked at the four elven lords opposing him.

"All four may not be against you" Nickelo pointed out in their shared space. *"I calculate the two older males are the ones to watch. The high lord and the old female may remain neutral if it comes to a fight."*

"If someone's not with me, then they're against me as far as

I'm concerned," Richard replied continuing to grow more irritated as the situation spiraled out of control. Reaching out with an active scan, he located each of the four lords' links to their Power reserves. As he expected, they were unprotected. He wrapped Power around them in preparation for disabling the links but left the links as they were for the moment. All four lords appeared oblivious to their danger.

"What do you expect?" asked Nickelo. *"Few magic users in the current time know how to protect links. Even your bondmate's link was unprotected until you started placing traps on it last week. By the way, what are you going to do about Jeena's brother and sister-in-law?"*

Reaching out with two more lines of Power, Richard wrapped the links of his new relatives as well in case either tried anything.

"Six lines of Power out at the same time is stretching it," said Nickelo. *"Are you sure you can control all six at once?"*

Richard didn't know, and he really didn't care at the moment. He faced the old elf Jeena called Lord Sheshna. "You know, it never ceases to amaze me how things change. Nine days ago, before all of your staffs and magic items were recharged, it was 'Oh, thank you, Elf Friend.' Now, when you're standing there with your staffs fully charged and your necklaces, rings, and wands that you carry glowing with energy, you're giving me an ultimatum to turn over my own equipment."

High Lord Trenadine raised a free hand. "Ultimatum is much too strong a word, Elf Friend. I believe what Lord Sheshna and Lord Thalos meant to say was that we should discuss things and—"

"You may call it an ultimatum or whatever you want," said Lord Sheshna. "The end result is that we will not allow you to keep your weapons or any of your other equipment until we have thoroughly checked it out. We will not allow you to wander around Silverton carrying those abominations."

Eyeing the four lords, Richard had a feeling his battle computer's earlier analysis was correct. Neither the high lord nor the old female looked as if they wanted to fight. Even the military lord Jeena called Thalos seemed leery of escalating the situation. Only Sheshna seemed eager to force the question.

"Just remember," said Nickelo in their shared space, *"you can*

block the links to their Power reserves, but they will still have their staffs and other magic weapons. Your victory is by no means assured."

A part of Richard didn't care, but another part had no wish to harm his bondmate's family members. *"I suppose killing Jeena's brother or adoptive father might put a damper on any future family get together."*

"No doubt," said Nickelo.

"Then I will leave Silverton," Richard said speaking to the high lord. "Problem solved." He glanced to his left. "Jeena, you once told me that you would go with me to live with my people. I've tried yours, and it obviously isn't working out. Are you prepared to leave with me now?"

To her credit, his bondmate didn't hesitate to answer. "Give me five minutes to go inside and pack a few things. Call your spirit-horse. We can leave as soon as he gets here."

Jeena stepped toward the door of the home, shoving Ceril to the side. Richard fought down the desire to force his way past Jeena's brother as well to prove a point, remaining where he stood.

"Wise decision, Rick," said Nickelo. *"There is no use aggravating the situation. Maybe we can return to the physical dimension without a fight after all."*

The lingering burning sensation around Richard's stomach made him want to argue he'd already been in a fight, but he kept the thought to himself.

"Go if you want, High Priestess," said Lord Sheshna, "but the staff you carry belongs to the Lady, not you. It stays here."

Jeena let the staff fall from her hand, landing in the grass to the side of the dirt path leading to the door. She kept walking without looking back. When she got to the door, she reached out for the handle.

"Wait," said the old female lord standing near the high lord. "This does no one but our enemies any good."

Jeena stopped with the door partially opened, remaining that way for a dozen heartbeats. No one said anything, not even Richard. Slowly, Jeena closed the door and turned to face the old female. "You are ever the wise head in the crowd, Lord Othellian," she said. "I think that is why I have always respected you. Unfortunately, this time I see no way out of the hole we have all dug for ourselves." She pointed at Richard. "My bondmate came here based upon our promise of friendship. Yet he has been attacked and accused. The humans in his dimension treated me with far better courtesy while I was among them. What I have witnessed here tonight has made me ashamed to call myself an elf."

"Jeena," said High Lord Trenadine, "I—"

"Why?" asked Lord Othellian.

Richard saw Jeena frown. He was puzzled by the old female's question as well.

"Why what?" asked Jeena. "Why am I ashamed?"

Lord Othellian shook her head. "No. I mean why does the elf friend need his weapons and equipment while he is in Silverton?"

Richard snorted, gesturing at Ceril with the handle of his phase rod. "You mean besides the fact this guy tried to run me through with his fancy sword?"

The old female looked at Richard, giving what he took to be a faint smile. "Yes, besides that. Why do you need your weapons and equipment while you are here? You seem like an intelligent being…" she said this time giving a definite smile, "…for a human. I am sure you can understand our concern about the demon presence in your weapon."

"Oh, she's good," said Nickelo. *"I bet she could teach you a few things about tact and defusing situations."*

Richard had to admit the old woman's attitude was growing on him. Instead of automatically giving a flippant reply, he decided to answer honestly. "I have many enemies. I may need to protect myself. Also, if I get called away, I will need my equipment on short notice."

"Actually," said Nickelo in their shared space, *"I do not believe that is true any longer. Your bondmate has an agreement with* 'the One.' *He will no longer send you on missions without consulting you first. In return, your elf said she would not short-circuit the entire tele-network and take out* 'the One' *and every other computer in the galaxy."*

"Can she do that?" Richard asked.

"Well," said Nickelo, *"I do not have enough information to calculate the odds. However, at least a small probability must exist because* 'the One' *certainly has changed his ways a little. I*

calculate when 'the One' *placed part of himself in you that he made himself vulnerable."*

Richard didn't bother pointing out that his battle computer was part of *'the One.'* He had no desire to hear Nickelo claim he had no knowledge of such in his databanks.

Richard refocused his attention on the old female. "Anyway," he told Lord Othellian, "those are the two main reasons."

The old female didn't seem put off. "What if the lords of the Council of Light guaranteed your safety while you are here?" asked Lord Othellian. "If you turn over your weapons and equipment just long enough for us to check them out, I promise that I will fight to the death to protect you until you get them back."

"As would I," said High Lord Trenadine.

"And I," said Jeena sending an emotion down their link, leaving no doubt she meant what she said.

Lord Othellian faced the two remaining lords.

Lord Thalos broke first. "I am a soldier. My duty is to protect anyone in our lands. Of course I will fight to protect the elf friend if his enemies try to harm him while he is here."

The old female lord switched her gaze to Lord Sheshna. It seemed to Richard that they were having a staring contest for several seconds.

Finally, Lord Sheshna looked away before turning to speak to the high lord. "My only concern is and has been the safety of the citizens of Silverton. If the elf friend surrenders his weapons and equipment—"

"*Temporarily* surrenders," said Lord Othellian.

"Of course," said Lord Sheshna. "If he were to give us his equipment long enough to allow us to verify its safety, then I swear as a lord of the Council of Light that I will fight to protect him as I would any other resident of Silverton. The elf friend's enemies will be my enemies...if he surrenders his equipment."

"And if I choose to leave or need to go on a mission?" Richard asked. "What then?"

"Then your gear will be returned to you, Elf Friend," said High Lord Trenadine seeming to grow relieved at the possibility of averting a crisis.

Richard pointed a thumb in Ceril's direction. The silver-haired elf had remained silent during the interchange, but the flames of hatred still flared in his eyes. "What about this guy? I don't feel like walking around town always wondering if I'm going to be attacked."

"Ceril?" said Jeena. "What say you?"

Jeena's brother stepped next to his bonded and daughter, placing an arm around Terika. "I care not what the human does as long as he stays away from my family. If the human gives up his demon weapon and stays clear of Therasia and Terika, I will cause him no harm."

"Your word?" asked Jeena.

Ceril didn't look at Richard but instead stared at his sister. "I give my word as a member of the Thoraxen clan. Just keep him clear of my family. You will always be welcomed in our home Sister, but he is not."

Jeena said nothing, but Richard felt her emotions. *She will never set foot in her brother's home again,* he thought. *I'm sorry I brought my bondmate trouble.*

Lord Othellian pointed a wrinkled hand at Richard. "So, Elf Friend. Are you satisfied?"

Richard locked eyes with Jeena. The mix of emotions coming down their link told him all he needed to know. She would go with him wherever he asked, but her home was in Silverton. *She wants to stay, but she will never ask.*

Sighing, Richard removed his pack and dropped his phase rod into the open flap. Reaching through the slit in his robe, he took off his utility belt and dropped it in as well. He left his battle helmet hooked to the outside of the dimensional pack.

"You know, Rick," said Nickelo in their shared space, *"if you put me inside your dimensional pack, maybe we can get* 'the One' *to teleport one of your replacement packs to you. Then you could summon me back. No one here would be the wiser."*

"No," Richard said. *"I'm not a liar. If I make a bargain, I'll keep it. Besides, unless they somehow take you off-planet or put my pack in some high-tech security vault, I'll still be able to talk to you."*

"True," admitted Nickelo. *"We have communicated up to a quarter of a light year distance before. Plus, your dimensional pack and this battle helmet have been previously tagged. If push*

comes to shove, you can always summon them back to you. But then you already knew that, didn't you?"

Richard resisted smiling as he held out his pack. "I can get this back whenever I want, right? No questions asked?"

"Of course," said the high lord reaching out. "It will be in the palace armory anytime you need it."

Richard pulled his pack out of reach of the high lord. "No."

The look of relief that had been building on the high lord's face disappeared.

Walking to stand in front of Lord Sheshna, Richard held out his pack with the attached battle helmet. "I want you to keep it. That way there can be no claim of someone giving me my equipment behind your back."

The old elf's eyes widened to be replaced by a look of triumph. Taking the pack from Richard, Lord Sheshna raised the flap and peered inside. His eyes widened again before narrowing. Looking up he said, "It is empty. Where is the demon weapon?"

"It's back in my home dimension," Richard said.

"I demand that you bring it back," said Lord Sheshna.

"Why?" Richard asked deciding to use Lord Othellian's method of asking a simple question to defuse a potential crisis.

Lord Sheshna's face turned red in the light from the silver elms. "Why? Have you not been listening, human? So we can determine if the weapon is dangerous."

Richard gave the old elf the version of a smile he normally reserved for his brother Gaston. "I will save you the trouble. It is extremely dangerous. That's why it's called a weapon. But unless my memory is going bad, your concern was about having the weapon in Silverton. I've done you one better. It's no longer even in this dimension. The only way I have to get it back is with that pack. So…"

"So," said Jeena walking past Ceril to stand beside Richard, "as long as you have my bondmate's pack, his weapon will pose no danger to the citizens of Silverton. Also, without his pack, Rick cannot summon any of his equipment. He is keeping his part of the bargain. Are you suddenly changing your end? Or do you have some reason other than desiring to protect the citizens of Silverton for wanting my bondmate to give up his equipment?"

How the old elf could turn any redder was beyond Richard, but

Lord Sheshna did.

"How dare you question—"

"I have worked with you far too long not to question your motives, my dear Lord Sheshna," said Jeena. "I ask again. Are you changing the bargain?"

Richard had to give the old lord credit for not blowing his stack.

After a dozen heartbeats, the elf's face returned to a more normal color. He turned away from Jeena to look at Richard. "My word is my bond, human. I will store this bag as agreed. If you want it back and are prepared to leave Silverton, I will return it without question." With that settled, Lord Sheshna turned and made for his mount.

Lord Thalos followed close on his heels. Ceril guided his family to the road, staying well clear of Richard.

Once they were all gone, Lord Othellian spoke. "I hope the bonding ceremony tonight goes smoother than your homecoming, Elf Friend." The old elf laughed.

"What is so funny?" asked High Lord Trenadine.

"I was just thinking the elf friend has a habit of shaking things up whenever he is around." Facing Richard, she laughed again. "I think I am beginning to like you, Elf Friend. It was worth all the stress of the last few minutes just to see someone get the better of Lord Sheshna for once." She laughed even louder.

High Lord Trenadine and Jeena joined in.

Richard did not. He had a feeling he'd made a powerful enemy.

"What else is new?" asked Nickelo in their shared space.

"Not a thing," Richard thought back. *"Not a blessed thing."*

CHAPTER 32

Matthew followed the two women as they walked down the warehouse corridor a few steps to his front. Despite his professed desire to help with the tour, Brachia had quickly become bored and left for his lab.

Well, Matthew thought, *Tia and Dren have certainly hit it off. Tia hasn't spoken two words to me since Dren showed up.* He shook his head and smiled, wondering if he was getting jealous. *I suppose because I've been away from Tia for nigh on a year that I want every second to myself. I'm smart enough to know that will never do. Tia won't put up with a smothering relationship. Neither would I come to think of it.*

A strange feeling touched the edge of Matthew's senses. It came from a side corridor they were just starting to pass. He'd felt the sensation many times in the past whenever his uncle had activated his phase rod. The feeling was one of hunger.

"We're near Rick's gear, aren't we?" he said stopping to face the direction of the hunger.

Dren and Tia halted and looked back.

"That's right," said Dren. "This warehouse stores a lot of the small arms and miscellaneous equipment. There's a room at the end of that corridor devoted to Rick's standard weapons along with his extra battle suits and helmets. His phase rods are there as well. Last time I checked, he still had over ninety of them."

"Can we take a look?" Matthew asked unsure why he wanted to visit the source of the hunger but certain he needed to do so.

Dren shrugged. "Sure. It's not like we're on a schedule or

anything. I just thought you'd find some of the miscellaneous stuff more interesting. A few of the things in this warehouse are strange, to say the least."

"I'd kinda like to see Rick's gear," Matthew insisted. "If that's all right with you, Tia?"

Tia shrugged. "Makes no never mind to me. I find it all pretty interesting. I wouldn't mind having one of those dimensional packs of Rick's myself. It would come in handy."

"No doubt," Matthew agreed as he followed the women toward their new destination. Along the way, they passed several octopods wearing orange suits. He unconsciously moved to the side to avoid touching what he assumed were slimy creatures. While he was used to being around a myriad of species, something about the multi-tentacle Storageans rubbed him the wrong way. He noticed several of the octopods greeting Dren as they passed.

"You seem to be well known," said Tia.

Dren laughed. "When you're one of a dozen or so humans on a planet consisting mostly of land-roving octopuses, you tend to stand out in a crowd."

Tia joined Dren in laughing. "I see your point." Gesturing at a door ahead, Tia asked, "Is that the place?"

Nodding, Dren passed her hand over a box at the left side of the door. The double door slid open, revealing neatly folded battle suits stacked on shelves opposite the door.

Following Dren and Tia through the doorway, Matthew noticed a line of battle helmets plugged into chargers on a long metal table. He counted seven empty charging stations.

"How many battle helmets does Rick have?" Matthew asked. "I'm assuming these are all his."

Nodding at an orange-suited octopod sitting at a work table, running tests on a battle suit, Dren walked over to the long table and picked up the first battle helmet past an empty charger, then tossed the helmet to Matthew.

Catching the battle helmet in one hand, Matthew flipped it over and checked the inside for the manufacturing tag. He saw only an embossed '8 of 55' on the inside rim.

"Fifty-five, huh?" Matthew said placing the helmet back on its stand. "Why so many?"

Tia laughed. "You've been around Rick long enough to know

he's not exactly easy on equipment. If he's only lost seven over the years, I think he's done pretty well."

A metallic click from the direction of the orange-suited octopod drew Matthew's attention to the translator box on the Storagean's belt.

"Actually," said the octopod rising from his bench on four of his eight tentacles, "the requestor has only had five battle helmets damaged beyond repair. The requestor currently has two helmets checked out of inventory."

"Two?" asked Tia.

"That makes sense," Matthew said. "Rick gave Gaston one of his battle suits when we fought those vampires on Portalis. Gaston still uses the battle suit Rick gave him. I've seen him in it. He's got one of Rick's phase rods as well."

Speaking to the octopod, Dren asked, "So two complete battle suits are checked out?"

"Negative," said the Storagean. "Two battle helmets are out, but only one battle suit. Only one phase rod is out as well. There were two checked out, but only one now." Gesturing at a meter-wide teleport pad in the corner of the room with a free tentacle, the Octopod explained. "The other battle suit and phase rod appeared on the teleporter an hour ago. I just finished installing a fresh isotopic battery in the phase rod a few minutes ago. The returned phase rod is on the rack over there now."

Matthew followed the gaze of one of the Storagean's eye stalks to a weapons rack along the far wall. In addition to a variety of rifles and pistols, the rack held a line of phase rods. The sensation of hunger he'd been feeling came from three rods separated from the others. He noticed an empty fourth spot next to the other three.

The Storagean must have noticed Matthew gazing at the empty spot. "Brachia modified four of the requestor's phase rods with energy sources he salvaged from another requestor's phase spears. I do not like maintaining those special phase rods, that's why I keep them separate from the others. One of the special rods is still checked out.

Matthew wandered over to the three special phase rods. The feeling of hunger grew stronger as he approached. He reached out a hand toward the nearest rod but pulled back before touching the weapon.

"Yes, you feel it, do you not?" asked the octopod. "Something has changed in the last two weeks. The sensations from the special phase rods grow stronger every day." Gesturing at the long line of phase rods located away from the three, the octopod said, "I much prefer working on those."

"Is something wrong, Matt?" asked Tia. "I mean, I don't like the feeling from those special phase rods either, but we've felt it before. It's that demon essence Brachia and Dren put in them."

"Don't involve me," said Dren. "Brachia can take all the credit for that. I only helped modify the battle suits so they would protect Rick from creatures in the void. The demon-essence thing was all Brachia's idea."

Matthew stared at the special rods for a couple of seconds before turning to look at Dren and Tia. "I know those phase rods have helped Rick during his missions, but I don't trust them. They seem to be getting stronger. I've never sensed the feeling of hunger before while they were deactivated."

A sensation of hate came from the rods.

"It's almost like they can understand what we're saying," Matthew said.

"Doubtful," said Dren. "It's just an energy source; that's all. I wonder why Uncle Rick turned his phase rod and battle suit back in but kept his battle helmet checked out. It's too bad. If Nick was here, I'll bet he could enlighten us on a few things."

The three of them remained silent while looking at the special rods. The feeling of hate dissipated. Matthew noticed the sensation of hunger did not. While he continued looking at the rods, he sensed the octopod return to his worktable.

Dren was the first to turn away and head for the door. "Come on, you guys. I want to show you something else in this warehouse before I take you to one of the heavy weapons warehouses. Those warehouses are in another city, so we won't be coming back here after we leave."

"Show us what?" asked Tia as she turned to follow her new best friend.

"Oh, you'll see soon enough," laughed Dren. "I don't want to spoil the surprise."

* * *

The Dalinfaust sensed the three humans leave the room.

So, they suspect my parts are getting stronger. I shall have to take more care to keep the growing strength of my connection hidden. It would not do to have them do something foolish like attempt to remove my essence from the phase rods ahead of schedule.

"*Fate is working to our advantage, brother,*" said Zenthra. "*The master's variable has sent his phase rod back to the planet Storage. My special operations team can retrieve all three of your parts and take them to Portalis. With the fourth part carried by your time-commando, we can open the gate enough to free us.*"

Anger burned in the Dalinfaust at his brother's intrusion into his thoughts, but he kept his irritation hidden. *I still need him,* he thought taking great care to prevent his brother's intrusion again. *Once the gate is open and I am free, I will place Zenthra back in his prison to start a new thousand-year period of torture.* The Dalinfaust laughed.

"*What is so humorous?*" asked Zenthra growing suspicious.

The Dalinfaust got control of his emotions before replying. "*Nothing to concern you, dear brother. I was merely thinking of the tortures you and I will inflict on Cancontus and Efrestra when we are free.*"

Zenthra laughed. "*Yes. Their torture will be good practice for what I will do to the human who destroyed my computer avatar. While our brothers' pain will only last a thousand years, his will be for all of eternity.*" Zenthra's laughter increased. "*I can picture all three of them now, screaming together.*"

So could the Dalinfaust, only the image in his mind was of all three of his brothers screaming along with the human. "*Yes, he will pay,*" agreed the Dalinfaust. "*In the meantime, you must concentrate on the task at hand. Your Dragar minions must get the three phase rods and take them to the point on Portalis where I tell you.*"

Zenthra stopped laughing. "*I told you their ship cannot penetrate the protective shield around the planet.*"

"*Two shields,*" said the Dalinfaust. "*Have you forgotten there is a separate shield protecting the elves' continent?*"

A sensation of hate came from Zenthra. "*I have not forgotten. Perhaps you are the one who needs reminding. The best my*

Dragar warship can do is orbit Portalis. They cannot take the parts of you that are in the human's phase rods onto the planet's surface. That is unless you have a plan you have not told me."

The Dalinfaust laughed. *Oh brother,* he thought. *I have many plans you know nothing about. Your infinitesimal brain could not handle all the plans I have made.* Laughing again, he sent his brother an image of the creature he planned to use to transport the demon parts to the desired location on Portalis.

Zenthra began to laugh. *"Yes. You have done well, Brother, to keep control over one of the spirit-cats while in our prison. I am curious why you did not just have the creature take your time-commando to the planet Storage to fetch the phase rods containing your parts. Why bother sending my Dragars?"*

The Dalinfaust wasn't in the habit of explaining his reasoning to any of his brothers, but this time he relented. He still needed Zenthra's cooperation to escape his prison. *"I deem it best not to let my time-commando know he can travel between dimensions using his mount. Your Dragars can fetch my parts and return them to the magic dimension. Once your black ship is orbiting Portalis, my time-commando can use his spirit-cat to fetch the phase rods from the Dragar ship and bring them to the surface of Portalis."*

"Then we will be free," said Zenthra.

"Yes," agreed the Dalinfaust. *"Then we will be free."*

CHAPTER 33

The inside of Jeena's home was clean but cluttered. Richard soon realized Terika hadn't exaggerated about the number of books and scrolls in the house.

"Get used to it," said Nickelo in their shared space. *"It is your home now as well."*

Home, Richard thought as a warm feeling washed over him. *I've never had a home before.*

Jeena scooted a small basket overflowing with scrolls out of the way with her foot. "I apologize for the mess. I suppose I really should return some of these books back to the library."

Shrugging his shoulders, Richard continued looking around the room Jeena had called her living room. As soon as they'd entered, she had pulled a thin chain on the wall near the door. Richard noticed the chain ran to a louvered opening in the ceiling that gave off light. He detected magic behind the louvers.

"I calculate a permanent light spell is in the cavity behind the louvers," said Nickelo.

"Calculated that all by yourself, did you?" Richard asked.

"Yes, I did," replied Nickelo ignoring the intended sarcasm.

Two comfortable-looking chairs were positioned near the broken front window. A cool breeze sent the silken curtains fluttering. A long wooden bench large enough to hold four elves was located on the opposite wall and stacked to overflowing with pillows.

Glancing at the floor, Richard noticed it was fully carpeted in a thick gray fur. Bending down, he rubbed his hand through the carpet, then smiled. "It's soft."

Jeena smiled back. "It is luxamar fur. Most of our home is carpeted with their fur. I have a set of slippers lined with it as well. Luxamar fur is warm in the winter and cool in the summer."

The word luxamar triggered a memory in Richard of a rabbit-sized animal with gray fur. "The entire house, huh? Must've taken a lot of luxamars, if I'm thinking of the right animal."

Jeena smiled. "Yes, it did, my bondmate, but not in the way you think. Elves don't kill luxamars for their pelts. We comb them to get their excess fur. It took many hundreds of years of combing to create all of the carpets in our home. I have certainly done my share of combing over the years."

Standing up, Richard said, "It's a nice house, Jeena. I wouldn't change a thing. Besides, the books and scrolls are stacked and sorted. I doubt they'll be in the way."

Jeena laughed. "Do not be so sure. Reale and Meshoan obviously spent some time straightening the place up." She glanced around the room. "To be honest, I normally have to move books off the furniture in order for guests to sit down."

Richard shrugged again. "I'll get used to it. How about giving me the rest of the grand tour?"

Nodding her head, Jeena led the way around the small, two-bedroom bungalow while explaining the various magical devices. Richard soon found the home had the equivalent of all the modern conveniences, the only difference being they were run by magic instead of technology.

After his bondmate explained how to operate the bathroom shower, Richard laughed. "I'm afraid that I'm a little short in the magic department. If I have to cast spells to make the shower work, I'll probably have to get used to being dirty. Or you'll just have to turn the hot water on and off for me."

Jeena gave him one of the smiles that made the world seem right. "Fret not, my bondmate. We will get one of the mages to cast some longer lasting spells in our home. It is something that homes with younger children have to do. Elf children are not born with the ability to cast spells, so we have ways of modifying homes to accommodate them. In the meantime, I will get the shower ready for you. We both need to change clothes before we leave for the Midnight Blessing." She eyed Richard. "Do you want to take your shower first, or shall I?"

Richard smiled. "You know, I'm not sure I trust myself operating this shower the first time all by my lonesome. Maybe we should try it together... uh, just for safety reasons."

Jeena returned his smile. "Yes, perhaps we should."

* * *

As they walked along one of the many white-stone paths in Silverton's central park, Richard smiled. Every silver elm in the park glowed with silvery light. Hundreds of elves were walking along the path in the direction of the Tree of Light.

"So you see," said Jeena continuing to explain the problem with the tree, "neither of the two bonding ceremonies conducted after we left resulted in a seeding. The Lady seems to believe it is but a minor problem. We can only hope. Six bondmates have volunteered to participate in the ceremony tonight."

"Only six couples?" Richard asked. "I thought there was room for ten pairs in the Presence of the Lady."

Laughing, Jeena tightened her grip on Richard's left hand. "Eligible bondmates do not grow on trees, Rick. Twenty sets of new bondmates participated in the previous two ceremonies. High Lord Trenadine had to scour the lands far and wide to find six more pairs who had yet to conduct their bonding ceremony. Typically, only a few dozen elves a year become bondmates. If the ceremony tonight does not produce seeds, it could be two or three months before we have another Midnight Blessing."

"Oh, I didn't know."

Jeena laughed again. Richard liked it when his bondmate laughed. In addition to the musical quality of the sound, the feeling of joy he sensed through their bond link was a pleasure all in its own.

"Well, now you know," said Jeena. "The Council of Light sent messengers to all the villages within riding distance to bring their depleted magic items to the ceremony tonight."

"I wonder if the council is a little too confident we'll be able to fix the problem."

Jeena smiled. "You are the elf friend. I have a feeling the Silvertine elves are growing used to expecting miracles from you."

Richard shook his head. "That's not exactly what I wanted to hear. I'm just a man."

"Yes, you are," agreed Jeena. "Be that as it may, I also have begun to expect miracles from you."

Grinning, Richard said, "Great. No pressure. By the way, where do you want me to be during the ceremony? I've a feeling sitting anywhere near your brother wouldn't be a good idea."

The smile on Jeena's face disappeared. "No, it would not. I am very sorry, Rick. I suppose we both brought baggage into our bonding. As far as where to sit, Leethor and Meshoan have offered to have you and I perform the watch-over with them tonight. You like them, right?"

Richard nodded, remembering how Leethor had led the elf guards who'd accompanied King Halmafad and him to Silverton. He thought about how Meshoan had been injured during an orc ambush, forcing him to heal her. "I do like them. Even their children were friendly to me the night of our bonding ceremony."

Reaching the center of the park, Richard and Jeena stood admiring the Tree of Light hand in hand for several minutes. He would've been content to remain that way longer, but a forester came and fetched his bondmate away. Before she left, Jeena pointed him in the direction where Leethor's family normally sat. Richard wove his way through the crowd, finding himself besieged by children and adults alike.

"Guess they do not share your brother-in-law's opinion of you," said Nickelo in their shared space.

"Good thing," Richard said. *"Otherwise I'd probably be tarred and feathered by now."*

"Elf Friend," came a shout from the left.

Looking over, Richard spotted Leethor standing near a blanket, waving a hand to get his attention. Meshoan sat near him holding on tight to two small elf children trying their best to escape their mother's grasp. Richard remembered the children's names were Leenador and Meenish.

Weaving around several elf families sitting on blankets, Richard stopped at the edge of the colorful red and blue blanket upon which Leethor's family sat.

"Elf Friend," said Leenador and Meenish at the same time.

"You get to sit by me," said Leenador. If the young boy had

been a human, Richard would've guessed his age at four or five.

"That would be between eighty and a hundred in elf years," said Nickelo.

"Yeah. Thanks for the biology lesson," Richard thought back.

"You're welcome. That is what I am here for, oh most eager to learn of all wizard scouts."

Pointing at an empty spot on their blanket, Leethor guided Richard to a position between the two children. With the boy sitting to his right and the girl on the opposite side, Richard crossed his legs, making himself as comfortable as possible. The children began showing him the contents of their family's picnic basket, but in less than two minutes the novelty of having the elf friend with their family apparently wore off. The children soon wandered off to play tag with some of their friends.

"We heard you had a rough day," said Meshoan.

Richard noticed Meshoan had let her long brown hair down. Both Leethor and she were dressed in what Richard took to be standard scout clothing of brown and green pants and tunics. The two wore daggers but no swords.

"News travels fast," Richard said. He gestured at the elves' outfits. "Going casual, I see. Last time you were both dressed a lot fancier."

Leethor smiled. "Last time we were attending the bonding ceremony of an elf friend and a high priestess. Most bonding ceremonies are a lot less formal."

"Well, thanks for letting me stay with you 'til Jeena's free," Richard said appreciating the fact he had at least a couple of friends among the elves.

"And me," said a squeaky voice from behind Richard. He turned to see Rembis working his way toward them. The gnome magic user wasn't much taller than some of the smaller children, but his long white beard made him stick out.

"There you are," said Meshoan gesturing to one of the free spots on the blanket vacated by the children. "I thought you might not be coming."

"Ha," said Rembis. "I wouldn't miss it. I have never been to a bonding ceremony. Besides, I am not in the habit of passing up a free meal, even if it is at midnight."

"Are you staying at the palace," Richard asked.

Rembis shook his head. "No. Master Jathar found a room for me at the mages guild. Seems I am an adjunct instructor now if I want the position. Since I have nothing special going on, I thought why not?"

"The gnome is very logical," commented Nickelo in their shared space. *"I like him."*

"So do I," Richard replied back. *"And it has nothing to do with logic."* To the gnome, he said, "I guess I figured you would be leaving to go live with the gnomes in the western mountains."

Rembis snorted. "Not hardly. Nothing against the Portalis gnomes, but I was born off-planet twenty thousand years in the past. I have no ties to the gnomes in this land other than we look similar."

"Twenty thousand years in the past?" said Meshoan. She leaned toward the gnome. "How can that be?"

"Oh, it can be, believe me," Richard said. "Rembis and I were slave labor in some mining tunnels on an asteroid…err that's a small planet in outer space." He scratched his head and laughed. "It's a long story involving time-bubbles and starships. I'll tell you the whole boring tale one of these days."

"I doubt it will be boring," said Leethor. "Jeehana has told us of metal ships that sail between the stars. I will admit I have never fully believed it. But…" He turned away from Richard to the gnome. "So you come from twenty thousand years in our past?"

The gnome smiled. "Actually, I have been even farther back in time. Rick and I fought a battle together to destroy the Dragars' temple a hundred thousand years ago. After that, I spent most of my time with Queen Emerald and her dwarves in New Drepdenor. Then like a fool, I got captured again by the Dragars. That's how I wound up as a slave in those tunnels where I met Rick."

"So how'd you get captured?" Richard asked. "While you're at it, how'd you get off Portalis?"

The old gnome glanced at Meshoan and Leethor before looking back at Richard. "Maybe I shouldn't go into specifics right now."

Curious at the gnome's sudden secrecy, Richard waved a hand at the two elves. "Leethor and Meshoan are my friends. Whatever you have to say to me, you can say in front of them."

With a shrug of his shoulders, the gnome mage began his tale. "At Queen Emerald's request, I led a small band of adventurers back to the dwarves' home in Old Drepdenor."

"I take it you're talking about the original one near the Dragars' spaceport and not the one on the elves' continent, right?" Richard asked.

"That's correct, Wizard Scout. After your friends and you departed, Queen Emerald cleared the tunnels of Old Drepdenor of the vampire scum. She had us gather as much of the dwarves' wealth as we could carry and take it with us to the elves' continent. Once we arrived, the Oracle directed us to the mountain the elves now call New Drepdenor. Queen Emerald established the dwarves' new home there."

"So why did she send you back to Old Drepdenor?" Richard asked. "Was it to get more of the dwarves' treasure?"

Rembis shook his head. "No; at least not the treasure you think. You see, New Drepdenor has a gate similar to the gate here in Silverton."

A forgotten memory of a dragon ride to a mountain with a gate a hundred thousand years in the past popped into Richard's mind. "I left a three-headed dragon there to guard the gate," he said. "Were they still there when the dwarves arrived?"

"Aye, they were," said Rembis. "Or he was, or she was. I guess the gender depends on which part of that three-headed dragon you're talking to. Personally, I think the female is the wisest of the three, so I usually talked to her."

"And?" Richard asked.

Rembis frowned. "And…? Oh, yes. I almost forgot where I was headed. Anyway, the dragon you left guarded the gate, but she said her kin could only hold the lock in the gate for so long. To permanently lock it would require four locking stones."

"Locking stones?" Richard looked over at Meshoan and Leethor. The bewildered looks on their faces told him they were as confused as him, so he turned back to the gnome. "All right, I give up. What's a locking stone?"

A smile crept over Rembis's lips. "You should know, Wizard Scout. You helped destroy one. The Mountain's Heart was one of the four required locking stones."

"You mean that blue gem the dwarves used to make magic items?" Richard asked.

Rembis nodded. "The one and the same. The dragon guardian

told us that if locking stones were placed in the four corners of the gate, the gate would be permanently closed."

"Corners of the gate," said Leethor getting in on the conversation. "Are you talking about the four corners of the gate located under the Tree of Light?"

Shaking his head, Rembis said, "Not specifically. The dragon guardian was referring to the four corners of the gate under New Drepdenor. I suppose the same principle holds true for the Tree of Light's gate."

"Nick?" Richard said in his shared space. *"Are you getting this? Did you know it already?"*

"Sorry, Wizard Scout. It's not in my—"

"Databanks?" Richard said. *"Yeah, I know. Sometimes I get more than a little tired of hearing that same old excuse from you."*

"Well," huffed Nickelo, *"next time I will just make something up if that is what you want. Otherwise, all I can do is tell you the truth. The information is not in my databanks."*

"Fine. Sorry I asked."

An idea popped into Richard's mind. He looked at Rembis. "So, are you saying all we have to do is collect some pieces of the Mountain's Heart and stick them in those corner thingy's to lock the gates permanent-like? I've seen plenty of those blue gems in magic items over the years. We should just pry them out of a few pieces of magic equipment and lock the gates now."

Richard's enthusiasm for his idea went down in flames when the old gnome shook his head.

"Unfortunately, it is not that easy," said Rembis. "The part of the Mountain's Heart would have to be at least the size of your fist. The small slivers used in magic items wouldn't work." He pointed at the dagger on Leethor's waist belt. "Your dagger has a part of the Mountain's Heart. It is too small to be of use as a lock."

Meshoan shifted position to get a better view of the gnome. "You mentioned going to Old Drepdenor to get something. What?"

"Ah," said Rembis. "Queen Emerald sent us to find Thoagmar's Hammer. That was her father's war hammer. It was lost when the vampires overran the dwarves' home. The gem in the hammer is large enough to hold a lock on a corner of a gate."

"Did you find it?" Richard asked. "The war hammer, I mean."

Looking down at the blanket, Rembis shook his head and

remained quiet for a couple of seconds before looking back up. "No, we did not. You destroyed the Dragars' temple during the rebellion, but something evil was left behind. The tunnels under Old Drepdenor were re-infested with vampires and other...err, *things* when we arrived. My team was captured. What few of us weren't killed outright were given to a group of Dragars."

"I thought all the Dragars had left the planet," Richard said struggling to remember details of his previous mission. "The shield around Portalis should keep their starships from taking off or landing."

Shrugging, Rembis locked eyes with Richard. "We didn't get off the planet by a starship. We were teleported. I heard one of the Dragars say their god Zenthra did it."

"That can't be right," Richard said in his shared space. *"I destroyed Zenthra's computer avatar. He's supposed to be locked up in the demonic plane for a thousand years or something like that."*

"The demon is...now," replied Nickelo. *"However, you only destroyed the avatar a little over a hundred and fifty years ago. The events your gnome is describing happened a hundred thousand years earlier. Zenthra was still alive and kicking in his computer avatar then."*

Richard shook his head, thinking, *I really hate time-commando stuff.*

"You do not believe me, Wizard Scout?" asked Rembis. "I swear by all I hold dear that I tell the truth."

"It's not that," Richard said sensing a note of irritation in the gnome's voice. "The time stuff just gets a little confusing for me." He studied the gnome before asking his next question. "So you were captured before finding the king's war hammer. Do you think it's still under Old Drepdenor? If we went there and found it, could we use the gem to lock the gate under the Tree of Light?"

The gnome spread his hands. "As to whether the king's weapon is still there, who am I to say? A lot can happen in a hundred thousand years. As to locking either of the two gates, a piece of the Mountain's Heart can only be used to lock one corner of a gate. The remaining corners require other sources of energy."

"What?" asked Meshoan. "What other energy?"

Rembis smiled before shrugging. "You are asking the wrong

gnome. I am only a mage. My mission was to retrieve Thoagmar's Hammer. Whether Queen Emerald knew what was required to lock the other three corners of the gate, I do not know."

"Well, that was a waste of time," Richard told his battle computer. *"I wish he'd have said that in the first place."*

"It wasn't a complete waste," said Nickelo. *"At least we know the gates can be locked. We just need to discover how."*

"Well, I think—" A murmuring in the crowd drew Richard's attention. He looked toward the far side of the Tree of Light to see Jeena facing twelve elves. There were six males and six females positioned in pairs.

"Leenador; Meenish," said Meshoan motioning to her wayward children. "Come here. The ceremony is starting."

As children throughout the crowd rejoined their families, the elves grew still.

Richard easily made out Jeena's voice in the ensuing silence.

"My friends, we come here as witnesses to the sacred bonding of the elves before us. As they make their pledges to each other, let us swear to honor their commitment and to defend the lands against all who may try to overcome it."

Richard noticed his bondmate lift her staff high, sending out a blue glow from its tip that spread out until it encompassed the entire crowd. "We are the elves of Silvertine. Although I do not wish to detract from this joyous occasion, I would be amiss if I did not tell you all that the time of a great battle is fast approaching. We must be ready. As these bondmates make their offerings to the Tree of Light in order to strengthen the gate he protects, let us be as willing to sacrifice all we have if necessary to keep the coming darkness at bay."

As he watched, Jeena lowered her staff and turned to look at the eight elven lords assembled behind her. "The Lady has entrusted us with the great responsibility of leading her people during the upcoming crisis." She seemed to stare at Lord Sheshna as she said, "We must not let hidden agendas or petty quests for power prevent us from working together for the betterment of our nation."

Turning back to face the six sets of bondmates, Jeena led them through their oaths. As Richard watched, branches reached out from the Tree of Light and placed wreaths of glowing leaves on the heads of the twelve. The new bondmates' closest friends tied each pairs' hands together at the wrist with a soft vine.

Once the binding was complete, Jeena faced the crowd. "Let the tying of these vines symbolize the binding of these bondmates for all eternity. Let no one challenge their bonding. They have been blessed by the Tree of Light, and they will never be alone again."

The crowd cheered. Richard cheered with them. As the six sets of bondmates were led down the path toward the Presence of the Lady, Richard thought the Tree of Light glowed even brighter.

"Hmm," said Nickelo. *"Shandria seems to be expending more Power. I calculate she is confident you'll be able to fix whatever is wrong with the tree's offering link. I hope you do not let her down."*

An image of Shandria before she'd become the Lady of the Tree flashed in Richard's mind. In the image, she smiled at him. *I hope not either,* he thought.

CHAPTER 34

The black dreadnaught shimmered as it made its final jump. A moment later, the warship appeared in a completely different part of space. The twin-suns of the planet Storage glinted off its blackened hull.

"Status?" said the Dragar admiral making the question sound like the command it was.

A Dragar sitting in front of an array of misty globes turned around to look at his leader. "Our information was correct. A total of four transport ships orbit the planet. The primary spaceport is nearly empty. Only a single recon ship is currently positioned on the launching docks. Our scans are picking up some ground-based defenses, but they should pose little problem. Shall I order the bombardment to begin?"

The Dragar admiral's features remained stoic, but his eyes flashed red fire. The mention of a recon ship bothered him. On two previous occasions, a single recon ship had caused him problems.

"No," replied the admiral. "Send in the special operations unit to retrieve the three weapons. Tell them they have exactly thirty minutes to complete their mission and get off the planet before we turn it into a glowing ball of molten rock."

The Dragar technician nodded as he turned to concentrate on his communications spheres. Within seconds, the admiral felt his dreadnaught shudder as four shuttles shot out her open bay door heading directly for the planet the primary computer called Storage.

The Dragar admiral knew what a smile was from the many

slaves he'd owned over the years and had the feeling that if he could smile, he'd be smiling right now. Everything was going according to plan.

CHAPTER 35

"Telsa, Omar says my sister's taking Matt and Tia to see the rings. Do you want to go?" said Brachia.

Wizard Scout Telsa Stremar glanced up from her computer console rubbing her brow. She was tired. Not physically tired, of course. Her self-heal took care of that. Nevertheless, she was mentally beat. She was also frustrated. The civil war with the Conglomerate was already two weeks old, and she still hadn't seen any action. Instead, the high command seemed intent on keeping her on Storage to oversee experiments.

"You know it is not the high command," said her battle computer in their shared space. *"They do not even know of Storage's existence. Face it. You are working for* 'the One' *all the way."*

"Aren't we all?" Telsa replied remembering how she used to scoff whenever her friend Tam talked about a galaxy-wide conspiracy of computers working toward some unknown end. *"If it wasn't for the fact I know we need better defenses against magic-based weapons, I'd have shoved off this planet as soon as the war with the Conglomerate started."*

"Easy to say," said Raj, *"but harder to do. It is a long walk back to Velos."*

"Yeah, well, the Defiant *is here now,"* Telsa said. *"Sergeant Ron would take me on in a heartbeat."*

When Raj didn't try to counter her argument, Telsa turned her attention back to the young boy. "I thought Keka said those rings were off limits."

"Oh, they are," smiled Brachia. "However, I have never let a few rules stop me from looking at them in the past. Omar and I have a few tricks to get us through security."

Smiling back at Brachia, Telsa weighed the hours of boredom she still faced going through test results versus a little diversion accompanying the boy. The diversion won hands down.

"Sure, I'll go, but why do you want to bother if you've seen them before?"

"Well, for starters, I don't want my sister thinking she can pull a fast one over on me. Dren's got some monitors on the rings. She told me the next time she went to the small arms warehouse, she'd take me with her to validate any changes. Besides, you're almost as smart as Dren and me. I want to see what you make of them."

Coming from anyone else, the words might have irritated Telsa. Since the boy and his sister were probably the two smartest people she'd ever met, she took it as the compliment the boy intended.

"Then let's go," Telsa told the boy as she reached next to her chair and picked up her modified M12. She checked the fireball wand under the main barrel to make sure it was fully charged, then walked to the door where the boy waited. "I assume we're taking the tube train?"

"No way," laughed Brachia. "We'd never get there in time. Since I do a lot of work on Uncle Rick's equipment, I've got a small teleporter in my lab connected to the pad in the room where his battle helmet and other equipment are kept. We'll take that." Brachia suddenly broke out in laughter in a way only young boys could do.

"What's so funny?" Telsa asked trying to remember when she'd been that young.

Brachia stopped laughing long enough to reply. "I was just thinking how surprised Dren is going to be when we show up. She hates surprises."

* * *

Tia followed Dren to the metal door. When Dren passed her palm over an indentation in the wall located at waist level, the door slid open.

Matthew stepped next to Tia. "Geesh, Dren. This is the fourth set of security we've passed. Even my mother doesn't have this much protection."

Grinning, Dren glanced over her shoulder as she walked through the open doorway. "Well, this is the last one. Truth be told, we shouldn't be able to get in here, but Brachia installed a couple of backdoors in the security for us."

Growing a little nervous, Tia glanced over her shoulder. The corridor was empty. "So should I be expecting armed guards or something to show up and drag us off to the brig?"

Dren laughed. "Not hardly. The Storageans are a peaceful race. They don't even have an army or navy. Some heavy-duty ground to space defensive cannons are around the more important parts of the infrastructure like the main teleporter, but other than that, they rely on secrecy for protection."

Her friend's statement went against the grain of Tia's military upbringing. "Security through obscurity isn't very secure if you ask me. A fleet of dreadnaughts orbiting the planet would serve them a lot better."

With a shrug, Dren said, "Maybe so, but then the Storageans wouldn't be who they are if they had them. Like I said, they're a peaceful race. Besides, a fleet of warships would require a lot of space traffic to keep them supplied. It would just draw attention to the place. There are powerful force fields protecting the more important installations. At least that's something."

Unconvinced, Tia kept further opinions to herself. Having been raised in the military since she was six, the idea of a peaceful race was foreign to her.

Following Dren, Tia turned a corner of the corridor into a room not much larger than the inside of the X-shuttle. Four gray-metal pedestals were located in the center of the room. Each pedestal had a different colored placard at its base. Tia noticed the four colors were blue, green, red, and yellow. The blue, green, and red pedestals held a fist-sized gem the same color as their pedestal. The yellow pedestal didn't hold a gem. Below the empty slot on the yellow pedestal were two solid-gray rings. Tia glanced at the other pedestals. The green pedestal held two rings positioned below the green gem. Each of the two rings contained a paper-thin sliver of a green gem. Glancing at the pedestals for the blue and red gems, Tia noticed two empty ring-sized slots below each gem.

"What are these things?" asked Matthew. "What's with the gems? They seem almost alive."

Looking closer at the blue, red, and green gems, Tia noticed they appeared to be swirling almost as if a living gas were inside. Her passive scan picked up potent Power from them. She sensed the same potent Power coming from the two rings with the slivers of the green gem.

"Well," said Dren, "I don't know the stories on the other gems, but the blue one was found by Uncle Rick during his first mission on Portalis. He actually found two of them. One we attached to a staff to close a gate. The second gem was put in Uncle Rick's dimensional pack and sent here."

"Why?" Tia asked.

"Why did Rick send it here?" asked Dren. "For safekeeping, I guess. Anyway, the Storageans removed two small slivers of the blue gem and placed them in two rings. They did the same when the red and green gems showed up."

Tia looked back at the blue and red pedestals and their empty ring slots. "So where are the blue and red rings?"

Matthew's face brightened as he snapped his fingers. "Wedding rings."

Momentarily caught off guard by her companion's answer, Tia asked, "What?"

"The rings Rick summoned when Sergeant Ron married Jeehana and him had red gems," said Matthew. "I sensed their Power. The frequency was the same as the Power coming from the red gem on that pedestal."

Nodding her head, Dren smiled. "That's right. And the two missing rings with the blue gems were summoned by Rick when wizard scouts Trinity and Jerad were married."

Tia looked closer at the two rings inset with the slivers of the green gem. "All right, so they're wedding bands. Very nice. That doesn't explain the super security on the room."

"No," said Dren, "I suppose it doesn't. Brachia and I have been conducting some experiments with the gems. We think they are parts of a lock."

"A lock on what?" Tia asked growing suddenly interested. She had some knowledge about the blue gem. "Matt and I were part of a mission for *'the One'* to destroy a man-sized blue gem called the Mountain's Heart. From what I've been told, the gem was blown to hell and back with the pieces being lost on some unknown planet." She pointed at the blue gem. "Is that a piece of the Mountain's Heart?"

"That's my guess," replied Dren. "As for what it locks, Brachia and I think it is part of a lock system that can be used to open or close a dimensional gate."

"You mean like to the magic dimension?" asked Matthew.

Shaking her head, Dren stared at the blue gem before turning back to look at Matthew. "No. Something far worse. My parents developed a device that could be used to open and close gates to the demonic plane. We—"

"What?" said Matthew and Tia at the same time.

Matthew recovered first. "Who in their right mind would want to open a gate to the demonic plane?"

"No one in their right mind," admitted Dren. "I'm guessing it won't be a surprise to you that not everyone in the galaxy is altogether sane. As for the device my parents created, they intended it to close gates. The other blue gem Rick found supplied the energy for our parents' device. A friend of ours used the device to close a partially-opened gate a long time ago."

Tia looked at Matthew before turning her attention to Dren. "Okay, another interesting story. I'm guessing you had a point in bringing us here?"

After returning Tia's gaze for several heartbeats, Dren said, "I did. Both of you can sense Power. Wizard Scout Telsa has checked the gems and rings out, but she's not a diviner. She told us the gem slivers in the rings are so closely intertwined with their parent gems that the rings could be conduits for the gems' Power. Unfortunately, she couldn't tell how to activate the Power using the rings. I'd like the two of you to check the rings out in case you can spot something Telsa couldn't."

"Us?" Tia said. "We're not diviners either. We received some training from Rick and Gaston while we were with them on that time-commando mission, but we're far from wizard scouts. If Telsa didn't know how to do it, I doubt we can figure it out."

"Will you at least try?" Dren asked.

After glancing at Tia, Matthew said, "Might as well. What can it hurt?"

"I suppose we could try," Tia said only partially convinced. She formed an active scan and reached out toward the green gem. "The green gem is the only one with completed rings, so I suppose we should start there."

Tia sensed Matthew reach out with a scan of his own as he probed the two rings containing the slivers of the green gem. She kept her scan concentrated on the fist-sized green gem. Other than sensing the immense Power in the gem, she detected nothing useful. Glancing over at Matthew, she noticed beads of sweat forming on his brow.

"Are you all right?" Tia asked becoming concerned.

Matthew appeared to concentrate even harder on the two rings. "They're fighting me for some reason. I may need some help."

Unsure how she could assist but determined to try, Tia shifted her active scan down to the rings. The line of her active scan brushed against Matthew's. The moment it did, a green flash erupted from the rings, blowing both Matthew and her against the wall.

Tia hit the deck hard, but not before she sensed the flow of Power from the two rings and the green gem merge with the lines of Power from Matthew and her active scans. The green gem's Power intertwined with the line to her Power reserve. She sensed the line of Power from Matthew merge with her line as well. More than that, she sensed Matthew as if for the first time through the link that now connected them. She felt his concern for her safety as he picked himself off the metal deck and rushed to her side. She felt an overwhelming emotion come down the link. The emotion was love.

"Oh my," Tia said, unable to voice her true feelings more than that.

Matthew's eyes widened. "Tia. I… I had hoped, but I didn't know for sure. Now I do."

Tia didn't have to ask what he'd hoped. She knew. Her emotions were flowing down the link to him. *He knows I love him.*

"Are you two all right?" asked Dren bending over to help Tia to her feet. "I don't understand what happened. It shouldn't have been dangerous."

Tia wanted to gaze into Matthew's eyes and savor his emotions through their new link, but she forced herself to address Dren's need for information first. "The rings are designed to be used in pairs. I'm guessing they didn't react to Telsa because she was by herself. When the green rings sensed Matt and me, they modified the links to our Power reserves. Matt and I are connected now."

"We're connected to the rings as well," said Matthew. "You feel it, don't you?"

Tia reached out with her mind and levitated one of the green-gemmed rings toward her. As if under its own volition, the ring slipped onto her left ring finger. When she glanced at Matthew, he nodded. A line of Power reached out from Matthew and pulled the remaining green-gemmed ring toward him. The ring slipped on his left ring finger as well.

"Uh, what are you guys doing?" asked Dren. "We're not really supposed to be in here. I'm pretty sure the Storageans aren't going to be happy if you try to steal their rings."

Tia locked eyes with Matthew. Emotions passed between them. He gave her one of the smiles she loved before he turned to Dren.

"The rings don't belong to the Storageans," said Matthew speaking for both of them. "They've been waiting for us the same as the other rings were waiting for Jeehana, Rick, Trinity, and Jerad." He pointed at the yellow pedestal. "Do you have any idea where the yellow gem is located? I think the rings for all four gems are needed to close a gate."

Looking confused, Dren glanced at some flashing security lights on the wall before turning back to Matthew. "I think the yellow gem was a failed mission. I believe Uncle Rick retrieved the blue, red, and green gems on missions for *'the One.'* I've talked to him about it, and he only remembers the mission for the blue gem. There is no yellow gem, as far as I know."

A sensation through the ring on her finger told Tia all she needed to know. "The rings cannot complete their purpose without the yellow gem."

Frowning, Dren said, "I told you we don't have it. What do you ex—"

The building shook. Alarms began sounding. The unmistakable sound of small-arms fire came from the corridor.

"We're under attack," Tia said.

"Impossible," said Dren. "I told you the Storageans are a

peaceful race. They don't even carry weapons."

Tia picked up the frequency of life forms that suddenly appeared on her passive scan. She'd sensed the same frequency before when she'd accompanied Rick on a time-commando mission to Portalis. She had no doubt who was attacking.

"Dragars!" she shouted as she made for the door with Matthew and Dren hot on her heels.

A shudder of fear ran down Tia's back. She was a soldier born and bred, but even soldiers got scared on occasion. She thought of the unarmed Storageans trying to fight the vicious Dragars and their Tharg allies.

Creator help us, Tia thought. *I don't even have a weapon.*

CHAPTER 36

"May I join you?" said a familiar voice.

Richard looked up to see Jeena standing next to the blanket. He smiled and patted an empty space next to him. "I wondered when you were going to make it. I think you must've talked to every elf on the way here."

Jeena laughed as she crossed her legs, sitting down next to Richard. She placed her staff on the grass near the blanket to keep from disturbing the sleeping children.

"Oh, I missed a few. They are all very concerned about whether a seeding will occur."

"We will see soon enough," said Meshoan. "The bondmates have finished their swim in the lake. They should be…ah…"

Richard thought he noticed the brown-haired Meshoan turn a little pink. "I've been there," he said taking his bondmate's hand in his. "You don't need to explain. They should be sharing Power with the Lady soon."

Meshoan nodded. "Yes, sharing Power."

Leethor grinned, giving Richard a wink. "I did not realize my bondmate was so shy."

Murmuring in the crowd made Leethor turn his head in the direction of the tree. Richard followed his gaze to a band of silvery Power forming at the base of the tree. The band of silver slowly rose to the top of the Tree of Light as another band formed at the base. The progress of the bands sped up with each new band."

"Are you ready?" asked Jeena.

Richard nodded as he formed an active scan, reaching down into the earth. He found the offering link from one of the mating pairs of bondmates and felt the presence of Jeena's scan in his own. Surprisingly, he sensed Power from the red gems in his and her rings intertwined with their links.

"That's different," said Nickelo in their shared space.

"Is it dangerous?" Richard asked ready to pull the plug and shut down his active scan.

"I calculate that is a negative, Rick. I would advise continuing the scan. Finding out why the elves' offerings are not being completed is important. We can analyze the situation with your rings later."

"Roger that," Richard said renewing his concentration on his scan. He sensed Power leave his bondmate and travel down the offering link. At the spot where he and Jeena had previously deactivated the parasitic link during their own bonding ceremony, Richard spotted a weak point.

"That's not good," Richard said out loud. "Some of the Power is leaking through the opening. It's feeding Power to something at the other end. I don't know who or what is receiving the Power, but I doubt it bodes well for us."

"Can you block the opening?" asked Jeena. "You did so before."

"Apparently not good enough," Richard said as he probed the patch he'd previously placed on the opening. He located the weak points in the patch. "Yeah. I can do it, but I'll need your help. We'll do it just like last time."

"I am with you," said Jeena backing her words up with an emotion that was as much a promise as it was a feeling.

Using his bondmate as an anchor point, Richard made his way down the opening created by the parasitic link while avoiding the traps he'd set when he'd originally created the patch. As he continued into the blackness of the parasitic link, he sensed hate and demonic evil. He knew the creature at the other end. It was the Dalinfaust.

"Stay calm, Rick," said Nickelo. *"I'm with you; so is the elf. The demon is weak. I can sense it. He must be using the Power siphoned off the elves' offerings as fast as he is getting it because I sense he is still weak. I recommend closing the link off as quickly*

as possible and getting out of here."

"Roger that," Richard said.

Wrapping Power around the parasitic link, Richard twisted it back on itself. For good measure, he twisted the link three more times, locking each twist with Power. He surrounded each lock with traps and finished off by placing traps on the traps. Following the line of Power Jeena previously attached to him as an anchor, he drew back to survey his work.

In the distance, Richard heard Leethor say, "There was no seeding. Another offering is starting. I hope whatever you are doing, you are doing it fast."

Sensing Jeena next to him, Richard monitored the next wave of donated Power as it made its way up the offering link. The Power passed over the patch without diminishing as far as he could tell.

"Nick?" Richard asked.

"I detected no drop in Power, Wizard Scout. Whatever the demon was doing with the stolen Power, he is going to have to do without it now. I will continue to monitor any additional offerings, but I calculate it is repaired for good this time."

Richard heard shouting from the elves around him. Withdrawing his scan, he looked at the Tree of Light. It seemed to be glowing brighter. He heard the sound of raindrops even though no clouds were in the sky.

The smile on Jeena's face told him all he needed to know. "It is a seeding," she said. "We did it." Leaning over, she kissed Richard on the cheek. "I expected a miracle, and you have not let me down, my bondmate. What could go wrong when you are near?"

* * *

Lord Crendemor watched the elf and human out the corner of his eye as he continued to play the part of guest with the high lord's family.

They are all fools. They don't even know how to protect the links to their Power reserves. With a simple twist of magic, I could cut the links of both the high lord and his bondmate before killing them in front of their children. Not yet, though. I must complete my part of the plan first. There will be time enough to kill them all later.

As he glanced at the high priestess, he saw her lean over and kiss the human on the cheek. His anger burned even hotter. *I will kill them slowly. The human will rue the day he took my bondmate from me. His fool brother should be gathering the sacrifices even now. Soon the time for the ceremony will be here. Then the gate will be opened.*

Looking around the crowd of elves, he envisioned the tortures his demon army would inflict on them.

Laugh away, he thought. *Your time is fast approaching. I swear it.*

* * *

When the flow of Power from the parasitic link stopped, the Dalinfaust reacted quickly to shift some of the Power he had stored over the years to the communication link he had established for Zenthra.

The Dragars have begun their attack. It would not do to have Zenthra lose control now. I have enough Power stored to complete the task. Once the gate is open and I am free, I will have all my Power at my disposal again. Until then, I must not let Zenthra or that fool Crendemor know I have been weakened.

The demon traced the parasitic link back to its point of origin. The new blockage and the numerous traps told him what had occurred.

So, the human has closed the hole in his patch. Perhaps I should have used more caution and only siphoned off a small part of each offering, but no matter. I have enough stored Power for my needs. The master's variable will soon pay for his part in trying to hinder my plans. Oh, how he will pay.

The Dalinfaust thought of how he would punish the human once he was free, then laughed so hard the demon guards outside his cell shrunk away in fear. He cared not. Soon he would be free.

Let them all beware. My time is nigh. I will be the master soon enough. All will grovel before me. I swear it.

CHAPTER 37

The moment the tingling from the teleporter stopped, Telsa knew something was wrong. Even before Raj's warning shout of *"Dragars!"* reverberated in their shared space, Telsa was shoving Brachia behind her while forming a defensive shield and raising her M12.

Although apparently surprised, two four-armed Thargs reacted faster than their Dragar masters. A flurry of magic-energy rounds flew out their rifles, peppering against the shield Telsa had created. She returned fire. A Tharg went down before Telsa sensed one of the Dragars form a defensive shield between the second Tharg and her.

"Stay down!" Telsa yelled at Brachia as she dropped her M12 and leaped for the nearest Tharg. She drew her phase rod, activating it in destructive mode as she went.

The initial surprise of the Dragars and Thargs didn't last long. Four Thargs and two Dragars formed a line behind the Dragar's defensive shield as three of their companions ran out the room carrying what looked to Telsa like phase rods. She ignored them as she passed through the Dragar's defensive shield swinging her phase rod at the head of the nearest Tharg.

"Lucky for you the Dragar's defensive shield is only attuned to energy," said Raj. *"If it had been attuned against physical attacks as well, you would have bounced off."*

"No kidding, Sherlock," Telsa said using a modified phrase she'd read in a book her friend Richard had once loaned her. *"Now*

how about using that nanosecond brain of yours to help get me out of this mess?"

"Compliance."

The legs of Telsa's battle suit kicked out, catching a Tharg in the throat and sending him flying into one of his companions. Ignoring the other Thargs, Telsa sent a blast of pure Power at the two Dragars. Her specialty as a wizard scout was projection, and she was inside their defensive shield. The Dragars didn't stand a chance. Her wall of Power hit the dragon-like creatures and blew them apart. Cauterized pieces of flesh and bone accompanied the Power into the shelves behind, scattering pieces of metal and parts of battle suits everywhere.

"You just took out half of Wizard Scout Shepard's battle suits along with the Dragars," said Raj. *"I calculate your friend is going to be none too happy next time he sees you."*

Telsa didn't care at the moment what Richard might like or dislike. She had three more Thargs to deal with first, and there'd be time enough for apologies later if she was still alive to see him.

Burrp!

Spinning to her left, Telsa saw two of the Thargs falling amidst a stream of plasma rounds. She noticed Brachia on one knee, firing the M12 she'd dropped. He was using the stream of plasma like a water hose to push the fallen Thargs into the back wall.

Overextending her left arm, Telsa shoved the tip of her phase rod into the joint between the neck and chest armor of the remaining Tharg. She sensed the subatomic explosions of phase energy tearing the Tharg's throat apart. He went down before firing a shot.

"Cease fire!" Telsa yelled at Brachia who was still spraying the two Thargs' bodies. At her command, he released the trigger on the M12.

Glancing at the blood leaking out the joints of the two Thargs by the wall, Telsa said, "I think they're dead, Tex." Reaching into the ammo pouch on her belt, she extracted a replacement isotopic battery and tossed it to the boy. "You know how to reload that thing?"

Without a word, Brachia removed the near-empty battery in the M12 and swapped it with the fresh one.

Telsa heard the sound of small arms fire coming from the

corridor.

"No rest for the wicked, eh?" said Raj in their shared space.

"I haven't got time for jokes, Raj," Telsa snapped. *"Give me an analysis."*

"Compliance. Based upon the data from your passive scan, I calculate the warehouse is under attack by at least fifty Dragars and Thargs. They appear to be special ops. I calculate an eighty-two percent probability they are on a snatch mission. Since those other Dragars left with the three special phase rods belonging to Wizard Scout Shepard, I calculate that was their mission. You obviously surprised them."

More firing came from the corridor. Looking back at Brachia, Telsa said, "Stay here. I'll be back as soon as I can."

Without waiting for a reply, Telsa pulled her Deloris-model phase pistol from its holster while running through the door to the hallway beyond. Life forms appearing on her passive scan told her the special ops troops were bunched together near an intersection down an adjacent corridor. She noticed three other life forms down the opposite hall across the intersection. The frequencies of the three life forms were all too familiar.

"Dren, Tia, and Matthew," said Raj stating the obvious.

With a burst of speed, Telsa headed in the direction of the intersection.

* * *

More firing spurred Tia into an even faster pace. She rounded a corner right into a pair of four-armed creatures in full armor with rifles at the ready. After spending a year on Portalis, she didn't have to be told they were Thargs. Reaching through the chest armor of the nearest Tharg with a line of Power, Tia wrapped the first vital organ she found and pulled hard with telekinesis. She wasn't sure what she'd gotten hold of, but apparently it was important enough that the soldier went down before he could fire a shot in return. His companion went down as well. Tia noticed a line of Power withdrawing from inside the second Tharg's helmet and returning to Matthew.

Reaching down, Tia grabbed the rifle dropped by the first soldier before continuing to run down the corridor. She sensed

Matthew running behind her. A glimpse at her passive scan told her that Dren was heading in the opposite direction, away from the fighting.

I knew she was smart, Tia thought. *Only an idiot would run toward the fighting.* Laughing, she picked up speed in the direction of the small arms fire.

Tia didn't have far to go. As she came into view of an intersection, a blaze of energy rounds came streaming down the corridor.

Magic, she thought as she dove to the floor returning fire with her confiscated rifle. A large thud to her right rear confirmed Matthew had hit the floor as well. A flurry of magic energy passed her right side before hitting a shield in front of the opposing soldiers as Matthew began returning fire.

Tia threw up a hasty defensive shield of her own, angling it the way Richard and Gaston had taught her. The shield formed just in time as the Thargs lowered their aim. Rounds ricocheted off the shield, hitting the ceiling and continuing down the corridor.

"There's too many," yelled Matthew, his voice barely audible over the din of weapons firing. "We've got to pull back. Our shields only stop energy rounds."

Tia was about to agree when two round metal balls came bouncing down the corridor from the direction of the Thargs.

"Grenades!" Tia shouted. Reaching out with her mind, she knocked the grenades back the way they'd come using telekinesis.

Boom! Boom!

The grenades exploded in a burst of magic fire and smoke at the feet of the first rank of Thargs. Their armor stopped some of the shrapnel, but apparently not all. Tia noticed two of the Thargs go down spewing blood out of cracked visors. The fire of the remaining Thargs momentarily slackened.

"They've got magic users," said Matthew low crawling up to join Tia.

A glance at her passive scan showed at least a half dozen Dragars were behind the lead Thargs. The size of their Power reserves confirmed they were magic users. Tia sensed a large ball of energy forming in the hands of the lead Dragar as the other five fed him Power.

"Spell!" Tia warned Matthew doubting either of their defensive shields would hold against the magic. From experience, she knew their shields were nowhere near the quality of a wizard scout's.

Just as the lead Dragar released his spell, Tia sensed a wall of Power form to her front, creating a defensive shield. The shield wasn't from Matthew. A line of Power was coming from behind the special ops soldiers. Tia recognized the frequency.

"Telsa," said Matthew just as the spell hit the wizard scout's defensive shield.

Boom!

The lightning bolt spell was unable to penetrate Telsa's wall of energy, and the majority of the electrical charge deflected back the way it had come. A dozen of the lead Thargs caught the brunt of the spell, causing them to fly back into their comrades. Before they could recover, large balls of phase energy passed over Tia's head, striking Thargs and Dragars alike.

Boom! Boom! Boom!

Risking a glance to her rear, Tia saw Dren standing in the corridor with a 20mm phase cannon strapped to her side and firing in full automatic. A cartridge belt ran from the auto-cannon back to a four-wheeled cart holding a large metal container of ammo.

Tia noticed Dren's mouth move. Although she couldn't hear the words over the sound of the auto-cannon, she caught the girl's meaning anyway. Standing with her back to the side wall of the corridor, Tia edged back toward the young scientist. Battle-hardened as she was, the sight of balls of phase energy passing a half meter from her face still sent a chill down her back. A glance at the other side of the corridor showed a wide-eyed Matthew doing the same.

Once Tia was safely behind Dren, she knelt and began returning fire with her rifle.

"I grabbed this out of one of the storage rooms," shouted Dren between rounds. "I hope you approve."

Tia did, but she didn't take the time to answer as she concentrated on returning fire at the remaining Thargs and Dragars. As she fired, the six Dragars threw up a defensive shield in the center of the intersection. The shield buckled under the onslaught of the 20mm auto-cannon, but it held long enough for three of the Dragars to slip down a side corridor.

"Some of them are getting away," shouted Matthew.

"Does it matter?" Tia shouted back. "There's still plenty trying to kill us as it is. Keep firing."

Matthew did, and so did she. Glancing out the corner of her eye, Tia noticed that the container on the cart was nearly empty. As she watched, the last length of the cartridge belt snaked out of the metal container and made its way toward the auto-cannon.

Tia aimed at a Tharg and pulled the trigger of her rifle.

Click.

Empty. Now what am I going to do?

* * *

Telsa came upon the special ops' rear guard firing her phase pistol at one soldier as she swung her phase rod at the neck joint of another. At the same time, she sensed a group of Dragars forming a spell farther down the corridor. She had no doubt the spell's target was the life forms she'd identified as Dren, Tia, and Matthew.

Reaching out with a line of Power, Telsa formed a defensive shield in front of her three friends just as the ball of magic burst into a lightning bolt. The spell's energy was reflected back and hit a group of Thargs that were firing at her companions. Dropping the defensive shield to conserve Power, Telsa tried to fight her way toward the six Dragar magic users. Her progress was slowed by a dozen Thargs firing at her fleeting form as she returned fire. She sensed the Dragars forming a defensive shield at the intersection to reflect the fire of her friend's auto-cannon.

"Where'd they get an auto-cannon anyway?" Telsa wondered as she formed a defensive shield against the Thargs' firing at her.

"Does it matter?" asked Raj. *"Three of the Dragars have slipped past the intersection. They are the ones carrying the special phase rods. I highly recommend you stop them."*

Telsa was about to say "How?" when a ball of magic energy passed over her right shoulder hitting the closest Tharg.

Boom!

A magic-based ball of fire filled the confined area of the corridor, sending white-hot flames in both directions of the hallway. Telsa sensed Brachia behind her with her passive scan. Turning, she noticed him preparing to fire another fireball from the wand under the modified M12. Diving on top of the boy, she surrounded them both in a defensive shield just as the wave of flames washed over them. As soon as the fireball passed over, Telsa stood and jerked the rifle out of the boy's hands.

"Never," she told the boy, "do that again. A fireball in a confined space? Are you crazy?"

"I just wanted to help," said Brachia.

Tia handed the boy her Deloris phase pistol. "Then help me with this. I'll keep the M12."

"Raj," Telsa said out loud. "Analysis."

The battle helmet's external speakers crackled. "Between the lightning bolt and the fireball, the corridor is clear. You're lucky. I calculate Dren ran out of ammunition for her auto-cannon. Otherwise, you'd be dodging 20mm phase rounds right about now. Your passive scan indicates the three Dragars are heading to an exit. I recommend you hurry if you want to catch them."

Telsa pointed her phase rod at Brachia, being careful not to touch him with the rod. "Stay here this time. I mean it."

The boy nodded his head.

Telsa took off running. She jumped over scorched bodies as she made her way to the intersection. Tia and Matthew met her, picking up a couple of the scattered rifles as they came. She noticed Dren unhooking herself from the harness for the auto-cannon.

"Take care of your brother," Telsa yelled. Glancing at Tia and Matthew, she weighed the odds. They weren't wizard scouts, but they were both good fighters. "Stick close but stay behind me. I can self-heal. You can't. We've got to stop those three Dragars."

"Why?" asked Matthew as he came running behind with Tia at his side. "What's going on?"

I only wish I knew, Telsa thought.

CHAPTER 38

The communication officer on the Dragar dreadnaught approached the admiral holding out his computer pad with the screen facing out. He waited for his commander to acknowledge his existence before speaking.

"What is it?" hissed the admiral.

"The special operations team is experiencing heavier resistance than expected, Admiral. They have the objects but are having trouble returning to their shuttles. They are taking heavy losses."

The admiral walked behind the Tharg and looked at the officer's scrying spheres. The leathery skin between the admiral's eyes wrinkled as his face took on a darker shade of gray. "So, our strike leader suspects several of the Empire's wizard scouts are opposing them, do they? Order a squadron of our fighters to provide support. Dispatch troop shuttles with an armor company for good measure."

As the Tharg turned to carry out his leader's commands, he overheard the admiral give orders to the dreadnaught's captain. "Bring our ship out of stealth mode and commence bombardment. Attack everything as per the priority list from our primary computer."

"What about the main spaceport?" asked the ship's captain. "It is close to the small-arms warehouse. Our troops would be caught in the blast of any of our heavier bombs and missiles. Should I order atomics be used on the spaceport anyway?"

The admiral raised a scaled hand to rub his brow. After a few rubs, the admiral shook his head. "No. Avoid using atomics on the spaceport until our troops have departed. We cannot risk losing the objects. Destroy everything else on the planet. Save the spaceport and the small-arms warehouse for last. If anything still lives on that planet in two hours, your life will be forfeit."

The communications officer was thankful he wasn't the captain. He had a feeling that at this moment the captain wished he wasn't either.

* * *

The Storagean left the tube-train the same as he had at the start of every shift for the last seventy-five years. The only difference now was that his recent promotion to shift leader put him in charge of the heavy-weapons warehouse. Raising two eyestalks, he sought out the top of the building. Its distinctive red color contrasted with the gray metal of the buildings around it.

A feeling of pride swept over him. *Perhaps this will be the day a new request comes in for my team. The odds are low, but it could happen. We have kept every piece of equipment in perfect shape for so many years. We must be ready when they are needed. I am now the shift leader. I will make sure we are ready.*

The octopod noticed a streak of light coming out of the sky. Twisting his eye stalks to follow the path of the streak, he noticed two more streaks behind it. The first streak slammed against the force field protecting the warehouse and exploded in white light so intense the Storagean's optic nerves were burned to a crisp. He did not see the impact of the second missile as it destroyed the force field. Neither did he see the third missile tear into the heavy-weapons warehouse and explode in a ball of magic radiation. The last thing the octopod felt was enormous heat consuming everything in its path. After a microsecond of pain, the Storagean felt nothing ever again.

* * *

"We are under attack," said Margery over the *Defiant's* intercom.

Sergeant Ron came staggering out of the captain's quarters, into the cockpit, still shoving an arm through the sleeve of his shirt. After pulling an all-nighter working on the X-shuttle's modifications, he was in no mood for jokes.

"What d' ya mean under attack? By who?" said Sergeant Ron jumping into the pilot's seat while activating the ship's sensors.

"Unknown," replied Margery. "A dreadnaught is orbiting the planet. It appears to be bombarding locations on the planet with warehouses. The missiles appear to be those magic radiation type nukes the Crosioians used to attack the Empire. I calculate a thirty-eight percent probability the dreadnaught overhead is a Dragar warship from the magic dimension."

Not one to waste time, Sergeant Ron didn't bother asking how or why. All that mattered was that they were. Scanning the ship's internal sensor display, he noticed most of the crew was on the *Defiant* resting up from the previous night's endeavors. Only Wizard Scout Terrie Shatstot, Comstar, and Timerman were still at the hangar with the X-shuttle.

Slapping the intercom switch, Sergeant Ron said, "Battle stations. Charlie, prepare for emergency takeoff. Margery, contact Terrie's battle computer and have them get the X-shuttle off the ground pronto. Tell them to meet us in orbit."

To his crew's credit, they didn't bombard him with questions that he didn't have the answers to anyway. He noticed the light for the rear cargo bay hatch go from red to green.

"Rear hatch secure," came Charlie's voice over the intercom. "Hyper-drive engine will be online in thirty seconds."

After a quick check of the pilot's control panel, Sergeant Ron flicked the launch button on his control stick. He shoved the lever for the sonic-wave jets as far forward as they would go. The *Defiant* jumped upward, pressing him down into his seat. Two nylon-mesh belts slid out of his seat back and secured him in place.

"Really, Sergeant Ron," said Margery. "The least you could have done is buckled yourself in before taking off. You should also have waited for the crew to give the okay. Poor old Charlie was still in the cargo bay. A stack of ammo crates are pinning him down."

"He'll live," said Sergeant Ron hoping he was telling the truth. "Send a couple of the dwarves to help him get out."

"*Defiant*, this is tower control," came a mechanical voice from what Sergeant Ron recognized as one of the Storageans' translators. "You are not authorized for take—"

Flipping the switch on the communications' control to a different frequency, Sergeant Ron triggered the ion thrusters to maximum. The recon ship shot forward a mere five hundred meters above the spaceport. He tilted the controls upward until the *Defiant* was nearly vertical and climbing twice the speed of sound.

"Analysis," ordered Sergeant Ron using the ship's intercom so the crew could hear his conversation with Margery.

The intercom crackled. "The Dragar dreadnaught is in orbit at four hundred kilometers. Their commander has launched a squadron of fighters and three troop shuttles. I calculate their destination is the small-arms warehouse located east of the spaceport. In case you have forgotten, Dren, Tia, and Matthew went there earlier. I am in contact with Telsa's battle computer. Raj says his wizard scout is also at the warehouse. Telsa has Brachia with her. They have been in a skirmish with a special operations team composed of Dragars and Thargs. I calculate—"

"I've heard enough," said Sergeant Ron still speaking over the *Defiant's* intercom. "If'n anyone isn't at their battle stations, you'd best be getting there. We're going to engage that dreadnaught before they wipe out half the population."

After adjusting his course to intercept the dreadnaught, Sergeant Ron checked the tactical hologram located between the pilot and copilot seats. Two dozen orange dots denoted fighters and troop shuttles heading for the small-arms warehouse.

"Should I plot an intercept course?" asked Margery sounding hopeful. "Wizard Scout Telsa and the kids won't stand a chance against all that firepower."

Weighing options, Sergeant Ron shook his head. "Negative. Stay on the dreadnaught. We've got to slow down their aerial bombardment. Contact Terry's battle computer and have them use the X-shuttle to support Telsa and the kids. That's the best we can do at the moment. We're going to have our own problems."

"Compliance."

Reaching out with his mind, Sergeant Ron located the dreadnaught. A sudden realization hit him as he recognized the warship's energy frequency. His hand shook on the controls, causing the *Defiant* to jerk left.

"You are drifting left," said Margery. "Do you want me to take over control of the ship?"

Forcing himself to concentrate on flying, Sergeant Ron maneuvered the recon ship back on track. *It's the black dreadnaught,* he thought. *The one that killed my wife.*

Hate began to overwhelm Sergeant Ron. Through sheer force of will, he regained control of his emotions. *I let my hatred get the best of me once. It almost cost me my grandson and my ship. I won't give in again. I've got to stop the bombing. Thousands are dying every second.*

"You are back on course," said Margery. "The crew reports all weapons are online and ready. Are you sure you do not want me to take control of the *Defiant?*"

Sergeant Ron had a feeling the ship's computer was remembering when he'd lost control the last time they'd encountered the black dreadnaught. He didn't care what Margery thought. He wasn't giving up control of his ship.

"Negative," he said. "I'll do the flying. You just concentrate on doing your computer stuff." He pushed the intercom switch again. "Angela, get up here and take the copilot's station. I'm going to need help with our shields. Charlie, you and Asquan get in the fighters. Launch as soon as you're strapped in."

"What about engine?" asked Charlie.

"Daniel can take care of the hyper-drive, can't you, Daniel?" said Sergeant Ron.

"Affirmative," said Daniel, his voice sounding shaky but only slightly so. "I can also help guide missiles and still monitor the hyper-drive if you want."

"I want," said Sergeant Ron.

The *Defiant* shuddered as the recon ship cleared the atmosphere. A glance at the control panel told him the dragon-fighter in the right wing pod had launched. *I'll say this for Asquan. He might be young for an elf, but he doesn't waste any time.* A second later the ship shuddered again as the zip fighter in the left wing pod launched. *Of course, Charlie doesn't waste any time either.*

Leveling the *Defiant*, Sergeant Ron fired a half-second burst of the hyper-drive. He noticed a red dot on the tactical hologram growing larger. Looking out the pilot's windscreen, he zoomed magnification to maximum. That's when he saw it. The black dreadnaught lay dead ahead. Even as he watched, colored beams of light from her main guns lashed out at the planet below. Dozens of missiles launched from her sides, their fiery glow disappearing into the clouds below. Seconds later, dots of brilliant light flashed through the cloud layer.

Sergeant Ron aimed the bow of the *Defiant* at the center of the black dreadnaught's port side. He brought the sights for the recon ship's forward missile tubes to bear. Pressing the intercom switch again, he gave his crew what he knew might be their final orders.

"Fire everything you've got as she comes to bear. The Storageans are being slaughtered down there. Their salvation depends on us. We ain't going to let those Dragars get away with murder again!"

CHAPTER 39

Wizard Scout Gaston Myers dragged the limp elf off the spirit-cat. His mount snapped at the form of the male elf as the body fell unconscious to the stone floor of Crendemor's lab. Myers's knocked the cat's head away with the heel of his boot. The spirit-cat growled and bared its teeth. Drawing his phase rod, Myers activated it in destructive mode. The cat creature snarled as the feeling of demon-hunger filled the space. Continuing to snarl, the creature nonetheless left the elf alone and shifted into the void, merging down into the floor.

Dragging the elf to one of the two remaining empty cages, Myers tossed the limb body inside being none too gentle. After securing the door, he turned to survey the dimly-lit lab. His night vision filter picked up every detail. It wasn't a pretty sight. He detested the stink of evil in the place.

"You humans and your thoughts about good and evil," came the voice of Myers's battle computer in their shared space. *"There is no such thing. What care you about the fate of these measly life forms? The bottle of DNA gas will soon be yours."*

Myers glanced down the row of ten cages before replying, *"I'm beginning to wonder if it is worth it."*

"Oh, come now, Wizard Scout. You are too close to the prize to falter now. You have nine of the ten prisoners. Only one more elf is needed for the ceremony to proceed."

Looking at the row of cages, Myers felt a sense of shame. The four female and five male elves had been all too easy to capture. As a diviner, he'd only needed to cut off the link to their Power reserves to defeat them. None of them had even a single trap on their links.

"They were all fools," Myers decided, forgetting to keep his thoughts in his private space.

"Exactly," said his battle computer Wanda. *"They are all fools. None of them are worth the life of your precious Diane. With the DNA gas, you can extend her life and keep her young forever. You will finally be a family."*

"Stay out of my head, demon. Where is Crendemor? He was supposed to meet me here."

"Alas," replied the demon, *"he is attending one of the elf ceremonies. He will be here on the morrow. I do not think he will be pleased that you insist on bringing him adult elves. As I have explained, the blood of elf children is more potent. The gate-opening spell requires the most potent blood you can gather."*

"No!" Myers said speaking out loud for the first time. "There are lines even I will not cross. Do not speak to me of it again."

"As you say, Wizard Scout," said the demon. "I am merely your humble battle computer. I calculate you have time to get a final captive before the dark elf arrives. I highly recommend you make it a child. Even now the Dragars are recovering the other phase rods required for the ceremony. The Dalinfaust would not be pleased if his freedom were delayed because you did not do your part."

Myers bit his lip. He had much to say, but this time he kept his opinions in his private space. *The demon is right. I am too close to getting the DNA gas now to quit. I must see it through to the end.*

"Summon my mount," he ordered his battle computer.

"Compliance."

The lizard-skinned spirit-cat rose from the stone floor until its entire body was above ground. Mounting the cat, Myers sent it an image of the mountains a day's walk from Silverton.

There are isolated villages there, he thought. *I should be able to find another captive without drawing suspicion.*

With that thought, the cat disappeared into the floor taking Myers with him.

CHAPTER 40

Three troop shuttles were on short final as Telsa ran out an opening that the Dragars had apparently blown in the side of the building. Pieces of still glowing white-hot metal littered the concrete surface beyond. Using her passive scan, she spotted three life forms heading in the direction of the incoming shuttles.

"Watch out," warned Raj. *"Two fighters are rolling in for a strafing run from your ten o'clock."*

Scanning the sky, Telsa spotted the incoming streaks of light and ten more fighters circling the spaceport, looking for additional targets. Reaching out with her mind, she probed the rightmost of the two fighters that were making their gun run. She found what she was seeking. Sending a line of Power into the skull of the life form inside, she pulled hard with her telekinesis. The fighter wavered a moment before it dove straight toward the ground and exploded in a blast of fire and smoke.

"Shield," ordered Raj.

Without taking the time to think, Telsa threw up a hasty defensive shield to her front. Balls of magic energy hit, ricocheting into the air. She sensed two life forms to her rear as Matthew and Tia dove for cover behind her shield.

"He's coming in for a bombing run," said Raj. *"Your shield is only good against energy weapons."*

Telsa knew that only too well. She looked around for cover but saw nothing useful. Reaching out with her mind once again, she sought the occupant in the attacking fighter but missed. *"It's coming in too fast. I can't get a lock."*

Raising her Deloris phase pistol, she began firing as fast as she could pull the trigger. A flurry of plasma rounds joined her return fire as Tia added the modified M12 to the fray.

All of the rounds glanced off the force field surrounding the fighter. As the fighter leveled off in preparation for dropping its bomb, Telsa reached out with her mind in a last desperate effort to tear out the pilot's heart. Before she could get a lock, the fighter exploded, sending a shower of flaming wreckage in all directions. Telsa turned and pulled the two teenagers to the ground beneath her to protect them from the falling wreckage as best she could. Most of the smaller bits of flaming metal bounced off her battle suit. She heard a moan from Tia.

"My legs," said Tia. "I'm hit."

Something passed overhead at low altitude. Telsa glanced up in time to make out the distinctive shape of the X-shuttle heading in the direction of the three troop shuttles touching down five hundred meters away. Beams of energy reached out from the X-shuttle, seeking the landing ships.

Boom! Boom! Boom!

All three troop shuttles exploded as the combination of beams of magic and plasma energy did their job.

"It is Wizard Scout Shatstot, Timerman, and Comstar," said Raj. *"Taylor says his wizard scout is having Timerman try to take out some of those other fighters before they come back to pick you up."*

Telsa jumped off the two teenagers and made a quick survey of Tia's leg injury. The teenager's lower calf was a bloody mess, but Telsa figured it wasn't life-threatening. Pulling an emergency bandage from her utility belt, she tossed it at Matthew.

"Take care of her, then collect Brachia and Dren," Telsa ordered as she began running in the direction of the burning troop shuttles.

"Where are you going?" shouted Matthew as he began ripping open the bandage pack.

With a final shout over her shoulder, Telsa said, "I've got to stop those three Dragars with the phase rods. I'll be back."

At least I hope I'll be back, Telsa thought sensing two more fighters turning in her direction as they lined up for a strafing run.

She gauged the distance to the three life forms she'd sensed ahead. They were turning to face her and forming a defensive shield as they did.

"You've got to close with them before those fighters complete their turn," said Raj. *"I calculate that's your only chance."*

Telsa kicked her battle suit into high gear. *Some chance,* she thought. She kept running anyway.

CHAPTER 41

The *Defiant* bucked again as another salvo of Dragar missiles slammed against her shields.

"Angle the shields more," Sergeant Ron ordered. "Too much radiation is getting through."

The redhead sitting in the copilot's seat bristled. "Don't be telling me how to angle no shields," snapped Angela, sweat flying off her forehead as she glanced from her console to the tactical hologram and back. "If you spent as much time trying to fly this bucket of bolts you call a ship as you did worrying about how I handle the force fields, maybe we wouldn't be getting hit so much."

Sergeant Ron opened his mouth to respond but got sidetracked when his passive scan picked up another dozen missiles heading his way.

"They are the magic nukes," said Margery over the ship's intercom. "I recommend you avoid getting hit. The *Defiant's* shields are down to thirty-seven percent. Our force field cannot take more than two more hits by those nukes before it gives out."

Inverting the *Defiant* in a hard roll, Sergeant Ron triggered the hyper-drive for a split-second burst. Bright bursts of light behind the recon ship confirmed his maneuver worked.

"Hey," said Margery, "the *Defiant* is not a fighter. You will exceed her stress points."

Leveling off, Sergeant Ron pointed the recon ship's bow at the black dreadnaught once again. "A dozen nukes would've exceeded a few stress points as well, so can it, Margery. Find me a weak point in that behemoth's shields. We can't keep trying to slug it out with them."

"Amen to that," said Angela angling the shields against a series of magic beams from the black ship.

The intercom crackled. "Charlie is online," said Margery. "He says he has found a possible defect in the rear shields. We may be able to slip a few missiles through."

Touching the icon for the zip fighter, Sergeant Ron said, "Charlie, what ya got? I don't mind telling you I'm ready to grasp at straws."

"No straws," came Charlie's voice over the intercom. "I run maintenance scan on black ship. Magic different, but close enough. I notice generator for force field at position three nine six intermittently reduces energy flow when you attack their forward shields. Suspect bad relay switch."

Sergeant Ron didn't care what the reason for the reduction was. Years of association had taught him Charlie was the best mechanic in the Empire. If his friend said the magic generator was faulty, then it was faulty. "What are you proposing?"

"*Defiant* attack shield in forward position one three two. Asquan and I attack rear shield at three nine six when weak. Might work."

Sergeant Ron shifted his attack run to the front of the dreadnaught. "All weapons concentrate on position one three two. Give it everything ya got, including the kitchen sink."

"Kitchen sink?" asked Angela angling shields with her right hand as she entered targeting information to the forward torpedo tubes with her left.

Sergeant Ron grinned. "Yeah. I know. Guess I've been reading that *Cute Sayings* book of Rick's too much." Checking the gun sights for the forward plasma cannons, he flicked the safety cover up and placed his finger over the trigger.

"Daniel," said Sergeant Ron into the intercom. "Between the port, starboard, and forward tubes, we'll be firing eighteen torpedoes. Can you handle guiding all of them at the same time?"

"I can try," replied Daniel.

"Well, if you can't do it, we'll all be dead in about five minutes, so I'd appreciate it if you told me now. That way I'll have time to make peace with my maker."

"I can do it, Captain," said Daniel, his voice taking on a sound of confidence.

"I had no doubt you could," Sergeant Ron replied. "And don't call me Captain. I'm a sergeant. I work for a living."

CHAPTER 42

Calem awoke with a start. Someone was shouting to his father. As an elf, Calem was blessed with excellent hearing, but even so, he couldn't make out the yells. He did hear his name mingled in the jumble of words. That in itself was strange. At three hundred and ten years, he was still considered a child by most of the adults in the sleepy little mountain village of Ivy Borough.

Straining to make out the voices, he concentrated on making out the tones even if he couldn't make out the words. Any kind of a commotion in his village was cause for concern. Making a split-second decision, Calem jumped out of his hammock and quickly began dressing. Just as he was finishing, the curtain door to his room was pulled back. There stood his father.

Jacobarak nodded his approval. "Good. You are dressed. The chief wants to see you outside." Without any explanation, the elf turned and walked out of his son's modest room.

Calem froze in confusion. *The chief?* he thought. *Surely he doesn't know about the kidnapped totem already? I knew our prank would get some notice from the elders, but confronting me in the middle of the night is not the chief's way.*

Grabbing his moccasins, Calem followed his father out the door. Once outside, he noticed the old, white-haired village chief surrounded by what looked like half of the village's inhabitants.

As his father approached the chief, Calem heard the chief shout to the crowd, "Now go! Fetch them and return as quickly as you can."

The crowd dispersed.

The chief turned narrowed eyes to look at Calem.

Deciding to throw himself on the mercy of the chief, Calem opened his mouth to offer an apology for the *borrowed* totem. After all, he and his friends were going to give it back.

"Calem!" said the chief looking grim. "The elves of Ivy Borough have need of your speed. You are the best runner in the village. Will you serve us this day?"

Taken aback, Calem glanced at his father who gave him a slight nod. Knowing there was only one answer he could give, he spoke in his most formal voice. "The family Stonemoss is ever ready to serve our village and our chief. Ask, and it will be done as long as breath is in my body."

"Good! As I knew you would," the chief stated before he turned to confer with the rest of the village's council of elders.

Temporarily ignored by the chief, Calem turned to his father. He had a thousand questions on his lips.

Jacobarak raised his hand. "Hush, my son. I will explain. A rider from Silverton arrived a short time ago. High Priestess Jeehanathoraxen and the elf friend have returned. The Council of Light has called for all magic items to be brought to the city for recharging."

Unable to contain himself, Calem said, "What has that to do with—"

Jacobarak raised his hand again. "Will you ever learn to let your elders finish talking before you start asking questions?" With a patient smile, Jacobarak continued, "Our village was too far to make the high priestess's own bonding ceremony before it ended nine days ago. As you know, the recharging stands did not work during the two bonding ceremonies conducted without the high priestess and the elf friend. We have magic items that need to be recharged. They must be placed in the recharging stands before the sun rises. No one can be sure the high priestess and the elf friend will be available during future ceremonies. This may be our only chance to charge our items. This is a lot to place on you, my son. Do you understand your responsibility?"

Calem glanced at the night sky, noting the position of the stars. "It is already past midnight, Father. The ceremony has already begun. Surely the rider can make it back in time if he hurries. What does the chief need me f—"

Jacobarak frowned at his son. "That is enough questions, Son. The rider continued on to Upper Borough. The chief told him there would not be enough time to get to Upper Borough and back before sunrise, but the rider said he had his orders. He left, vowing to stop for our magic items when he passes back through our village."

"The chief was right," said Calem knowing full well the mountain paths large enough for a horse were three times the distance of the footpaths used by the village runners. "The rider will never make it back here in time."

"That is why we need you," said Jacobarak placing a hand on his son's shoulder. "Can you do it?"

For a moment, Calem was confused, but then he understood. The Chief and his father wanted him to carry the village's magic items to the City of Light. Calem did a rough calculation of distance and time. No matter how he calculated it, he came up short. "The distance is too far for the time we have. No runner can make it."

"I know that is how it seems, my son. It will be hard leagues, with half of that a narrow mountain path. And it must be done in the dark. It is a lot to ask, but I have faith in you. There is more strength in you than you know. You have the blood of the family Stonemoss flowing in your veins, and they have always been the fastest runners of all the elves."

Despite his father's words, Calem didn't see how it could be done. Nevertheless, he stifled the protests struggling to get out. Nodding to his father, he accepted the charge. "When do I leave?"

"Soon," replied his father.

In less than five minutes, the chief handed Calem a small backpack filled with most of the village's magic items consisting of broaches, necklaces, and rings. Calem didn't have to look to know the magic items were expended. They were magic items with potential but currently held no Power. Still, they were a symbol of the village's connection to the elves of yore when magic abounded in the land of Silvertine.

Calem noticed several elves at the far end of the village heading his way, carrying a long, slender object wrapped in deer hide. As he watched, they solemnly handed their package to the chief. The chief removed the hide, revealing the item inside. An elf-high shaft of highly polished black root-wood glistened in the moonlight. The shaft was tipped with a luminescent head of ivory thick as a large elf's wrist at its base, converging to a deadly point at the end.

"Mendera's Lance," mouthed Calem reverently as the chief placed the village's most cherished treasure in his trembling hands.

Calem thought back to the tale he'd first heard from his father. In the old days, the elves of the Eastern Mountains and those of Silverton were threatened with extinction by a powerful demon inhabiting the body of a giant. Impervious to even the most powerful enchanted weapons and spells of the time, the demon-giant and its minions seemed destined to overwhelm even the strongest of elven warriors. If his father's tale were true, the event had occurred almost 45,000 years ago when the power of the elves was at its peak. Even so, the elves had failed to prevail against the demon-giant and its army.

On the eve of the final battle outside the gates of Silverton, the unicorn Swiftmane, his elven maid Mendera, and threescore unicorns presented themselves to the elven high lord to offer their aid. The Council of Light had declared the unicorn Swiftmane an elf friend. Even aided by the unicorns, the fighting had been terrible, or so the story went. Finally, after a day and a half, Elf Friend Swiftmane ridden by Mendera and accompanied by the remaining unicorns and the best of the elven warriors and spellcasters made a last-ditch charge through the enemy's center. The unicorns and elves fought their way deep into the enemy's formation. Once there, Elf Friend Swiftmane had challenged the magical shields surrounding the demon-giant. After destroying the shields, the unicorn had rammed his horn deep into the demon's heart. The resulting explosion blew open the giant's chest and destroyed the foul darkness inhabiting the demon's avatar. Like most tales of old, the victory had a tragic end. The unicorn's valiant charge also shattered the base of Swiftmane's horn. The unicorn and his rider were thrown back when the point of the broken horn delved into the giant's body.

A dying Swiftmane, surrounded by those unicorns that still lived, ordered the high lord to remove the horn from the chest of the demon's avatar and use it to create a lance. Elf Friend Swiftmane had then prophesized that the lance would one day save the elves from certain destruction. Once his words were spoken, the elf friend passed from this world into the next. The high lord had done as he was asked, creating Mendera's Lance. Since Ivy Borough was the birthplace of Mendera, it had been kept there ever since

The chief released his grip on the lance. The full weight of it forced Calem's arms downward. It was no lightweight spear, but a full-blown battle lance. The heft of the shaft combined with the weight of the unicorn-horn tip surprised Calem.

How am I supposed to run carrying this? he thought, wisely keeping his mouth shut.

"It is imperative that you place this lance in a recharging stand before sunrise," the chief said sternly. "My dreams have been troubled of late. I believe the day is fast approaching when Elf Friend Swiftmane's horn will once again be needed to save our race from destruction. Go! Go now, Calem Stonemoss. Let nothing prevent you from keeping your date with destiny!"

"But, holy one, the lance is too heavy! I will never—" began Calem.

"I said go!" shouted the chief with a well-aimed kick to Calem's backside.

Sufficiently motivated, Calem took off at a blistering pace all the way to the edge of the village. Once the last of the lights from the village were behind him, he slowed his pace to what he hoped would be maintainable to the base of the mountain. The lance was heavy and awkward. Within a few minutes, he was panting heavily.

"I can't do it," he told the stars in the sky. "This pace will kill me before I get halfway to the river." In spite of his words, Calem continued running at the much too fast pace because that's what he had to do.

A shadow came out of the wood line and began running beside him.

"You will never be able to keep this pace up, Calem," said Generve, the chief's granddaughter.

Relief overcame the initial shock of the appearance of the elf girl. *I should have known my best friend would find me,* he thought. As the all-around instigator of most of the things that got Calem into trouble, Generve and he were practically inseparable.

Although he knew his friend wasn't that great of a runner, he hoped she could pace him for a few minutes. Even a short time would help keep his mind on the task at hand instead of visualizing why it couldn't be done.

"I know," Calem panted, "Still, I have to try. I have to make it by sunrise."

"Actually, you probably need to get there before sunrise," replied Generve. "The recharging stands only activate when the couples mate. What are the odds their last mating will be timed with the sunrise?"

The logic of Generve's argument hit Calem hard. He started slowing his pace. "Then it is a lost cause. Why should I even try?"

"Don't slow down!" shouted Generve. "You are not alone in this. I heard my grandfather talking to the rider. I knew their plan was doomed to failure. Fortunately for you, I think outside the basket."

"What do you—" began Calem.

"Quiet! Save your breath. You are going to need it. Corby and Ivy are at Dobson's Corner. They are rigging a rappelling rope for you. Instead of following the path down the mountain, you can rappel down the cliff face. It will save you ten leagues."

"Are you crazy?" Calem said slowing down again. "There's nothing below Dobson's Corner besides—"

"The river," finished Generve placing a hand behind Calem and forcing him to keep his blistering pace. "You can rappel to the end of the rope and drop into the river."

"Loaded down with this lance? Are you crazy?"

Generve laughed. "My grandfather often asks me the same thing, but yes, with the lance. Of course, you will need to close your eyes before you drop."

Calem glanced at his friend. "You mean to keep the silt in the water out?"

"No," said Generve giving a devilish laugh. "Because even you would not be stupid enough to drop so far if you could see what you were doing."

His friend's plan seemed farfetched to Calem, but he gave in to Generve just as he always did. He wondered if the reason he gave in so easily was force of habit from all the years his friend's harebrained schemes had actually worked. Regardless of the reason, he soon found himself rigged for a rappel and standing on the edge of the cliff face that was Dobson's Corner.

The lithe figure of his friend Ivy strapped a makeshift harness for Mendera's Lance across his back. "There," she said. "Now you will not lose it when you make the drop from the end of the rope."

"I don't know," said Calem giving a final argument. "The chief said to run. He made no mention of rappelling or swimming."

"My grandfather couldn't think of a new or better way to do things if it fell out of the sky and hit him on the head," said Generve placing a hand in the center of Calem's chest and giving a shove.

With the decision made for him, Calem bounded down the cliff face, covering ten paces with each bound. Though the moon had set, he could see the river far below. The end of the rope appeared to be dangling much too far above the water.

The least they could have done is gotten a longer rope.

A shout from Generve drew his attention. "We will meet you in the city as soon as we can get there!"

"You can do it," shouted his friends Ivy and Corby in unison.

Losing sight of his friends, Calem continued rappelling down the rock face. He made the descent as quickly as possible. Although he could see with his night vision, distances were harder to judge than under full daylight. As if to prove the point, Calem slammed into the rock wall harder than intended. Shaking the blow off, he made a final bound to reach the end of the rope. Unfortunately, the end of the rope was at the same point where the cliff curved back into the mountainside.

Hanging freely in the air, Calem looked down to judge the distance to the swirling water below. *It looks a lot farther than I thought,* he decided. Nevertheless, he released the link of his rappel harness from the rope. When he did, he realized it was definitely a lot farther than he'd hoped.

The lance strapped to his back threw him to the side as he slammed into the water. Stroking as hard as he could, Calem broke the surface of the river and took in a breath of fresh air. The weight of the lance and the river's swift current drove him underwater almost immediately. When his feet hit bottom, he used the momentary leverage to kick back toward the surface.

Like many mountain rivers, the Dobson was fast but shallow in most spots. The curve in the river underneath Dobson's Corner formed a deep natural pool, which had cushioned his fall, but the swift current had already pushed him past that point. The river at the location where he now found himself was only shoulder deep. Grabbing a convenient branch, he pulled himself out of the river. Sodden and bedraggled, he made his way through the brush until he stood at the entrance to a narrow path with a rocky rift at the other end. Through the rift he could see the start of the flat plains, which he knew would eventually lead to Silverton.

Just as he was about to step onto the path, Calem froze. *Something is wrong. I sense it; but what?*

Glancing from one side of the ravine to the other, he searched for anything out of place but saw nothing. Again, he started to step onto the path. Again, he froze.

This is crazy. It is just my nerves. Time is running out. I have got to keep moving. There is nothing there.

CHAPTER 43

Wizard Scout Gaston Myers eyed the trail, waiting for the elf to make his way out of the river. When the young elf arrived on his side of the river, Myers saw him freeze in place. The elf's eyes scanned both sides of the rocky pass. Myers wasn't too concerned. His best stealth shield was up

Taking a closer look at the elf, Myers shook his head. *"This one's too young. I told you I wouldn't take a child for Crendemor's sacrifice."*

"You are too sentimental, Wizard Scout," said Wanda. *"Besides, do not fool yourself. This one is not a child."*

"He's a teenager," Myers replied determined not to cross the line he'd drawn for himself. *"I will not harm children."*

Myers felt a momentary sense of hatred from his battle computer before the demon got its emotions under control. *"Nonsense. You confuse human children with elves. This one may look similar to a human that is fifteen years old, but he is at least three hundred years of age. Do not deceive yourself. He is older than you. He is older by far than your dear Diane. He has already lived four of your human lifespans. Take him captive now. Do not let his false appearance of youth cause you to lose sight of your goal. You need one more prisoner else the Dalinfaust will be displeased. This young elf may be your only chance at redemption."*

"He would be no prisoner any more than the others are," Myers said. *"You know as well as I that Crendemor plans on*

sacrificing all of them."

"What care you?" growled the demon. *"Life forms are dying the moment they are born. What difference does a few short years make?"*

When Myers made no reply, the demon spoke again. *"Hurry, fool. This elf may be the key to achieving your dream. The DNA gas is within your reach. Take the elf now."*

Dislike for the demon nearly overrode Myers's desire for the bottle of gas, but not quite. In spite of his promise not to harm children, he thought the command for his mount to shift back into the void.

"I will come up under him," Myers said. *"I won't harm him unless necessary. I don't kill children."*

When his battle computer gave no reply, Myers guided his mount below ground until he was directly underneath the elf. Using his passive scan, he sensed that the teenager was still frozen on the trail. He imagined the elf's head frantically shifting from one side of the path to the other.

"Do not worry," said the fake Wanda. *"He cannot detect you. He is at your mercy. Grab the elf's leg, shift him into the void, and pull him below the surface. We can savor his terror together as you strap him to your mount."*

Trying not to think about what he was doing, Myers reached up with his left hand.

Just before Myers made contact with the teenager's moccasin, the demon shouted. *"Wait! We have to leave. Now!"*

Withdrawing his hand, Myers said, *"Why?"*

An image of a spaceport flashed into Myers's mind. Burning wreckage could be seen in the distance. Someone in a battle suit was running toward three Dragars. One of the Dragars held what appeared to be three phase rods. The knowledge that the phase rods were needed to free the Dalinfaust came into his mind.

"The Dragars are on Storage," said Wanda. *"They are your allies. Their escape route is no longer viable. You must fetch the phase rods yourself and bring them here."*

"How?" Myers said. *"I can't make the spirit-cat take me to the physical dimension. If I could, I would've been long gone."*

"Your mount will take you there now."

"What if I decide not to come back?" Myers said unsure

whether he would or not.

The demon that was his battle computer laughed. *"You will return. You need the bottle of DNA gas. Besides, the Dalinfaust is already making plans for an insurance policy to ensure you do your part."*

The demon's words and tone sounded ominous, but Myers decided to ignore the hidden threat. *I will fetch the phase rods,* he thought in his private space. *Once I have all four of the special rods in my possession, I will be in a stronger bargaining position.*

Envisioning the spaceport, Myers sensed the spirit-cat shift into another dimension. He pulled his phase rod out and activated it in destructive mode. He had recognized the short figure in the battle suit.

Only Telsa is that short. I have nothing against her. I won't kill her unless I'm forced, but I will have those phase rods. I'm going to save Diane. That's all that matters.

* * *

Empress Diane Deloris rose from her desk, surveying the office full of admirals, generals, and politicians. She walked around the end of the desk until she towered over the Conglomerate's Admiral of the Fleets. All others in the room stepped back, removing themselves from the vicinity of the man.

"I want my son found, do you hear me? I don't care how many ships you have to divert. I want him *found.*"

"My Empress, I assure you that every ship not in direct combat is even now searching the galaxy for your son. The rebels and their Trecorian allies press us hard. Even the Crosioians have begun fighting against us. Thanks to the arrival of those magic ships, the bats' losses were extremely high. The Crosioians believe we tricked them. We can spare no more—"

"You can spare what *I* say you can spare," the empress said spraying spittle in a most unladylike fashion. "Finding my son is your number one priority, Admiral." She glared at the man. "Don't make me say it again."

"My Empress," said a second admiral, a female who was standing to the left of the Admiral of the Fleets. "Surveillance videos confirm your son and the chief of security departed Risors on the X-shuttle together. One of our spies on the rebels' new space station orbiting Earth confirms they were there."

The empress frowned. "And…?"

The female admiral started to glance at the Admiral of the Fleets before she caught herself and locked eyes with the empress instead. "Although I cannot confirm it, I have reason to believe your son departed the space station on a ship called the *Defiant*. Our spy says—"

The empress held up her hand.

The twenty humans and humanoids in the office froze. They all knew better than to draw unwanted attention from their volatile empress.

The empress nodded her head. "You seem to be the only one here who knows anything. You are now Admiral of the Fleets." She smiled at the woman. "So tell me, Admiral, where is the *Defiant* now?"

The new Admiral of the Fleets glanced at the old admiral before looking back at the empress. "Uh, the ship has vanished, My Empress. Our spy submitted a preposterous story that the *Defiant* went to another dimension. According to him—"

The empress raised her hand again. "Leave me. Everyone. I need time to think."

When the crowd didn't depart fast enough to please the empress, she shouted, "Go now! Or I'll have you all placed in a disintegration chamber."

The remaining admirals, generals, and politicians rushed for the door determined not to be the one to draw the wrath of the empress. When the room was clear, the empress returned to the chair behind her desk and sat down.

Why did Gaston force my son to leave with him? I should've known he lied when he said he loved me. He has obviously lied about everything.

The empress opened the middle drawer of her desk and pulled out a reflector pad. After clicking the ON icon, she studied the hologram of her face. The reflector pad revealed every wrinkle in merciless detail. She touched the crowfoot at the corner of her left eye.

I am getting old. Gaston lied. There is no DNA gas. There never has been. He has used the lie to steal my son. Somehow I will get

Matthew back. I will order the entire fleet to attack the space station. We will acquire the ability to travel between dimensions.

The empress rose from her chair, slamming her fist on the intercom icon located on the lower left of her desk. "Send the admirals back in here. I have a mission for them."

Within seconds, a half-dozen admirals led by the new Admiral of the Fleets entered the office. Before the empress could speak, the gray-scaled figure of a horse-sized cat rose out of the plush carpet of the floor. An emotion of hatred and hunger filled the room. The empress screamed as the cat bit into her leg, pulling her into the floor.

The empress reached out for the Admiral of the Fleets as the woman drew her sidearm. Every cell in the empress's body tingled. Then all she saw was darkness accompanied by intense cold.

CHAPTER 44

As suddenly as it came, the strange sensation that something was wrong left Calem. He checked both sides of the ravine again. He shivered, not from fear, but from his plunge into the cold mountain river.

I have got to get moving before I freeze to death.

Taking a final look at the path to his front, Calem took off at a trot. His pace was slow at first but gained momentum as his muscles warmed. His speed increased even more when he hit the flat grasslands that he knew stretched all the way to Silverton's main gate.

A burning ache in his lungs forced Calem to slow. *I have to pace myself. I cannot keep a dead run all the way to the city. It is still too far. No one can do that.*

Risking a glance at the stars, he made a quick estimate until sunrise, comparing the time against the remaining distance. *I will never make it at this pace. I have to speed up.*

Calem sped up until he was once again at a dead run. Almost immediately, the low end of the lance strapped on his back got between his feet and sent him down face first. He twisted to the side enough to land in the lush grass instead of the hard-packed dirt of the path, then picked himself up and took a moment to catch his breath.

This will never do, thought Calem as he unslung the lance from his back and tried balancing it in one hand. *It is too heavy. What was the chief thinking?*

Propping the lance on his shoulder, Calem took off at a run. The awkward lance bounced painfully against his collarbone with each step. He kept running, picking up speed as he went. He ran for hours, only slowing down long enough to trick his fatigued body into thinking it was going to get a respite before speeding up once again. His lungs were burning reminders that he could run himself to death if he wasn't careful. Nearly blind from fatigue, Calem became aware that he was no longer running on a dirt path. The road beneath his feet was cut stone.

Taking a labored breath, Calem forced himself to take stock of his surroundings. Things seemed lighter. He risked a glance over his left shoulder. In the far distance, he spotted the peaks of the tallest mountains. They were no longer dark.

No! Calem thought. *They shine with the sun. It is almost dawn. I have to get to the Tree of Light before it is too late.*

His blurred vision made out a waist-high stone marker to the left side of the road. It was marked with a large number 2.

Two leagues? Calem thought. *Am I only two leagues away?* He wiped tears of pain from his eyes as he looked ahead. *There is the main gate. I can see it.*

In spite of the pain in his lungs, Calem sped up, using every last bit of energy in his body. After an eternity of one beleaguered step after another, a second stone marker caught his eye. It was painted with a large 1.

He tripped on a gap where a frost heave had raised one stone higher than another and fell hard on his knees. Ignoring the bloody scrapes, he jumped up and began running again. He felt a warm liquid running from his right knee, down to his ankle. *How serious is it?* he wondered knowing he didn't have time to look. He felt a sharp pain each time his right foot made contact with the road.

I can't do this! Calem thought. *It is too much to ask. I can hardly breathe. I can barely see.*

In spite of his admonitions, he continued to run although his pace did slow a little. Each wheezing breath was a symphony of torture. His very throat felt as if it was on fire.

Massive metal objects passed by Calem's left and right.

The gates. I am inside the gates.

Calem hardly noticed guards getting out of his way as they waved him through and cheered him on encouragingly. A glance over his shoulder confirmed the first pinkish promise of a sunrise soon to come was on the horizon.

A raspy voice said, "Hurry! Hurry! Don't quit now."

A part of Calem's brain recognized the voice as his own. He wiped mucus from his nostrils with his free hand. When he took his hand away, it was covered with blood. Coughing repeatedly, he continued to run though he tasted blood.

Soon Calem was running through the park and cutting corners on the white-graveled paths to save time. Ahead he heard a series of loud thunderclaps. He felt a stiff breeze pass through the glowing leaves of the park's silver elms.

The silver elms cleared. Calem found himself in the open with the Tree of Light just a few hundred paces to his front. Ripples of silver power were moving from the base of the tree to its top in rapid succession. Small bits of lightning were arching between the tree's limbs. The entire clearing was taking on a reddish glow as the sun prepared to peek over the mountains. The largest ripple of power yet began making its way up the tree.

This is it, Calem thought. *I can see the recharging stands, but the crowd is blocking my way.*

The realization that he was not going to reach a recharging stand before the last offering was made washed over Calem. In desperation, he drew the lance back and heaved it with all his might. Whether through adrenaline or possibly because Mendera's Lance still had a small amount of Power hidden inside, the heavy lance arched over the heads of the crowd, reaching its zenith, and began a descent toward the nearest recharging stand.

Four things occurred at the same time. First, Calem fell unconscious to the ground as his strength gave out. Simultaneously, the last ripple of Power reached the top of the tree and exploded into showers of lightning bolts. Finally, the first rays of sunlight swept into the clearing just as Mendera's Lance hit the recharging stand along with a final bolt of lightning.

* * *

Slowly the darkness faded away as a glow of light coaxed Calem out of the bliss of unconsciousness. His first sensation was the feel of soft hands gently wiping his face with a cool cloth.

Opening his eyes, he saw a white tunic with a small emblem depicting a crescent moon enclosed by two concentric circles sewn on the collar.

"Good. You are awake," said the medic.

Wiping Calem's face once again with a wet cloth, the female made him take a sip from a bottle containing some foul concoction.

"You've damaged your lungs," the medic said sounding sympathetic. "I'm not sure how bad, but it doesn't look good."

The elf must've seen the panic in Calem's eyes because she added, "I'm just a healer of the second circle, so don't lose hope. I'll get one of my seniors to take a look at you in a few minutes. Just sit here and rest. Do not drink anything else until I get back."

When the medic turned, Calem saw her look at a trio of nearby elves. "See that he stays still and keep him warm. I will be back as soon as I can." The medic departed at a trot toward a group of elves standing near the trunk of the Tree of Light a bowshot away. Calem tried to rise. He grabbed onto the stone wall next to where he lay, but a fit of coughing forced him to lie back down.

"Calem, how are you feeling?" asked Generve sounding as if she were unsure she wanted to hear his answer.

Calem looked at the worried looks on his three friends. Ivy was near tears, and even Corby's eyes were glistening.

"How...how long?" Calem croaked.

"The medic said you have been unconscious for over half an hour. We got here a couple of minutes ago," Generve replied. "How are you feeling?"

As if in answer, Calem began coughing again. He pulled his hand away, noticing flecks of blood in his palm. His friends saw it as well. When Generve looked at Ivy and Corby, Calem knew there was no need to answer her question. She already knew. They all knew.

I have damaged my lungs, Calem thought. *My running days are over.*

Once his coughing subsided, Calem glanced at his friends. All three were looking at him, unable to speak. He noticed the small pack with the village's magic items lying on the ground next to his side, still full.

"I failed. It was all for nothing. I didn't get them to a recharging stand in time."

"What about Mendera's Lance," asked Corby. "Where is it? Did it get recharged?"

With a rising panic in his voice, Calem realized he no longer carried the lance. "I threw it at a stand. There wasn't enough time to—"

"And a mighty throw it was," came a deep, throaty voice.

Calem and his friends looked at the newcomer approaching from the direction of the Tree of Light. He was an old elf, wearing a dark brown robe. A staff in his left hand shone with Power as he used it to help hold his aged body upright. Calem didn't recognize the old elf, but he did recognize the staff.

It is a lord's staff. He must be one of the lords of the Council of Light.

Calem lost all curiosity in the elf's identity when he noticed the item held in the elf's right hand.

"Mendera's Lance," Generve said pointing to the lance. "It is glowing. It has been recharged!"

"So it has," confirmed the elven lord. "Your young friend's throw got it to the recharging stand just in time. It was the fifth and final time the stands recharged this night. You must have run very hard to get here from Ivy Borough before the sun rose."

"How did you know we were from Ivy Borough?" asked Generve sounding suspicious. "Err, Lord ah...?"

"Lord Sheshna, at your service, young elf maid," the elf said with a slight nod of his head. "As for knowing where you are from, even an old addled mind like mine can remember that Mendera's Lance has been at Ivy Borough these past few thousand years."

"Of course," said Generve sounding unusually meek to Calem.

"May I inquire who you are?" Lord Sheshna asked Generve, apparently assuming she was the leader of the four elves.

"Oh, sorry," replied Generve blushing. "I am Generve, granddaughter of Chief Theodcrat of Ivy Borough. These are my friends Calem, Ivy, and Corby."

"Well met," said Lord Sheshna. He glanced down at Calem. "May I ask how you came by the lance, mightiest of elven throwers?" The old elf tried his best to smile.

Calem had a feeling the elf lord didn't smile very often. Lifting the pack of magic items off the ground, Calem looked at the elven lord. "Our chief tasked me with placing the lance in a recharging stand along with this pack of magic items. I failed."

"I see," Lord Sheshna said. He hefted the glowing lance in his hand. "At least you partially succeeded. The lance appears to be fully charged. I suspect it was the more important of your items."

"Yes, but I was unable to get the remainder of the village's magic items recharged," Calem said. "The distance was too far. I—"

"Nonsense," said Lord Sheshna. "I do not want to hear you speak of failure again. You did your best. Anyone can see that. Your throw of Mendera's Lance was a sight to behold. I am going to mention you to my friend, Lord Thalos. He is in charge of our army. Should you ever desire a career in the military, I am sure he could find a place for you."

"May we have Mendera's Lance back," Calem asked trying to be polite, but attempting to sound firm at the same time. "We must return it to our chief."

Lord Sheshna hefted Mendera's Lance high and looked at it admiringly. The horn at the head of the lance radiated Power. Even at a distance, Calem could feel the weapon's magic. From what he could tell, the lance held even more Power than the elven lord's staff.

"This lance is a lot of Power to entrust to four young elves, do you not think?" Lord Sheshna said. "What assurance do I have that Mendera's Lance will make it safely back to Ivy Borough?"

"Calem's father, Jacobarak, and some of the men from the village are coming in a wagon," said the normally shy Corby. "They will be here soon to see the lance safely back."

Lord Sheshna looked at the brightly glowing lance again before speaking. "Well, my young elves. I will return Mendera's Lance to you for safekeeping for now. You must promise me you will not leave until Jacobarak and the other adults arrive to see you safely home. Do I have your word on that?"

Calem and his friends nodded in unison.

"Good," continued Lord Sheshna, "As for you, young Calem. I want you to guard this lance with all your might. I believe it responded to you when you threw it. For some reason, I think Mendera's Lance and you are destined for greatness, although I have no idea what that might entail."

Lord Sheshna laid the glowing lance next to Calem. As he

turned to leave, the old elf looked back at the young elves. "I believe the Lady has something for all of you to do. Again, I cannot say what, but I believe it is so. I feel it is so. Should any of you ever need my help, please feel free to ask. I may be old, but you may find even these old arms can provide aid when you need it most." The old elf departed heading in the direction of a white-stone path that Calem knew led to the palace.

"A lord," said Ivy grinning with excitement. "Can you believe it? We actually talked to a lord of the Council of Light! No one in Ivy Borough is going to believe us."

Corby bent down to touch the lance before looking at Calem. "Did you hear him say he would talk to Lord Thalos about finding you a place in the military? Maybe you could be a general someday." Bringing his arm across his chest in a mock salute, he laughed. "General Calem, I salute you."

Calem coughed before shaking his head. "I will never be in the military. I have damaged my lungs. I can feel them. If I do more than take slight breaths, I start coughing up blood. I may not be fit for anything ever again."

"You are the most pessimistic elf I have ever met," said Generve. "Your lungs may not be as bad as you think. Even if they are, the healers may be able to help you. My grandfather says those who give up before they even begin to fight have already lost." Somewhat more kindly, she added, "Besides, you never know what kind of aid the Lady will send your way."

CHAPTER 45

The sixth and final sharing of Power by the new bondmates occurred just as the new day's sun peeked over the eastern mountains. The morning glow bathed the Tree of Light with its warmth. Richard squeezed his bondmate's hand as she sat cross-legged beside him, leaning on his shoulder.

Jeena yawned before looking at Richard and bursting out in laughter. "Sorry. Sometimes I get a little giddy when I do not get enough sleep."

Richard smiled. "Ah. That's another tidbit of information about you I'll store away for future memory. Give us a few more years, and we'll probably know everything there is to know about each other."

"Ha!" laughed Jeena. "I suspect I can live another thousand years with you and still not know everything."

The idea of a thousand years with the beautiful elf passed through Richard's mind. He wondered if even that would be long enough.

Meshoan started packing things into the basket her family had brought the night before. She chuckled at the young couple and said, "So, Jeehana, I suppose your work is just beginning." She pointed at the gray seeds underneath the Tree of Light's outstretched limbs. "I for one am glad I do not have to rake all that up."

"Well, although I may not be doing the raking, I will certainly be busy today," replied Jeena.

Leethor stopped rolling up a blanket long enough to smile at Jeena. "It will do my heart good to know that while I go home to my comfortable bed, you will be here making sure every last seed is inventoried and stored away for future use."

Richard released his hold on his bondmate's hand and stood up to get a better look beneath the tree's limbs. "What do you do with all the seeds? There looks like a lot of them."

Reaching up for Richard's hand, Jeena pulled herself to a standing position. "Looks can be deceiving. Our land used to be covered from one shore to the other with vast forests of silver elms. Most are gone now. Only the forest of Silvertine remains."

"I believe what Jeehana's trying to say," said Meshoan, "is that the seeds are very important. They will be used to replant our continent with silver elms trees."

"Hmm," Richard said remembering the vast tracts of the elven lands he'd traveled over during previous missions on Portalis. "That will take a lot of seeds. Why bother? I've been all over this continent over the years. There are already vast forests from one end to the other. I'll admit the silver elms are pretty when they're lit, but trees are trees." Richard felt irritation through his bond link. He looked at his companions to see Jeena and Meshoan staring at him. "Uh…aren't they?"

"Open mouth, insert foot," said Nickelo in their shared space. *"You should learn to listen more."*

"I listen," Richard told his battle computer.

"Sure you do," replied Nickelo.

The feeling of irritation from Jeena didn't last long. "Rick, I am afraid you have touched on a sensitive subject. How ever goes the silver elms, so goes the elves. Our Power is linked to the silver elms in ways too subtle for even elves to understand. As the stands of silver elms have lessened, so has the magic of the Silvertine elves."

"At least that's how the story goes," said a voice Richard didn't recognize.

Looking in the direction of the voice, Richard saw a young male elf about Jeena's age. He was dressed in an elaborate blue robe. In his left hand, he carried a staff. Richard recognized the elf as one of the lords of the Council of Light but couldn't remember the elf's name.

"His name is Lord Linustanoi," volunteered Nickelo in Richard's shared space.

Jeena nodded her head at the newcomer before looking back at Richard. "Elf Friend, may I present Lord Linustanoi."

The young elf lord nodded.

Richard nodded back. "I take it you don't agree with the theory about the elves and the silver elms."

The elf shrugged. "Who am I to say? I am still learning my way around as a lord of the Council of Light. Still, I cannot help but wonder if the silver elms are as important as some among us believe." The elf lord looked at Jeena. "After all, the elves' magic was at its height during the time of the ancient Letians. That was well before the time of the Tree of Light or the silver elms."

Jeena smiled at Richard. "Lord Linustanoi and I have had this same discussion often in the past fifty years. I point out that the Lady says the silver elms are important. He counters that the elves' magical abilities have deteriorated over the last hundred thousand years despite the Lady's presence."

Lord Linustanoi gave Richard what appeared to be an attempt at a friendly smile. "I am afraid I am a creature of logic, Elf Friend. I see cause and effect. Since the planting of the first seeds of the Tree of Light, the elves magical skills have deteriorated. Cause and effect. What else can I think?"

Richard got the impression the young elf didn't smile much.

"His logic is a little skewed," said Nickelo. *"Based on his logic, the elves' magic should have increased as the forests of silver elms have disappeared. Instead, the magic has continued to deteriorate."*

Richard had to agree with his battle computer. During his time-commando missions, he'd found the farther back in time his mission, the more skilled at magic were the elves. For that matter, the abilities of all magic users regardless of species was stronger. He didn't know why, but the abilities of magic users during the current time were the weakest of any magic users he'd encountered over the years. The only exceptions were those who'd been transported from the past to the current time.

Richard scratched his chin before looking at the elf lord. "Maybe there's another reason the abilities of the elves and other magic users have declined."

The smile on Lord Linustanoi was momentarily replaced with a frown, and the elf looked at the grass-covered ground before returning his gaze to Richard with his smile back in place. "Ah. An interesting theory. Perhaps we can meet together sometime when we aren't so busy and discuss your idea in private." The elf spread his hands in an open-armed gesture. "Alas, I have other duties demanding my attention this morning as I am sure the high priestess does as well."

"That I do," agreed Jeena. "Then we will not keep you, Lord Linustanoi."

"Nor I you," said the elven lord with a deep bow. "Until another time, Elf Friend."

Richard nodded but said nothing. Once the elf was out of earshot, he turned to his bondmate. "What's his story? He strikes me a little strange."

Jeena glanced at the retreating elven lord before turning back to her bondmate. "Ah. The story of Lord Linustanoi is a sad tale. He was called as an applicant for a vacant position on the Council of Light about the time you freed me from the Dalinfaust. As he traveled to Silverton from his home village of Silver Glade, his party was attacked by a large band of orcs. All were killed save Linustanoi. His friends gave their lives that he might escape and return to their home village to give warning. Unfortunately, the marauders beat him to Silver Glade. Every elf, including the children, had already been tortured and killed. The orc army had also wiped out the entire populations of the surrounding villages."

"Must've been tough on him being the only survivor," Richard said.

"It was," agreed Jeena. "When our scouts found him, he was single-handedly trying to bury those that had been murdered by the orcs. He has never fully recovered. To be honest, he is the weakest of the elven lords. He probably should not have been selected as a lord, but after his tragedy, no one on the council had the heart to deny his appointment. We pretty much leave him to his own devices." Jeena looked back in the direction Lord Linustanoi had gone, but the elf was no longer to be seen. "I would not say this to his face, but try as he might, Lord Linustanoi is not the friendliest of elves. The high lord says to give him time. Perhaps one day he will be able to forget enough to move on with his life."

Richard looked in the direction the elven lord had gone. "The weakest you say? Maybe so, but he has one heck of a stealth shield. I didn't even detect him behind us until he spoke."

"I suppose," said Jeena surveying the foresters busy raking underneath the branches of the Tree of Light.

Looking at the tree, Richard got the impression the two dozen foresters were determined to keep as many seeds as possible from being crushed under the feet of the two hundred plus children playing tag under the tree's branches. Another score of children high in the tree's limbs jumped from one branch to another, staying out of reach of their pursuers. Terika and Matisa were among the children playing in the tree's branches.

Jeena must've noticed what he was looking at because she placed a hand on his shoulder. "They will come around," she said. "Matisa has no grudge against you. I think you just frightened her last night."

"And Terika?" Richard asked regretting his short-lived fight with Ceril had placed a seemingly insurmountable wedge between his new niece and him.

Jeena squeezed his shoulder. "It will pass, my bondmate. Have faith."

Richard noticed her glance back at the foresters. He forced a smile on his face. "Go. You don't need to babysit me."

Still hesitant, Jeena said, "What will you do?"

Meshoan spoke up. "You are welcome to come with us." She pointed at the forms of Leenador and Meenish playing tag under the Tree of Light's branches. "Once I gather up those two bundles of energy, we will be returning to our home for some much-needed rest. You can spend the day at our home if you wish, Elf Friend."

"That is right," said Leethor. "As far as we are concerned, you are family." The elf commander hugged his bondmate. "We owe you much. You saved Meshoan's life as well as that of our unborn child. We are eternally in your debt."

Richard felt his face growing warm. He'd never liked being the center of attention. "Thanks, but I think I'll stick around here for a while and watch the kids play. It's kinda relaxing." Turning to Jeena, he said, "I may go to the library later before returning home if you don't mind."

Jeena smiled. "The library? Ah, I can think of no better place to spend your spare time. I will see you this evening, my bondmate."

"Yes, you will," Richard said smiling.

Another look at the departing crowd and children playing in and under the Tree of Light sent a feeling of peace washing over him. He looked back at Jeena.

"What is it?" Jeena asked. "Is something wrong?"

Richard shook his head. "No, just the opposite. I was thinking I've found what I've been searching for my whole life."

The swirls of molten silver in Jeena's eyes sped up. "What is that?"

Richard smiled. "A home."

CHAPTER 46

After Leethor and his family departed and Jeena left to take charge of the seed cleanup, Richard made his way toward the stone wall he'd sat on the previous day. He made for the spot where an indentation in the stone wall made a comfortable seat. Once there, he looked around.

There was a group of four young elves about forty meters away; two males and two females. Two of the elves were standing while one of the females knelt beside a young male. The male was sitting down with his back against an extension of the wall Richard stood next to. He noticed looks of concern on the faces of the two standing elves and the kneeling female.

Something about the kneeling female drew Richard's attention. Looking closer, he noticed that she had three earrings dangling from one ear and what he could swear was a small nose stud in her right nostril that had an embedded glow-stone chip. Her knee-length robe was a bright multi-colored affair instead of the single earth tones that seemed to be the standard for most other elves.

As Richard studied the oddly dressed female and her companions, he made a snap decision. *"Teenagers!"* he said in his shared space. *"They're probably rebels or misfits as well. I'll bet they keep their parents on edge."*

"No doubt," agreed Nickelo. *"Isn't causing adults trouble part of a teenager's job description?"* Nickelo laughed before growing serious again. *"Although I am not there with you, I can still analyze the data you are picking up with your senses and your*

passive scan. You forgot to mention the kneeling female's brown hair has streaks of purple in it. Also, do me a favor and scan the object on the ground next to the male with his back against the wall."

Looking near the boy, Richard noticed a long object resembling a spear or a lance. Forming an active scan, he detected strong magic from the object—very strong magic. He sensed only good from the weapon and a familiar frequency from the tip of the lance. It was part of a unicorn's horn. Since it didn't appear to pose a threat, he decided to ignore it for the moment. He touched the four elves with his scan. The male with his back to the wall was injured. Richard sensed moderate damage to the boy's lungs along with some minor damage to both knees. The teenager's right lung appeared to be bleeding internally.

As if feeling his gaze, the injured boy looked at Richard. Their eyes made contact. Richard registered a sadness in the boy.

"He's got to be having trouble breathing," Richard thought. *"I wonder what happened?"*

"No idea, Wizard Scout," replied Nickelo. *"Why not try asking? People have been known to do that when they are seeking information, or so I have been told."*

Richard was intrigued enough to walk toward the four teenagers. When he drew near, all four elves looked in his direction. The eyes of the two standing elves widened. They both took a step back before regaining their composure. The kneeling girl rose, but she did not step back.

"You are a human," said the rising girl. She glanced back at her two standing companions. "It is all right. My grandfather described him. He is the elf friend." She looked back at Richard. "Aren't you?"

Nodding, Richard said, "So they tell me." He pointed at the boy with his back against the wall. "He's hurt."

The teenage girl nodded. Several strands of purple and brown hair came loose, dangling in front of her face. She brushed them back with a motion that seemed to be a familiar habit. "That's right. Calem ran all the way here from Ivy Borough. The medic said Calem's lungs are damaged. She went to get a couple of the senior medics to see if they can help." The girl took a step forward folding her arms across her chest.

Richard got the feeling she wasn't at all intimidated to be in the presence of the great elf friend.

"My grandfather told me you are a healer. He said you healed the Tree of Light. He also said you healed some elves. My grandfather says you are the only person to ever heal an elf through magic."

Richard didn't bother trying to explain that he didn't use magic to heal. He used pure Power. Walking closer to the injured elf, he knelt beside the boy. The teenager tried to rise, but a fit of coughing forced him back against the wall. When the boy moved his hand away from his mouth, Richard noticed specks of blood in the boy's palm.

"Calem, right?" Richard asked. The boy opened his mouth to speak, but Richard raised a hand to stifle his reply. "Don't answer. No use starting another coughing fit." As he spoke, he reached out with his mind and drew Power from the reserve he used to heal others.

"Are you sure you want to do this?" asked Nickelo. *"His injuries are not life-threatening. You do know it's going to hurt, don't you?"*

"What do you want me to do, Nick? Look at the scan I did on his lungs. The medics aren't going to be able to help much besides relieving the pain. At best, the scar tissue in the lungs will pretty much haunt him the rest of his life. Besides, the injury is relatively easy to heal. I don't think it will hurt all that much."

"So says the man who forgets how much healing hurts a few minutes after he does it."

"Whatever," Richard said having already made up his mind. *"Now stop distracting me."*

Wrapping healing Power around the teenager's injuries, Richard compared the way the elf was now with the way his body should be. He drew the injuries in the lungs into his own body as well as the cuts and bruises on the boy's legs. Almost immediately, he began coughing as his lungs caught on fire.

"They are not on fire," came Nickelo's thoughts. *"They just feel that way. Hang in there, Wizard Scout. The healing is almost complete."*

Once Richard's body replicated all of the boy's injuries, he sensed his healing Power repair the damage in the elf's lungs and to his legs. After the boy was entirely healed, he sensed the pain in his own lungs begin to fade as his Power healed the replicated damage to his body. Richard also felt something else. He felt an emotion of near panic coming through the link to his bondmate.

"Get away from him," he heard Jeena shout in the distance. "What are you doing to him?"

"Nothing, High Priestess," Richard heard the purple-haired teenager say. "We are not doing anything. Honest."

Opening his mouth to calm his bondmate, Richard began coughing. He noticed blood on his hand as he pulled it away from his mouth. He felt gentle hands wrapping around his shoulders as silver hair flashed in front of his face.

"Rick. What is it? What have you done?"

Fortunately, injuries replicated from others healed much faster than those he acquired on his own. By the time Jeena finished asking her questions, Richard's lungs were healed enough to reply. He looked up into her tear-streaked face. "It's all right. I'm fine."

"No, you are not," insisted Jeena. "You are bleeding. I felt your pain through our bond link."

Richard shook his head. "Not anymore. I'm already starting to forget how much it hurt. That's just the way—"

The molten silver in his bondmate's eyes flashed with a hint of anger. "Well, I haven't forgotten. The burning pain is still fresh in my mind. You were hurt. I…" The anger in her eyes disappeared. "I was frightened. I thought you were being attacked."

The realization that he was no longer alone in the world hit Richard hard. His actions affected others.

"Your actions have always affected others," said Nickelo in their shared space. *"You just rarely cared before."*

"I'm sorry, Jeena. I… I wasn't thinking. Calem here needed help. I didn't think about the fact that you would feel the pain as well. I'm sorry I hurt you."

With her eyes softening even more, Jeena said, "I didn't feel the actual pain. I felt your emotions as you went through the pain." She looked at Calem who was now standing next to his three friends. She turned her attention back to Richard. "I am glad the boy is healed, but you must promise me that you will never do that again without speaking to me first." She wiped at something near her eye. "I was scared, Rick."

"I'm really sorry, Jeena. I will try to talk to you first from now on before I try healing someone."

"Promise me," said Jeena. "I want wizard scout honor."

"I'll try," Richard said hating to deny his bondmate anything. "You wouldn't want me to let someone die just because you weren't around, would you?" The feeling Richard got through his bond link was mixed.

Finally, Jeena shook her head. "No, but when I am around, you have to talk to me first. Promise me."

The pleading look on his bondmate's face made Richard give the only answer he could. "I promise. That's wizard scout honor."

Jeena stared at him for a couple of heartbeats. "I am going to hold you to that, Rick." She continued to stare until he nodded his head. When he did, Jeena turned to look at the four youths. She pointed at the boy Richard had healed. "So you are Calem?"

The boy nodded. "Yes, High Priestess." He waved his right hand to indicate his three companions. "These are my friends Ivy, Corby, and Generve. We are all from Ivy Borough."

Glancing down, Jeena studied the lance near the boy's feet. "Ah. That explains why you have Mendera's Lance. I saw you throw it during the last offering. You got it to the recharging stand just in time."

Bending down, Jeena picked up the lance. The unicorn horn point glowed with Power. "It has been fully recharged," she said. She glanced at Richard. "Mendera's Lance is a powerful weapon. It has meant the difference between victory and defeat for the elves on more than one occasion." She pointed at the arm-length tip of the lance. "The lance point came from the unicorn Swiftmane. He and his maid Mendera fought—"

Richard nodded. He had already recognized the frequency of the unicorn horn. "Yes, I know. I was there, remember? I saw Mendera and Swiftmane's charge against the demon-giant." Richard touched the horn with the fingertips of his left hand. "They were both good friends."

A feeling of awe mingled with sadness came down the link Richard shared with his bondmate. She stared at him without saying anything.

Looking at the four teens, Richard said, "May I hold it?"

"Uh, of course, Elf Friend," said Calem.

The other teens nodded their heads. Jeena held the lance out to Richard. He took it reverently with both hands. Memories of the half-elf Mendera and the unicorn Swiftmane passed through his mind. He couldn't remember everything, but enough to know he missed his friends and allies.

"I should've been with them during that final charge," Richard said out loud. "I let them down."

"Don't do that, Rick," said Nickelo in their shared space. *"You had your own battle. You did all you could."*

Richard wasn't so sure.

Sensing his sadness, Jeena laid a hand on Richard's shoulder. "I do not know all that happened that day, but I would bet my life you did not let them down. I do not believe you would ever willingly let anyone down."

"Swiftmane died," Richard said. "A lot of others died too."

Jeena glanced at the Tree of Light before looking back at Richard. "I am sure they did. Victory almost always comes at a cost. The legends tell us Swiftmane died fighting for all that is good." She pointed at the lance in Richard's hands. "Elf Friend Swiftmane's last wish was for his horn to be formed into this lance so that he could continue to defend against evil long after his death."

Richard contemplated the weapon in his hands. The lance was heavier than he'd expected. He could feel the Power emanating from the horn at the weapon's tip.

"It seems a little short for a lance," Richard said remembering pictures he'd seen of old knights on Earth riding into battle on their chargers with long lances to their fore.

"Oh," said the purple-haired Generve. She took a step toward Richard. "May I?"

Unsure what the teen wanted but seeing no harm, Richard nodded and handed the weapon to the teen girl.

Generve pointed to a thumb-sized protrusion halfway down the shaft of the two-meter-long lance. "My grandfather showed me this," she said. "You press on this and slide it." The girl slid the protrusion in the direction of the unicorn tip.

Richard heard a click. The end of the shaft extended out until the unicorn-horn tip was a full five meters from the base. "Ah," he said. "Now that's more like what I expected a lance to look like.

I'm assuming it will retract."

The purple-haired elf smiled as she pressed down on the protrusion and slid it back slightly. After another click, the shaft retracted until the lance was back to its two-meter length.

"Cool," Richard said.

The girl frowned. "Cool?"

Richard laughed, and so did Jeena.

Taking pity on the teenager, Jeena said, "It is just a saying my bondmate uses when he is trying to say he is pleased with something."

Generve glanced back at her three friends before returning her gaze to Richard. "Cool," she said as she handed the weapon back to him with a smile. "I think we have just discovered another word to confuse the adults."

Jeena laughed again, her silver eyes sparkling. "Then you must spend some time talking to my bondmate. He has all kinds of *cool* sayings."

Richard laughed as he practiced extending and retracting the lance a few times. When he was done, he handed the weapon back to Calem. "I think this is yours."

Calem accepted the lance, looking a little relieved to have it back. He turned and conferred with his friends a few seconds before turning to Richard. "Elf Friend, I want to thank you for healing me. I am sure my father will want to thank you as well. If I may be so bold, my friends and I would like to invite you—"

A wave of intense evil washed over Richard. A few of the children playing under and in the Tree of Light's branches screamed. He felt a rush of fear from the link he shared with his bondmate.

"The Tree of Light is under attack!" yelled Jeena. "The Lady says someone is attacking the Presence of the Lady." She took off running in the direction of the path leading to the cavern underneath the tree.

Richard took a step to follow.

"*Wait,*" said Nickelo in their shared space. "*You are unarmed. Summon your dimensional pack. Get your weapons and armor first.*"

"*No time,*" Richard said.

"*Make time. Look at your passive scan.*"

Power flared on his scan to the north. Richard looked in time to see a bright blue beam of light shoot up into the air from the northern obelisk. He remembered Terika and Matisa telling him the obelisk was one of the corners of the Tree of Light's gate. The beam of energy arched downward until it touched the top of the Tree of Light. Bright silver Power from the tree rippled up from its base to meet the blue beam, pushing it back and forming a shield. Power flared from both the blue beam and the silvery shield. Richard sensed an all too familiar evil in the blue beam of energy. It was demonic in nature.

"The beam has the same frequency as that in your special phase rod," said Nickelo. *"Only your brother has one of those rods. He must be here. Summon your pack and get your battle suit on. Now!"*

Richard glanced in the direction his bondmate had gone. She was running for all she was worth toward the path leading to the cavern. He sensed Power flare beneath the Tree of Light as if a battle was taking place below ground.

"I can't be in two places at once," Richard mentally yelled.

"Then don't try," said Nickelo. *"Your bondmate is the high priestess. The other lords will come to her aid. You have got to stop your brother. Except for your Jeena, the other elves links to their Power reserves are unprotected. They won't stand a chance against your brother."*

Torn but seeing his battle computer's logic, Richard thought the command to summon his dimensional pack. When it appeared in the air to his front, he grabbed it with one hand, ripped his battle helmet off the side with the other, and shoved the helmet onto his head. The visor slid down into three-quarters mode. He imagined his battle suit and weapons. No Power left his reserve, but he wasn't concerned because they were freebies. Lifting the flap, Richard reached inside the opening but felt nothing. He looked inside.

"It's empty," Richard said. *"What's going on?"*

"Try something else," suggested Nickelo.

Richard imagined an M12, sending the specs to his dimensional pack. No Power left his reserve. Raising the flap, he glanced inside. Again, the pack was empty.

"What's that big jerk in the sky think he's doing?" Richard

said. *"I thought Jeena and 'the One' had an understanding."*

"I don't think it is 'the One' causing the problem this time," said Nickelo. *"I am going to try and contact the Oracle. Hold on."*

Richard didn't have time to hold on. He was about to say so when another wave of demonic evil washed over him. He sensed a flare of Power to the east. Glancing in that direction, he saw a beam of red arch out from the eastern obelisk and join the blue beam in its assault against the Tree of Light's shield. The silvery shield surrounding the tree bent inward before regaining its shape.

Monitoring his passive scan, Richard detected a slight difference in frequency between the beam from the first obelisk and the second.

"I don't get it," Richard said. *"The second beam's frequency appears to be from a different phase rod. How did Myers get two phase rods?"*

"Rick, I am in contact with the Oracle. The planet Storage is under attack by one of the black dreadnaughts. All three of your phase rods that were on Storage have been stolen. The Oracle says the R12 planetary core generator on Storage is diverting all energy to the force fields around the most sensitive sites. The main teleporter is no longer operational. You cannot summon anything with your dimensional pack. You are on your own."

Richard spun to face south. As he did so, a flare of demonic evil washed over him and a green beam of energy arched out from the third obelisk to join in the assault on the Tree of Light. The sound of screaming children filled the air. Richard heard the sound of High Lord Trenadine's voice.

"Lords to me," shouted the high lord, standing at the edge of the Tree of Light's branches with his bondmate, Reale.

High Lord Trenadine and his bondmate each planted the butts of their staffs in the ground. Beams of blue light shot out, reinforcing the shield around the tree. Lord Othellian joined them. Richard noticed Lords Thalos and Sheshna running for the path Jeena had taken leading to the entrance of the Presence of the Lady.

"I've got to help Jeena," Richard shouted. "I need a weapon."

"Elf Friend," shouted a young voice behind Richard.

Turning, Richard saw Calem throwing Mendera's Lance in his direction.

"Take this," shouted Calem. "What should we do?"

Grabbing the lance in midair, Richard said, "Gather the children under the Tree of Light branches and keep them there. The tree's shield should protect them."

With weapon in hand, Richard took a step to follow Lords Thalos and Sheshna.

"No, Rick," said Nickelo. *"You've got to stop your brother. If he activates the last obelisk, I calculate the shield around the tree will be destroyed. Without the Power of the Tree of Light, the gate may be opened. If that happens, demon armies will destroy all three galaxies. You've got to stop him."*

"How?" Richard said unsure how he was supposed to get to the last obelisk in time. *"He must be teleporting or something. I can't get there in time by running."*

An image of a black stallion with flaming red eyes and claws instead of hoofs flashed in Richard's mind. Without thinking, he sent an emotional call for help into the universe, putting all the need he could muster into the call.

Almost immediately a black head came out of the ground followed by the black body of the spirit-horse. Taking no time to wonder at the speedy response, Richard jumped on the stallion's back. Black tendrils sprung out of the spirit-horse's back and sides, securing him in place.

"Where?" asked the stallion speaking the question in near-perfect Intergalactic Standard.

Richard sent his mount an image of the last obelisk.

The stallion shimmered, shifting into the void. Down into the ground they went.

Richard could only hope they would be in time.

CHAPTER 47

"Fire," Sergeant Ron shouted into the ship-wide intercom. "Give that black ship everything you've got! We've got to create an opening for Charlie and Asquan!"

The *Defiant* shuddered and bucked, partially from the outgoing weapons but mostly from the massive amount of return fire coming from the dreadnaught.

"Shields are down to thirteen percent," said Angela sounding very calm to Sergeant Ron, considering the circumstances. "I'm guessing their next full salvo will be our last."

"Roger that," Sergeant Ron said trying to sound matter-of-fact.

I've led a long life, he thought, *longer than I have a right. I should've died the day I first saw that blasted black ship. Sharon should've left me and saved the crew of the* Defiant *instead. My only regret is that I never got to pay back those who killed my wife and destroyed our ship.*

Sergeant Ron guided the *Defiant* forward until he was firing point-blank range at the huge dreadnaught. Something near the bow of the black ship drew his attention. He thumbed the zoom control for the video to max magnification. Rows of pieces of torn and scorched metal of various colors, sizes, and shapes appeared to be welded to the dreadnaught's hull underneath the black dragon insignia painted on the bow. Sergeant Ron could barely see unintelligible writing on some of the pieces of metal. A few others had letters in Intergalactic Standard; *Stargazer, Calypso,* and *Galaxy End* to name a few. He recognized them as ships supposedly lost to pirates over the last forty years, then scanned down the row until one scorched piece of metal caught his eye, blocking out all else. The name on the metal was all too familiar. It read *Defiant*.

Tears formed in Sergeant Ron's eyes. He squeezed the trigger on his forward guns, sending beams of plasma, phase, and magic at the dreadnaught. His weapon's fire might as well have been spitballs for all the good they did.

I can't let them get away, Sergeant Ron thought. *Not again. They murdered Sharon. I won't let them get away.*

* * *

The Dragar communication officer said, "Admiral, the ship to our front is concentrating fire on a single shield."

"Is the shield holding?" said the admiral not really concerned. The recon ship was proving tougher to destroy than he'd anticipated, but he had no doubt a couple more salvos would finish the job.

"Front shields are holding," verified the tactical officer standing to the admiral's left. "The two fighters to our rear concern me. They are holding back for some reason."

The admiral scoffed. "What do you think they are going to do? Fighters are no match for our dreadnaught. As soon as we destroy that recon ship, I want all guns brought to bear on the shield around the R12 planetary core generator. Once it is destroyed, the shields around all the other facilities will drop. They will be helpless."

"Yes, sir," said the tactical officer. "We have already destroyed seventy percent of our designated targets."

"I want them all destroyed, do you hear me?"

"Yes, sir," hissed the tactical officer, "but I must warn you that a relay for one of our rear shields is intermittently malfunctioning. There is a danger—"

The admiral glared, his forehead turning dark gray. "Do not give me warnings or excuses, fool! Blow that recon ship out of the sky, then concentrate on the planetary defenses. Do I make myself clear?"

The Dragar tactical officer brought his forearm across his chest.

"Yes, sir. It will be done as you command." He exchanged glances with the communication officer before returning his attention to his scrying globes. Eighteen missiles were heading toward the rear shield. Each missile appeared to be uncannily spaced the perfect distance to allow the missile to its front to explode without being caught in the blast of the next, but near enough to add its own force to that of its predecessor.

As the tactical officer continued to watch, the first missile hit dead center on the rear shield controlled by the faulty relay. The shield held. Two more missiles made contact with the same shield. Again, the shield held, but the tactical officer felt the deck of the huge dreadnaught shudder. Throwing caution to the wind, the officer rose hurriedly and made his way toward the admiral. Three more missiles struck home as he ran the short distance to his commanding officer. The third missile hit hard enough to rattle one of the scrying globes out of its mount. The globe shattered on the metal deck, spraying noxious vapor all around.

"Sir," said the tactical officer, "the ship is in danger. Our rear shield—"

Another missile struck the rear shield. The force was such that both the admiral and the tactical officer were knocked off their feet.

"Admiral," said the communication officer running the six paces to the admiral's station on the bridge. "Damage control is reporting fires in sections thirteen and fifteen. Engineering says one of the rear shields is at twelve percent and dropping."

"Impossible!" roared the admiral attempting to rise to his feet. "Those are just fighters back there."

The strike of another missile knocked the admiral back down to the deck.

"Rear shield is at three percent," said the tactical officer getting back in the conversation. "The next missile will hit in six seconds."

The admiral raged. *How can my ship be defeated by a mere recon ship?* Rage though he might, the admiral was no fool. "Jump!" he ordered. "Jump now!"

The admiral felt his skin tingle as the magic in the dimensional drive took effect. The walls of the ship began to shimmer, then everything went black.

* * *

Sergeant Ron continued to pour every weapon at his disposal into the dreadnaught's forward shield. At the same time, he monitored the strikes of the missiles into the rear shield of the black ship.

"Their rear shield is at three percent," said Margery. "The next missile should penetrate."

"Take it to 'em, Daniel!" Sergeant Ron yelled into the intercom. "You've got them on the ropes. Don't let up!"

Even as he said it, Sergeant Ron noticed the dreadnaught shimmer and disappear. The remaining missiles that had been targeting the black ship's rear shields passed through empty space.

"Noooooo!" Sergeant Ron shouted. "Not again! I can't let them get away again!"

"Incoming," said Margery. "The last ten missiles are heading toward us now."

Sergeant Ron pressed the missile self-destruct button on the arm of his command chair. Bright flashes of light filled the cockpit.

"All missiles have been destroyed," said Margery. "As for the dreadnaught, I calculate you will meet it another time. In the meantime, your grandson and the others are fighting for their lives on the planet below. You have got to help them."

"Matthew?" Sergeant Ron asked before regaining control of his emotions. "Margery, I want you to set a course for the spaceport. We're going in at max throttle."

CHAPTER 48

The two Dragar fighters came roaring in eager to make a kill. Glancing to her front, Telsa gauged the distance to the three Dragars who had stopped running to turn and face her. One of the trio carried the three phase rods.

"It is going to be close," said Raj in their shared space. *"I highly recommend you speed up."*

Telsa didn't bother replying. Her battle computer knew as well as she that the battle suit was already at max speed. She saw flashes of light from the three Dragars as they opened up with pistol and automatic rifle fire. Multicolored beams of magic came streaking toward her. Throwing up a hasty defensive shield, Telsa angled it so the balls of magic ricocheted into the air. She was tempted to project a wall of Power against the Dragars and crush them into the concrete taxiway.

"Bad idea," came Raj's thought. *"The moment you kill those Dragars, the fighters will be free to bomb you into nonexistence."*

"I wasn't going to do it," Telsa said. *"I was just thinking about it."*

"Sure you were," said Raj unconvinced. *"Now get ready to slide."*

At exactly the right moment, Telsa twisted to her side and slid feet first into the Dragars. She felt a tingle of energy as she passed through their defensive shield, but it wasn't attuned to physical attacks. She came to her feet inside the Dragars' shield swinging her phase rod at the neck joint of the closest. The Dragar ducked under the blow and fired his pistol at Telsa's head. His aim was no better than her swing. The pistol's ball of magic went wide of the mark.

As Telsa swung at a second Dragar, the roar of engines filled the air from the two Dragar fighters passing overhead a mere ten meters. Wind vortices knocked one of the Dragars off his feet. The tip of Telsa's phase rod caught a second in the side of the helmet. She sensed the microscopic explosions of phase energy scrambling the brain inside. Telsa reached out with her mind to the third Dragar, wrapping what she hoped was the creature's heart with Power and jerking with telekinesis. The Dragar dropped to the ground, spraying a flurry of magic rounds from his rifle as his finger reflexively tightened on the trigger. When the Dragar hit the taxiway, his rifle flew from his hands and he moved no more.

"For Creator's sake," said Raj, *"stop killing them. They are the only reason the fighters didn't drop a bomb in your lap on that last pass."*

"I didn't kill all of them. I kept one alive."

The live one rose to his feet holding the three phase rods in one hand and a pistol in the other. Before Telsa could react, a solid slug of metal tore into the Dragar's visor and out the back, spewing blood and bone onto the concrete beyond.

Spinning, she raised her phase rod into a guard position. Telsa saw a man dressed in black armor twenty meters away, holding a phase rod in one hand and a pistol in the other. She recognized the armor as a battle suit and the pistol as one of Rick's .44 caliber AutoMags. She knew the man as well.

"Gaston," Telsa said.

"I calculate this does not bode well," said Raj in their shared space.

"No sh—" Telsa started.

"Move to the side, Telsa," shouted Myers walking slowly toward her with phase rod and pistol at the ready. "I've got no wish to harm you, but I'm short on time."

"He must want the phase rods," said Raj. *"I calculate that would not be a good idea."*

"I can't do that, Gaston," Telsa said as she jerked a thumb at the burning wreckage of the troop shuttles behind her. "I don't know how you got here, but your ride off this planet is gone. Just turn and walk away, and I promise I'll cover for you long enough for you to find alternate transportation."

Myers didn't reply. Instead, Telsa sensed a line of Power reach out in the direction where the Dragar had dropped the phase rods. She sent out her own line of Power, knocking Gaston's aside.

"That was a mistake," said Myers changing the visor of his helmet to clear, showing his face. "I know my brother has protected the link to your Power reserve, but you still can't hope to stop me. I'm a shifter. Face it. You're outgunned."

Telsa switched her visor to clear as well, then flicked the dial on her phase rod to maximum destructive mode. The miniature lightning bolts of red energy crawling up the brerellium-steel rod brightened sharply. "I guess that remains to be seen," she said trying to keep her voice steady. "I'm not one of your cadets anymore. I won't be intimidated."

Myers looked at her for a second, then gave a tight-lipped smile. "No, I guess you won't. It's a shame. I always liked you."

Telsa noticed her ex-TAC officer thumb the dial on his phase rod. The rod glowed bright red with phase energy. She sensed a wave of hunger from the rod. The thought of the demon essence inside yearning for her life force caused a drop of sweat to track down Telsa's face.

Myers gave a small laugh. "You already know how this will end. I can see your fe—"

Firing her Deloris blaster as fast as she could pull the trigger, Telsa charged forward.

Myers twisted to the side, avoiding the phase energy. He shimmered, shifting into the void.

Telsa didn't care. She continued her charge, swinging her phase rod at the side of Myers's helmet so fast even her ex-instructor was caught by surprise. He ducked below the swing, but not quite fast enough. The tip of her phase rod drew a thin gouge in the forehead of his battle helmet.

Myers kicked back and swung wildly with his phase rod, forcing Telsa to keep her distance. She continued firing her phase pistol trying her best to hit the fleeting target that was the wizard scout.

"I could use a little help, Raj," Telsa thought. *"He's in the void, but if I can get a hit with one of my phase rounds we've got a*

chance."

"I am doing my best," said Raj. *"His battle computer is anticipating your moves just like I am anticipating his. We are evenly matched."*

Click.

The Deloris blaster stopped firing.

"Oh, by the way, you are out of ammo. I recommend you reload."

Telsa dropped the now useless pistol and gripped her phase rod with two hands. Although Myers still had ammo, he smiled and holstered his AutoMag. Changing his grip to two hands, he charged forward. Telsa met him halfway, but the force of the blow knocked her back a step. She swept with her leg, hoping to catch her opponent off balance. Her foot passed through Myers's leg, throwing her off balance instead. Myers swung downward. She barely got out of the way, swinging her own phase rod to keep him out of reach.

"He is in the void," said Raj. *"Only your phase rod can touch him."*

"No kidding," Telsa said as she took another swing at Myers.

Myers smirked before disappearing down into the concrete pavement.

"Use your active scan," said Raj. *"Do not let him sneak up on you."*

Reaching out with her mind, Telsa located two life forms underground. "What the—"

A gray-skinned paw with finger-length claws reached out of the concrete right below Telsa's feet. She swung downward with her phase rod, hitting the side of the gray paw. It retracted into the ground.

"Behind you," yelled Raj in their shared space. *"He had his stealth shield activated."*

A life force appeared on Telsa's passive scan right behind her. She spun in a desperate attempt to block the blow she knew was coming, but she was too late. Halfway through her turn, she caught a flash of red before her side erupted in the worst pain she'd ever felt. Her organs gave way to phase energy as they ruptured, spewing their contents inside her body. Through the intense pain, she felt something greedily sucking life force out of her.

Power from Telsa's reserve wrapped around her injuries in a desperate attempt to return her to baseline, but it was no match for the demon essence in Myers's phase rod. She sensed death's cold embrace reaching out for her.

* * *

Myers pulled his phase rod away from the curled-up ball of black armor that was his ex-cadet.

"More," said Wanda. *"Keep the phase rod touching the wizard scout until you drain her dry. The Dalinfaust needs all the energy he can get. The more you take from her, the more he will feed me."*

"Kiss off," Myers said. He looked at Telsa lying helpless before him. *"I'm here to get the phase rods, not to kill wizard scouts."*

"I am hungry," said Wanda. *"Feed me or—"*

"Or what?" Myers said knowing full well the demon that was his battle computer was a dangerous partner.

"Or...or the Dalinfaust will be displeased."

"Then he'll just have to live with disappointment," Myers said distrusting his battle computer more than ever. *"Now summon my mount and inform the Dalinfaust we've got the weapons. I hope your master still has enough Power to get our mount back through that shield surrounding Portalis. Otherwise, we came here for nothing."*

"He has the Power and more," said Wanda. *"Pray you never find out the extent of his Power."*

Before Myers could reply, the gray-skinned head of the spirit-cat followed by the rest of its body emerged from the ground. He noticed the cat limp on its bloody right foot.

"Great. He's injured," Myers said. *"Can he still take us back to Portalis?"*

"He can," said Wanda. *"Now fetch the rods and let us be gone. The Dalinfaust must be freed, or you will not get the DNA gas for your precious Diane."*

Myers's face grew warm, but he controlled his anger. He hated having ever gotten Diane involved in the mess where he now found himself. Regardless, all he could do now was see it through to its end. He reached out with a line of Power toward the three phase rods. Another line of Power struck his, knocking it aside

312

before wrapping around the phase rods and levitating them to his rear.

Turning, Myers saw a young man standing ten meters away catch the phase rods in midair.

"Matt, give those here. I don't have time for this."

Matthew pointed at Telsa's still body. "Is she dead?"

Shaking his head, Myers said, "No. Her self-heal is repairing her injuries now." He tried to smile. "We'll need to work on your passive scan when we get the time. You should've been able to figure that out on your own. By the way, that's a good stealth shield. I didn't even sense you."

Matthew looked at Myers without smiling. "Rick and you taught me well when we were on Portalis."

"So we did," Myers said knowing he didn't have time for discussions but unwilling to fight his own son. "I need those phase rods, Matt. I need them to help your mother. Trust me. In a few days, we can be a real family. We can all be together, but I need those rods. You've got no idea what's going on."

"Maybe not, but I'm going to find out. I'm going with you."

"The hell you are," Myers said feeling fear for the first time in many years. "I don't want you anywhere near where I have to go."

"Then you're going without these rods because I'm not giving them up without a fight."

Reaching out with a line of Power, Myers split it apart, sending the separate lines in two directions toward the phase rods in his son's hand. He sensed a line of Power reach out from his son and knock one of his lines away. His other line grabbed onto the rods and pulled them out of Matthew's grasp. The phase rods made it halfway back to Myers before another line of Power from his son grabbed onto them, holding them frozen in midair.

"Let go, Matt," Myers said pulling the rods with telekinesis. They moved a couple of meters toward him before freezing in place once again as his son redoubled his efforts.

"You're not taking them without me," said Matthew.

Another line of Power joined Matthew's and jerked the phase rods back to the center point between Matthew and Myers.

"You're not taking them at all," said a feminine voice.

Myers glanced to his left to see Tia limping forward, using a rifle as a crutch. Blood oozed out of a bandage on her leg, leaving a trail of red back toward the warehouse two hundred meters away. He noticed two figures running from the building carrying rifles and recognized them as Dren and Brachia.

I don't have time for this, Myers thought in his private space. *What do I do now? Tia and Matt are stronger than they think. I'm not going to be able to wrest the phase rods from their combined Power without hurting one of them.*

"Incoming!" yelled Wanda over the external speakers of his battle helmet. "Those two fighters are making a bombing run. Your shield will not protect you against physical attacks."

Sensing with his passive scan, Myers saw the two fighters leveling off for their bombing strike. Turning in their direction, he made out two bombs underneath each fighter.

"We've got to knock out those fighters, or we're all dead," Myers yelled. "Matt, Tia, take the one on the right. I'll take the left."

Temporarily forgotten, the phase rods fell to the concrete taxiway as three lines of Power reached out toward the attacking fighters. Myers reached into the trigger mechanism for one of the bombs under the wing of his fighter, twisting hard with telekinesis.

Boom!

The leftmost fighter disintegrated in midair.

Myers sensed the lines of Power from Tia and Matthew probing for the pilot's heart in the remaining fighter. Their control was sloppy. He sensed the teenagers miss on their first attempt. Weighing the odds, he decided they would get the pilot on their next attempt. Making his decision, he ran toward his spirit-cat and jumped onto the saddle as he pulled the three phase rods into his waiting hand with telekinesis.

"Go! Go now!" Myers yelled at his mount.

Just as the spirit-cat began to shimmer, a pair of arms wrapped around Myers's waist.

"Not without me," shouted Matthew locking himself in place with Power.

Myers grabbed his son tight as the spirit-cat completed its shift into the void between dimensions. "You fool. If you fall off, you'll die."

Myers gripped his son even tighter as his mount shifted into another dimension. The die was cast. It was too late to take his son back now.

* * *

Tia missed the pilot on her first attempt. She made a second attempt, forcing herself to concentrate despite the pain in her leg. She expected to see a line of Power from Matthew make a second attempt as well, but instead, it withdrew for some reason. As the remaining fighter closed, Tia located the pilot's heart and wrapped it with Power. When she jerked, the aircraft dove for the ground, exploding in a blast of magical fire and smoke.

"We did it!" Tia shouted as she turned to share the victory with Matthew. She caught a glimpse of a gray-skinned cat carrying Myers. Matthew's father was holding onto his son with one hand. The cat sank into the concrete, taking Myers and Matthew with them.

"Noooo!" Tia shouted hobbling to the spot where they'd disappeared. She fell to the ground doing her best not to cry and failing miserably.

The sound of running feet drew Tia out of her grief. She glanced up to see Dren and Brachia standing over her.

"They're gone," Tia said. "Myers took Matthew with him. Why? Where?"

Dren looked at her brother before glancing back down at Tia. "I don't know why, but it's a pretty safe bet Myers is going to Portalis. That was one of those spirit-cats Uncle Rick described. It must be taking them and the phase rods to Portalis. We need to go after them."

Hope surged in Tia. "How?"

Pointing to a bright light in the sky, Tia said, "That's how."

Tia reached out to the light with her senses. She recognized the frequencies of the crew of the incoming X-shuttle. She grew more confident. Terrie was onboard. He could heal her. Once the X-shuttle was docked to the *Defiant*, Tia was sure Sergeant Ron could convince the triplets to take them to the magic dimension.

Tia sensed a tingle in her left hand. Looking at the gray-metal ring with the inset sliver of green stone, she reached into the link connecting her to Matthew. She felt him on the other end. She felt fear and confusion, but the mere fact that he was alive gave her hope.

She sent an emotion of hope and courage through the ring.

"Don't worry, Matt. We're coming. That's a promise."

CHAPTER 49

The nine bottles of red liquid glistening on the table in the hidden lab contrasted sharply with the older containers of blood and organs. Lord Crendemor held one of the bottles up in front of the sphere. The yellow eye looked unimpressed.

Sneering with disgust, Lord Crendemor said, "The fool brought me adult elves. On top of that, he only brought nine elves for sacrifice. The spell will be weak without the blood of ten children."

"Do not fret, elf," said the Dalinfaust. "The blood will be sufficient to begin the spell. Other sacrifices will be made available when you need them."

"I need children," Lord Crendemor insisted.

"You shall have them. One step at a time, elf. I have everything under control."

Lord Crendemor burned with anger. He hated being reliant on the demon. *I must play along for now,* he thought. *When my chance comes, I will take it. The Dalinfaust will rot in his prison for his full thousand years if I have anything to do with it.*

Grasping a larger vial, Crendemor recited the spell taught him by the demon as he transferred the contents of the nine bottles into it. By the time he tapped the last drop of blood out of the ninth bottle, the vial was nearly full.

Placing the vial on the table next to the Staff of the Lady of the Tree, Crendemor faced the sphere once more. "We are short, as I suspected. I suppose I can kill one of the caretakers in the Presence of the Lady and use their blood, but it will be weak."

"No," said the Dalinfaust. "I have already arranged for the tenth sacrifice. She will meet you there." The Dalinfaust laughed. "I must keep my promise, after all."

The demon's comment confused Lord Crendemor. "You are talking nonsense. We need the blood of children, I tell you."

The yellow eye in the sphere narrowed. "*Never* think you have the right to *tell* me anything, elf."

Lord Crendemor bit his tongue. "Of course. I merely meant—"

"I know what you meant. You think you know much, but your infinitesimal knowledge falls far short of what is needed. As it so happens, since I am not at my full abilities, opening the gate completely will take the sacrifice of two hundred elf children to succeed; not ten."

"What?" Lord Crendemor said taken aback by the impossibility of such a task. "Elf children are too well protected. We could never get—"

"You fool," said the Dalinfaust the yellow eye growing even narrower. "Do you think I have not thought my plan out considering every eventuality? The required sacrifices are even now scampering under and among the limbs of the Tree of Light. Once the spell I taught you begins, it will suck the life force from the children playing around the tree. As the blood of the children spill, the gate will open. Once I am free, the demon armies will be mine to command."

A vision of the two hundred plus children Crendemor had seen under the Tree of Light when he'd left flashed into his mind. For the merest instant, a twinge of conscience caused him to doubt his resolve, but he shoved it aside and swore never to think on it again.

I will wrest control of the spell from the demon with the aid of the staff, Lord Crendemor thought. *The lives of a few children are nothing compared to what I will gain. The demon armies will be mine to control. Once I have conquered the three galaxies, I will bring my bondmate Lillia back from the land of the dead to rule at my side.*

Lord Crendemor noticed the yellow eye in the sphere staring at him as if guessing his thoughts. Before the Dalinfaust could say anything, a disturbance in the void touched Crendemor's mind.

"They are coming," Lord Crendemor said eager to change the

subject. "I sense multiple instances of your essence." Concentrating harder, he picked up something else. "The spirit-cat is bringing two life forms with it. Is your time-commando bringing the tenth sacrifice?"

"No. The last sacrifice will join you in the Presence of the Lady. The fool is bringing his son with him. That may work to our advantage. My demon servant says the human is becoming more difficult to control. Be on your guard."

I am always on my guard, Crendemor thought.

The life forms drew closer. A gray-scaled cat head rose out of the lab floor until its body was completely clear of the stone. Its black-clad rider carried three deactivated phase rods in his right hand. Behind the rider sat a human male in his late teens, holding tight to the black-clad rider.

Lord Crendemor gave his best false smile. "I see you have brought us company, Wizard Scout. I wish I had known so I could be more hospitable. As it is, I have nothing to offer your...son."

The wizard scout frowned. "He is no concern of yours, elf." Myers raised the three phase rod handles. "I have brought the other parts of the demon. Take them. I am done with you and your schemes. Now give me the DNA gas, and we will be gone."

Lord Crendemor reached out with his mind and probed the teenager. He sensed a large Power reserve with a heavily trapped link. Frowning, he glanced at the yellow eye in the sphere.

When the demon said nothing, Crendemor shrugged. "Alas, I cannot do as you ask, human. Your task is almost done, but not quite. You must take the phase rods and plant them in the center of each corner of the gate as we discussed. Once you are done, you are to meet me in the Presence of the Lady. You will receive your reward then, as you deserve."

"Now?" said Myers. "I thought you said it was too dangerous today. You said it would be tomorrow."

"The situation has changed," Crendemor replied. "If what the Dalinfaust tells me is true about the Dragar's debacle on Storage, I have no doubt forces are even now being assembled against us. Time is of the essence."

The teenager grasped Myers's arm and said, "Father, this place stinks of evil. We need to leave. Now."

The wizard scout glanced over his shoulder at his son. "I have to do what he says," said Myers. "I am too close to stop now. We must go to the corners and place the phase rods."

The yellow eye in the sphere swiveled to look at the human father and son. "Just you, time-commando. Your son will stay here where he will be safe."

"Like hell," said Myers. "He goes with me. Otherwise, the deal's off. I'll take these phase rods back where I found them. You can stay in your prison until—"

Instead of the angry shouts Lord Crendemor expected, the Dalinfaust laughed. "Life forms continue to amaze me with their audacity. How do you plan on returning to your dimension? Your mount obeys me, not you. Even if you could control it, the spirit-cat cannot pass through the shields surrounding Portalis without my assistance. You go when I say and not before."

Glancing at the wizard scout's face through the man's visor, Lord Crendemor detected a deep shade of red. *The human's hands are beginning to shake. He is going to rebel,* Crendemor thought. *That will not do. My plan is too close to success to fail because of petty concerns over a human boy.*

"Remain calm, human," Lord Crendemor said keeping his voice soft and even. "Your son will be safer here than he would be going with you. Can he self-heal? Can you defend him against the elves while you complete your mission? You brought him here, not us. We gain nothing by doing him harm. Think before you do something foolish."

The redness on the human's face lessened somewhat.

"No," said the boy looking at his father. "I will not stay here. I am not helpless. If you try to leave me in this place, I will find a way out. I will—"

Unseen, Lord Crendemor waved his right hand as he whispered words of a spell. A ball of blue shot out of his hand, encasing the boy in magic. Before either of the humans could react, the spell jerked the teenager off the back of the spirit-cat and levitated him into the nearest cage. The door of the cage slammed shut.

"Nooo!" shouted the boy sending a wall of Power at the cage door. When the Power touched the bars, it dissipated into nothingness.

Out the corner of his eye, Crendemor saw the wizard scout leap off his mount and activate a phase rod in his left hand.

"I'll kill—" started Myers.

"Your son is unharmed," Lord Crendemor said. "He is more powerful than he knows. He would have caused trouble for all of us. The cage contains both Power and magic. I have done you a favor by placing him inside."

Myers took two steps forward and raised the activated phase rod in his hand. "Let him out. Now!"

"Calm, human," said the Dalinfaust. "The elf did you a favor. Even you could not control your son without harming him. He will be here safe and sound once you complete your mission. When you return with the bottle of DNA gas in your hand, you can free him and return to your dimension with my blessing. Live the remainder of your days with your son and your precious Diane. You are too near your goal to throw it away in a fit of anger. Think, human. Think."

Lord Crendemor readied a lightning bolt spell except for the final word and placed his free hand on his sword hilt. After a dozen heartbeats, he noticed the muscles in the wizard scout's face relax. Crendemor returned the spell's Power to his reserve but kept his hand on the hilt of his sword.

The wizard scout turned to his son. "I've got to go, Matt. I'll be back for you. I promise."

"Father, no," said the teenager. "Don't leave me here. Don't do what they say. They're evil. Don't you feel it? We need to get away now."

Without replying to his son, Myers turned his back and mounted the spirit-cat. Once strapped into the saddle, he locked eyes with Crendemor. "If you harm one hair on his head, I swear—"

"Do not worry," said the Dalinfaust. "Your son is as safe as your precious empress. He means nothing to me. Do your part of the plan. He will be here when you return."

"Father, please."

"I'll be back, Matt. Trust me. We'll be a family. You'll see."

The spirit-cat shimmered before disappearing into the floor.

"Noooo!" yelled the teen boy as his father's head sank from view.

Lord Crendemor turned to the sphere.

The yellow eye glared at him. "Do you know what to do, elf?"

"I know my part," Lord Crendemor said placing the vial of blood in a satchel and slinging it over his shoulder. He nodded in the direction of the boy. "What about him?"

"Leave him alone for now. He may come in handy if the human balks at the last moment. Once the gate is open, you may kill him at your leisure."

Lord Crendemor smiled. "Your time-commando will not be happy."

The Dalinfaust laughed. "My time-commando will be dead as will the boy's mother." He laughed again. "They must be given their just rewards. After all, I am a demon of my word."

Lord Crendemor smiled before reciting a teleport spell. The area around him shimmered in and out of focus. Then everything went black.

CHAPTER 50

Time passed slowly for Matthew. Surveying the dimly-lit cavern for what seemed like the hundredth time, he saw nothing that would aid in his escape. What he did see sent shivers down his spine. He had no doubt if by some miracle he lived that he would be visited by nightmare visions of the dark elf's laboratory the rest of his days.

Rattling the bars of his cage with both hands, Matthew slipped down to his knees. A dark-red liquid on the metal floor soaked into the legs of his jumpsuit. He quickly rose, trying not to think about the source of the fluid. He reached out with his mind and probed into the locking mechanism on the cage door the way his uncle had shown him. The lock resisted his probe.

It's magic, Matthew thought. *Rick can disable magic locks. I can't. I've got to think of another way to escape. There has to be a way.* The words of the voice from the sphere haunted him. *My parents are in danger. I've got to help them.*

Glancing at the sphere resting on the bloody table, Matthew looked to make sure the yellow eye was no longer visible, then breathed a sigh of relief when it wasn't. Turning to look around the room again, he caught a glimmer of green as the dim light from a nearby lamp reflected off the ring on his left hand.

I wonder…

Reaching into the ring with his mind, Matthew sought and found the link that had been established between Tia and him on Storage. He felt Tia's emotions. She was frightened. More importantly, she somehow felt nearer than she had a few minutes earlier.

She's in the magic dimension. That's the only answer.

Concentrating on the link, he searched for the source. The magic of his cage tried to fight him. He was not trained to combat magic. The ring and its gem, on the other hand, were partly magic and partly something else as well. He wasn't sure exactly what they were, but it didn't matter. The Power of the ring was too much for the magic of the cage. With the ring's aid, Matthew succeeded in circumventing the cage's security. He reached out for Tia; the other part of his soul. He sensed her high overhead. She was close. He didn't know how; he just knew she was there. He touched her, putting his need in the touch.

Tia responded with a joy measuring that of his own. Neither he nor she were alone anymore.

Tia sent an emotion through the link in their rings. Although he heard no sound, Matthew knew the meaning just the same.

"I'm coming."

* * *

"I tell you Matt's in trouble," Tia told Sergeant Ron. "We need to get down there now."

Sergeant Ron looked at the planet below through the cockpit's forward viewing screens. "And just how do you propose I do that? Portalis has a shield around it. The elves' continent has another. The *Defiant* can't get through. Neither can our two fighters. Charlie and Asquan have tried."

"Maybe the X-shuttle can," came Charlie's translated voice over the cockpit's intercom. "She hard to see. Maybe she get through shields."

Sergeant Ron scratched his beard. "I don't know. Even if the X-shuttle could get through, which I doubt, she might not get back out."

"It's worth a try," said Terrie standing behind the copilot's seat with his right hand on Angela's shoulder. "We aren't going to do any good just orbiting the planet. If we don't try something, we wasted our time coming here."

Tia nodded her head at the retired wizard scout, thanking him for his support. She glanced at the elf Comstar, then at Calatron, the leader of the gnome mages, and the dwarf Felspar. They all nodded.

"We've got to try something," said Felspar. "I can have my security team on the shuttle in nothing flat. If the X-shuttle can't get through, then we're no worse off than we are now."

Tia noticed Sergeant Ron glance at the viewing screens again. He turned, nodding his head. "Fine. We'll give it a shot." He punched an icon on the armrest of his pilot seat. "Sergeant Hendricks, you're in command of the *Defiant*. Daniel will stay here with you. Charlie and Asquan will cover you in their fighters in case one of those black ships shows up. Everyone else to the X-shuttle pronto. Bring every phase weapon we've got. If'n Gaston's there with that blasted lizard cat, they can shift into the void. Creallium's our only defense."

"And Holy Metal," said Felspar twisting his battle axe to let the light reflect off the blue gem in the handle."

"Roger that," said Terrie. "I'd recommend bringing one of the Warcats as well. Sergeant Hendricks has infused Warcat number two with flecks of creallium. That should help."

Tia wondered how Terrie thought they were going to cram a Warcat inside the soon to be crowded X-shuttle. She didn't ask questions. All she cared about now was getting to Matthew.

"All right," said Sergeant Ron. "What are you sluggards standing around for? We've got a job to do. Let's get to it. Or do you expect me to do everything myself?"

Tia joined the rush for the door and sent an emotion to Matthew through her ring.

"I'm coming."

CHAPTER 51

Lord Crendemor came out of his teleport ten meters in front of the double doors leading to the Presence of the Lady. They were open. As he'd expected, there were no guards.

Why should there be? he reasoned. *Elves are too honorable to violate the sanctity of the Presence of the Lady without authorization.* He smiled, hefting the Staff of the Lady of the Tree. *I, on the other hand, make my own authority.*

Checking the stealth spell he'd placed around the staff, Lord Crendemor stepped into the tunnel entrance walking quickly. As he passed the first bend, he spotted an old elf raking the sandy floor.

The elf looked up from his raking, eyes growing wide before he recognized who approached. "Ah, Lord Linustanoi. I am sorry, but you are not allowed—"

Lord Crendemor flicked his hand, saying a single word. A ball of magic shot out and caught the old elf in the chest.

Boom!

Pieces of the elf splattered the sides and roof of the tunnel.

Blast the luck. I hoped to get farther in before the alarm sounded. I am going to need help after all.

Sensing the energy of the Tree of Light turning toward the tunnel entrance, Lord Crendemor raised the Staff of the Lady of the Tree, forming a shield around him. He cast a spell taught him by the Dalinfaust the previous day. Lord Crendemor stepped back as an elf-sized glowing orb appeared in the tunnel. Two orange demons a head taller than him with arm-length horns stepped out.

As soon as they were clear of the orb, the spell blinked out of existence. One of the demons waved a clawed hand, casting a spell of its own. A second glowing orb appeared. Two demon-hounds with four snake-like appendages growing out of their necks walked out to stand next to the spell-casting demon.

The demon that had cast the spell glared at Lord Crendemor. "Go. The Dalinfaust has commanded us to hold the entrance." The demon waved its arm, sending an emotion of intense evil. "Go now, elf. Free our master."

Despite previous encounters with demons, Lord Crendemor felt a cold chill run up his spine. He convinced himself he wasn't afraid, then turned and ran down the tunnel.

At the next bend, Crendemor halted to cast a second spell taught him by the Dalinfaust. Six lizard-skinned spirit-cats crawled out of the tunnel floor.

"Guard this place," Lord Crendemor ordered. "Let no one pass."

The lion-sized cats growled. Their hate washed over Crendemor, but he knew they would obey. The magic of the Dalinfaust's spell would allow nothing else. Running forward, he drew his sword. It had been Lillia's sword. Forged of Holy Metal, the weapon felt warm in his hand.

If all goes well, I will gain revenge for my bondmate's death this day. I will gain revenge for all the wrongs that have been done me over the years.

The tunnel opened up into the Presence of the Lady. Although it had been 90,000 years since his bonding night, the lit cavern was just as he remembered.

Lillia, you were so beautiful in your bonding dress.

Shoving the memory aside, Crendemor continued forward, approaching two of the elven caretakers standing near the tunnel opening with rakes in hand. He beheaded both with a single swing of Lillia's blade. Before the heads stopped rolling on the sand, he cast a spell that sent out balls of energy in four directions. Each hit a caretaker and blew holes in the right side of their chests. He sensed no other life forms in the cavern.

Suddenly a ball of blue energy reached out in his direction from one of the thousands of glowing spheres of Power suspended from the roots of the Tree of Light. The blue energy glanced off his shield doing no harm.

Lord Crendemor dropped his polymorph spell of the fool Linustanoi and replaced it with the dark elf form he'd grown to prefer over the years.

"Your time has come, Lady," Lord Crendemor shouted. "I have your staff. You cannot fight yourself."

Two more balls of blue energy left the dangling globes of Power hanging from the roots. They too glanced off his shield without effect.

"You are weak, Lady. You have allowed too much of the tree's Power to be used to create gates between the physical and magical dimensions. Now you are going to pay the price for your generosity."

Lord Crendemor laughed stopping only long enough to cast the third spell taught him by the Dalinfaust. The magic of the spell reached upward and encompassed a dozen of the dangling globes of Power overhead. Using the Power of the tree's globes, the spell reached down into the crystal-clear lake in the center of the cavern and drained the lake dry.

Rushing forward, Crendemor ran to the house-sized boulder in the now dry lakebed. He levitated to the top of the stone. Reaching into the pocket of his robe, he pulled out the vial of elf blood and poured it onto the symbol etched into the center of the stone. As the dark-red liquid soaked into the boulder, the symbol began glowing with a greenish light. Lord Crendemor intuitively sensed it wasn't glowing enough.

"The fool Dalinfaust," he shouted in growing frustration. "I told him we needed another sacrifice. I told him it was not enough."

At that moment a gray, lizard-skinned cat emerged from the floor of the dry lakebed. A fear-stricken scream from a human female struggling in the cat's mouth to no avail filled the cavern. He sensed latent Power in the female. Sending out an active scan, he located her Power reserve. It was large, but her link appeared weak.

She's a novice, Lord Crendemor thought.

Tracing another link in the female's Power reserve, he sensed the boy he'd left in the cage in his lab. Crendemor smiled suddenly understanding the Dalinfaust's comments about promises of a reward for the time-commando and his empress.

The spirit-cat released the screaming woman before shifting back into the void and disappearing beneath the dry lakebed.

Wrapping the human female in magic, Lord Crendemor levitated her to the top of the boulder. She fell to her knees crying. The woman raised her right hand to her left shoulder in an attempt to staunch the blood oozing out of the holes created by the spirit-cat's fangs. As the blood dripped onto the outer edge of the symbol carved into the top of the boulder, Crendemor noticed the symbol grow brighter.

He smiled. "Ah, Diane. Your wizard scout has told me so much about you. How good to finally meet you after all these years."

"Gaston!" screamed the woman looking around.

Lord Crendemor laughed. "I fear your Gaston is busy on a mission of his own. It is just you and me here."

The woman looked up. Appearing to gather her courage, she wiped the tears from her eyes. "I demand you release me. I am the empress. What is it you want? I will give you anything."

"Yes, you will," Lord Crendemor said levitating the woman into a prone, face-down position directly over the carved symbol in the stone. "Just a few more seconds, human, and you will get the reward you have so long desired."

The woman struggled to rise, but her diminishing strength from blood loss was no match for the levitation spell. She turned her head to look up, fear evident in her gaze. "Please. I am the empress."

Laughing, Crendemor pulled the bottle of DNA gas out of his pocket. He knelt down and held the bottle of swirling gas in front of the woman's eyes. "This is what you seek, is it not? Is not this your heart's desire?"

"Please," pleaded the woman. "I will give you anything. I just want to go home."

"Too late, my sweet," laughed Crendemor enjoying the woman's misery. "The Dalinfaust needs your blood to complete his spell." He glanced at her for a second before asking, "Tell me, are you scared?"

"Yes," whimpered the woman. "Please. Let me go."

Lord Crendemor sensed that the woman's fear was not yet sufficient. *The more fear in the sacrifice, the more potent the blood.*

"You want to live forever, do you not?" Lord Crendemor asked continuing to monitor the woman's emotions closely. "Soon the dream of immortality shall be yours. I shall spill your blood on this stone. When I add the DNA gas, the Dalinfaust's last spell will be complete. You will be happy to know that your essence will merge with his. The demon will give your soul his undivided attention for the rest of eternity. Be assured your suffering will give the Dalinfaust much pleasure. Does that make you afraid, my sweet Diane?"

"Yes!" cried the woman. "I admit it. I'm afraid. Are you happy? Please—"

Sensing the woman's fear was at its maximum, Lord Crendemor place his sword under her throat and slid the blade across. As the stream of blood soaked into the boulder, the engraving in the stone shone brightly. When the gushing blood slowed to a trickle, he kicked the lifeless body of the woman over the side, removed the stopper on the bottle of DNA gas, and poured the contents onto the symbol as he cast the final spell taught him by the Dalinfaust.

The engraving's glow forced Crendemor to step back and look away. He sensed the Power of the Tree of Light flowing into the gate, attempting to stop the spell. The spell began to dissipate.

"No!" Crendemor shouted sensing pending defeat. "The spell is not strong enough. I told the fool we needed the blood of children."

Something inside Crendemor made him reach up with his senses. He detected the life force of two hundred plus children. Instinctively he knew where the required sacrifices would come from. At the same moment, he felt a source of energy strike the Tree of Light and sensed demonic evil as well as a color. Blue. The demon's spell attempting to unravel the lock around the gate strengthened as the Tree of Light was forced to divert Power to defend itself. A second wave of demonic evil joined the first with the color red. Soon, a third wave of evil followed with the color green.

One more to go, Lord Crendemor thought. *Then the gate shall be mine to open. Nothing can stop me now. Nothing.*

CHAPTER 52

The spirit-cat stopped directly underneath the first corner of the gate located in the north quadrant of the city. For some reason, Gaston Myers sensed the color blue. He reached out with an active scan to search for guards, but only found several magical traps.

"Based upon the deterioration in the lines of magic, they are ancient," said Wanda. *"Your scan indicates a connecting link leads from the corner back to the elves' Tree of Light."*

Myers had already figured out the obvious. It was the potential for other not so obvious details that concerned him. He probed the traps protecting the corner. It didn't take long to locate several weak points.

"The elves haven't maintained the traps," Myers told his battle computer. *"My brother taught me a few tricks on how to circumvent magic. I should be able to disable these easy enough."*

"I calculate you are correct, Wizard Scout. The current elves are weak. They cannot even protect the links to their own Power reserves, much less maintain the ones established by their betters. If you give me control of your scan, I can assist you. After all, I live to serve."

Myers ignored his battle computer's offer. They both knew the last thing he planned on doing was giving the demon embedded in his battle helmet's processing unit any more control than it already had.

Reaching out to the weakest of the traps, Meyers twisted the magic back on itself. When he did, the magic unexpectedly began unraveling at a rapid rate with the weakest trap giving way first followed by another and then another.

"What the—" Myers started to say before catching himself.

"Ah, I see what the old elves did," said Wanda giving a laugh. *"Do you not recognize the pattern?"*

Myers refused to admit to his battle computer that he didn't. However, much as he despised the demon that was his battle computer, he knew it was usually correct when conducting analysis. He forced himself to concentrate on the unraveling traps. As he did, he noticed minute links between each. Expanding his scan to include the entire corner of the gate, Myers noticed something he had initially missed.

"Each point of magic is connected to its neighbor," Myers said. *"It's one of those Circle things like Shepard created, isn't it?"*

"Very good, Wizard Scout," replied Wanda sounding much too smug for Myers's liking. *"You are correct. It is a Circle. The original spellcasters used each point of magic to reinforce the other. The elves a hundred thousand years ago were very proficient at magic. It is unfortunate for the elves in the current time that they no longer have those same skills. If the Circle had been maintained, you would not have been able to disarm the traps. Based upon the results of your scans, I calculate the four corners of the gate also form a Circle. Once the first corner is disabled, the others should be easier to defeat in turn."*

The demon laughed.

Myers frowned. Whenever the demon laughed, it usually meant trouble. *"What's so funny?"*

"Oh, Wizard Scout, you have so much to learn. Do you not see the full pattern? Each corner of the gate is a Circle in itself. The gate's four corners form a larger Circle. This makes our mission all the easier. Every Circle must have a center. When you destroy the center, you destroy the Circle. All you must do now is place one of the phase rods you carry in the center of each corner. Once the demon essence gains control of the four corners, the center for the gate to the demonic plane will be vulnerable."

Myers was unsure where the demon's logic was heading. *"So what is the center of the Circle for the gate?"*

The demon laughed even harder. *"Foolish mortal. Is it not obvious? The Tree of Light is the center. The tree has tied its*

Power to the four corners by becoming the Circle. Once the four corners are destroyed, the tree will fall. I see the logic of the Dalinfaust's plan even if you cannot. You must destroy the corners, which will then destroy the tree, causing the lock on the gate to fail. The dark elf is already in position. Complete your mission so he can complete his. Woe be unto this world, for my master will soon be free."

Regret nearly overcame Myers's resolve. After so many missions for the Dalinfaust over the years, he well knew what woe was coming.

It will take many years for the Dalinfaust to conquer the magic dimension, Myers reasoned in his private space. *I am sure of it. Diane, Matt, and I can live out our lives in the physical dimension. We can be happy. I just need to get the DNA gas. What happens in the magic dimension is not my concern.*

"Of course it isn't," said the demon apparently intruding on his thoughts. *"Your reward is near. Complete your mission so you can join your Diane and your son. Hurry. You must act now. The dark elf has been detected. The Tree of Light is gathering its Power to stop him. You must act now before it is too late."*

Myers guided the spirit-cat upward. Once his mount broke the surface, Myers didn't bother shifting out of the void. While the inside of the hollow obelisk appeared empty, he sensed the center of the corner. He moved his mount forward, activating one of the spare phase rods as he did. Once in position, he jammed the glowing rod directly into the keystone of the corner's center. A wave of hunger from the demon essence in the phase rod washed over him. The demon essence consumed Power from the center, using it to attack the keystone. Slowly, the demon essence gained mastery over the magic of the Circle. Once it did, a beam of blue light shot upward through the roof of the obelisk. Myers sensed the beam reaching out toward the elves' tree. Before the beam made it to the Tree of Light, he sensed a shield of pure Power form to block its path.

"Hurry," said Wanda. *"The tree's Power will reestablish control of this corner soon. You must get to the next corner to keep the tree off balance."*

Myers formed an image of the red colored obelisk located in the eastern part of the elves' city. The spirit-cat sank down into the floor, turning east. Myers reached out and probed the links forming the Circle of the next corner. By the time his mount arrived under the obelisk, he was already unraveling the elves' traps. The magic in the traps seemed weaker, giving way much easier than those of the first corner.

"It is as I told you," said Wanda. *"Each corner depends on the other. Now hurry."*

Guiding the spirit-cat next to the corner's center, Myers activated the second of the four phase rods and plunged it deep into the keystone for the corner's Circle. The demon essence easily gained control, and within a dozen heartbeats, a beam of red light shot out from the obelisk and added its magic to that of the blue-colored beam. Myers sensed the shield surrounding the Tree of Light bend slightly inward before steadying.

"It is working," said Wanda sounding excited. *"Some of the lords of the elves' council are attempting to aid the tree. I calculate they will not be enough if you hurry. You must take out the next corner before elf defenders arrive at the two remaining obelisks."*

The spirit-cat didn't wait for Myers to give a command. It immediately sank into the floor and headed toward the third obelisk in the south portion of the city. Once again, Myers reached out with an active scan and probed as his mount closed the distance. The traps on the third corner fell away without any trouble. Activating another phase rod, Myers stabbed the keystone. The demon essence in the phase rod appeared stronger to Myers, overcoming the corner's defenses with little problem. A beam of green light joined the assault on the Tree of Light's shield. Myers sensed the shield being forced back to the very edge of the tree's branches. He sensed life forms hiding behind the shield.

"Those are children," Myers said. *"They will be killed."*

"What care you?" said Wanda. *"Hurry. You must disable the last corner. The dark elf has already begun his part of the plan. The blood of the ten sacrifices has been poured onto the keystone for the gate. All is ready. You must not fail."*

A thought crossed Myers's mind. *"Crendemor only had nine sacrifices. Where did he get ten?"*

"The Dalinfaust provided the necessary sacrifice," said Wanda. *"Now do your part."*

Myers held his mount where it was. *"Who did he get?"* The thought of his son waiting in the cage in the dark elf's lab flashed into his mind.

"Rest easy, Wizard Scout," said Wanda. *"Your son is safe. If you doubt my words, check for yourself. You share the same Power reserve."*

Distrusting the demon, Myers followed the link to the Power reserve he shared with his son. He found the link leading to the primary reserve. Touching one of the links on the large reserve, he immediately shrank back. The link was that of his deceased father. Moving on, he found another link. Following it, he found his son. He sensed his son was alive and well.

"All right," Myers said breathing a sigh of relief. *"He's alive. Let's get this over with."*

Who the Dalinfaust had gotten as the tenth sacrifice, Myers didn't know or care. He had his own priorities. Sending the spirit-cat an image of the final obelisk, Meyers reached out with an active scan to probe for traps. Without warning, a line of Power reached out and knocked his line aside.

He recognized the frequency of the new line of Power. *"Shepard!"*

"Kill him," said Wanda. *"He is trying to keep you from your Diane. He is going to try to stop you from disabling the last corner of the gate. Hurry. Time is crucial. The Tree of Light is starting to recover. Do not give the tree the time it needs."*

A life form appeared on Myers's passive scan. He recognized it as his brother's spirit-horse. Although he didn't detect his brother, he had no doubt Shepard was on the stallion. The spirit-horse was directly under the last obelisk, effectively blocking his way.

The spirit-cat roared a challenge using an emotion of hate for its mortal enemy. A roar of emotions reverberated from his brother's mount in reply.

"You have the advantage," said Wanda. *"Your fool brother gave up his armor and weapons. The primary teleporter on Storage is still down, so he cannot use his dimensional pack to summon them. Kill him quick. Kill him now."*

The trouble was Myers knew his dimensional pack wasn't working either. All he had was his basic load of ammo and the last phase rod.

Sending out another active scan, Myers split it into two parts. One he sent to locate his brother's exact position, and the other he sent toward the keystone of the corner to look for traps. He sensed a line of Power reach out once again from the direction of the stallion. The line split into two parts, knocking both of his lines to the side.

Anger raged inside Myers. The realization his brother was determined to keep him from being with Diane and Matthew burned into his mind. *You stole my father,* he thought. *I won't let you steal my son.*

Activating the remaining phase rod in full destructive mode, Myers kicked his mount in the ribs, urging it forward. The spirit-cat required little urging. Its anger and hate encompassed Myers as it streaked forward, eager to kill. The spirit-cat's emotions infected Myers. His eyes blazed with jealous anger. As his mount charged forward to meet his brother, one certainty came to Myers's mind.

One of us is going to die today.

CHAPTER 53

The X-shuttle glanced off the shield, rebounding back into space.

"That's the third time," said Angela. "Our force field is down to forty-seven percent. Let's face it. We aren't getting in using brute force."

Sergeant Ron picked himself up off the deck, again standing behind the pilot's seat. "I can count, blast it." He leaned closer to Timerman in the pilot's position. "Divert more power to our stealth shield. Whatever sensors are controlling the shield around Portalis is still detecting us."

"Aye, aye, Captain err…Sergeant," said Timerman adjusting controls on the X-shuttle's console. I can get another three percent by shutting down life support, but I doubt that's going to be near enough to make a difference."

Tia unbuckled from her bench seat and squeezed past the Warcat Sergeant Ron had somehow crammed into the middle of the shuttle's passenger compartment. She made her way next to the *Defiant's* captain.

"I sensed the planet's shield that time," Tia said. "I believe it's a combination of physics, magic, and spiritual energy. I sense the stealth shield for the X-shuttle is also a combination of all three energies. The problem is that the shuttle just isn't powerful enough on its own to completely hide our presence from the shield surrounding Portalis."

Sergeant Ron looked at Tia and scratched his beard. "So are you trying to tell me it's hopeless? If so, think again. My grandson's down there. I ain't-a gonna leave him all alone regardless of what you may think."

Heat rose in Tia's face. She controlled her temper as best she could. "Do you honestly think I'm trying to tell you to give up?" When Sergeant Ron remained silent, Tia said, "I'm just thinking we've got other resources on this ship. You're a diviner, untrained according to Rick, but still a diviner. Comstar, Terrie, and I can create stealth shields. What if we all use our Power to supplement the X-shuttle's stealth shield?"

"Do not forget about me," said Bright Wing in perfect intergalactic standard. "I can cast a stealth shield as well."

Despite the tenseness of the situation, Tia smiled. "We could never forget the only dragon in our crew. The X-shuttle's engine will be your responsibility. We'll need you to keep it as efficient as possible. We'll need every bit of Power it's got." Tia switched her gaze from the two-meter-long silver dragon to Sergeant Ron. "Err, that is assuming you approve of the plan, Sergeant Ron."

"I haven't quite made up my mind," said Sergeant Ron starting a fresh session of beard scratching. "I think there's more to that force field than just detection. It's the strongest energy I've ever encountered."

Wizard Scout Terrie Shatstot spoke from his seat in the rear of the passenger compartment. "I think Tia's got the right idea. But you're right as well. It's more than just us being detected. That's where you've got to come in, Sergeant Ron. You can use your diviner ability to find us a weak point. The rest of us with the ability to use stealth shields can strengthen the shield around the X-shuttle."

Calatron rose from his seat and moved forward until he stood next to Tia and Sergeant Ron. "That includes my magic users and me." He waved an arm to encompass the members of the *Defiant's* crew jammed into the shuttle. "I dare say we've got more power crammed into this little space than most dreadnaughts. If we all work together, we might get through."

Sergeant Ron stopped scratching his beard long enough to nod. "Fine. We'll give it another go." He placed a hand on Timerman's shoulder. "I'll feed you the coordinates for any weak point I find in that blasted force field. The rest of you will reinforce the shuttle's stealth shield." He pointed at Bright Wing. "Except you. Get inside the engine and give us all the power you can make the blasted thing generate. I've got a feeling we're going to need every bit of it."

The silver dragon scurried past Tia before shifting through the floor in the direction of the X-shuttle's engine. Tia drew Power from her reserve and merged it with the shuttle's stealth shield, reinforcing it as best she could. She sensed other lines of Power from her fellow crewmembers doing the same.

"Taylor," said Sergeant Ron speaking to Terrie's battle computer. "I've found what might be a weak point. Take control of the shuttle's computer and help Timerman get us through."

"Compliance," replied Taylor over the battle helmet's external speaker.

"Full throttle," ordered Sergeant Ron. "It's all or nothing this time."

As Timerman shoved the thruster controls all the way forward, Tia grabbed hold of the back of the copilot's seat, steadying herself against the increasing G-force. Calatron wasn't so lucky. The little gnome rolled head over heel before being caught by the pot-bellied dwarf Stovis.

Tia was tempted to reach out with her mind to locate the force field's supposed weak point but forced herself to concentrate all of her Power on the shuttle's stealth shield.

"This is it," said Timerman. "Contact is in five, four, three, two, one."

The X-shuttle shuddered slightly, but other than a mild tingle, Tia felt nothing.

"We're through," said Timerman. "I'm making for the second shield around the elves' continent."

"Don't let up yet," warned Sergeant Ron glaring at the rest of the crew. "We're not done 'til we're done."

Again, Tia forced herself to concentrate on reinforcing the shuttle's stealth shield. It wasn't easy. Thoughts of Matthew being tortured or worse kept entering her mind.

Timerman banked the X-shuttle hard to the left. "Contact in five, four, three, two, one."

The X-shuttle shuddered more violently this time. Despite her hold on the copilot's seat, Tia was thrown to the deck.

"We're through!" shouted Timerman. "Which way, Tia? I'm

flying blind. I need a destination."

Pulling herself upright, Tia reached into the ring on her left hand with her mind and followed the link attached to Matthew. "That way," she said pointing to the shuttle's two o'clock position. I'd guess about two hundred kilometers."

"This is it guys," said Sergeant Ron. "I don't know what we'll be up against, so be ready for anything. Timerman, take us in real careful like. I don't want any surprises."

A tense five minutes followed as the crew readied phase rifles, pistols, battle axes, and a variety of equipment.

"There," Tia said pointing to a dark cut in the face of a cliff ten kilometers ahead. "Matt is in there. I can feel him."

Comstar stood. "That place is surrounded by powerful magic. I can sense it. From what I can tell, it would take an army of mages to get through."

Sergeant Ron smiled, saying, "Or an old diviner with a half-crazy crew of misfits." He touched a switch on the hologram pad between the pilot and copilot seats.

An image of the cliff appeared. As Tia watched, the *Defiant's* captain continued fiddling with the pad's controls until a red dot appeared at the base of the cliff.

Placing a hand on Angela's shoulder, Sergeant Ron said, "Fire everything the X-shuttle's got at that point. It's the keystone for the spells. Alternate between physical and magic weapons."

Angela looked over her shoulder at Sergeant Ron. "Everything? Are you sure? Sergeant Hendricks installed two missiles with tactical nukes on the shuttle. One's magic-based; the other's a standard nuke. You're telling me to fire those as well?"

"No, dagnabit," said Sergeant Ron. "I don't mean those. Do I have to do all the thinking? I want to force a hole through the spells, not blow my grandson to kingdom come."

Tia noticed Angela bite her lip. To the red head's credit, she said nothing. Instead, she just turned and grabbed the firing controls while staring hard straight ahead.

Sergeant Ron looked down at the deck before glancing back at Angela. "I'm sorry. I...I'm just worried about Matt. There's not a gunner in the galaxy I'd trust more than you with my grandson's life."

Angela glanced back. Tia sensed the tenseness in the redhead's shoulders leave.

"I've got it covered, Sergeant," said Angela. "You can trust me."

"Believe me, I do," replied Sergeant Ron. "Otherwise, I'd be on the gun controls myself." He turned to face Comstar. "I'm no good at magic. The moment those spells fall, let us know. The phase cannon on the X-shuttle will make mincemeat out of that cliff if we don't stop firing in time."

The old elf nodded but didn't bother replying. Tia saw the elf's eyes get a blank stare as if looking at something unseen.

"I'm ready, Sergeant Ron," said Angela. "Timerman, hold the shuttle at a hover. I need a stable firing platform."

The X-shuttle slowed to a stop facing the cliff. Tia gauged the distance at four hundred meters. *Point-blank range,* she thought.

"Fire," ordered Sergeant Ron.

The X-shuttle vibrated as every phase, plasma, and magic weapon Sergeant Hendricks had on the ship opened up. Multicolored streams of energy blasted against an unseen shield in front of the cliff. Tia sensed energy forming a wall between the shuttle and the cliff. She sensed evil as well.

"Fire the 30mm chain gun," said Sergeant Ron. "Solid slugs of metal can confuse magic if it's done right."

Timerman reached for the gun control on the armrest of the pilot's seat. When the orc teenager pulled the trigger, a bee-like buzz was added to the sound of weapon's fire. Tia sensed the wall of energy and the evil giving way. She sensed Terrie and Sergeant Ron send out lines of Power against the wall of energy, forcing it back even more. She added her own line of Power to the fray drilling into the wall of energy the way Rick had taught her. Suddenly the wall of magic disappeared.

"Cease fire," yelled Comstar.

A few beams of delayed energy blasted into the rock face, sending shattered pieces of stone in all directions before Angela could stop firing. With controlled desperation, Tia followed the link between her ring and Matthew's. She sensed an emotion of hope coming from his end of the link, then sent the same emotion back double fold.

"He's still alive," Tia shouted. "Land this thing next to the opening. Now!"

"Hey," said Sergeant Ron. "I'm still in charge." Turning to Timerman, Sergeant Ron said, "Uh, land next to the opening."

"Aye, aye," said Timerman giving Tia a wink.

As soon as the X-shuttle touched the ground, Tia reached past Timerman and hit the icon for the rear ramp. Spinning, she took off running and knocked down two dwarves and a gnome in the process.

"Wait!" yelled Sergeant Ron. "We don't know what's in there. We need to go together."

Tia was already halfway down the ramp before the *Defiant's* captain finished speaking. She jumped over the side, heading to the black cut in the cliff's face, then ran inside the obvious tunnel using an active scan to guide her way. A faint light ahead drew her like a moth to a flame. Sensing a trap ahead, she slowed long enough to circumvent it the way Gaston and Rick had taught her.

I may not be a diviner, she thought, *but after spending a year on Portalis, I can at least work my way past a few magic traps.*

Tia disabled two more traps as she made her way through the tunnel before stepping into a large, dimly-lit room cut into the rock. A quick glance picked up row after row of shelves along the walls stacked with bottles and vials of every size and shape. She specifically avoided trying to figure out their contents. The stench of death and evil in the place told her all she needed to know.

A stack of white limbs in one corner drew her attention. Tia made out the arms and legs of lifeless bodies stacked like so much cordwood. A fleeting glance told her none of the bodies was Matthew. She moved on with her scan. Her link told her Matthew was alive. She just needed to find him. Ten cages lined up against the wall opposite the entrance were all empty save one.

"Tia!" came a yell from the farthest cage.

"Matt!" Tia yelled back running to the cage to jerk on the bars of the door. She glanced at the locking mechanism, detecting no latch.

"It's magic," said Matthew. "Do you have a weapon?"

Tia mentally kicked herself. A vision of her rifle leaning against her bench seat flashed in her mind. She opted not to mention the fact to Matthew. Pulling the Deloris phase pistol from her holster, she said, "Stand back."

As soon as Matthew cleared the way, Tia fired twice. The phase rounds ricocheted off the lock and hit the opposite wall, breaking several bottles without making so much as a scratch on the lock.

"Hold," said a voice behind Tia.

Tia turned to see Comstar waving his hands while speaking words she heard but quickly forgot. A ball of blue energy formed to the elf's front before moving forward to wrap around the cage's lock.

Click.

The cage door popped open.

Matthew rushed through the opening with outstretched arms. Tia met him halfway, squeezing her arms around him with all her might. Their lips met. She pulled Matthew even tighter.

"Enough already," said Sergeant Ron. "Let's get out of her while the gettin's good. Matt's not the only one we came to Portalis to save, you know."

Reluctantly, Tia released her hold on Matthew. He seemed just as hesitant to let go of her. Their eyes met, giving a promise neither would break. Finally, Matthew looked away and pointed at a red-stained table near the center of the room. A globe containing a swirling white gas was the only thing on the table. Tia sensed evil from the sphere of gas.

"Grandfather, we need to take that with us," said Matthew.

"Are you crazy?" replied Sergeant Ron. "This whole place stinks to high heaven of evil. I'm going to blow it all to hell and back once we're safely on the X-shuttle. I'll be doing the world a favor."

Matthew shook his head. "You don't want to destroy that. It's important. Trust me."

Before Sergeant Ron could speak, a yellow eye appeared in the white gas of the sphere. The feeling of evil in the room increased noticeably.

A shiver ran up Tia's back.

"You pathetic mortals," growled a deep voice from within the globe. "You are too late. Even now my plan is set in motion. The gate will soon be open. The Tree of Light shall cease to exist. Flee back to your dimension while you can. You may have a few short years of life before my demon armies destroy all you hold dear."

Tia froze unable to move or even breathe despite struggling to do so.

Comstar seemed to be the only one in the room capable of movement. The old elf jerked off his cloak and cast it over the sphere of white gas.

As soon as the view of the yellow eye was broken, Tia released her breath. *I can move again,* she thought.

"This is my dimension," said Comstar wrapping his cloak more firmly around the sphere without touching it directly. "And your plan shall not succeed, foul demon. We are not alone."

Unsure what to do, Tia looked at Sergeant Ron.

Sergeant Ron took another glance around the room, then in a voice with a hint of shakiness said, "All right, bring that blasted thing and let's get out of here. We've got places to go and people to save."

Everyone began running for the entrance at once.

"Where are we going next?" Tia shouted as she ran hand in hand with Matthew.

Sergeant Ron didn't reply. He just took up a position in the rear and hustled everyone out of the tunnel opening. Once all were onboard the X-shuttle, Timerman raised the ship to an altitude of a thousand meters and a distance of four kilometers.

Sergeant Ron ordered the teenage orc to turn the shuttle toward the cliff face. Once lined up, he said, "Angela, put one of our tactical nukes down that black hole. I don't want whoever created that room from hell slinking back to use it again."

"Roger that," said Angela touching an icon on the gun control. A missile shot out from the front of the shuttle streaking into the black rift in the cliff. The forward video screen blacked out for two seconds before coming back online to reveal a billowing mushroom cloud. The X-shuttle bucked violently before Timerman got it under control.

"Where to now, Sergeant?" asked the teenage orc.

Sergeant Ron didn't hesitate. "Silverton. Apparently, we've got a tree to save."

CHAPTER 54

The double doors leading to the Presence of the Lady were fifty paces ahead when a ball of orange energy streaked out of nowhere straight toward Jeena. She raised her staff and mouthed two words, throwing up a hasty shield in time to deflect a blast of fire and brimstone. Heat rolled over her, singeing a few strands of silver hair but doing no serious damage.

Looking around for enemies, Jeena noticed the air in front of the open doors shimmer accompanied by a wave of hate along with the smell of demonic evil. Two horned, orange-skinned monstrosities appeared. Slightly taller than elves, they were twice as broad with three arms and a long forked tail. Two hound-sized demons with snake-like appendages protruding from their necks stood on either side of the two demons.

Jeena shivered. Rick had told her stories of demon hounds with snakeheads that could heal their bodies faster than damage could be meted out. She reached out with her mind, praying to the Lady that the two demon-hounds had the weakness her bondmate had once described.

I am a diviner. If their links are not trapped, maybe I can stop their flow of Power.

The hounds' links were easy to find. Detecting the presence of traps was another story. Her bondmate had not had time to train her sufficiently. Praying there were no traps, Jeena twisted each link back on itself. The demon-hounds yelped, then rushed forward with teeth bared and snakeheads hissing.

Pointing her staff at the charging demons, Jeena shouted a word of magic asking the air around the demon-hounds to do her will. The air obeyed, converting into acid completely engulfing the four-legged demons. The hounds stumbled before falling to the ground writhing as the noxious liquid ate into their flesh. Some of the snakeheads reacted instinctively, attempting to bite anything within reach. Two snake heads bit into the neck of one of the demon-hounds before the spell's acid turned the heads into a soupy liquid. The other hound wallowed on the ground, trying to rise but hampered by the acid eating away at its eyes.

One of the orange demons looked down laughing. It waved a hand at the whimpering demon-hound, sending a ball of orange magic into the beast. The four-legged demon exploded into a thousand pieces of flesh and bone.

"Very good, elf," said the orange demon speaking not in words but somehow speaking just the same. "Someone has taught you well. You will find my brother and I are not such easy foes. Our links are protected the same as I see are yours. Skill and Power will decide the outcome of our battle."

The second of the orange demons spoke. "Enough talk, Sister. Our master will be freed today. Kill the elf and summon more of our kind. You always talk too much."

Jeena sensed anger combined with pain through the link to her bondmate. *Rick is in battle. The Tree of Light is still under attack. There is no time for this.*

Raising her staff in her left hand, Jeena drew Power from her reserve and formed a ball of magic over the outstretched palm of her right hand.

The sister-demon laughed again. "Good, elf. You wish to fight. I could summon more of my brothers, but you are no match for us. I will feast on your flesh from—"

The ball of magic shot out from Jeena's hand, turning into a multi-forked bolt of lightning. Fingers of electrical energy reached out for both demons. The lightning struck invisible barriers to the demons' front before rebounding into the sky.

"Foolish elf," laughed the sister-demon. "It will take more than the abilities of a single elven lord to get past us."

A sphere of bright blue magic passed over Jeena's right shoulder, exploding against the demons' shields and forcing them to take a step back.

"Then try three elven lords!" shouted a voice from behind.

Jeena had no trouble recognizing the voice. "Sheshna! We've got to get to the Presence of the Lady. Someone is trying to open the gate."

Another ball of magic streaked past Jeena, hitting the shields protecting the demons. She recognized the frequency of Lord Thalos. The old general's spell burst into a fierce ball of fire totally engulfing the two demons. The flames dissipated quickly, revealing the two demons standing shoulder to shoulder unharmed.

Two spheres of orange magic reached out from the demons. One sphere headed toward Lord Thalos while the other went for Lord Sheshna. Jeena sensed magic form shields in front of the two elven lords. The orange balls ricocheted off the lords' shields, shooting into the air.

Pulling more Power from her reserve, Jeena formed it into a finger-sized beam and sent it directly against the force field in front of the brother-demon. Twisting the beam of magic in a drilling motion the way her bondmate had taught her, Jeena dug in hard and created a small hole in the demon's shield.

"Sheshna!" Jeena yelled. "Use the breach. I cannot hold it open long."

Jeena heard her fellow lord yelling words she quickly forgot. She sensed a mass of magic building as Sheshna's spell took form.

"Not so fast," said the sister-demon as a line of magic reached out and split into two separate parts.

Jeena sensed the two lines wrap around the links connecting lords Thalos and Sheshna to their Power reserves. The demon's lines twisted, kinking both lords' links. Lord Sheshna's incomplete spell dissipated into the universe from which it had come.

"What happened?" shouted Lord Sheshna falling to the ground.

"You pathetic mortals," snarled the sister-demon. "You do not even know how to protect your links. You are powerless now."

"Not quite," shouted Lord Thalos rising to his feet holding his staff aloft.

Magic energy shot out from the top of the general's staff, forcing its way through the opening Jeena had created in the brother-demon's shield. The concentrated ball of Thalos's blue magic burst against the brother-demon's forehead, splattering bone and brain matter on his sister. Jeena sensed the life force that was the brother-demon being jerked back from whence it had come.

The ring on Jeena's left hand tingled. *"You have no time to fight this battle,"* said Danny. *"The two lords lost the links to their Power reserves, but they still have the magic of their staffs. Leave the remaining demon to them. You have got to stop the gate from opening. Rick is in his own fight. He cannot do it. You are the tree's only hope."*

Hard though it was, Jeena turned her back on her fellow lords. In the confusion of Lord Thalos's attack, she ran past the sister-demon and through the double doors leading into the tunnel beyond. She sensed magic leave the sister-demon heading in her direction. A wall of magic popped into existence behind Jeena. She recognized Sheshna's frequency. The demon's magic exploded against the wall, lighting the tunnel for a brief second but doing her no harm.

"Go, Jeehana," shouted Lord Sheshna. "Save the tree. We will handle this monster."

Putting on a burst of speed, Jeena rounded the first bend, jumping over the contorted body of one of the Lady's caretakers. The shocked look frozen on the face of the hapless elf burned deep into Jeena urging her to seek revenge.

"Do not give in to anger," warned Danny. *"You need all your wits about you. Whoever is at the gate knows what they are doing. Be careful. I calculate that— Watch out!"*

A fleeting image of a gray shape emerging from the tunnel wall was all the warning Jeena got. Twisting to the side, she avoided the main brunt of the beast's attack. The claws of one outstretched paw ripped through the cloth of her sleeve, leaving trails of blood along their path. Jeena only had time to hope the scratches were superficial. Swinging her staff at the underside of the large cat-like creature, she released its magic just as the jeweled end made contact with the cat's belly.

Boom!

The blast threw Jeena rolling across the tunnel floor. She was up in an instant. Her attacker lay on the stone floor covered in blood with its legs twitching in the final spasms of death.

"It is a spirit-cat," said Danny. *"There may be more in the void. I recommend—"*

What the battle computer's recommendation would've been, Jeena didn't know. She sensed life forms approaching from below and dove to the side, pulling her Deloris phase pistol from its holster as she fell. Firing in mid-air, two phase rounds struck a gray, lizard-skinned cat's head as it emerged from the floor. The phase rounds left two bloody circles in lieu of the cat's eyes. Blood, brain, and bone sprayed against the wall beyond. The dying beast shifted out of the void still partially embedded in the stone floor.

Sensing two more life forms coming from one wall and two more from below, Jeena raised her staff and pistol prepared to go down fighting. She sensed an emotion of pain from her bondmate and Power draining rapidly from Richard's reserve, leaving it near empty. In a final act of sacrifice, she sent part of her Power down the link to her bondmate.

Goodbye, my love, she thought using the human's term for how she felt. *I have failed, but I will be waiting in the next world for you.*

Two gray shapes emerged from the floor five paces away. At the same time, two more came flying from the wall to her right. Choosing her targets, Jeena sent a blast of magic through her staff at the nearest cat. She simultaneously pulled the trigger of her phase pistol as fast as it would fire, sending phase rounds at a second cat.

Jeena's eye caught a glimpse of bared teeth as the two remaining cats leaped for her exposed throat. Before the teeth got close, a ball of blue magic caught one of the cats in the chest and threw it back. Two black arrows flew at the remaining cat, catching it in the neck just below the base of its skull.

"Go!" shouted voices to Jeena's rear.

Turning long enough to see her rescuers, Jeena saw the old gnome Rembis flanked by Leethor and Meshoan. The two elves dropped their bows and drew swords as they took the fight to the wounded cats. Jeena noticed the gnome mage preparing another spell as one of the wounded cats charged.

"Help us," came a tingle in Jeena's head.

"Lady," Jeena said forcing herself to turn her back on her friends and continue running down the tunnel toward the Presence of the Lady.

A series of explosions echoed through the tunnel from the direction where she had left her fellow lords fighting the sister-demon. She knew the sound was more than could be made by either Lord Thalos or Lord Sheshna's spells alone.

"What was that noise?" Jeena mentally asked.

The ring on her finger tingled. *"The demon has gated in more of her brothers."*

"I have to go back," Jeena said torn between loyalty to her fellow elves and the Lady's need.

"No," said Danny. *"The two lords are not alone. They already have help."*

"Who is helping them?" Jeena asked as she renewed her run toward the Presence of the Lady.

Danny laughed. *"Humans."*

CHAPTER 55

The large life form came charging straight at Richard. He recognized the frequency of a spirit-cat, only it seemed much more potent than the ones he'd dealt with in the past. Although he couldn't detect the rider, he had no doubt who it was.

"Myers."

"I calculate a ninety-nine percent probability you are correct," said Nickelo. *"He will have armor and weapons. You only have that glorified pig sticker those elf teenagers called a lance. You do not even have armor."*

Richard didn't need to be reminded of his lack of equipment. He kicked himself for giving up his weapons and armor to the old elf lord.

"Too late for recriminations," said Nickelo. *"Get ready. Your brother will be here in five seconds."*

Richard had been a marine. Marines weren't in the habit of waiting for fights to come to them. Picturing the life form charging his way, he sent the image to his mount. The stallion bolted forward, sending out an emotion of battle fury. A wave of angry emotions came back from the spirit-cat. Leaning forward, Richard braced his legs against the sides of his spirit-horse. He wrapped Power around the hilt of Mendera's Lance to hold the heavy weapon in place and braced for contact.

"Don't forget you can extend the lance," reminded Nickelo.

Richard disregarded his battle computer's advice. He knew his brother too well. *"No. He's going to try and get in close and stay there. A shorter weapon will be easier for me to use."*

The distance between them closed to fifty meters. Four lines of Power reached out from Myers, coming at Richard from all four corners of the compass at once.

"You cannot handle four attacks simultaneously," warned Nickelo. *"Not from someone as skilled as your brother. Recommend you retreat."*

"Fat chance," Richard thought as he drained all but a single drop of Power from his primary reserve. He sent the massive blast of Power directly at Myers in an all-or-nothing endeavor to stop his brother in his tracks. He sensed an emotion of surprise and fear from Myers as the four attacking lines withdrew to form a hasty defensive shield at his brother's front. Richard's Power exploded against Myers's shield, bending it inward almost but not quite to the breaking point.

Two seconds later, the stallion and spirit-cat collided. Two cat claws reached out, raking at Richard's face. The stallion twisted to the side opening his mouth and clamped down with his finger-length fangs on one of the cat's legs, jerking the spirit-cat off balance. One clawed cat-paw partially caught Richard across the neck, missing his jugular but tearing deep gouges in his flesh nonetheless.

The stallion twisted, raising his forelegs with clawed hoofs extended, and caught Myers across the right leg with the razor-sharp claws. The blow caught Myers in the act of swinging his phase rod at Richard's head. Myers changed direction, thrusting the tip of his phase rod at the stallion's chest. Richard brought his lance downward, deflecting the phase rod enough so the tip missed his mount's chest, scraping along the stallion's ribs instead.

The spirit-horse roared in agony as the demon essence in the weapon sucked out life force. The phase energy of the rod left a bloody gouge along the spirit-horse's side. Giving tit for tat, Richard thrust out with Mendera's Lance, sticking the unicorn-horn point into the spirit-cat's left haunch. The spirit-cat screamed and twisted to get away from the lance.

Both the spirt-cat and the stallion separated, heading for the surface. As soon as Richard broke through the stone floor of the obelisk, he jumped free of his mount and ran toward the spot he sensed Myers and the spirit-cat would appear. He wasn't quite fast enough. Myers leaped clear of the cat in time to swing his phase rod at Richard's head.

As Richard dodged his brother's blow, he glimpsed their surroundings. They were inside the hollow obelisk. The room was about thirty meters across and twice as high. A yellow glow from the center of the room provided enough light to see even if he hadn't been wearing his battle helmet.

"Rick, get back on your stallion," said Nickelo. *"Your physical muscles cannot compete with the speed and strength of your brother's battle suit. Wanda is bound to be helping him. Without a battle suit of your own, I can only give advice. I cannot help control your movements."*

Richard wasn't in the mood to cut and run. He sensed his bondmate in a desperate battle of her own near the Tree of Light. *"I have to get to her."*

"I recommend you try concentrating on staying alive first," said Nickelo. *"You drained your primary Power reserve dry. You cannot fight Myers toe to toe."*

Power came flowing down the bond link he shared with his bondmate. Richard sensed an intense emotion as if Jeena was telling him goodbye. The drop of Power he had in his reserve mixed with Jeena's, creating more Power.

"You are now at seventeen percent Power," said Nickelo. *"I calculate that is still not enough to defeat your brother."*

"It'll have to be," Richard said as he charged forward, catching his brother in the stomach with the butt of the lance and knocking him back a step.

The stomach armor of his brother's battle suit was too strong for the non-magical butt of the lance to do any real harm. Myers quickly thrust out with his phase rod, catching Richard in the left shoulder.

"Arrgh!" Richard screamed as microscopic explosions of phase energy ripped his shoulder muscle apart. Worse than the physical wound was the tearing of life force from his soul. He had attacked others often enough with the demonic phase rod, but this was the first time he'd ever felt the agony of the demonic essence stealing life force. Pain such as he'd never felt accompanied by dark evil and absolute hate swept over him.

Richard's left arm fell to his side totally useless. He nearly dropped the lance but was able to hang on with his right hand. In desperation, he swung Mendera's Lance as hard as he could against Myers's head. Although the physical part of the blow wasn't all that powerful, the fully-energized magic of the lance multiplied the force many times over. Myers was thrown to the floor. Shattered pieces of battle helmet flew into the air.

If he'd been unwounded, Richard might've been able to take advantage of the situation. As it was, he was only able to fall to the floor swinging the lance wildly in a vain attempt to keep his brother at bay.

For his part, Myers rolled on the floor with blood streaming out the cracked side of his helmet. He rose to his feet four meters away, well outside the reach of Mendera's Lance. Richard noticed the visor was up on his brother's damaged battle helmet, apparently out of action.

Myers locked eyes with Richard. "I'm not going to let you stop me!" he shouted as he pulled his .44 caliber AutoMag from its holster and aimed the weapon at Richard's head. "You've stuck your nose in my business for the last time, Shepard."

Sensing the tightening of his brother's finger on the trigger, Richard pointed Mendera's Lance at Myers's chest. Pressing the protrusion on the shaft of the lance the way Terika had shown him, he braced the butt of the weapon with telekinesis as the shaft extended outward driving the glowing unicorn horn straight into the chest armor of Myers's battle suit and deep into his brother's chest.

At the same moment, Myers pulled the trigger of his AutoMag. The heavy brerellium steel slug slammed into the right side of Richard's chest, throwing him head-over-heels into the wall. Mendera's Lance went flying out of Richard's grasp, landing near the center of the room.

"Don't pass out, Rick," shouted Nickelo.

Richard heard, but the darkness swept over him anyway. When he dug his way back to reality, he heard Nickelo shouting.

"Move, Marine. Move now or you'll never move again."

Richard sensed his self-heal working overtime to return his body to baseline. The pain in the right side of his chest was less. Even the pain created by the demon essence in his left shoulder was more bearable. He felt blood gushing out his wounds, letting him know he'd only been unconscious for a few seconds.

"You have been out for five seconds," said Nickelo reading his wizard scout's thoughts. *"Your brother has been unconscious as well, but he is starting to move now. He dropped the AutoMag after he fired. You've got to get to it before he does."*

Richard made out the blurry image of a blood-soaked Myers dragging himself across the floor as he reached out for the AutoMag. He knew he couldn't get to the pistol before his brother. Sending out a line of Power, he knocked the AutoMag against the far wall using telekinesis.

Myers pushed himself off the floor with one hand while grabbing at the bloody wound in his chest with the other. He succeeded in pulling the 9mm pistol out of the battle suit's shoulder holster. Blood dripped off the end of the pistol's barrel, but Richard knew a little blood wouldn't hinder the weapon's operation. He sensed his brother's self-heal attempting to heal the damage caused by Mendera's Lance and that the self-heal wasn't going well.

"I calculate you are correct," said Nickelo. *"Magic from the unicorn horn is still inside the wound. Your brother's self-heal is barely keeping up. An inordinate amount of Power from his reserve is being used for the healing. I calculate the wound will only get worse before it gets better. If you can keep your brother at bay for another minute or so, you may gain the advantage. The demon essence in your wound is also resisting your self-heal, but your previous experience healing wounds created by the demon essence is helping. I calculate you will be fully healed well before your brother."*

Richard stopped dragging himself on the floor and looked at his brother.

Myers staggered to his feet using his battle suit's assistors to overcome the weakness from his wounds, then pointed the 9mm at Richard's chest.

Richard had a feeling he wasn't going to have another minute to heal.

Myers gave a half smile. "Tricky to the end, eh Shepard, but your usefulness is over."

Richard noticed Myers glance at the spirit-cat and the stallion. The two spirit creatures had stopped fighting, separated, and were panting hard, apparently trying to catch their breaths before resuming their fight. Blood dripped down several parts of their bodies. Although Richard could tell both of the mounts were badly injured, he sensed neither was ready to give up.

Myers took a step forward, sighting down the barrel of the 9mm. Richard's brother gave a final tight-lipped smile. "You're a fool, Shepard. You always have been. Once I drive my phase rod into the keystone of this corner of the lock, the gate can be opened. Then I'll get the DNA gas I need. Diane, Matt, and I will be together forever."

Richard shook his head continuing to lock eyes with his brother while ignoring the pain in his chest and shoulder as best he could. "You're the fool if you think any demon is going to give you what you want."

Myers laughed. "I'll see soon enough. You, on the other hand, won't be alive. I'm going to put all seventeen rounds in you, and then use my phase rod to drain you dry. You're going to die knowing the weapons you gave me are the same ones that are killing you."

A memory popped into Richard's mind. He remembered the time when he'd walked into his brother's room as they were preparing to fight vampires under Old Drepdenoris Mountain. He remembered giving Myers his battle suit and weapons before summoning another set for himself. He remembered giving his brother the phase rod lying on the floor where his brother had dropped it.

"Rick—" started Nickelo.

"I know," Richard said as he thought the command to summon the 9mm.

The pistol disappeared out of Myers's hand and reappeared in the air an arms-length from Richard. Still too weak to even grab the pistol, he let it fall clattering to the floor.

Myers glanced at his empty hand. "What the—"

"You said it yourself, Myers. Those are my weapons. That's my battle suit as well. I tagged it long before I ever gave it to you; and what I tag, I can summon."

A line of Power reached out from his brother toward Richard's chest. Richard knocked it aside with his own line of Power. Myers turned, stumbling in the direction of the spirit-cat. Richard thought the command to summon his battle suit, battle helmet, and weapons. Myers fell to the floor as his battle suit disappeared. Richard's brother was up in a flash, dragging himself onto the back of the spirit-cat. Both the cat and Myers shimmered before disappearing into the floor.

"This isn't over," said Nickelo.

"I know," Richard said trying to stand but failing miserably.

"You have lost too much blood," said Nickelo. *"Plus, that demon essence is still eating away at your wound. Your self-heal is making progress, but the healing is taking longer than usual."*

Despite his pain, Richard sent an active scan into the wound on his left shoulder seeking out the demon essence. He found a nearly invisible link between the mass of evil in his shoulder and the phase rod on the ground nearby. Using some of the Power created when Jeena sent him Power from her reserve, he wrapped the demonic link twisting hard. The link didn't kink as he expected. Instead, it snapped completely apart. The demon essence in his shoulder sent out an emotion of hate before succumbing to his self-heal.

"Hmm," said Nickelo. *"I calculate that will drastically speed up the healing process."*

"How long before I'm able to get around," Richard asked desperate to get to his bondmate. He had no doubt the cavern the elves called the Presence of the Lady was his brother's destination.

"At least five minutes before you are fully battle ready," said Nickelo.

"I can't—" Richard started.

"Let me finish," said Nickelo guessing his wizard scout's argument. *"Put the battle suit on. Use telekinesis if you must. The hole the lance made in the chest will prevent the suit from sealing, but none of the major systems in the suit are damaged. If you give me full control of the suit, I can use the assistors to get you around long enough for you to get to your bondmate."*

Understanding came to Richard. He tried reaching for the battle suit's pants, but a wave of pain washed over him. Using telekinesis, he tore off his robe and replaced it with his battle suit. The arms and legs of the suit began moving of their own accord. The battle suit rose off the floor, taking Richard with it. He felt the arms of his suit strapping on his weapons and reloading, then levitated the still activated phase rod into the suit's left hand. He noticed the cracked battle helmet on the ground. The lower portion of the brerellium chip containing the helmet's CPU was visible through the crack. Richard thought the command to make his suit bend down and reach for the damaged battle helmet.

"No!" said Nickelo stopping the movement of the battle suit.

"What do you mean no?*"* Richard said wondering if he should override his battle computer's control of the suit. *"We've got to save Wanda. Myers is our enemy, not his battle computer. The helmet's damaged. Wanda will die as soon as the backup emergency isotopic battery runs out."*

"That's not Wanda," said Nickelo sounding certain. *"It is a demon. When you cracked the helmet with that lance of yours, the demon momentarily lost control of its connection to the tele-network. Its true thoughts appeared for a nanosecond. Wanda is dead. Your brother killed her after the battle with the vampires."*

The idea that a wizard scout could purposely kill their battle computer was too much for Richard to comprehend. He shook his head. *"No. Even Myers wouldn't—"*

"Check it yourself. You have part of 'the One' *in your DNA. Use it to scan what is in that chip."*

Short on time, Richard reached into the brerellium chip with his mind expecting to find a battle computer. What he found instead forced him to beat a hasty retreat. The evil of what was inside was too much for a mere human mind to bear for long.

Without asking his battle computer's opinion, Richard touched the tip of the phase rod to the exposed end of the helmet's CPU chip. He sensed a scream of agony as the demon essence in the rod hungrily sucked out whatever the demon in the chip used as life force. The scream diminished before stopping altogether. Richard noticed the miniature lightning bolts running up and down the length of the phase rod were glowing brighter.

"I would have advised against that," said Nickelo. *"I calculate you just made the Dalinfaust that much stronger."*

"Whatever," Richard said ending the conversation.

Calling his spirit-horse, Richard deactivated the phase rod and reattached it to the utility belt on his left hip. Once his hand was free, he levitated Mendera's Lance into his waiting hand. At the same moment, the stallion rose out of the floor beneath him, saving him the trouble of mounting. As if sensing the importance of the lance, two tentacles of black protruded out of the stallion's right flank and formed a carrier of sorts for the weapon. Richard retracted the lance into its two-meter length and slid it into the carrier.

"I need information," Richard thought as he sent his passive scan outward the way his friend Trinity had taught him. What he found was not what he expected. It was worse.

"I see it," said Nickelo converting the passive scan's data into visual information on Richard's heads-up display. *"Multiple demons are at the entrance to the presence of the Lady. At least two elf lords and a magic user are fighting them there. Your friends Leethor, Meshoan, and Rembis are engaged in the tunnel. Your bondmate is locked in battle inside the cavern. To top it off, the Tree of Light is still being attacked by the demon essence from three of the obelisks. The other elven lords are trying to help, but the tree is in danger.*

"What do you want to do, Wizard Scout? You cannot help everyone. You need to make a decision. Who are you going to help first?"

Richard didn't need to think. He only had one destination in mind. *"Jeena."*

CHAPTER 56

As soon as the tunnel opened into the Presence of the Lady, Jeena saw the bloody bodies of two of the Lady's caretakers. She raised her staff, searching for whatever foul monster dared to attack the sanctity of the Tree of Light's inner sanctum. Her eyes were immediately drawn to the dry lakebed. On the boulder in the center stood a single elf lord.

"Lord Linustanoi," Jeena said momentarily wondering how the young elven lord could have beaten her to the cavern. She was even more confused when she saw what the elf held in his hands. "The Lady's staff," she said. "How?"

The elf lord loosed a ball of magic in her direction.

Drawing Power from her reserve, Jeena mouthed the words of a defensive-shield spell in time to form a barrier between her and Lord Linustanoi. The elf lord's spell hit her shield, glancing up to the ceiling where it exploded in a blast of fire. A dozen globes of Power dangling from the roots of the Tree of Light exploded as well, sending pieces of jagged stone raining down onto the beach below.

"Are you sure you want to do this, Jeena my sweet?" said Lord Linustanoi with an out of place smile. He pointed at the many roots dangling through cracks in the ceiling. "It would only take a few misplaced spells to start a chain reaction. This whole place would crumble into oblivion. Your precious Tree of Light would come crashing down."

Jeena squelched the spell on her lips. "Are you mad? What do you hope to accomplish? You are an elven lord."

Lord Linustanoi gave a smile that was more a sneer. The mocking sneer was one Jeena had never seen on the young elf lord, but it seemed familiar nonetheless.

"Jeena, I am hurt," said Lord Linustanoi. "After spending an intimate year together, do you mean you do not recognize me?"

Jeena frowned. She had no time for riddles. Already she felt pain through the link to her bondmate telling her that Richard was in battle with someone or something.

"Of course, I know you," Jeena said walking cautiously forward to close the distance to her fellow lord. "Now give me the Lady's staff. We can use it to stop whatever is being done to the Tree of Light."

"Stop it?" laughed Lord Linustanoi. "Now why would I want to do that? As soon as the Dalinfaust's time-commando disables the last corner of the gate, I am going to use this staff to call forth an army the likes of which the three galaxies have never seen." The elven lord's sneer took on an evil look. "You could have ruled by my side, but instead you cast your lot with a filthy human."

More confused than ever, Jeena continued moving forward at a pace she hoped would close the distance without spooking the young elven lord into another attack.

"Hold where you are, Jeena," said Lord Linustanoi pointing the staff he carried at the thickest mass of Power-filled globes overhead. "I swear I will cast a spell so powerful, every bit of tree root above will be destroyed."

Jeena froze where she stood. The ring on her finger tingled. *"You are running out of time,"* said Danny. *"Nickelo says your bondmate is preparing to do battle against his brother right now. You must do something."*

"Do what?" Jeena thought back. *"You are the battle computer. How about giving some advice?"*

"Sorry," said Danny. *"I have nothing logical with greater than a one percent chance of success. In desperate times, battle computers rely on their wizard scouts to come up with illogical solutions or to just plain get lucky."*

"Well, I am not a wizard scout."

"Hmm. Then I calculate we may have a problem."

"You remain quiet, my sweet," said Lord Linustanoi. "You were ever the fool. You still do not know who I am."

Although confused by the elven lord's words, Jeena decided her only chance was to keep her fellow lord talking while she tried to think of some way to overpower him and get the Lady's staff without bringing the cavern down around their ears.

"You are Lord Linustanoi. You are a lord of the Council of Light. You are sworn to protect—"

The young elven lord laughed. "Ha! I am sworn to protect nothing other than myself. As to the fool Linustanoi, he has been dead these last fifty years. My orcs and I ambushed and killed him as he made his way to Silverton to interview with the council. I killed all in his party as well as everyone in his village to make sure no fool could later challenge who I was. Then I took his place using a polymorph spell taught me by the Dalinfaust." Waving a free hand at his body, the elven lord laughed again. "It is a very good spell. Even the vaunted Master Jathar has not been able to penetrate my disguise. I had hoped I would never have to wear this form again, but I decided to cast the spell back on myself when I sensed you coming through the tunnel."

Too much unexpected information was coming too fast for Jeena. "I do not under—"

"Of course you do not," sneered the elven lord. He waved a hand in the air. "Here, let me help jar your memory."

The air around the elven lord shimmered. Linustanoi's features changed, his light skin taking on a darker hue as his hair turned white.

"Crendemor!" Jeena shouted, all thought of her purpose and where she was forgotten. Her long-buried hatred of the dark elf came roaring to the surface. Shouting a word of Power, Jeena sent a ball of deadly magic at her hated enemy. Even as the magic glanced off the dark elf's defensive shield, Jeena continued running forward while sending ball after ball of magic at the white-haired elf.

Crendemor staggered back under her sudden assault, nearly falling off the boulder in the process. The sneer she'd so grown to hate during her year of captivity was no longer on the dark elf's face. She heard Crendemor shout a quick spell to shore up his defensive shield before sending balls of magic out the end of the Lady's staff, in her direction.

As the oncoming magic drew close, Jeena sensed Danny angle

her shield in such a manner to make the dark elf's spells ricochet into the sandy beach instead of up into the globes of Power dangling overhead. Jeena was too angry to care where the magic went or what damage it did. The only thing she wanted was to shove her staff down Crendemor's throat.

As Jeena drew close to the boulder, she spoke the one-word incantation for a levitation spell, raising herself onto the large stone. Crendemor met her with a swing of the Lady's staff at her head. Ducking, Jeena thrust her staff into the dark elf's belly. A flash of blue magic burst from the end of her staff, forcing the dark elf back. Even in her anger, Jeena could tell her foe was unharmed.

"He is wearing magic armor underneath his robe," said Danny. *"I can sense it. Fortunately, you are inside his defensive shield. Use your pistol."*

Switching hands on her staff, Jeena pulled the Deloris blaster out of its holster and fired rapidly at the swiftly moving dark elf.

Boom! Boom! Boom!

None of the rounds hit their intended target. Forcing herself to take the time to line the barrel of her weapon on the dark elf's chest, Jeena pulled the trigger again.

Click.

"Out of ammo," said Danny. *"I calculate you should have reloaded when you had a chance."*

A smile grew on Crendemor's face as he drew a jewel-handled sword from a scabbard at his waist. He thrust the weapon at Jeena's chest. She turned just in time to avoid the attack, but the keen edge of the magic blade left a line of red droplets across her right breast and shoulder.

Throwing her pistol at Crendemor's face, Jeena cast a spell at the dark elf's feet. Vines appeared out of the boulder, wrapping around the white-haired elf and tripping him to the boulder's surface. He smacked the side of his face on the stone hard, leaving a splattering of blood and a broken tooth behind as he struggled to rise.

Raising her staff high overhead for a killing blow, Jeena drew Power from her reserve determined to end the dark elf's life once and for all. Before she could bring her weapon down, an unseen force jerked the staff out of her hands. The staff flew through the air and landed in the sand twenty paces away from the boulder.

Sensing a line of Power withdrawing to her rear, Jeena turned to see a man on a horse-sized lizard-skinned cat. The cat was dripping blood from claw marks across its chest and flank. The man was unclothed and bloody, but she recognized him immediately.

"Myers!" Jeena exclaimed half disbelieving what she saw.

"Watch out," said Danny in their shared space.

Catching a glint of blue, Jeena turned her attention back to Crendemor in time to see him thrust the Lady's staff at her chest. The blue gem at the tip of the staff glowed bright blue as it forced its way through her defensive shield. Jeena sensed the staff struggling against Crendemor as if hesitant to do her harm, but the dark elf's will prevailed. Jeena was slammed backward, her head hitting the top of the boulder hard enough to make everything go black for three long seconds.

Only semi-conscious, Jeena heard Crendemor shout words she quickly forgot. Lines of magic twisted around her chest, arms, and legs. By the time her vision cleared, she was already wrapped in magic and unable to move. Jeena tried pulling Power from her reserve, but it didn't work. She sensed Crendemor had somehow used the Lady's staff to circumvent the traps her bondmate had placed on the link to her reserve. Her link was blocked completely.

"Danny, I need help," Jeena said in her shared space.

"I can do nothing," said Danny sounding genuinely sorry. *"I have informed Nickelo and the others. That is all I can do."*

As her mind cleared, Jeena noticed Crendemor standing over her. He kicked her hard in the ribs. "That is for trying to oppose me." The dark elf turned his head toward Myers. "Why are you here? The last corner of the gate is still active."

"Shepard," moaned Myers clutching his chest. "He took my armor and weapons. He's got some kind of magic spear he shoved through my chest. I'm trying to self-heal, but I need a few more minutes. Shepard was hurt, but he'll be coming here. I'll need a weapon when he does."

"Fool!" shouted Crendemor. "Why am I forced to work with fools?"

Sensitive to emotions, Jeena detected anger welling up in her bondmate's brother. Her mind began churning furiously as she tried to think of a way to use the obvious animosity between the two males to her advantage.

"Shepard has the last phase rod," said Myers still clutching his chest. "Give me your sword. I'll go back and stop him. Once I get the phase rod back, I'll disable the last corner. Then I'll expect the bottle of DNA gas."

Although she couldn't move, Jeena could speak. "Just like a human to betray his own brother. I am surprised even a dark elf can force himself to work with you. Only elves are honorable enough to—"

Crendemor laughed. He spat a mouthful of blood and saliva at Jeena's face, hitting the stone instead. "You think so highly of elves. I despise humans more than you, but they can be useful at times, even if it is only to take the blame for what I do."

The dark elf's reply wasn't what Jeena expected. Her confusion must've shown on her face.

Crendemor looked down and laughed. "Of course you do not understand. Allow me to explain."

The dark elf waved a hand at his body while reciting a spell. The words of the spell reminded Jeena of a reverse polymorph spell. The air around Crendemor shimmered as the dark elf's features changed again. His skin color lightened until it was almost white. When the shimmering ceased, a tall, handsome high elf stood before Jeena.

"You look surprised, my sweet," said the high elf. "Allow me to introduce myself. I am Kreathin. Perhaps you remember the discussion you had with my dark elf form in Drakomar?"

Jeena did remember. She had been reading about a high elf called Kreathin who'd been lured into the art of necromancy. She had not fully believed it then. She still didn't. No high elf could do such evil as far as she was concerned.

"I remember our talk," she said. "If you are that Kreathin, then you are no high elf. What is your true form? How many more layers of polymorph spells do you have before you reveal your true self?"

Kreathin smiled. "Foolish to the end are you not, Jeena? You think too highly of your race. Your mother did not want to believe a high elf could betray her either."

"My...my mother?" Jeena couldn't fathom what her mother had to do with the hated foe standing before her.

"Oh, my sweet Jeena," laughed Kreathin. "How I have so

wanted to tell you the true tale of your parents' demise and that of your equally sweet sister. You and your brother should have been with them that day, but fate cheated me out of my true prize."

"What are you saying?" Jeena said, her mind still reeling from the blow to her head. "My parents and sister were killed by hu—"

"Yes, by humans," finished Kreathin squatting on his heels to better see her face. "Or so I made it appear. The Dalinfaust taught me a mass polymorph spell that has come in handy many times over the years. It was so easy to use it on two companies of orcs and my dark elf assassins and I. Combined with some stolen equipment from a camp of humans we killed, it was easy to make the high elf scouts who found your slaughtered parents believe humans had done the deed."

Jeena struggled for breath. Her anger rose, giving her strength, but still she could not free herself from the magic binding her. "You monster. I swear I will kill you if it is the last thing I do."

Again, Kreathin laughed before giving the mocking sneer Jeena had so grown to hate in Crendemor. He seemed to be enjoying her misery.

"That is the same thing your mother said before I had my way with her. After that, I gave her to my orcs. As for your sweet sister, I had her taken away to avoid seeing what was done. I raised her as my own for many years, treating her with kindness until she was of a mature age. Then I gave her as a gift to the Dalinfaust. I made sure she remained a virgin while she was in my care, so the demon could heal her between torture sessions. I still remember her screams. They were delicious. She died on the same sacrificial stone where I had you chained."

An animal-like cry came out of Jeena's throat. She redoubled her efforts to free herself. Despite her efforts, she was unsuccessful.

Kreathin stood sneering down at her. "So you see, my sweet Jeena, it was not humans who destroyed your family. It was I, one of your own kind. Now I am going to kill you as well."

"No!" screamed a male voice full of rage.

A blue ball of magic struck the defensive shield around Kreathin. The shield buckled, but the magic was reflected upward, exploding among the Tree of Light's roots overhead. Spheres of Power exploded, raining fire and brimstone down. Several bits of hot ash landed on Jeena's legs, but she cared not. She sensed the frequency of the magic. She knew who had come. Straining to look out the corner of her eye, she saw two figures near the tunnel entrance running in the direction of the boulder upon which she lay.

Hope flared inside Jeena. Hope that she could kill the monster that had destroyed her family. She knew the two coming to join the fight. She sensed the Power of Kreathin and Myers, comparing it with her two newfound allies. The two who were coming were woefully outgunned. She had to get free to help them. She had too.

"Danny," Jeena thought. *"Help me."*

"I wish I could," replied Danny, *"but I cannot. It is up to them. I calculate the odds are not good. There is no logical way they can win."*

Jeena remembered something her battle computer had said earlier. *"Then we will have to pray we get lucky."*

CHAPTER 57

Ceril ignored the stray bits of energy landing around the defensive shield just outside the Tree of Light's outstretched arms. He saw High Lord Trenadine and Lords Reale, Renere, Othellian, and Crenashal standing at the edge of the clearing, adding the Power of their staffs to the tree's defensive shield. Priestess Aldriss, Priestess Kantaria, and old Priest Tobias were there with a dozen acolytes of the priesthood, trying to shore up the flagging defenses around the tree as the beams of blue, red, and green energy continued their unrelenting assault on the Tree of Light. Ceril ignored them all. He had only one concern.

"Terika," Ceril yelled turning to face the Tree of Light. "Where are you? Answer me."

"Father!" came a shout from inside the silvery shield surrounding the tree.

Relief flooded through Ceril when he saw his daughter standing at the base of the Tree of Light with her arms wrapped protectively around two young elf children. Over two hundred other children were grouped near Terika, their unofficial leader.

Terika took a step toward him.

"No!" Ceril shouted, fear adding to the volume of his voice. "Stay where you are. The Lady's shield will protect you. You will be safe if you stay near the tree. Remain with the children. Keep them together until this is over. I will be back for you, I promise."

With a display of courage that filled Ceril's heart with pride, his daughter nodded her head. "I will keep the others safe, Father. I swear it."

The sight of his daughter standing helpless among the other children tore at Ceril's heart, but he forced himself to take his gaze away. The Tree of Light was under attack. He was a mage of the fifth circle. He had to help. A shout from the high lord drew his attention.

"Lords and priests help hold the shield," yelled High Lord Trenadine. "Master Jathar, take all the mages to the Presence of the Lady. Help Lords Thalos and Sheshna and the high priestess when you get there."

"Mages, follow me," shouted Master Jathar taking off at a run for the white-stoned path leading to the Presence of the Lady.

A dozen mages and novices along with a score of soldiers ran behind the old mage.

Ceril took off after them. When he reached the part of the path leading down to the tunnel entrance, he glanced over his shoulder for a final look at the Tree of Light. Bright beams of blue, red, and green light continued to explode against the translucent shield surrounding the tree. A stray bit of magic ricocheted off, blasting a section out of the stone wall near the Council of Light's ceremonial mound. Jagged pieces of debris shot into the air, falling around the scrambling crowd of elves below. The limbs of the tree twisted back and forth as if in agony. Ceril just made out the children crowded near the base of the tree. They appeared to be hunkered down with the older children trying to protect the younger as best they could. Try as he might Ceril could no longer make out his daughter, but he had no doubt she was there protecting those younger than her. A part of him wanted to go back, but the more logical part of him knew the best way to help lay forward.

The Tree of Light is on the verge of being destroyed. I have to get to the Presence of the Lady and stop the attack. That is the best way to help Terika. It may be the only way.

An emotion of fear and anger came to Ceril from the link his bonded Therasia had attached to him during their bonding ceremony years earlier. He sensed she was nearing the northern obelisk. *She must be trying to stop the blue beam at its source,* he thought. *She is in danger, but I cannot help her now.*

Ceril wished he could share his emotions with her, but they

were not bondmates. He had never given his bond back to her, only she to him. The thought that one or both of them might die this day without being full bondmates sent a wave of icy fear into his heart.

I swear if we get out of this alive, I will give myself to you in bonding, Therasia. I cannot bear the thought of an eternity without you.

With that thought, he was over the lip of the path and descending down to the valley where the entrance to the Presence of the Lady was located. He picked up speed, passing those ahead of him as he went.

I have to stop the attacks, he thought. *The lives of my bonded and daughter depend on it.*

By the time Ceril arrived, the battle in the small valley containing the entrance to the Presence of the Lady was in full swing. He saw a company of elves dressed in the blue chainmail of the Council of Light's personal guards arrayed around two elven lords. He recognized the lords as Thalos and Sheshna. He noticed a splattering of his fellow mages interspersed within the soldiers' formation.

Opposing the elves was a sight out of Ceril's worst nightmare. A score of monstrously shaped creatures of every size and shape were engaging the elven force. Ceril sensed intense evil coming from the nightmare creatures.

"Demons!" shouted Master Jathar as he sent a lightning bolt at the largest of the creatures.

The lightning bolt glanced off the demon's thick skin, shooting into the sky. The demon roared with rage and charged in Master Jathar's direction. Two soldiers met the demon with swords at the ready. The demon, twice the size of the elves, grabbed one of the soldiers and tore her in half, chainmail and all. A ball of magic from another demon hit the second soldier. The screaming elf burst into flames. The charred corpse of the soldier fell to the ground, breaking into blackened pieces when it hit.

Ceril charged into the fray, casting a ball of magic as he drew his sword.

"Magic weapons only," shouted Lord Thalos. "Soldiers form a line on me. Mages to the rear."

Soldiers and mages alike hastened to obey the old general, but the demons hindered their way. An orange-skinned demon waved one of its clawed hands, and a wall of magic appeared to its front. A black opening appeared in the wall. Out of the opening walked a four-armed demon twice the size of an elf. As the wall of magic disappeared, the new demon raised a flaming whip and struck out at a trio of soldiers trying to make their way toward Lord Thalos. The whip cut completely through the soldiers, leaving charred body parts in its wake.

"The orange one," shouted Lord Sheshna. "We have to kill it before she summons more."

A half dozen balls of magic shot out from the rank of soldiers as mages sought to obey. Ceril added a lightning bolt of his own to the mix. Before any of the magic reached their intended target, Ceril sensed lines of magic reach out from several demons and create a defensive shield to the front of the orange demon. The elves' magic burst harmlessly against the shield.

When the smoke cleared, Ceril saw the orange-skinned demon wave her arms again. Another of the walls of magic appeared and out ran two hounds with what appeared to be snakes growing out of their necks. As the gate spell dissipated, the two demon-hounds charged into a squad of soldiers. Wolf-like fangs tore through armor as the snakeheads struck out at any elf within reach.

"We cannot fight them," yelled a soldier before a horned demon resembling a six-legged bull gored him. The demon-bull tossed the unlucky elf over its shoulder as it sought another target.

Above the din of battle, Ceril heard someone shout, "A dragon!"

Looking skyward, Ceril saw a shiny object high in the sky and closing fast. *If that is a dragon, it is the strangest looking dragon I have ever seen,* he thought. Strange or not, he prepared a lightning bolt anyway as he waited for the *dragon* to get within range. As the shiny object drew closer, it began looking less and less like a dragon and more like some flying metal golem in the form of a stubby-winged dragon want-to-be.

Without warning, a streak of light shot out from the front of the metal dragon and hit the bull-shaped demon in the chest. The bull-demon flew back rolling on the ground, spattering blood and gore as it went. More beams of light shot from the metal dragon, striking other demons. Smaller objects resembling miniature dragons shot out from the metal dragons' wings, trailing flames of fire behind them. Ceril sensed magic in some but not all of the smaller dragons. The miniature dragons slammed into several demons and exploded into multi-colored balls of flame and energy.

The larger, metal dragon came to a hover fifty paces in the air. Ceril saw the back part of the dragon open up. Out of the opening came what appeared to be a black golem half again as tall as an elf. Behind the golem came smaller, dwarf-sized figures in strange suits of armor. Other elf-sized figures followed them, falling toward the ground before jets of energy from their backs cushioned their fall.

The black golem hit the ground running toward the orange-skinned demon. It shoved its way past two smaller demons and, raising its left arm, shot out balls of energy that struck the orange demon before she could cast another spell.

Ceril charged forward casting a spell of his own at one demon while swinging his sword at another that was engaging one of the dwarf-sized humanoids. Ceril's sword barely missed the smaller humanoid before biting into the demon's left arm. The dwarf-sized humanoid raised a strange-looking staff, sending a stream of energy into the demon's face. The demon was knocked back a step before another of the small humanoids jumped at the demon and swung a battle axe into the creature's chest.

Ceril pulled his sword back as he glanced into the clear visor of the nearest of the small humanoids.

A red-bearded dwarf stared back at him. "Well?" asked the dwarf. "Are you going to stand there gawking all day? Or are you going to help us with these demons?"

Ceril loosed a spell at another demon as an elf-sized figure joined the dwarf. A glance in the visor of the newcomer revealed the face of a young human male in his late teens or early twenties. The human carried one of the strange-looking staffs in his right hand and a balled-up cloak containing what appeared to be a round object in the other.

"Storis," the human male yelled at the nearest dwarf. Holding up the balled cloak, the human said, "We've got to get this inside that tunnel. It's the only way to stop whatever is happening in there. I sense it."

The dwarf raised his staff, sending a series of energy balls at another demon before looking back at the human. "It's too dangerous, Matt. We've got to consolidate out here first. Give Angela and Timerman a couple of minutes with the shuttle's blasters to clear out the riffraff. Then we can worry about getting inside the tunnel."

Ceril noticed the human shake his head. "It will be too late then."

Without waiting for a reply, the human ran toward the entrance leading to the Presence of the Lady while dodging balls of magic from demons blocking his way. The human shot balls of energy from his staff as he ran carrying whatever was stored in the cloak in his free hand. Something in the human's desperate charge told Ceril the boy's mission was one of utmost importance.

Ignoring his usual disdain for humans, Ceril ran after the young man casting a fireball spell to clear the boy's way. By the time the human entered the tunnel, he had caught up. Ceril took the lead with the human close behind.

Ceril passed the body of a fallen caretaker before rounding a bend in the tunnel. When he cleared the bend, he saw Leethor and Meshoan fighting a desperate battle with two lizard-skinned cats the size of ponies. Four cat bodies littered the ground in testimony to the fierceness of the fight. A gnome near the two elves cast a spell, striking one of the cat creatures in the chest and knocking it back.

When Ceril slowed with the intent of helping his comrades, the human male rushed past. Taking only a moment to make his decision, Ceril ran after the human and caught up just as the young man entered the Presence of the Lady. As soon as they entered, Ceril's eyes were drawn to the dry lakebed with the large engraved boulder at its center. On top of the boulder, a male elf with a glowing staff in one hand and a jewel-handled sword in the other stood over the unmoving form of his sister.

The male elf said, "So you see, my sweet Jeena, it was not humans who destroyed your family. It was I, one of your own kind. Now I am going to kill you as well."

"No!" shouted Ceril casting a hasty spell at the male elf.

The blue energy of the spell hit a shield surrounding the elf and glanced up into the cavern's roof. A dozen globes of Power dangling from tree roots exploded, sending rocks and burning debris into the cavern below. Ceril charged forward casting another spell as he ran. The human boy followed for a few steps, firing balls of energy from his metal staff before stopping suddenly and looking to his left.

Out the corner of his eye, Ceril noticed a naked man on a horse-sized lizard cat. With no time to worry about the mounted human, he continued his charge hoping to draw attention away from his sister

"Please, Lady, don't let her be dead," Ceril prayed silently while drawing Power from his reserve for a third spell. Even running as fast as he could, he doubted he could make the top of the boulder before the male elf was able to bring his sword down on Jeena.

CHAPTER 58

Matthew began to run with his elf companion fully intending to assist in attacking the other elf on top of the boulder. Although he didn't know magic, he did know Power, and the energy being radiated from the top of the boulder told him all he needed to know.

Whatever I'm going to do, it needs to be done on top of that stone.

Movement to his left drew his attention. Matthew saw his father mounted on a larger version of the lizard-cats that he'd seen in the tunnel. Something else drew his attention. There at the base of the boulder was a crumpled body covered in blood. Recognition came to him. He stumbled, dropping his plasma rifle and the cloak with the sphere of white gas. He didn't care. Only one thing mattered now.

"Mother! No!" Matthew cried putting all his pain and misery into the two words.

* * *

Kreathin was in the act of bringing his sword down on the hated high priestess when the first spell hit his shield and threw him back a step. Following the line of magic, he saw the high priestess's brother and a human male running in his direction. He sensed Ceril casting another spell. Making a hand gesture for a counter-spell, Kreathin knocked Ceril's spell aside. He sensed the elf drawing

Power for a third spell from his reserve.

Not this time, Kreathin thought as he sent a line of magic out to locate a weak point in Ceril's link to his Power reserve. Kreathin suppressed a laugh when he sensed how pitifully weak the elf was. *Not even trapped,* he thought as he wrapped his line of magic around the link, twisting it back on itself.

Ceril stumbled and fell to the ground before jumping back to his feet with sword in hand.

Kreathin laughed. *Good luck getting up here quickly without your magic,* he thought.

"Mother! No!"

Tracking the voice to the running boy, Kreathin sensed Power in the human's reserve. He sensed a lot of Power.

An idea came to Kreathin. *The fool time-commando of the Dalinfaust failed to disable the final corner, but maybe I can succeed anyway. The boy is not a child, but he is still young and his Power is potent. His blood may be enough for me to use as a catalyst to make the Lady's staff open the gate. I can add the high priestess's blood for good measure. Victory will yet be mine.*

Kreathin sensed traps around the boy's link to his Power reserve. He glanced down at the high priestess lying helpless at his feet. She had succumbed to his spell thanks to the help of the Lady's staff. He knew the staff wasn't linked to the boy, so he couldn't use the same trick, but an idea came to him anyway. He remembered the time when his orcs and he had captured the high priestess.

Perhaps the spell the Dalinfaust taught me to disable the high priestess then will work on the boy now.

Reciting the spell, Kreathin cast it at the cavern's roof. The spell grew rapidly in size, sending a funnel downward toward the human boy. Traps on the boy's link detonated, reducing the effectiveness of the spell, but enough magic remained to fight its way to the core of the boy's link and drain Power from his reserve. The human fell to the ground unable to move as the paralysis part of the spell took hold. Wrapping magic around the human boy, Kreathin levitated him to the top of the boulder. As the boy flew through the air, Kreathin watched him pass over the head of the fool Ceril still trying to find a foothold to climb up the slick side of the house-sized boulder.

You will be too late, Kreathin thought. *The deed will be done long before you get up here.*

Levitating the human into a kneeling position at his feet, Kreathin grabbed the boy's hair and jerked his head back to expose his neck. At his touch, the paralysis part of the spell broke, but Kreathin held the struggling human in place with his levitation spell.

Placing his sword at the boy's throat while positioning the staff in such a manner that it would be covered with blood, Kreathin locked eyes with the high priestess. "Today you will see your foolishness, sweet Jeena. You could have ruled by my side, but now you will see the doom of your people. Once I make a sacrifice of this human boy's blood, I will slit your throat as well. Using the Power of his blood sacrifice, I will destroy the final lock on this gate and take command of the demon army."

Switching his gaze to the human, Kreathin waited for the boy's fear to grow to a suitable level. Once satisfied the boy's fear was at its peak, Kreathin shouted, "I sacrifice your blood, boy, the same as I sacrificed that of your mother. You will join her in hell for all eternity. Die, boy! Die now!"

* * *

Ex-wizard scout Gaston Myers sat on his mount waiting for his self-heal to counteract the pain in his chest and shoulder. The wound from his brother's spear was like none he'd ever received. Even now the spear's magic that remained in the wound continued eating away at his flesh, counteracting his self-heal. Myers sensed his self-heal slowly gaining the upper hand, but he had no doubt if his Power reserve had been less full, he would've succumbed to the wound by now. Through his pain, he heard a shout and recognized the voice as that of his son.

"Matt," he said barely able to whisper as the spear's wound made a last-ditch effort to overcome his self-heal.

Myers diverted all Power in his reserve to combat the spear's magic. He didn't need his battle computer to know it was going to be close. *I'm going to need every drop of Power in my reserve to win the fight against this wound.*

Magic flared near the cavern's ceiling.

Myers barely noticed as he continued to battle for his life. The lizard-cat beneath him grew restless.

I can't stay on this cat. It may shift into the void again. I can't afford any distractions. I must heal this wound and then get a weapon. Once I do, I'll go back and kill Shepard. I'll retrieve my phase rod and finish my task. I can still succeed. I'll get the bottle of DNA gas for Diane if it's the last thing I do. We can still be a family.

As he slipped off his mount to the lakebed, something drew Myers's attention. Through blurred eyes, he saw his son flying through the air and landing on top of the boulder. An elf carrying a sword was at the base of the boulder, trying to climb up. He also saw another elf on top of the house-sized stone, holding a sword in one hand and a staff in the other. Although the figure wasn't a dark elf, Myers knew it was Crendemor just the same.

Why the dark elf changed his appearance, I don't know or care, but the elf is definitely Crendemor. I wish I could send an active scan to the top of the boulder to see what's happening, but I can't. I need every drop of Power to heal this blasted wound. Once it's healed, I'll deal with Crendemor, but not before. Hang on just a few seconds, Matt, until I'm healed!

Wiping tears of pain from his eyes, Myers got a better look at what was happening on the boulder. Fear washed over him when he saw his son kneeling before Crendemor. As he watched, the elf jerked Matthew's head back and place a sword to the boy's throat.

"No," Myers tried to shout. The sound came out only slightly above a whisper. He started gathering Power from his reserve but stopped. *I can't yet. I need every drop for my self-heal. Matt will be okay for a few seconds. He'll have to be.*

Myers heard Crendemor speaking. The sound was muffled, but by concentrating, he caught the elf's final words. "I sacrifice your blood, boy, the same as I sacrificed that of your mother's. You will join her in hell for all eternity. Die, boy! Die now!"

Fear drove Myers to act. He began drawing Power from his reserve, trying his best to ration it. *I just need to use enough Power to distract Crendemor long enough for my self-heal to finish.*

Before the drawing of Power was complete, something at the base of the boulder caught Myers's eye. He saw the crumpled body of a blood-soaked animal. He had a fleeting thought that

Crendemor had probably sacrificed the animal before flinging it off the side of the boulder.

A sacrifice? Myers thought, keying in on the word. He looked at the animal closer. *It doesn't look like any animal I've seen on Portalis.* Recognition hit him all at once. Burning anger rose up, consuming everything but the image of the bloody sacrifice. *Diane!*

"Crendemor!" Myers shouted as the hate welled up from the inner depths of his soul. Drawing every bit of Power from his reserve, he sent it as one massive blast of pure Power against the elf the way his brother had done against him. Myers sensed his Power slam into Crendemor's shield, knocking the elf away from Matthew. He saw the staff fall from the elf's hand and clatter onto the boulder's surface.

With the total loss of his Power, Myers sensed his self-heal stop working. The magic in the spear's wound immediately began expanding, digging deep into his soul as it ravenously began eating away at his flesh. He started to fall to the ground but sensed magic wrap around him, levitating him through the air onto the top of the boulder next to his son. The magic forced him to a kneeling position. He felt a rough hand grab his hair and jerk his head to expose his throat.

"You made your last mistake, human," hissed Crendemor. "I should have killed you long ago. You have always wanted to be with your precious Diane forever. Now you are going to get your wish. Your blood is powerful. Once it mixes with that of your Diane and the others, I have no doubt the gate will open. The Dalinfaust will drink your soul along with that of your Diane. For good measure, I will add the blood of your son and the high priestess. Die, fool!"

Myers felt the cold edge of the elf's blade slice into his neck. He sensed something evil clawing its way through the stone below him, eager to be free. He sensed emotions resembling screams. One of the screams reminded him of Diane. His scream of emotions joined hers as evil beyond compare pulled him down into eternal darkness.

CHAPTER 59

From her position on the boulder, Jeena saw the blood of her bondmate's brother splatter onto the design carved into the top of the boulder. As soon as the blood touched the stone, she sensed it mingling with the blood of others already there and Myers's blood combining with a source of energy that could only be DNA gas.

As the blood and gas mixed, the top of the stone cracked. The earth shook. The movement of the boulder rolled Jeena onto her back as everything in the cavern was tossed from side to side. Jeena saw the globes of Power dangling from roots overhead swaying violently. She noticed Kreathin fall still clutching his bloody sword. At the same time, she saw the lifeless body of Richard's brother fall over the side of the boulder, disappearing from sight.

As the crack in the stone widened, the shaking grew more intense. Jeena sensed evil beyond compare attempting to make its way out the opening. She recognized the evil as the Dalinfaust. The demon wasn't alone. She sensed others of its kind coming behind him.

"Lady," Jeena pleaded in her mind. *"Help us."*

The Lady didn't reply, but a glint of blue caught Jeena's eye as the Staff of the Lady of the Tree rolled back and forth on the stone where it had been dropped. The cavern continued to shake, and the staff edged ever closer to Jeena's outflung left hand.

Kreathin apparently saw the staff's movement as well. He shouted, "No!" as he rose to his knees and dove for the butt end of the staff.

Before Kreathin's outstretched fingers made contact, the blue gem at the top of the staff touched the palm of Jeena's left hand. A blaze of blue shot out the gem and freed Jeena from the spell binding her. Jerking the staff out of Kreathin's reach, she jumped to her feet at the same time Kreathin rose to his.

Her hated foe thrust his sword at Jeena's chest while sending a ball of magic from his left hand at her face. She dodged to the side avoiding the sword thrust while drawing Power from the blue gem. Blue light shot out from the gem, deflecting Kreathin's magic into the ceiling where it exploded violently enough to ignite a score of Power-filled globes dangling from the tree roots.

Swinging the Lady's staff with both hands, Jeena struck out at Kreathin but hit an invisible barrier instead. The elf's defensive shield buckled inward but held. She sensed Kreathin sending another spell her way and deflected the ball of magic to the side.

The crack in the top of the boulder widened. The cavern shook harder, knocking both Jeena and Kreathin toward the lakebed below. Jeena noticed Matthew falling as well and reached out with a levitation spell, cushioning the fall of Richard's nephew and herself. Glancing at the top of the boulder as she fell, she saw black tendrils the thickness of an elf's waist reaching out of the stone. The tendrils stretched upward and tore away at the tree roots dangling overhead. The cavern shook as if the entire world was coming to an end.

A thunderous voice full of hate and everything vile echoed off the cavern walls. "The blood of the children above will set me free. The tree cannot protect them. They will all die screaming in fear. I will devour them all. Then I will be free to command the demon armies that follow."

Jeena reached out with her senses, feeling the emotions of the two hundred plus frightened elf children overhead. The children were huddling near the Tree of Light, seeking the tree's protection. Struggling to her feet, she wrapped herself in Power from the Lady's staff, determined to fight whatever was trying to escape from the gate. Before she could act, a ball of magic streaked toward her. Deflecting the magic into the sand, Jeena saw Kreathin charging at her, sword raised high. She heard the roar of the lizard-cat as if it was in full battle as well.

Time slowed as Jeena sensed a presence through the link she shared with her bondmate. Power flowed down her bond link into her Power reserve. The spell preventing her from accessing Power in her reserve disappeared.

Jeena smiled. *He is here. I am not alone.*

CHAPTER 60

A limb crashed into the ground not two paces from Terika, barely missing one of the younger children huddled nearby. The two young elves in her arms screamed. Terika wanted to scream as well, but she forced herself to remain brave for the sake of those younger than her.

"Where is Linther?" shouted a panicked teenage male a few paces from Terika. "Has anyone seen Linther?"

The young female in Terika's arm pointed up at the tree. "He was playing hide and seek. He told me he was going to hide at the top. He said no one would ever find him there."

A shiver of fear ran down Terika's spine. Young though he was, Linther was the best climber out of all the children. Looking up through the shifting and twisting limbs and leaves, Terika tried to find the top of the Tree of Light.

He would not be there now, Terika thought trying to convince herself using logic. *He would have come down with the others when the attack first started. He must be somewhere in the crowd.*

Despite the attempt at self-assurance, Terika continued to look overhead. She spotted a flash of yellow through the ever-shifting limbs and tried to remember what the young elf had been wearing that morning.

She envisioned Linther in her mind. *He had on a yellow tunic and brown pants,* she thought growing even more fearful.

Hoping against hope, Terika searched the treetop, catching another glimpse of yellow.

"Oh no," she said out loud spotting the young elf holding on for dear life to a limb three-quarters of the way up the tree. Even at that distance, she could see the fear on the young elf's face. The boy's fear forced her to ignore her own growing panic.

"Matisa," Terika said shoving her two young charges into the arms of her relative and best friend. "Watch them. Keep them safe."

Grabbing hold of the two elves, Matisa frowned as she asked Terika, "Where are you going?"

Terika merely pointed in the direction of the frightened Linther before making a running jump at the massive trunk of the Tree of Light.

"Terika, no!" came the frightened shout of her friend. "It is too dangerous. Come back."

The warning from Matisa was not needed by Terika. She knew only too well the danger. She had never been that good at climbing. Heights scared her, but the image of fear on the young Linther overrode her phobia. She jumped from one swaying branch to another while taking risks she'd never have taken before. Twisting branches lashed across her face leaving white-hot tracks of pain, but she continued upward nonetheless. Slowly but surely, she drew closer to the young elf.

A particularly strong blast from the attacking beams of energy caused the limb upon which the elf-boy clung to crack, dropping an arms-length before the limb held.

"Linther, hang on," Terika shouted. "I am coming for you."

The young elf stared wide-eyed at her. Tracks of tears streamed down his face. "I want my mommy. Terika, help me. Please."

Terika sought out a path to the elf-boy but saw none. Gauging the distance between the boy's limb and the branch where she stood, she made her decision. She ran two steps before jumping toward the boy's perch. She made the mistake of looking down in midair, spying the ground through the shifting leaves a dizzying distance below. In spite of her resolve, Terika screamed.

I am not going to make it, she thought sensing her leap was going to be a half-step short.

Reaching into the depths of her soul, Terika pulled Power from her reserve desperately trying to remember the low-level levitation spell Master Jathar had unsuccessfully been trying to drill into her head over the past few weeks. She knew she had never gotten the spell right. In desperation, she whispered the single-word spell, trying with all her might to get the pronunciation right.

Warmth gathered around Terika, momentarily defying the law of gravity before it disappeared as suddenly as it had come. The short-lived spell was enough. Terika's outstretched fingers caught hold of a thin branch growing off of the limb where the desperate Linther clung. The branch started to break, but she grabbed another and pulled herself up onto the swaying main limb holding the boy. Panting heavily, Terika balanced on her feet as she ran the short distance to the elf-boy. His wide eyes locked with hers.

She forced a smile on her face. "Come, Linther," Terika said trying her best to sound calm. "I am going to get you down."

The boy clung to his limb, still locking eyes with her. "How?"

Terika glanced down. The tortured limbs of the Tree of Light twisted violently, making any descent a potential death sentence.

How indeed? Terika wondered before a large blast of energy coming from underneath the very roots of the Tree of Light caused the tree to shake even more violently. A massive branch broke free of the main trunk, taking others with it as the limb fell toward the crowd of children huddled below. The limb holding Linther and Terika broke free as well.

As Terika and Linther fell, Terika reached out with her right hand and pulled the younger elf to her chest. She heard him scream, then heard a feminine scream join his. Branches smacked into her back. She felt a stab of pain in her right leg accompanied by the sound of snapping bones. Down they fell. Terika pulled the boy even tighter using her body in an attempt to shield the young elf from harm.

"I will not let you die," she shouted. "I swear it!"

Crack!

A momentary flash of white-hot pain exploded at the back of Terika's head.

Then everything went black as the world around her disappeared.

CHAPTER 61

As the stallion moved upward in preparation for shifting out of the void, Richard sent an active scan into the cavern the elves called the Presence of the Lady. He took everything in at nanosecond speed with the aid of his battle computer. He sensed demonic evil tearing its way through the boulder that was the lock for the gate. He sensed the life form he knew was the elf Kreathin charging toward his bondmate and sensed his nephew Matthew lying helpless on the dry lakebed from some type of paralysis spell. Based upon the frequency of another life form, Richard knew that his brother-in-law Ceril was also in the cavern. The life form of Myer's spirit-cat showed up on his scan as well. However, he found no sign of his brother.

"Myers must have his stealth shield up," Richard told his battle computer.

Two orange dots appeared on the heads-up display of Richard's visor.

"No, he doesn't," said Nickelo in a tone that told Richard something unexpected was up. *"Look closer."*

Concentrating his active scan on the location of the two dots, Richard sensed two lifeless forms. He recognized the frequencies of the bodies. *"It's Myers and the empress."*

"I calculate you are correct," replied Nickelo leaving it at that.

Before Richard could say anything further, the demonic evil breaking through the gate reached up and attacked the base of the Tree of Light. Richard followed the demon's attack, sensing the life force of elven children above. He sensed the demonic evil from the boulder strengthening the attacks from the demon essence in the three obelisks.

"I calculate the Dalinfaust is going to kill the children," said Nickelo. *"If the demon succeeds, the lock on the gate will break. The Tree of Light will be destroyed. I highly recommend you not allow that to happen."*

Reaching out with his mind, Richard sent half the Power in his reserve down his bond link to Jeena. As he did, he sensed a spell blocking Jeena's link to her reserve. He twisted the magic back on itself, tearing it away as he did. He sent an emotion of hope to his bondmate letting her know that she wasn't alone.

Richard instinctively knew he could either help Jeena or fight the demon trying to get through the gate, but not both. He forced himself to make the most important decision of his life. While he wanted to be at his bondmate's side, protecting the gate was more important. Even so, he refused to do anything until he got Jeena some help. Shifting his line of Power to Matthew, Richard found the keystone to the spell imprisoning his nephew. He ripped the spell apart, freeing the boy's link to his Power reserve the same as he'd done for Jeena. He moved his line of Power in the direction of Ceril and found his brother-in-law's link to his Power reserve also blocked. Richard untwisted the kink to Ceril's reserve. Almost immediately he felt Power begin to flow to Jeena's brother.

Kreathin's a tough opponent, Richard reasoned. *I've fought him before. But Jeena is no slouch. She's got her Power back now, and Ceril and Matthew will back her up. My job is to stop the demon from escaping.*

Having done all he could do to help his bondmate, Richard directed the stallion to shift out of the void, onto the dry lakebed near the boulder that was the gate. Jerking Mendera's Lance from the sheath on the stallion's flank, he jumped off the spirit-horse and ran in the direction of the boulder. He pulled his 9mm pistol from his shoulder holster, gripping it firmly in his right hand.

"Your dimensional pack is still not working," said Nickelo, *"so watch your ammo. You cannot get resupplied. Also, I have to point out that I calculate that popgun of yours will do no good against the demon trying to break free of the gate, so I hope you are not depending on it. Just a little FYI."*

Richard didn't plan on using his handgun against the demon. Tossing his pistol in Matthew's direction, he wrapped himself in Power and used telekinesis to gain the top of the boulder. A large rune etched into the stone glowed bright red. Black tendrils thick as a man's waist reached out from cracks in the stone, stretching to the ceiling high overhead. They were tearing out tree roots while tossing globes of Power to the side. An image of the elf Shandria in pain flashed in Richard's mind.

Thrusting Mendera's Lance down with all the force of his battle suit's assistors, Richard drove the unicorn-horn point deep into the largest crack, seeking the demon inside. A blast of white, blue, and black energy shot out the crack and blew Richard into the air. Somehow he was able to keep hold of the lance. Even with the lance removed, Richard sensed the magic of the unicorn horn inside the crack battling the demon within. Reaching out with his mind, Richard matched frequencies with the unicorn's magic, reinforcing and strengthening it as best he could.

Hitting the lakebed, Richard felt his battle suit roll and cushion the impact.

"Thanks, Nick."

"That is what I am here for, oh greatest of all wizard scouts."

For some reason, Richard got the strange feeling his battle computer actually meant it this time. Glancing up at the withering tendrils still digging at the cavern's roof, he thought they were having difficulty tearing out the stone. Even so, he could tell they were a long way from being defeated. He sensed magic from a spell at the top of the boulder aiding the demon by weakening the lock on the gate. While the magic in the wound made by Mendera's Lance continued its battle against the demon, Richard had a feeling it wasn't going to be nearly enough.

"The lance cannot destroy the Dalinfaust," said Nickelo. *"The demon has anchor points in this dimension supporting it."*

Richard knew his battle computer was right. He sensed the demon essences in the three obelisks attacking the Tree of Light from above as the demon in the boulder attacked the tree's roots from below. Although separate from the Dalinfaust, Richard sensed that the demon essences in the three phase rods were still linked in a way too subtle for his mortal mind to comprehend. He also sensed the demon essence in the phase rod attached to his left hip drawing energy from its surroundings and funneling it to the Dalinfaust

A tingle at the back of Richard's mind filled him with peace. An image of Shandria as he'd known her when they'd first met appeared in his mind.

"The eye," said Shandria's image. *"You must destroy the eye."*

"What eye?" Richard tried to ask, but it was too late. The image of Shandria, the Lady of the Tree, was gone. So too was the tingle at the back of Richard's mind.

Richard looked at the tendrils forcing their way through the boulder's cracks. Try as he might, he saw no eye on any of the black tendrils.

In desperation, he yelled through his battle helmet's external speakers at max volume. "What eye? I don't see any eye!"

CHAPTER 62

Charging forward, Kreathin raised his sword, determined to kill the high priestess before she could further set his plans back. Before he reached her, he glimpsed movement out the corner of his eye. A figure in a wizard scout's battle suit mounted on a black stallion with blazing red eyes emerged from the lakebed near the boulder. Kreathin sensed the spells he'd used to disable the links to Ceril and the high priestess dissipate. A second later, he sensed the spell he'd used to paralyze the human boy disappear as well.

I will not be defeated, Kreathin silently swore. *I am too close to the prize! I will have to help the Dalinfaust get free. I cannot allow my enemy to win. I will not let him win.*

Striking out at the high priestess with his sword, Kreathin's blow was deflected to the side by Ceril's counterthrust. The high priestess's brother switched directions with his blade, aiming a blow at Kreathin's head. Kreathin ducked, but a blow from the high priestess's staff knocked him back. He chanted a spell to reinforce his defensive shield just in time to deflect a ball of blue magic coming from the direction of the tunnel entrance.

Glancing at the tunnel, Kreathin saw Leethor, Meshoan, and a gnome running in his direction. He sensed the gnome drawing Power from his very large reserve in preparation for casting another spell and Ceril and the high priestess forming spells of their own. Even the human boy was drawing Power from his reserve while firing a pistol at the same time.

The combination of blows from the pistol, Ceril's sword, and the high priestess's staff caused his shield to buckle inward. Despite his hatred for the wizard scout, Kreathin was no fool. He made the only decision he could. Drawing Power from his reserve, he cast a teleportation spell.

As the cavern went in and out of focus, he heard the wizard scout shout, "What eye? I don't see any eye." Then everything went black.

* * *

Matthew fired two rounds from the 9mm handgun at the elf while drawing Power from his reserve and closing the distance to aid Richard's bondmate and the elf that was fighting at her side. Before he could reach them, the elf who had killed his father and mother shouted words Matthew heard but quickly forgot, then blinked in and out of focus.

As the elf disappeared from sight, Matthew heard his uncle shout, "What eye? I don't see any eye."

Hatred for the murderous elf was replaced by fear as the earth shook. Matthew finally saw the black tendrils reaching up from cracks in the boulder and tearing ever larger chunks of stone from the ceiling. He sensed demonic evil similar to what he'd sensed in the sphere of white gas.

The one with the eye, Matthew thought.

Spinning around, Matthew sought out the rolled-up cloak he'd dropped. He quickly spotted it twenty meters away. Running for the cloak, he sensed whatever was in the sphere reaching out to the demon clawing its way through the boulder. A black tendril popped out of a new crack in the boulder and slithered down the stone and across the lakebed, heading for the cloak-encased sphere of white gas. Jumping over the tendril, Matthew reached the cloak first and tossed it high into the air toward his uncle.

"Rick!" Matthew shouted trying to make his voice heard over the sound of rocks being torn from the ceiling. "The eye! Destroy the eye!"

The balled cloak flew into the air and the sphere came free, revealing a yellow eye in swirling gas. Hatred the likes of which Matthew had never encountered came out of the sphere. The sphere crashed to the lakebed as the black tendril made its way toward the eye.

A figure in black appeared next to the sphere.

Matthew watched his uncle draw his phase rod, activating it on the fly. The wizard scout drove the brerellium steel rod with its creallium core deep into the sphere.

Orange flames shot out, crackling through the air all the way to the ceiling. A scream that was more emotion than it was sound reverberated around the cavern's walls.

Matthew sensed the demon essence in the phase rod feeding off the demon essence in the sphere and lines of energy from the black tendrils being drawn into the phase rod as the demon began feeding on itself. He sensed his uncle draw Power from the Tree of Light's remaining globes overhead, using the additional energy from the tree against the demon. In his mind, he saw lines of Power reach out from Richard and latch onto the beams of energy above ground that were attacking the Tree of Light. He sensed his uncle drawing the beams from the three obelisks into the vicious cycle that was the demon devouring its own life force.

The high priestess raised her staff, shining the bright blue light of its gem onto the boulder.

The demon screamed again, this time withdrawing its tendrils back into the cracks. The sphere of white gas exploded, destroying the phase rod as well as itself. Somehow Matthew knew the phase rods in the three obelisks had been destroyed as well.

Deathly silence filled the cavern.

Ignoring everything else, Matthew ran to the base of the boulder and the two bloody bodies lying tangled together. He reached out, pulling his mother and father to his chest. They were all three together for the first time as a family. He cried as he'd never cried before. Matthew had a feeling he'd never stop crying.

CHAPTER 63

Richard surveyed the aftermath of the battle. The fight had been short-lived but fierce. Leethor, Meshoan, and Rembis had come running into the Presence of the Lady too late to help in the battle. The blood on their clothing had given mute evidence of the fierceness of their own fight in the tunnel. Jeena had quickly enlisted the aid of the gnome mage in securing the demonic gate.

A whinny drew Richard's attention. The stallion stood off to his left, over the limp body of the spirit-cat, tearing bloody mouthfuls of meat from the carcass and gulping it down. It was the first time Richard had ever seen the stallion eat. He hoped it would be the last.

Turning back to the boulder, Richard saw Jeena and Rembis on top. Jeena passed a beam of blue light from the gem at the tip of the Staff of the Lady of the Tree across the cracks in the stone. As the light touched the stone, the cracks closed, sealing the stone back together. Rembis walked behind Jeena casting spells onto the repaired cracks.

The sound of pain-filled crying tore at Richard's heart. He turned to see Matthew sitting with his back to the boulder, clutching the bodies of his parents in his arms. A part of Richard wanted to go over and comfort his nephew, but he couldn't think of any words that would help. He remained where he was, trying to come to grips with the fact that his brother was dead. Unlike his nephew, Richard found himself unable to mourn the loss.

"Time," said Nickelo. *"Your nephew needs time to grieve. I*

recommend giving him his space for now."

Ceril stood a half dozen paces from Richard's nephew staring at Matthew. The elf's expression was hard to read. Ceril said something to Matthew too low for Richard to hear before turning and walking over to join Leethor and Meshoan who were standing a dozen meters from the boulder. Richard heard his brother-in-law speak to the two elves.

"Tell Jeena I went to check on my family."

When Leethor nodded, Ceril took off at a run. Not once did Richard's brother-in-law acknowledge his existence.

Leethor approached Richard with a look of concern. "The demons were pressing our comrades hard when we left. We need to get back and help where we can."

Richard shook his head. "There's no need. My passive scan's clear. Whatever demons were there are either dead or gone."

"Nevertheless," said Leethor, "we need to report in and help. There are bound to be wounded."

Thinking of the wounded, Richard nodded. *I've done all I can here.*

Richard sent Jeena Power from his reserve along with an emotion of relief. He saw his bondmate look up from her self-imposed task of sealing the damaged gate. She only looked at him long enough to nod her head and return a little more Power through their link than he'd given her. Then she resumed the task of repairing the boulder.

As soon as Jeena's Power mixed with Richard's, Power was created. Glancing at the readings on his heads-up display for his reserve, he noticed he was at fifty-one percent Power. Turning away from the boulder, Richard ran for the tunnel. Leethor and Meshoan were already out of sight. He picked up the pace.

Signs of battle were evident all through the tunnel. Richard counted the bodies of six spirit-cats before he passed the body of one of the Lady's caretakers near the tunnel exit. Outside, Richard was taken aback by the apparent violence. Bodies and torn limbs of elves were strewn about like debris after a storm. At least a score of monstrous shapes from Richard's worst nightmare were mixed in with the bodies of the elves. The X-shuttle sat on the ground a hundred meters to his right, and most of the *Defiant's* crew were roaming around the battlefield trying to help the elves care for their wounded wherever they lay.

Sensing a flow of healing Power to his left, Richard's gaze found Terrie Shatstot kneeling next to a badly wounded elf. As the healing Power subsided, he sensed the elf's wounds heal. Then Terrie moved on to another elf.

"Must be nice to be able to heal without having to deal with the pain yourself," Richard said in his shared space.

"Do not get jealous," said Nickelo. *"At least with him here, you will not be tempted to try and heal the wounded yourself."*

"I wasn't planning on doing it anyway. My healing days are over." Although his battle computer remained silent, Richard had a feeling Nickelo was unconvinced.

While he discussed healing with his battle computer, Richard saw Leethor and Meshoan talking to one of the nearby elves. All of a sudden, Meshoan took off running in the direction of the Tree of Light.

Leethor remained behind long enough to yell, "The children!" before pursuing his bondmate.

An image of the children huddled near the Tree of Light flashed into Richard's mind. He sent an emotion of concern to Jeena before running after his two friends. Fast though the two elves were, they were no match for the battle suit's assistors. He passed them just as they crossed the point where the path leveled off and gave Richard a clear view of the tree beyond.

Richard stopped in his tracks. A crowd of adult elves, some with axes and saws, were hurriedly dragging branches away from a massive limb. As he began running again, he noticed Master Jathar and a half dozen black robed mages combine levitation spells to remove the large limb from what appeared to be bundles of bloody cloth on the ground. A great cry arose from the crowd, and Richard picked up his pace even more. Although he wasn't normally empathetic, Richard sensed intense anguish from the elves. As he drew close, he saw the bundles of cloth for what they were.

"Children," Richard told his battle computer. He sent an active scan toward the bodies of the children. Many of them were badly injured, but at least they were still alive. A few gave off no life force at all.

"Oh, no," Richard said out loud. "Not the children."

As parents and relatives gathered around the bodies, he stood awkwardly to the side.

"Nick, tell Terrie to get up here now. We need him."

"I already have. Sergeant Ron's bringing him up in the X-shuttle."

Richard saw Leethor and Meshoan hugging their son and daughter, both appearing unhurt. High Lord Trenadine and Lord Reale were standing near Ceril and Therasia, the two lords' daughter Matisa clinging to Reale. The young elf's right arm was in a sling. Tears streamed down Matisa's face. Richard noticed tears coming from the high lord and Reale as well.

Walking nearer, he looked closer at Ceril and Therasia. They were both kneeling by something on the ground. With a sinking heart, Richard realized it was the broken body of their daughter. The back of Terika's head was soaked with blood. Probing the elf child with an active scan, Richard detected no life force.

A shimmering in the air near Terika's body drew Richard's attention. He'd seen the same shimmer on thousands of occasions in the past, ever since he'd helped destroy the Dragars' temple on Portalis a hundred thousand years in the past.

"You know what the shimmer is," said Nickelo. *"It is the final life force of the person—their soul, if you prefer."*

Although Richard had seen a lot of death during his six hundred plus years, the sight of the lifeless body of the young elf hit him hard. He'd begun to like her in just the short time they'd been together.

In spite of his growing sadness, Richard forced himself to speak as emotionless as possible. *"Why is her soul still here? It usually disappears in a few seconds. From what I can tell, Terika has probably been dead for at least five minutes."*

Despite his effort to remain emotionless, the memory of the young elf smiling and laughing the previous day tugged at his heart. He remembered her last words about never wanting to see him again.

"Why is her soul still here?" said Nickelo. *"The answer is simple enough. The younger the life form, the more attached the soul is to the physical body. The souls of older creatures tend to leave for the next world immediately. Younger life forms such as the elf child tend to hang around longer. Her life force will dissipate soon enough."*

Looking around, Richard noticed other shimmers in the air. He counted twelve in total. The sound of loud voices turned his attention to several elves pointing at the sky behind him. He heard one of them say, "Dragon." Looking in the direction they were pointing, he saw the X-shuttle coming in on short final landing. He supposed the X-shuttle's stubby wings and silver hull might resemble a dragon to someone who'd never seen a spaceship before. The X-shuttle set down just outside the outer branches of the Tree of Light. As soon as the ship touched the ground, the rear ramp dropped open. Out ran Terrie and Sergeant Ron.

"Have Taylor tell Terrie to help the wounded," Richard told his battle computer in command voice.

"Compliance."

A shimmer of green in the direction of the Tree of Light caught Richard's attention. He looked to his right to see a translucent Shandria standing five meters away, tears streaking down her face. As far as Richard could tell, none of the elves nearby noticed their Lady.

"Would that I had never seen this day," said Shandria speaking in his mind. *"My bondmate and I are heartbroken. The elf children sought our protection. Instead, they died under the weight of our branches."*

Shaking his head at her obvious pain, Richard said, *"It wasn't your fault."*

"Does fault matter?" asked Shandria. She waved an arm to indicate the shimmers in the air. *"The children's last vestige of life force is fading fast. They will be gone soon. Neither the tree nor I can help them. We are not healers."*

Although the statement wasn't a question, Richard thought he detected the hint of a request in the Lady's words. *"They're already dead,"* he said. *"Even if I was somehow able to heal their bodies, I can't bring their souls back from the dead."*

"No, you could not," agreed Shandria locking eyes with Richard. *"No mortal can bring someone back from the dead. Once their souls have left this world, they can never return through the efforts of mere mortals such as you or me."*

Richard frowned. *"What are you trying to say, Shandria? If you're trying to tell me something, just say it. You know I've never been good at subtle nuances."*

In spite of her tears, the Lady gave a brief smile. *"No, you have not. I will do as you ask and speak plainly. As long as the children's souls remain in this world, they are not truly dead. If their bodies were healed, the soul could be enticed to return to its body. But the time grows short. They will soon be gone forever."*

The enormity of Shandria's unspoken request hit Richard. He looked at the broken bodies of the children around him, then took another look at the fading shimmers.

"I don't know how to entice a soul back to its body," Richard protested. *"I'm just a man."*

"You and I are connected, Richard Shepard," said Shandria. *"The tree and I can help. We will not lie. The pain would be unlike anything you have ever experienced. We will need to funnel Power through you to reconnect the children's life force to their healed bodies. It will be dangerous for you. There is a chance you may not survive such an endeavor."*

Richard looked down at Terika and the bodies of the other elf children scattered around the base of the tree. He reached out through the bond link to Jeena. He could tell she was on her way to him even now. He felt her fear as if she somehow sensed what he intended.

Turning to High Lord Trenadine, Richard said, "Bring the bodies of the dead children to me."

"What did you say?" asked the high lord staring at Richard as if looking at a crazed man.

"You heard me!" Richard said using a voice he normally reserved for speaking to battle computers in command voice. "Bring them to me. Now."

Without waiting for the astonished high lord to respond, Richard knelt next to Ceril. He removed his right glove and took the limp hand of Terika in his. He half expected his brother-in-law to interfere, but the silver-haired elf merely closed his eyes and began weeping.

"Rick, are you sure you want to do this?" said Nickelo in their shared space. *"No one has the right to expect it of you. You promised you'd discuss healing with Jeena. You gave her your wizard scout honor."*

Richard remembered. *"I said if she was here. She isn't yet."* He knew it was a technicality, but it was what it was.

A final look at the rapidly fading shimmer that he knew was Terika's soul confirmed his decision. Wrapping the broken body of the young elf with Power, Richard compared the bloody body with how he knew the elf child should be and pulled the difference into himself.

Pain flooded into Richard—not just pain to his body, but pain to his very soul. He sensed Shandria and her bondmate along with the Tree of Light funneling their Power into him. The wounds on Terika's body healed, as did the acquired wounds on Richard, but Terika's soul continued to fade away.

Richard's own soul threatened to tear out of his body. He saw and sensed things no mortal should ever bear. He sensed the creatures of the spiritual plane, and that they were not spirit creatures such as the dolgars or even his spirit-horse. In an instant of understanding, he knew the dolgars and his stallion resided in the outer spirit plane. The spirit-creatures he now sensed were from the deeper spirit-plane; the demonic plane. He sensed armies of demons waiting to be unleashed in the dimensions of the living. He sensed the Dalinfaust and his brothers and even their master and his plans to overwhelm the three galaxies. The death and destruction that would follow became a burning vision in his mind. Forcing himself to ignore the vision, Richard fought his way back to reality just as he sensed lines of Power wrapping around a nearby shimmer and bringing it back as well.

Screaming brought Richard out of his trance. The screams sounded familiar. He opened his eyes, squelching another scream before it escaped his throat. He hurt all over. The back of his head felt sticky inside his battle helmet.

"*Rick,*" said Nickelo. "*You're back. Praise the Creator, you did it.*"

"*How long was I out?*" Richard asked trying to get his bearings.

"*Only three point two seconds. You were operating at nanosecond speed.*"

Richard heard crying. Somehow he could tell it was happy crying. From his position on the ground, he noticed Ceril and Therasia hugging and kissing a blood-soaked Terika. The child looked extremely confused and more than a little frightened, but a quick scan confirmed she was completely healed.

Hands helped Richard sit up. The hands belonged to High Lord Trenadine. His eyes were wide as he looked down at Richard. "Elf Friend, I—"

"Where's the next child?" Richard asked.

"Rick, no," said Nickelo in their shared space. *"Do not do it. The pain will only get worse. You cheated death once. I calculate the odds will only get worse with each successive attempt."*

Before the high lord could answer his question, Richard glanced to his right to see an ancient elf holding a young elf boy in his arms. Richard recognized the ancient elf as Lord Sheshna. Tears were streaming down the elf lord's face. Although Lord Sheshna said nothing, the pleading in his eyes spoke volumes.

Reaching up, Richard accepted the body of the elf boy from Lord Sheshna and cradled the child to his chest. Again, pain washed over him. Like the previous time, he sensed Shandria and the tree pouring Power through him and felt his soul being drawn to even deeper regions of the spiritual plane. This time the inhabitants of the demonic plane seemed to sense his presence, and they began searching for him. He sensed their eagerness to tear his soul to shreds.

Richard returned to consciousness screaming once more. Jeena was there holding his head in her lap. He looked to find Lord Sheshna. The old elf was hugging a young boy in a bloody tunic tight to his chest. Although the young elf boy was crying, he was unhurt.

Looking around, Richard saw another child's body with a slight shimmering in the air nearby. Two elves were kneeling near the child and staring at Richard with tears in their eyes. Rolling out of Jeena's lap, Richard began crawling toward the child.

"No!" shouted Jeena grabbing onto his shoulders and pulling him back. "You have done enough."

"No, I haven't!" Richard said, desperate to get to the child before the shimmering disappeared completely. "You don't know the horrible things I've done. I've got to redeem myself. This may be my only chance. Please understand."

Using the strength of the battle suit's assistors, Richard broke free of Jeena's grasp. He reached out for the hand of the dead child, pulling the injuries into his own body. He began screaming as clawing hands reached out for his soul and tried to pull him into the depths of the spiritual plane. Then everything went black.

CHAPTER 64

The sound of breathing woke Richard. He recognized the sound as his own. The back of his head rested on something soft. *A pillow?* he wondered. The inside of his mouth was dry and cottony. He tried to speak.

"Wa-water," he finally croaked.

A calloused but surprisingly gentle hand raised Richard's head, supporting it as the rim of a wooden goblet touched his lips. Cool spring-wine trickled down his throat. Richard drew back coughing. Forcing his eyes open, he looked directly into two molten-silver eyes filled with concern. The eyes didn't belong to Jeena.

"Ceril," Richard rasped, pulling away. His head plopped back on the silken pillow. He glanced around for his bondmate. The bedroom was empty except for his brother-in-law and himself. *I don't understand,* he thought. *This is our house. This is our bedroom. Why am I here?* He tried to remember what had happened and how he'd gotten there, but his mind was a gray fog.

"Do you want more wine?" asked Ceril in what sounded like a concerned voice while shifting his position on the edge of the bed. "Jeena left not fifteen minutes ago to speak with the council. She will be kicking herself when she finds out you woke while she was away."

Clarity was slow in coming for Richard, so he decided to go for the obvious first. "How long have I been asleep?"

Ceril gave a timid smile. "It was not sleep. You have been unconscious for three days. Jeena has been with you the whole time until now. The messenger from the council had to beg her to go. I will admit you had us all worried."

A thousand questions popped into Richard's head, but he decided to ask the one that was bothering him the most first. "Why are you being so kind to me? I thought you hated humans."

The elf's face took on a red tint, but Richard got the impression it wasn't from anger. Ceril set the wooden goblet on the nightstand. His silver eyes swirled furiously as he locked gazes with Richard.

"How could I not be kind to you, Elf Friend? You saved my daughter's life. You saved all of their lives. I am ashamed of my past actions, Brother. I thought... But now..." Ceril glanced down at the floor, then back at Richard. "I have always thought humans killed my parents. I found out during the battle in the Presence of the Lady that I was wrong. I can only beg your forgiveness. I cannot blame you if you do not."

Something the elf said jogged a memory out of Richard's fogged mind. "Terika. Did you say she was hurt? Is she all right?"

A tear trickled down Ceril's face before he turned and wiped it away. When he looked back, his eyes were dry. "She is fine. You brought her back from the dead. You saved her as you saved the others. You are truly the elf friend. Please forgive me for doubting."

Partial memories flowed back into Richard's mind. Some he saw clearly. He saw enough of other memories to hope he would never remember them in full. He shrugged off the part in Ceril's words about bringing someone back from the dead. That was impossible. Still, one thing he knew for certain, the task ahead was too much for any one man or any one race.

Elf and human are going to need each other if they hope to survive what's coming, Richard thought. *We are going to need all the help we can get.*

Richard looked at his brother-in-law, sensing he was sincere. "I forgive you, Ceril. Grudges are a luxury none of us can afford any longer." A wave of fatigue washed over him. He yawned. "I'm very tired. I think I'll go back to sleep if you don't mind."

Sweet darkness enveloped Richard, wrapping him in its blissful peace. He tried to enjoy it while he could. He knew what was coming. Even asleep, he had a feeling times of peace would be long and far between in the foreseeable future.

CHAPTER 65

The crew of the *Defiant* and the Council of Light held an informal meeting outside the X-shuttle's rear ramp where it rested on its landing skids only twenty meters from the edge of the Tree of Light's outermost branches. Much had happened in the last week. Much still needed to be done. While a lot of the damage to the tree and the cavern below had been repaired, it was painfully obvious to those present that some damage would probably never be undone.

Standing just inside the Tree of Light's branches stood a green-haired elf. The Lady locked eyes with each attendee at the meeting one at a time before speaking. "The Tree of Light and I can hold the lock for only a short while longer. The demons on the other side of the gate have had a taste of freedom. They know the lock is weak. I fear our time is short. You must somehow close the gate permanently, once and for all, before the Tree of Light, my bondmate, and I are called from this world."

"How?" asked Jeena.

Richard thought his bondmate looked deadly dressed as she was in a black jumpsuit complete with utility belt and holster. The two wands and a wicked-looking dagger jammed into her belt added to the impression. She grasped the Staff of the Lady of the Tree firmly in her left hand as if it was a scepter.

"If it was possible for the gate to be closed permanently," continued Jeena, "why have you not done it before now?"

A slight smile appeared on Shandria's face as she spread her hands. "I think you believe I am more than I am, High Priestess. As to how the gate can be permanently closed, the four corners of the gate are the key. Four gems of Power were placed on this world by the Creator long before the elf friend and I retrieved the seed that grew into the Tree of Light. The tree was never intended to be a permanent lock on the gate beneath us. Only the four gems of Power can close the gate forever."

Glancing around, Richard saw looks of confusion matching his own on the faces of many attendees. "Then where are these gems. Let's go get them and lock the gate before the demons come up with another way to open the blasted door."

The Lady half turned to the Tree of Light and closed her eyes, taking on a blank look as if she were no longer in this world. After a half dozen heartbeats, Shandria turned back around and locked eyes with Richard. "Parts of two of the gems are here right now." She pointed at Richard's left hand. "You wear part of one on your finger, and so does my high priestess." Pointing at Tia and Matthew, Shandria said, "Your two friends wear parts of a second gem. The Oracle tells me two more of your friends are wearing a pair of rings bearing parts of a third gem."

"I don't know—" Richard started.

Dren said, "The gems used to create the three pairs of rings are in a warehouse on Storage. That is assuming the building wasn't destroyed during the attack. A blue, a red, and a green gem have been stored there for quite some time. A space also exists for a yellow gem, but the spot is empty."

Facing the teenager, Shandria nodded her head. "Yes. I have no doubt the yellow gem is missing. That particular gem of Power was destroyed over fourteen thousand years ago. The yellow gem had been entrusted to the care of the Ecarian giants. Someone broke into their vault, destroying the gem. Once the yellow gem was lost, our hope of closing the gate permanently was put on hold."

Richard glanced at Jeena. When she didn't speak, he looked back at Shandria. "Is there another of these yellow gems of Power mewhere? If so, just tell us and we'll go get it."

Shaking her head, Shandria said, "Not to my knowledge. vever, I must confess that despite what you may think, I am far all knowing. Perhaps the Ecarian giants have the information you seek. All I am sure of is that the gate must be closed permanently, and it must be closed soon."

A movement to Richard's left caught his eye. He turned as High Lord Trenadine rose from the chair Sergeant Ron had provided for him.

"I must admit," said the high lord, "that I have never heard of these Ecarian giants. If you tell us where they are, perhaps the council can send emissaries to make inquiries."

Chief Librarian Elisinsar was standing to the right rear of the high lord. He cleared his throat, getting everyone's attention. "I am afraid that will be an impossible task. Although it is not well known, Elf Friend Amirithoda was from the tribe of Ecarian giants. They all disappeared from the face of Portalis shortly after the yellow gem was reportedly destroyed. No one knows why. It has always been a great mystery to those specializing in giant lore."

Turning from the chief librarian to Shandria, Richard said, "What should we do? We need you to lead us."

The green-haired elf laughed. "My days of leading are long past, Elf Friend." She waved a hand at the tree behind her. "I am an adviser only, and a poor one at that, I fear. I agree you need a leader. That leader must come from one of you."

Richard noticed all eyes including those of the high lord turn to him. Even Lord Sheshna looked at him expectantly. Richard wanted to argue, but half-memories of what he'd seen deep in the spiritual plane were still clear enough to hold his protests in check.

"You are the obvious choice," said Nickelo speaking in their shared space.

"Whatever," Richard said already having made up his mind.

"You are the elf friend," said Jeena. "You will not be alone. I am with you." She waved her free hand at the other attendees. "As are we all."

Taking in the determined looks of those around him, Richard said, "Fine. But I'll warn all of you right now that I was a Marine. I learned long ago only one person can be in charge. If that's going to be me, then it's going to be me. If anyone can't deal with that, then now's the time to speak." Richard stared at Lord Sheshna since from all that Jeena had told him, he was the obvious troublemaker.

The old elf rose from his chair, glancing around at the other, before turning his attention back to Richard. "I cannot speak for the others, Elf Friend, but I owe the life of my grandson to you. Ingratitude is not one of my faults. Whatever you need me to do, you have only to ask."

"That goes for me as well, Elf Friend," said High Lord Trenadine.

"And me, partner," said Sergeant Ron. "I think I speak for the whole crew when I say we've got your back."

Richard looked at the other attendees in turn. Without exception, everyone present nodded their head.

As soon as he'd given everyone the chance to let their feelings be known, Richard got down to business. "Fine then. This is what's going to happen. Telsa, you'll stay here and work with Chief Librarian Elisinsar to find out all you can about these giants. Terrie, you'll stay as well. The elves need healers. I want you to start a school in Silverton and train their medics how to heal using pure Power. They can't be healed magically, but both you and I have been able to heal them using just Power."

Angela was standing slightly behind and to the left of Terrie and placed her right hand on his shoulder. "Well, if my husband's staying, then you can bet your last credit I'm staying as well, and I'll hear no argument about it."

The last thing Richard wanted to do was start an argument with the feisty redhead. He did the only smart thing he could and nodded, then moved on.

"Wise decision," said Nickelo in their shared space. *"She'll keep Terrie's nose to the grindstone."*

Richard continued giving orders. "Dren, Brachia, I need you back on Storage. I'm going to need my dimensional pack. Get the teleporter operational lickety-split. I don't know how much supplies are left, but whatever there is, I'm going to need them."

Dren and Brachia nodded.

"We'll get the Storageans organized," said Brachia. "Omar says he'll help as well."

Dren nudged her little brother. "The time for games is over. We ?d to be serious." She glanced back at Richard. "You can depend ıs, Uncle Rick."

ichard smiled. "I had no doubt." He turned to look at Tia and ıew. "I have a difficult job for you two—especially you, Matt.

I need you to go back and take charge of the Conglomerate. I need them back in the Empire's fold. Our civil war needs to stop. Tia can be your go-between with the Trecorians and the Empire's rebel forces. She can get Liz to help."

Richard had no doubt that he was giving a near-impossible mission to his nephew. Since the boy was still grieving for his parents, Richard had pretty much left him alone for the past week. However, the time for grieving was past.

When his nephew started shaking his head, Richard put his foot down. "We've all lost people we care for in this war," he said. "And we're going to lose a lot more before it's over. There will be time to grieve later, assuming we survive. I need you to get the Conglomerate on our side. You're the only one who can do it."

After looking at Tia, Matthew turned back to Richard. "You're asking the impossible. There are like fifty people in line to take over the Conglomerate. I may be my mother's son, but there are others way higher in the hierarchy who will be vying to take command."

His nephew's argument wasn't unexpected, so Richard was ready with an answer. "Sergeant Ron and I have already discussed it. He made a list of forty-eight people who will undoubtedly try to take over after the empress. From what he tells me, if the top ten or so are taken out of the equation, everyone else will fall in line."

Matthew shook his head. "I'm not going to kill my rivals, even if I could, which I can't. I won't do it even for you."

Sergeant Ron cleared his throat. "Don't get your feathers in an uproar, Matt. Rick didn't say kill. He's not an assassin. Fortunately for us, he's got a couple of spirit-wolf friends who can pretty much fetch anyone we want to accept our hospitality for a few months. That will give you time to consolidate your position as head of the Conglomerate. Just leave it to us. Trust me. You're not going to face as much opposition as you think. Most of the Conglomerate's rank and file think the civil war is as much of a waste as we do."

Matthew turned back to Tia, and they whispered in each other's ear. When Matthew turned back, he nodded. "I'll do my best, Rick."

"That's all I can ask, Matt," Richard replied.

"What about us?" asked High Lord Trenadine.

Glancing at each council member in turn, Richard phrased ¹

answer as tactfully as possible. "We need allies on Portalis—all we can get. I need you to make peace with the humans here. King Halmafad would be a good place to start."

"Humans," snorted Lord Sheshna. "Elf Friend, working with the humans from your dimension is one thing. The humans on our world are another. You are not an elf, so you cannot appreciate the harm they have done us over the years. How can we—"

"The same way I can work with a species that has done me harm," Richard said. "The Crosioians were responsible for my father's death. I watched them cut a close friend of mine in half right in front of my eyes. They killed a hundred million of my fellow soldiers. Regardless, I plan on making them allies. If I can forgive the Crosioians enough to work with them, you can do the same with humans here on Portalis."

"The Crosioians?" said Tia. "Are you crazy? They'd kill you on sight. How are you planning on getting them to stop fighting us and help? For that matter, why bother?"

Heat rose in Richard's face, but he forced his anger down. Tia was his friend. He had no doubt she was asking the same questions going through the minds of many others present.

"Why?" Richard said. "Because I've seen what we're up against. Trust me. Whatever harm other living beings have done to us is nothing compared to what will happen if the demon armies are loosed in our dimensions. They will torture and kill every living creature in the three galaxies." He glanced at Jeena. "Tia asked how. The only answer I can give is that I have absolutely no idea. All I know for sure is that I'm going to need help. Will you go with me, my bondmate?"

A smile crossed Jeena's face and her molten-silver eyes swirled faster than ever. "I will be by your side, my bondmate. And woe be unto anyone or anything that tries to stop me."

Richard returned his bondmate's smile. He knew trials beyond anything he'd faced in the past were coming his way. At the same *ime, he knew he wouldn't be facing them alone. "It's nice to have *ds,"* he thought.

·elo laughed in their shared space. *"I calculate a one *·rcent probability you are correct, Wizard Scout. It is *·iends."*

EPILOGUE

Pain racked through the Dalinfaust. Once the worst of the pain ebbed, the demon renewed his discussion with his brother, Zenthra. "Do not be a fool. I have only lost a battle. I shall win the war."

"You mean *we*, do you not, Brother? As to the fool, my part of the plan went perfectly. Your time-commando is the one who failed to use the phase rods I provided properly. Now there is no way to open the gates."

The Dalinfaust controlled his anger. He'd learned long ago working with fools like his brother was best done with sugar and honey. "Do not underestimate *our* abilities, my dear brother. The use of my essence stored in the phase rods along with the aid of the Lady's staff would have been the optimum way to open the gate. There are other ways."

"Hmm," said Zenthra. "What other ways?"

The Dalinfaust laughed. "You shall see, dear brother. All shall see soon enough. I am far from defeated. Let the three galaxies tremble. I shall be back one day to exact my revenge. By all that is unholy, I swear it."

[End Transmission]

ABOUT THE AUTHOR

Rodney Hartman is a retired US Army veteran with over twenty years of experience in military operations ranging from Infantry Private in the paratroops to Chief Warrant Officer flying helicopters during the Persian Gulf War. Mr. Hartman worked for many years as a computer programmer before retiring and pursuing a career as a full-time writer. Mr. Hartman lives in North Carolina with his wife and family along with their cat, McKenzie.

Printed in Great Britain
by Amazon